Headline Alberta

Deborah Ashton

Copyright © 2013 Deborah Ashton
All rights reserved.
ISBN: 1492393606
ISBN 13: 9781492393603

For Thelma and Pearl

Headline Families

ABBOTT

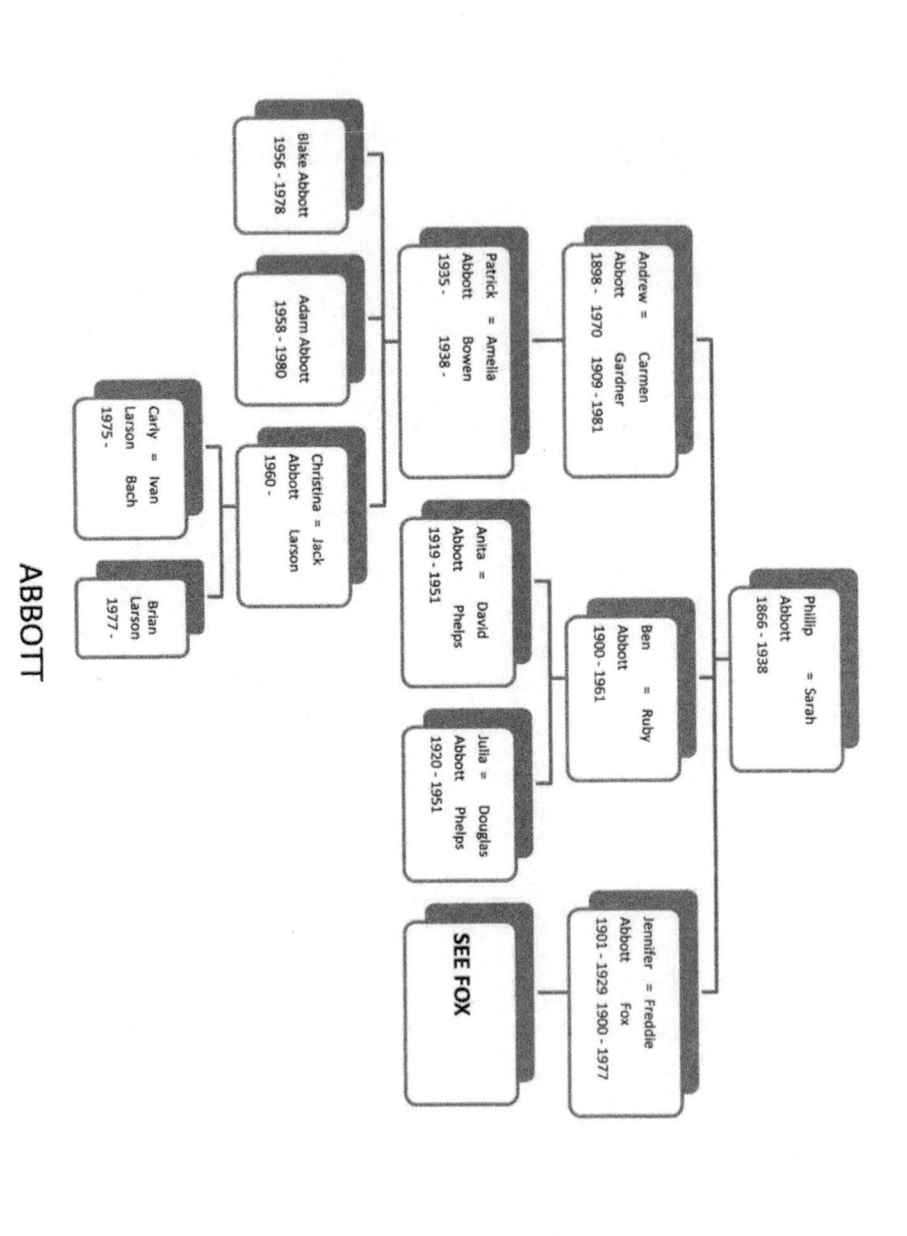

- Phillip Abbott (1866 - 1938) = Sarah
  - Andrew Abbott (1898 - 1970) = Carmen Gardner (1909 - 1981)
    - Patrick Abbott (1935 -) = Amelia Bowen (1938 -)
      - Blake Abbott (1956 - 1978)
      - Adam Abbott (1958 - 1980)
      - Christina Abbott (1960 -) = Jack Larson
        - Carly Larson (1975 -) = Ivan Bach
        - Brian Larson (1977 -)
  - Ben Abbott (1900 - 1961) = Ruby
    - Anita Abbott (1919 - 1951) = David Phelps
    - Julia Abbott (1920 - 1951) = Douglas Phelps
  - Jennifer Abbott (1901 - 1929) = Freddie Fox (1900 - 1977)
    - **SEE FOX**

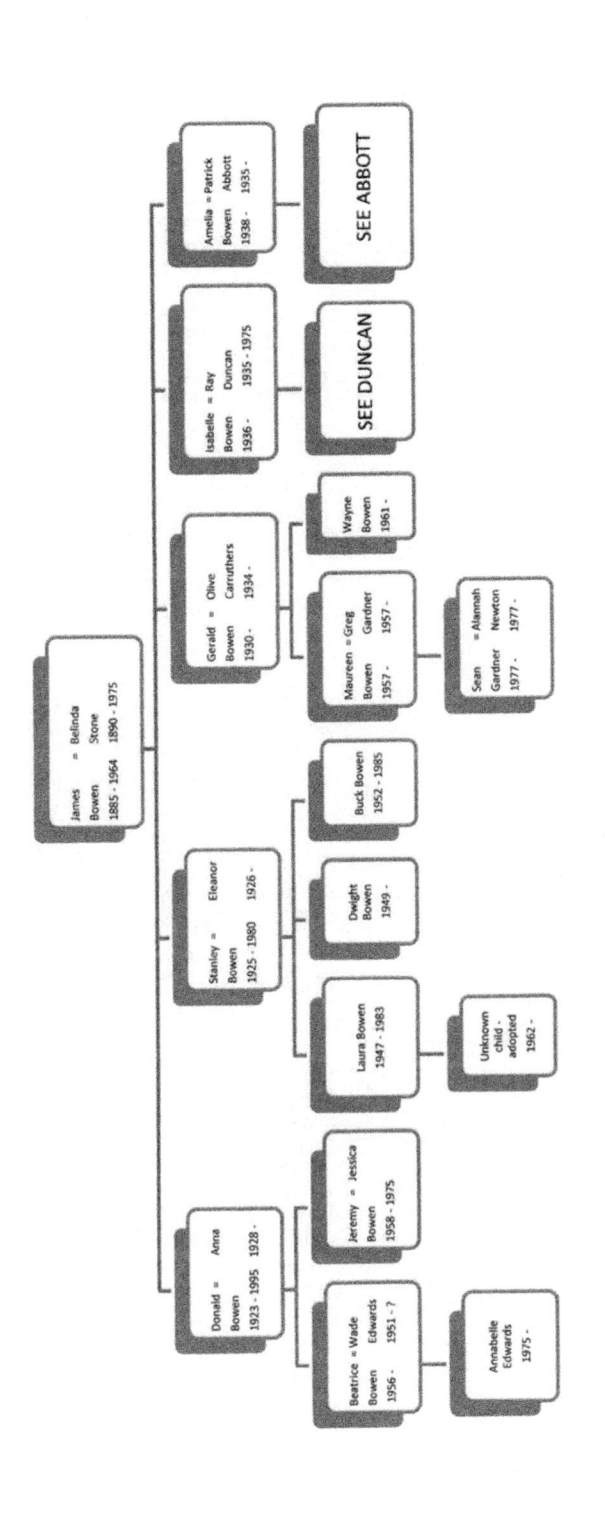

BOWEN

- James Bowen (1885 - 1964) = Belinda Stone (1890 - 1975)
  - Donald Bowen (1923 - 1995) = Anna (1928 -)
    - Beatrice Bowen (1956 -) = Wade Edwards (1951 - ?)
      - Annabelle Edwards (1975 -)
    - Jeremy Bowen (1958 - 1975) = Jessica
  - Stanley Bowen (1925 - 1980) = Eleanor (1926 -)
    - Laura Bowen (1947 - 1983)
      - Unknown child - adopted (1962 -)
    - Dwight Bowen (1949 -)
    - Buck Bowen (1952 - 1985)
  - Gerald Bowen (1930 -) = Olive Carruthers (1934 -)
    - Maureen Bowen (1957 -) = Greg Gardner (1957 -)
      - Sean Gardner (1977 -) = Alannah Newton (1977 -)
    - Wayne Bowen (1961 -)
  - Isabelle Bowen (1936 -) = Ray Duncan (1935 - 1975)
    - SEE DUNCAN
  - Amelia Bowen (1938 -) = Patrick Abbott (1935 -)
    - SEE ABBOTT

CARRUTHERS

Frank and Nora Carruthers

Ernest Carruthers (1906-) = Rebecca St. John (1910-1993)

- Rudy Carruthers (1930-) = Corem (-1994)
- Ollie Carruthers (1934-) = Gerald Bowen (1930-)

Dorothy Carruthers (1907-1919)

Theodore Carruthers (1908-1971) = Jane Mitulski (1912-1972)

- William Carruthers (1944-1975)
- Rhonda Carruthers (1950-1985) = Gerald Smith
- Terence Carruthers (1954-1995) = Ellen
  - Seth Carruthers (1982-)
  - Roxanne Carruthers (1984-)

Peggy Carruthers (1910-1973) = Jake Edwards (1909-1995) — SEE EDWARDS

Ethan Carruthers (1914-) = Janis Young (1920-1991)

- Ned Carruthers (1940-)

Lila Carruthers (1928-1989) = Rod Carlson (1932-1977)

- Lorna Carlson Webber (1945-1985)
- Peter Carlson (1948-)
- Vincent Carlson (1953-1987)

Mildred Carruthers (1919-) = Irwin Gardner (1915-) — SEE GARDNER

Justin Carruthers (1920-1933)

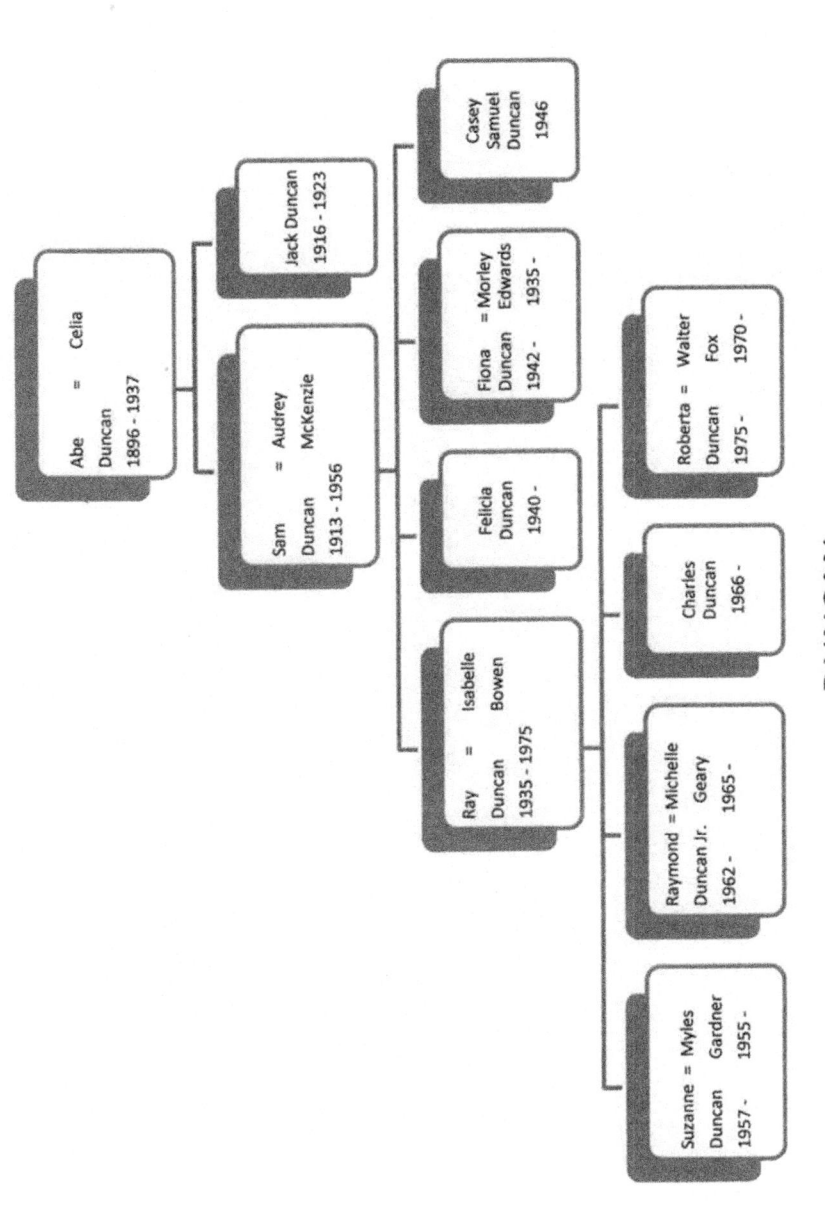

DUNCAN

- Abe = Celia Duncan 1896 - 1937
  - Jack Duncan 1916 - 1923
  - Sam Duncan 1913 - 1956 = Audrey McKenzie
    - Ray Duncan 1935 - 1975 = Isabelle Bowen
      - Suzanne Duncan 1957 - = Myles Gardner 1955 -
      - Raymond Duncan Jr. 1962 - = Michelle Geary 1965 -
      - Charles Duncan 1966 -
      - Roberta Duncan 1975 - = Walter Fox 1970 -
    - Felicia Duncan 1940 -
    - Fiona Duncan 1942 - = Morley Edwards 1935 -
    - Casey Samuel Duncan 1946

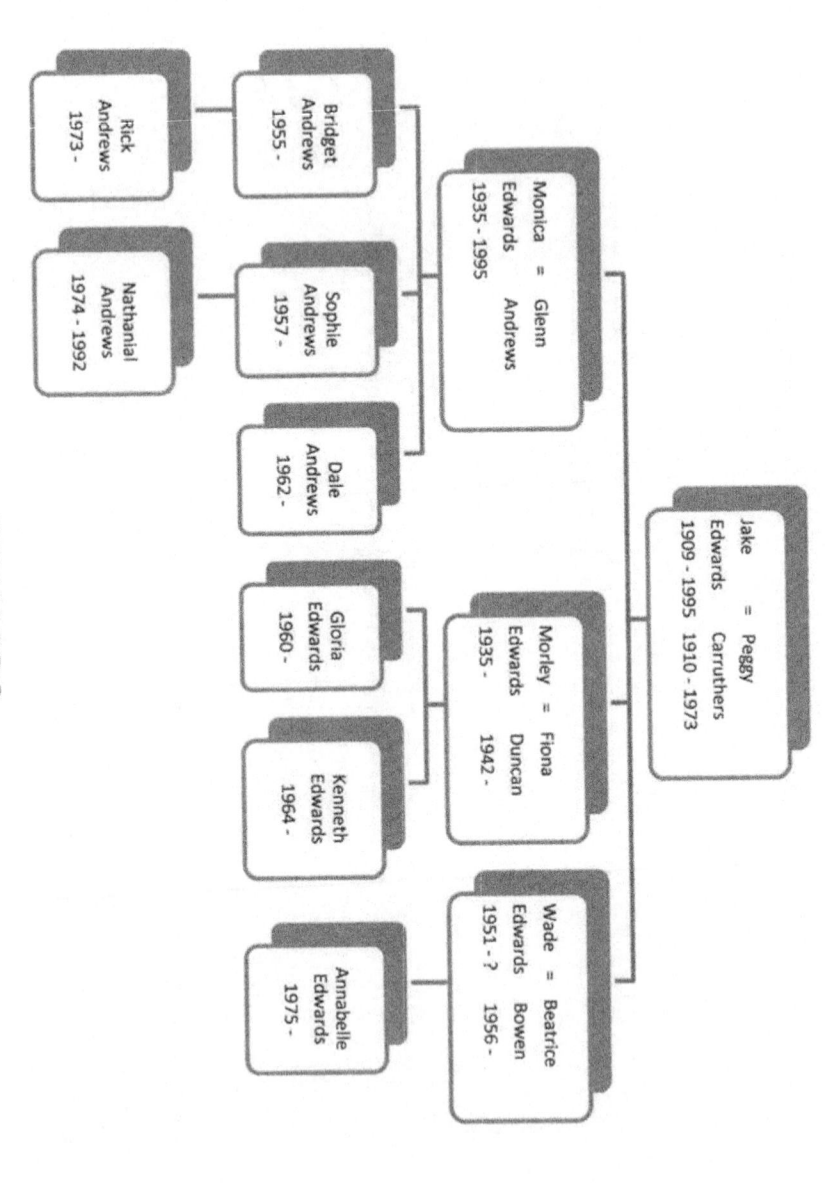

EDWARDS

- Jake Edwards (1909 - 1995) = Peggy Carruthers (1910 - 1973)
  - Monica Edwards (1935 - 1995) = Glenn Andrews
    - Bridget Andrews (1955 -)
      - Rick Andrews (1973 -)
    - Sophie Andrews (1957 -)
      - Nathanial Andrews (1974 - 1992)
    - Dale Andrews (1962 -)
  - Morley Edwards (1935 -) = Fiona Duncan (1942 -)
    - Gloria Edwards (1960 -)
    - Kenneth Edwards (1964 -)
  - Wade Edwards (1951 - ?) = Beatrice Bowen (1956 -)
    - Annabelle Edwards (1975 -)

FOX

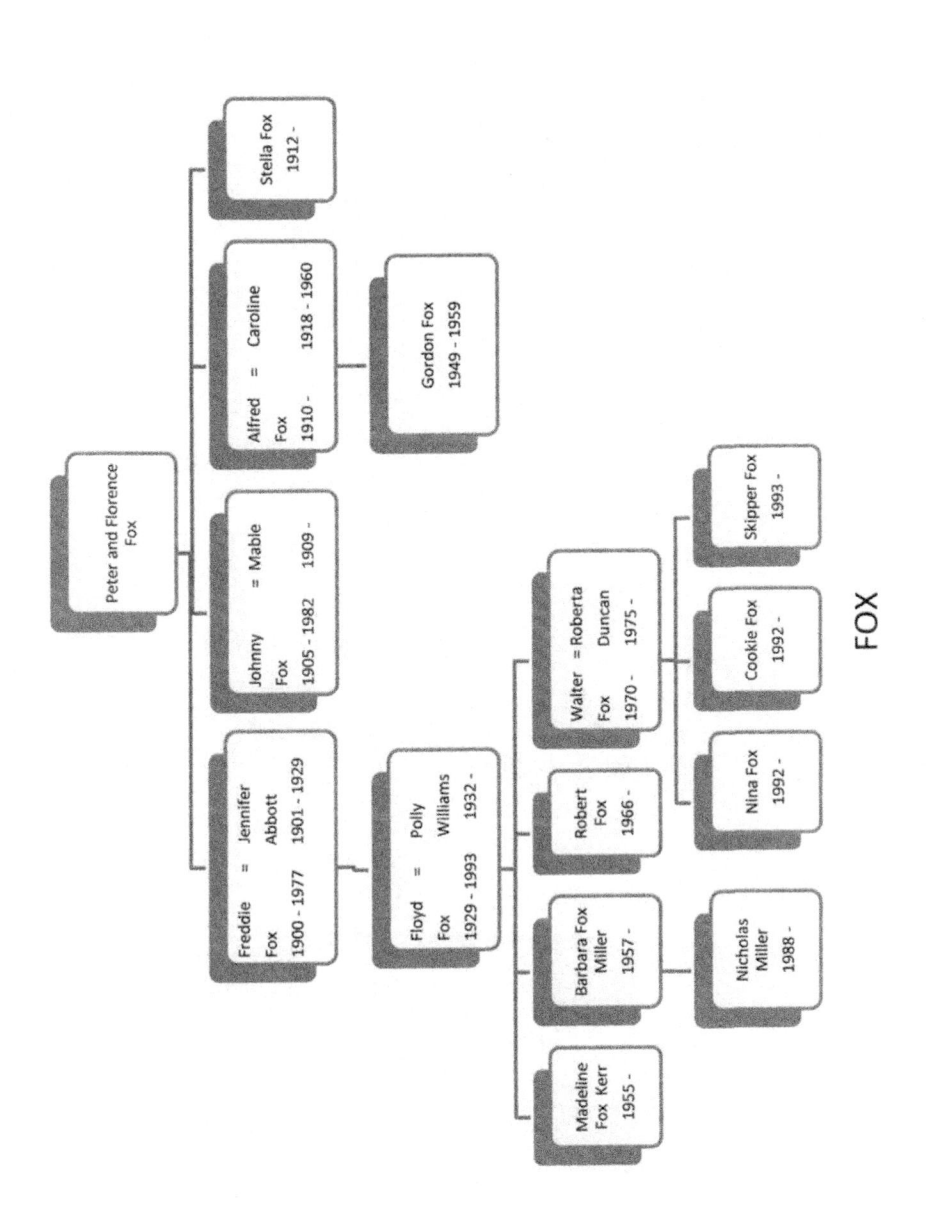

Peter and Florence Fox

- Freddie Fox (1900 - 1977) = Jennifer Abbott (1901 - 1929)
- Johnny Fox (1905 - 1982) = Mable (1909 -)
- Alfred Fox (1910 -) = Caroline (1918 - 1960)
- Stella Fox (1912 -)

Children of Alfred and Caroline:
- Gordon Fox (1949 - 1959)

Children of Freddie and Jennifer:
- Floyd Fox (1929 - 1993) = Polly Williams (1932 -)

Children of Floyd and Polly:
- Madeline Fox Kerr (1955 -)
- Barbara Fox Miller (1957 -)
- Robert Fox (1966 -)
- Walter Fox (1970 -) = Roberta Duncan (1975 -)

Children of Barbara:
- Nicholas Miller (1988 -)

Children of Walter and Roberta:
- Nina Fox (1992 -)
- Cookie Fox (1992 -)
- Skipper Fox (1993 -)

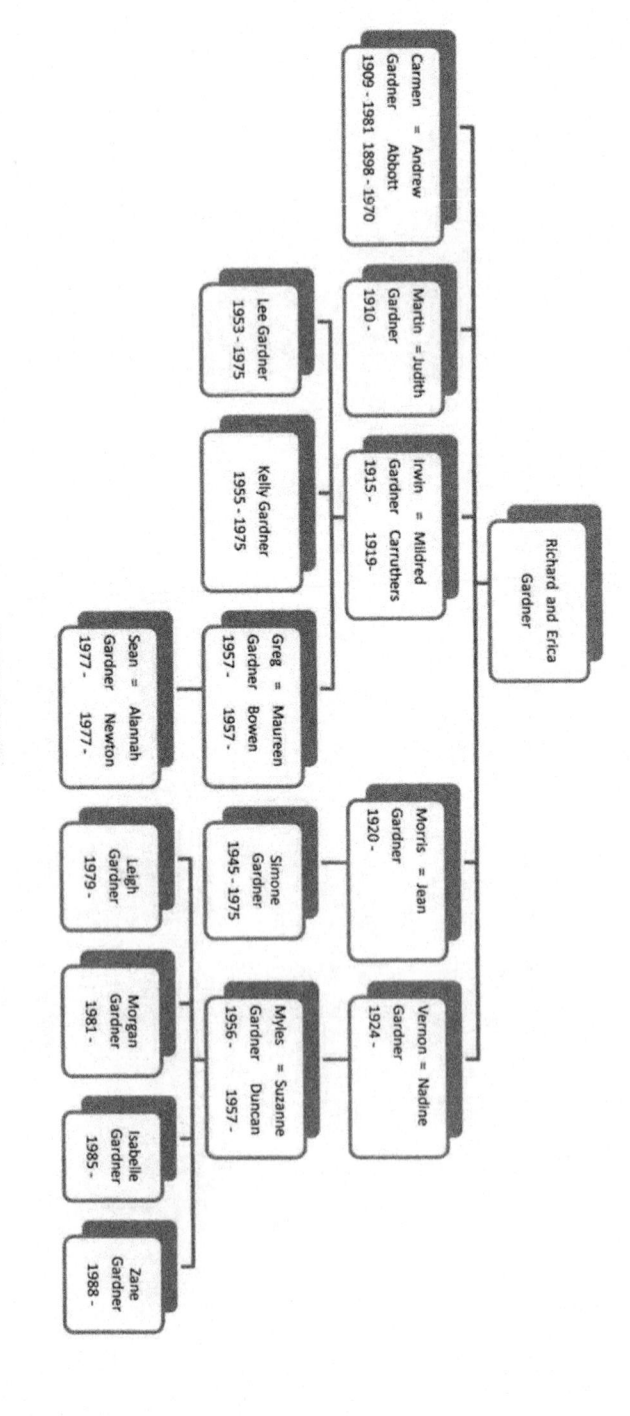

GARDNER

Richard and Erica Gardner

- Carmen Gardner (1909-1981) = Andrew Abbott (1898-1970)
- Martin Gardner (1910-) = Judith
  - Lee Gardner (1953-1975)
- Irwin Gardner (1915-) = Mildred Carruthers (1919-)
  - Kelly Gardner (1955-1975)
  - Greg Gardner (1957-) = Maureen Bowen (1957-)
    - Sean Gardner (1977-) = Alannah Newton (1977-)
- Morris Gardner (1920-) = Jean
  - Simone Gardner (1945-1975)
  - Myles Gardner (1956-) = Suzanne Duncan (1957-)
    - Leigh Gardner (1979-)
    - Morgan Gardner (1981-)
    - Isabelle Gardner (1985-)
    - Zane Gardner (1988-)
- Vernon Gardner (1924-) = Nadine

PART 1
Suzanne

Chapter 1

April 16, 1995

Thunder is good, thunder is impressive; but it is lightning that does the work.

- Mark Twain

Tomorrow, they will all eat their words.

When Terence Carruthers climbed behind the wheel of his 1977 Mercury Bobcat, he had a bottle half full of whisky and a head full of smug thoughts.

Yes indeedy-deed, tomorrow, the whole town will eat their words.

For nearly ten years, Terry Carruthers had known he was the brunt of sly winks and nudges in the ribs, both on the job site and in the pub down the street. He knew that the guys laughed at him behind his back, but that was only because they refused to believe what only Terry knew to be the truth. And tonight, at long last, it was all coming to pass.

Terry's rusted brown Bobcat sped down Highway 65, pelted with raindrops the size of beer nuts. He put some more weight to the gas pedal, anxious to get out of the storm and into his baby's arms. The worn little car sputtered in bitter retort, then roared as it edged into acceleration. The Bobcat was nothing special to look at, and would certainly win no drag races, but as Terry had often pointed out, it was good enough to get from Point A to Point B. Tonight though, Terry wanted to get to Point B a little quicker than usual. After all, he had been waiting for this special moment for ten years. Right now, the final few minutes of anticipation were the hardest to bear.

Terry found himself fantasizing about how the upcoming moment should unfold. Should he play hard to get, forcing Ellen to beg for his love and forgiveness? Or should he forget the little games, sweeping his one true love into his needy embrace as soon as he walked through the door? Terry decided that it didn't really matter. As long as the result was the same: that his Worst Mistake be erased and forever forgotten, wiped clean from the memories of his family, his friends, the good citizens of Headline, and most importantly, his ex-wife. Terry decided he should really be calling Ellen his wife now, what with the impending reunion. That was only one of many details he and Ellen would have to work out.

But as badly as Terry longed for the moment of reunion, he could not help return to relish in the self-satisfying moment when all his drinking buddies would have to eat every single one of their mocking words.

For the first few weeks after Ellen left Terry, the guys had been somewhat understanding at his difficulty in getting over the loss of his wife. They knew, some from experience, that having one's wife toss you out on your butt was tough to handle. But they expected Terry to stumble back to his feet within a few months like every other jilted man and start enjoying the single life that had suddenly been thrust upon him. Besides, it wasn't all bad. Terry wasn't even thirty years old yet; surely he had a few oats left to sow.

But the sowing of oats never happened. Terry simply refused to stop mooning over Ellen. He lamented incessantly to the fellows at the pub about how fabulous his dear Ellen was, and how much he truly loved her. Sometimes though, when the gush became too much to bear, someone more honest, like for instance, his foreman Tommy Armstrong would remind everyone of the unflattering truth of Terry's flawless marriage. Tommy brought up the many nights in the pool hall, when Terry, drunk out of his skull, would blather on about his heartless bitch of a wife to anyone who would listen. Tommy told the story of Candy, the barmaid from down at the Motor Inn: Terry managed to sneak away with that cute little bottled blonde after closing time on many a Saturday night, not to emerge until the grey Sunday dawn. Tommy disclosed stories of squandered pay checks, smashed fenders, and nights Terry passed out on Tommy and Bernadette's living room couch when Ellen refused to let him through the door of his own home. While hearing his buddies laugh and revel in tales of excess and wild abandon, Terry, a classic case of selective memory, would only look incredulously at Tommy and the boys with a look of hurt, then walk away.

"Hey, Terry, did you ever stop'n think that if you hadn't drank your family out of house'n home, Ellie wouldn't'a dumped your ass?"

"Terry, maybe Ellen'll take you back when the creditors stop pestering her 'bout all your bounced checks and maxed credit cards."

Terry could not comprehend these vicious comments. Didn't these people realize how much he agonized over his past sins? Didn't they know he had to live with these indiscretions each and every moment of each and every day?

Each and every day.

For ten years.

Until tonight.

Having just polished off a microwaved Swanson Salisbury steak dinner and a can of Molson, Terry had been getting ready to pop open a brand new flat of beer and spend the evening in front of the TV, either watching some Stallone action flick on the dish or a good wholesome porno video. But he didn't get as far as breaking the seal on the beer case, let alone making his viewing choice for the evening.

The telephone rang.

Terry burped, then picked up the receiver, only to hear a shaky female voice on the other end of the line. Ellen was distraught and very upset. She asked Terry to come over right away. He agreed and promised to be there in ten minutes and hung up before even asking why he had been summoned. Of course, there was no need to ask a pointless question like that. Terry knew exactly why Ellen had called. The moment of truth had finally arrived. She had come to her senses and decided she could not live another day without Terry by her side as husband and father to their two darling children.

Father? Children?

"How old were the kids now, anyway?" Terry mumbled to himself as he drove through the dark April night, a wet night that he failed to notice was only getting more and more blustery. Roxanne had to be eleven because she was not even walking when the Split had happened. That would make Seth twelve or thirteen years old. Terry was alarmed at the thought of being the father of teenagers. Not that he had ever been any type of a father to either of his kids. They used to come and stay at his trailer on the weekends when they were little, but they asked to stop the visits after a while. When Terry asked Ellen why, she said something about the children getting bored watching Daddy drink beer and fall asleep on the couch night after night. Terry thought that was a very insensitive thing for Ellen to say. He had a plenty good reason for self-medicating with the odd beer. His drinking was all her fault. She had no idea how deeply she had hurt him. What could Ellen expect after she had single-handedly destroyed his life?

Terry's glance fell to the brown paper bag resting on the bucket seat next to him. He had snatched it off the counter as he dashed out the door. His ramshackle trailer was parked on concrete blocks on his late father's farm some fifteen miles south of Headline, and he knew he would have to step on it if he expected to make it to Ellen's little bungalow in Headline in the ten minutes he had promised. He had found the time to grab his little brown paper sack though. His only thought at the time was that he may need it. For courage.

For all the excitement Terry felt about this long awaited moment, he felt strangely frightened too. It had been ten years since he had been with his wife. How could he ensure not blowing this golden moment? Terry grabbed the bag and pulled out its contents: a mickey of whisky, half full in the mind of a career optimist like Terry. He twisted the top off the bottle, letting the lid fall to the littered and dirty floor mats of the Bobcat. He raised the mouth of the bottle to his own.

But then he stopped. A voice spoke, a voice from the past that he did not quite recognize right away. It repeated a phrase that he had not heard in a long time.

"Please don't start drinkin', Terry. You know it turns you into a real asshole."

Terry pondered the voice, knowing he recognized it from somewhere. Of course! It had to be Ellen! She always encouraged him to give up drinking, and as badly as he wanted to please her, staying off the booze was the one thing that he had never managed to do for Ellen. And he knew it had disappointed her greatly.

Ellen was right. Tonight especially. Liquor was not the way to start a marriage anew. Ellen obviously had heard from those bigmouths in Headline that he was on the bottle worse than ever. But that hadn't stopped her from initiating things here tonight. Perhaps this night of passionate reunion was not appropriate to be half cut though. Ellen was such a titillating lover. Terry had so many fond manufactured memories of Ellen doing some incredible things to him in their bygone marriage bed. It had always amazed him that he could be so lucky to make love to such a beautiful woman---

Terry pulled the whisky bottle to his lips and took a quick swig. The thought of Ellen, naked and lustful, was too much for him to bear. He had to have just one drink.

"Terry, don't. You gotta stay sober. I need your help."

There was that voice again, louder and more desperate. Terry was puzzled. The voice was clearer now, and for the first time, Terry was unsure whether it really was Ellen after all. Ellen never took such a severe tone in her nagging. It had always been more of a whine; an annoying, almost nasal whine. God knows how he had hated that whine. Terry was sure though that Ellen would not whine at him when they got back together. She had learned her lesson.

"Terry," the voice said clearly, without a hint of a whine. "Do it for me, please."

Terry was suddenly frightened. The voice was familiar, and it definitely was not Ellen. For one, he realized he was hearing a man's voice. And though the voice was recognizable, he could not figure out who it belonged to. The voice rang in his foggy memory, traveling corridors that he had not ventured into for a very long time. Someone he had not talked to in a very long time was speaking to his addled brain. What was worse, the voice was so clear and precise; Terry could almost swear that it was coming from the passenger seat beside him. Imaginary voices from within his head were tolerable, almost commonplace. But when they moved to the seat next to him, he knew he was trouble. Maybe, just maybe, he had been dipping into the sauce too much after all.

Terry was overcome with a desire to take a look at the seat beside him, to the spot where the voice was coming from. But he was too petrified to do so. He had a strong feeling that if he did, he would see whoever it was speaking to him. The thought of seeing pink elephants, or worse, rattled Terry to the bone, and he took another longer pull on the whisky bottle.

The familiar sensation of warmth and calm that always came out of a bottle washed through his entire body. A blanket of mist clouded his mind and his vision and Terry relaxed into his seat, pressing his Bobcat even harder into the thunerous night. He decided it wouldn't hurt anybody for him to have a few more sips before he got to...where was he going anyway? Oh, yeah, Ellen's house.

After a few more numbing swigs of liquor, Terry found sufficient courage to swing his blurred gaze to the passenger seat. What he saw sobered him instantly. Terry screamed madly, and dropped his bottle on the floor. The remaining ounces of amber painkiller glugged onto the muddy floor mat. Terry didn't even notice what was happening to his whisky though. He continued to screech.

"No, no, no! It can't be!" Terry hollered hoarsely. Outside the rain was coming down harder than ever, and a bolt of lightning flashed across the sky. Seconds later, thunder boomed its retort.

"How did you get here?" Terry howled. "What do you want from me?" He stopped yelling. His face gained the expression of someone who was listening intently, though not truly comprehending.

"I don't understand! I don't know what you want from me! Please, just get outa my car!" He screamed in agony, staring into the invisible face beside him.

"Stop, no, you can't do this!" Terry shrieked. Suddenly the steering wheel of the car was whipping back and forth in Terry's tightly clenched fists, like there were two people fighting for control of the wheel. "Stop, I'll do what you say! You're gonna throw us into the ditch! You'll kill us!" The wheel continued to wind forward and back, throwing Terry's tiny beater all over the road.

"Stop! Please! Don't do this!" Terry howled. He looked out the front windshield of his car, just in time to stare directly into a set of oncoming headlights, spreading their bright beam over the rain soaked highway. Terry's hoarse begging turned into one long final scream.

2 DIE IN HEAD ON COLLISION
Headline Mail publisher killed

(Headline Mail - April 18, 1995)

Tragedy struck during the spring's first major thunderstorm which whipped across the Thunder region Sunday night. Two district men were killed in a head on collision 8 miles south of Headline.

Dead are Terence Carruthers, 37, a carpenter for Sureway Construction and Donald Bowen, 71, publisher of the Headline Mail, both from Headline. Carruthers' 1977 Mercury Bobcat car was in the wrong lane and in direct collision with the 1994 Mercury Sable driven by Bowen. Time of the accident was about 8 p.m. Sunday night. Death was reported to be instantaneous.

In a related story, Carruthers' 13 year old son, Seth Carruthers is in serious condition in hospital after falling from a tree early Sunday evening. Terence Carruthers was on route from his home near Thunder Ridge to the accident site at the Headline home of his ex-wife, Ellen Carruthers at the time of the collision with Bowen.

RCMP have confirmed that alcohol may have been a factor in the accident. The investigation continues.

Chapter 2

April 17, 1995

April is the cruelest month, breeding
Lilacs out of the dead land, mixing
Memory and desire, stirring
Dull roots with spring rain.

- "The Wasteland"
T.S. Eliot

    As usual, Polly Fox was late. That was to be expected though, since the business matriarch of Headline, Alberta was a very busy woman. She was a lady who turned heads wherever she went in town. These flourishes of sight and sound, of color and extravagance, were all a part of a very careful stage crafting. Even though she carried a look of incredulousness when attention turned her way, Polly knew exactly what she was doing. Today was no different.

    Polly screeched her 1995 Cadillac Fleetwood into two parking spots on Main Street. She emerged from the driver's side immaculately dressed in a large green hat and a sable trimmed jacket. Necks throughout the downtown area craned to see where the squealing tires came from. As soon as they saw that it was "just Polly", they went back to their business, the business of getting their own downtown Headline establishments up and running for the day. Dave at the barber shop continued to hose off the sidewalk in front of his barber pole. Steve at the dry cleaners across the street went back to cleaning up branches that had fallen in front of his store during last night's storm.

Local business people knew that few highway travelers made it into the downtown core of Headline. There were very few reasons for a tourist heading north to Alaska or the Yukon to make a detour into the town, when almost all their needs could be met at the businesses on two intersecting highways on the southern edge of town. Not that Headline was a particularly picturesque place, even Polly had to admit that. The downtown core was treeless and parkless, as too few businesses participated in her pet project, the Downtown Beautification Effort. But damn it! Downtown Headline had plenty to offer. Anyone who made one left hand turn from the main highway would find themselves at a busy little four way stop sign at the corner of Main Street and Thunder Avenue. The four corners of the intersection held Ken's Mechanical and Repair, Laura's Clothing Shoppe, a Rexall drug store, and the town's favorite eating establishment and more importantly, its designated gathering spot, the Fox Den.

Polly had a special place in her heart for the little café in the middle of town. While working as a waitress at the Fox Den when she was a mere teenager, she had met her future husband, Floyd Fox, who was manager at the time. From there, Floyd and Polly launched a marriage, a family, and a very successful business partnership. Floyd had died only two years ago, and Polly missed him desperately. But she was determined to soldier on. Currently, Polly owned no less than three local businesses and twelve apartment and duplex units, and they needed her full attention. She was also on the Headline Chamber of Commerce Board of Directors and needed to get inside the Fox Den for the breakfast meeting that started ten minutes ago.

Polly did take the time to pause outside the front door of the café to gather her composure and prepare for her grand entrance. She caught a glimpse of her reflection in the glass and smiled to herself with satisfaction, then she walked in. Polly immediately saw her group at their usual table at the back of the restaurant. She marched across the establishment in six long strides on four inch heels.

"Sorry I am late, everyone!" she announced.

"No problem, Polly," said the hefty middle-aged man in the corner. It was Leonard Kerr, owner of the Headline Market, the town's most profitable little grocery store. "We haven't started yet."

"We were just talking about that horrible accident last night," added the man to Leonard's left. Count on Glenn Andrews to wear his coveralls to a Chamber meeting. He may own Headline's oldest plumbing firm, but really! There are no toilets to plunge during breakfast. "Did you hear? Don Bowen and Terry Carruthers were killed. Slippery road out on ol' 65."

"Slippery road, my ass! You all know as well as I do what really happened out there!" Polly brayed loudly as she took a seat at the breakfast table with the rest of her Chamber executive members.

A mousy waitress wearing a nametag reading HEATHER, veered over to the group and poured coffee in five cups around the table.

"Are you'se ready to order?" asked Heather, pushing a stray piece of jet black hair back behind her ear. It was the consensus of all regulars at the Fox Den that no hair could attain such a color naturally. The regulars were correct.

"Yeah, sure," piped in Leonard. "I'll have your steak and eggs deluxe." Heather's forehead scrunched into a frown as she scribbled furiously on her pad, and then looked up in anticipation.

"Mr. Andrews?" she said, turning to Glenn.

"Bacon and eggs for me, sunshine. White toast and hash browns too."

"That sounds fine for me too, Heather," the red-haired man across the table said hastily. He appeared to be more interested in the agendas and files in front of him than ordering breakfast. Morris Gardner was a member of another of the more affluent families in the area. The Gardners were mostly businessmen, making their fortunes from small businesses, land deals and investments. Morris didn't say much, but when he did, Polly tended to listen.

"I'll have the continental breakfast," said the other woman at the table, a slim attractive lady in her mid-forties. Claire Robison ran Porcupine Oilfield Supply, a business started by her father in the '50's. Upon the death of Oliver Robinson, the town was shocked when his only child, thirty-one year old Claire, moved into her dad's office and picked up right where Oliver had left off. The rest was Headline history. Porcupine was now the biggest oilfield supply company in the Peace Country. Despite her involvement in the male world of oil, Claire retained her ladylike charm, actually thriving on it. Polly never could decide whether she admired Claire or not. Most of the time, she was just jealous of her.

"Oh, just coffee for me," Polly said hurriedly. "I never eat breakfast." Without another word, Heather bustled off to the kitchen.

Polly watched as Leonard dumped two heaping teaspoons of sugar into his coffee and took a sip. "So, Polly," he said in a slow deliberate manner. "What makes you think it wasn't the weather that caused Don Bowen's crash?"

"Oh, come on, Leonard," she exclaimed. "Everyone in Headline knows that Terry Carruthers character was nothing but a drunk!"

"Polly, please!" hissed Claire.

Don't play dumb with me!" Polly snapped back. She had little patience for Claire's lack of stomach for local gossip. "You know the stories as well as I do."

"Yes, but a Chamber of Commerce meeting is not the appropriate place to be discussing rumors and gossip."

"I think it's a little bit more than gossip, Claire," said Glenn.

"Glenn is right," agreed Morris, finally bringing his nose out of the documents in front of him. "You all know Terry worked for my nephew Myles for years. I have heard more horror stories than any one of you about that souse."

"That's right!" said Polly, running in high gear as soon as she sensed some consensus. "Why Val Osborne from the liquor store told me that he was coming in every day for his bottle."

"Please!" Claire exclaimed. "That is no way to speak about a young man who has come to the end of a very tragic life," Claire continued.

"You got a point there," said Leonard. "That boy was doomed from birth, what with that no-account father of his."

"All I can say," said Glenn, "is good riddance. There wasn't a good apple to be found under Ted Carruthers's entire tree."

"I just don't understand it. The rest of those Carruthers are good hard-working people. What went wrong with Ted and his kids is beyond me," puzzled Morris.

"I guess we'll never know now," Claire said crisply. "They're all gone now, never to speak a word in their own defense."

"There's no need for a defense," Leonard chided. "They were all losers: Ted, that hillbilly shack-up of his and their whole brood of bastards. And now a good hard-working man like Don Bowen is dead because of it too."

"It just goes to show you," Polly said, her voice rising in judgment and condemnation. "There is justice for no account losers, thieves, liars, whores and drunks like the Carruthers bunch. They all met their maker in the gruesome way they all deserved."

"All dead in automobile accidents out on the ol' 65," Morris puzzled. "It's just such a shame they had to take innocent people along with them."

"Like Don," Leonard said.

"Among others," Morris said. The entire group, even Polly, fell silent. Everyone around the table knew that Morris's only daughter Simone had been a passenger in a car that crashed over an embankment almost twenty years earlier. The driver of the car was Simone's boyfriend, Willie Carruthers, Terry's older brother; both Simone and Willie were killed instantly.

"Bastards," Polly seethed.

"Good morning ladies and gentlemen," a gruff booming voice pulled the group out of their unsavory discussion. They all looked up with a start, only to be faced with the lone individual that could instantly turn their faces into a collective red of embarrassment. That is, everyone except Polly.

"Good morning, Neil," Polly said smoothly, with nary a feather ruffled in her demeanor. Her eyes stayed wide and clear as she faced Neil Carruthers, cousin of the dearly departed. Neil was one of the few members of the Carruthers family that did not earn his living with his hands. The entire Carruthers clan was made up of farmers, tradesmen and oilmen. Neil, on the other hand, owned the Diamond Mine Jewelry Store, half a block down Thunder Avenue. "I'm so sorry to have heard about what happened to poor Terence," Polly continued. "We were all just talking about the tragedy."

"Yes, I heard," Neil said shortly. Polly blanched only slightly.

"It was a terrible shock to hear about the accident," Claire said sincerely. Unlike the rest of the group, Claire could express her condolences without a hint of hypocrisy, and she did so vehemently, not to be painted with the same brush as the rest of her breakfast party. "I know you were quite close to Terry, him being the only surviving member of your uncle Ted's family."

"Yes, we were all trying to help Terry out the best we could," Neil said. "He was a troubled man though, obviously not happy in life."

"I'm sure he's at peace now," said Claire sincerely.

"Absolutely, Claire. I appreciate your sentiments. Let's get in with business, shall we," Neil said gruffly, covering the choke that was building in his throat. "We have a meeting to conduct here."

"That's right," Claire said. "We have a lengthy agenda, and we're all busy people."

"Right, uh, okay," Glenn said, pulling himself into the business of the Headline Chamber of Commerce. "I see the first item of business is the Buck Bowen Scholarship. This is the tenth year of the scholarship following Buck's tragic accident, so we wanted to do something extra special this year. Any comments?"

By the time Heather brought the group their plates of bacon, eggs and pancakes, they were onto the third agenda item, and the topic of Terry Carruthers was forgotten. For the time being.

Headline Alberta

OBITUARY
(Headline Mail - April 18, 1995)

Terence Chester Carruthers passed away suddenly 10 miles south of Headline, Alberta on Sunday, April 16, 1995 at the age of 37.

He was born at Headline on January 22, 1958 to Theodore Carruthers and June Mikulski.

Terence Carruthers is survived by his children: Seth and Roxanne; uncles and aunts, Jake Edwards, Ernest Carruthers, Elton Carruthers, Mildred Carruthers (Irwin) Gardner; cousins, Monica Edwards (Glenn) Andrews, Morley (Fiona) Edwards, Rusty (Coreen) Carruthers, Olive Carruthers (Gerald) Bowen, Greg (Maureen) Gardner, Peter Carlson and Neil Carruthers.

He was predeceased by his parents Ted Carruthers and June Mikulski in 1971, his brother Willie Carruthers in 1975; his sister Rhonda Smith in 1985; his aunts Dorothy Carruthers in 1918; Peggy Carruthers Edwards in 1973, Lila Carruthers Carlson in 1989, Janis Carruthers in 1991, Rebecca St. John Carruthers in 1993; his uncles Justin Carruthers in 1931, Rod Carlson in 1977, his cousins Lee and Kelly Gardner in 1975, Lorna Carlson Webber in 1985 and Vincent Carlson in 1987.

Funeral services for the late Terence Chester Carruthers will be held on Thursday, April 20, 1995 at 4 p.m. at the St. Peter's United Church in Headline, Alberta, with Reverend Phillip Bentley officiating.

In lieu of flowers, donations may be made to the Janis Carruthers Memorial Fund. Funeral arrangements by Rosewood Funeral Chapel and Crematorium.

Deborah Ashton

OBITUARY
(Headline Mail - April 18, 1995)

Donald Herbert Bowen passed away suddenly 10 miles south of Headline, Alberta on Sunday, April 16, 1995 at the age of 71.

He was born at Headline on July 11, 1923 to James and Belinda Bowen.

Donald Bowen is survived by his loving wife Anna; daughter Beatrice Bowen Edwards; granddaughter Annabelle Edwards; brother Gerald (Olive) Bowen; sisters Isabelle Bowen Duncan and Amelia Bowen Abbott; nieces and nephews, Maureen Bowen (Greg) Gardner, Wayne (Sherry) Bowen, Suzanne Duncan (Myles) Gardner, Ray (Michelle) Duncan Jr., Charles Duncan, Roberta Duncan (Walter) Fox, Dwight Bowen, Christina Abbott (Jack) Larson.

He was predeceased by his father James Bowen in 1964; his mother Belinda Stone Bowen in 1975; his son Jeremy (Jessica) Bowen in 1975; his brother Stanley Bowen in 1980; his niece Laura Bowen in 1983; his nephews Blake Abbott in 1978, Adam Abbott in 1980 and Buck Bowen in 1985.

Funeral services for the late Donald Herbert Bowen will be held Wednesday, April 19, 1995 at 10 a.m. at the Mattson Lutheran Church in Headline, Alberta, with Reverend Christopher Stephens officiating.

In lieu of flowers, donations may be made to the Buck Bowen Memorial Scholarship Fund. Funeral arrangements by Rosewood Funeral Chapel and Crematorium.

Chapter 3

April 19, 1995

All I can say is that my life is pretty plain
I like watchin' the puddles gather rain.

- "No Rain"
Blind Melon

The Canadian prairies have the biggest sky in the world, they say. Not that Suzanne Gardner would know. She had never been further than three hundred miles from Headline, Alberta, and the sky was always the same size.

Standing on the crumbling sidewalk in front of her house, Suzanne was not impressed by what she saw. She peered cynically up into that so-called big sky and decided it was not so magnificent. Maybe today was not the best day to judge though. This gloomy April Wednesday felt more somber than ever to Suzanne. Low black clouds hung ominously over the town, rolling within themselves, threatening storm. They fell so low that the clouds almost touched the grain elevators that stood like sentinels down by the railway tracks. Suzanne could see all of Headline from her house on the top of the hill: the drab brown elevators, the mournful train engines and grain cars, and Headline's dejected little two street downtown. Suzanne rarely emerged from her own existence to allow herself to truly observe her little town.

Oh, Suzanne had read the cheery description of Headline and its historical significance on the big sign down at the tourist information center. According to the sign:

WELCOME TO HEADLINE!

First eyes on the majestic forests of the area were those of fur traders who established a Hudson's Bay Post at Thunder Lake some 15 km west of the present day location of Headline. Originally Headline was known as Willow Grove, named after the nearby Willow Creek. In 1906 the first pioneers settled in the area near the creek as its soil was rich for farming. The railroad, the lifeline to pioneer communities, arrived in 1910. In 1915, the town was renamed Headline by then mayor James Bowen, who in the same year started the town and indeed, the region's first weekly newspaper.

Oil was discovered in the 1950's and became one of the major industries of the area. That resulted in a sudden growth in population and services.

The Town of Headline is strategically located at important crossroads that lead to Canada's north. Excellent paved highways lead the traveler to northern adventure via Highway 47, the Mackenzie Highway that will take you to the Northwest Territories, and Highway 65 leading to Dawson Creek, the Alaska Highway and adventure in northeastern British Columbia, the Yukon and Alaska.

If one were to believe the faded words on the tourism sign (located conveniently next to two outdoor toilets and a weathered picnic table), one would think that Headline was a fabulous place to live! One would be wrong. Suzanne knew the truth that Headline was a town that thrived on the gossipy politics of isolation and boredom that kept its inhabitants ignorant and scared of the world of civilization some three hundred miles away. When she actually did think about the grand little town of Headline, it was all too depressing, reminding her that she had wasted her whole life here. Just these fleeting thoughts brought rare tears to Suzanne's eyes. Her lost youth and vanished dreams were the only things that could break through her tough exterior. Nothing else could hurt her.

A distant rumble erupted, like a growl in the back of the throat of a wild frothing beast. The thunder interrupted Suzanne's bitter thoughts and brought her back to the task at hand. She looked down from the sky to the plump green garbage bags hanging from each hand. It was garbage day on Wilcox Street.

Suzanne dropped the bags unceremoniously on the curb, and turned back towards the house. From here, she could see her house most clearly. She and Myles had bought this house proudly a half dozen years after they were married. It was the third oldest house in Headline, an original to the town, and they made great plans to renovate and refurbish to its original state, complete with music room for Myles and office for Suzanne. But these dreams, like all others made by Myles and Suzanne Gardner did not budge past the planning stage. Myles insisted he was too busy running the family business, but Suzanne knew the truth. They were simply too broke to do any renovations on their potential dream house. Now, nearly fourteen years since they moved in, the front porch sagged woefully, the shingles fell like autumn leaves with each gust of wind, and inside, the hardwood floors were still hidden by numerous layers of glue and ugly faded linoleum. During the winter, the house's embarrassing state of disrepair was thankfully hidden by hoarfrost and six foot snow drifts, in the summer by leaves and thick green foliage. Suzanne hated her house most during the spring and fall when the bare branches were naked, incapable of hiding its clutter and disarray.

Suzanne averted her eyes from her slouching house in disgust. She stared down at her feet and the cracked sidewalk beneath them. There resting on the edge of unkempt lawn, she saw a copy of the Headline Mail, the weekly local newspaper delivered to all residents each and every

Tuesday. The paper looked a bit soggy; it had obviously been delivered the previous evening, but not by an arm strong enough to toss as far as the front porch. Suzanne sighed, picked up the newspaper, walked up the steps and opened the front door.

Every house radiates some kind of disposition, some feeling of warmth or coolness, happiness or gloom, whether from the smells or tidiness or just that nameless something that hangs in the air. This is a home's very atmosphere. The inhabitants of the house are usually oblivious of these unspoken vibrations emitted by their own abode, being much too overcome by routine and familiarity. It is probably best then that Suzanne Duncan Gardner had that shield of routine to keep her from realizing her house's mood, or she would have been even further ashamed. As she stepped through the door of her residence of the past fifteen years, Suzanne was oblivious to the fact there was no rush of family warmth. The aura was actually that of fear, of foreboding anger and sadness, and it emanated from every faded piece of furniture and each cheap department store print on the wall. It was as if the mere existence of this cloud of unhappiness made it impossible for Suzanne to even attempt to personalize and add warmth to her family's home. It was all so unnecessary since no amount of "fixing up" could overpower the true tone of the house. As much as Suzanne loved her children, she has been unable to remove herself from the fear inside to create a home. But there was no time to even notice what was sorrowfully missing.

"Mom, I can't find my black jeans---"

"Mom, tell Morgan to quit pinching me."

"Mom, Zane said we're can't go to the movies tonight---"

"Mom, I need three dollars for school."

Suzanne waded through the cacophony of voices and made her way into the kitchen. There would be small sanctuary from the morning mayhem in making five paper bag lunches. As she began spreading peanut butter on bread though, Suzanne knew very well she was not safe from the persistent wants of her children.

"So, I'll pick you up about a quarter to ten," Myles said slowly and quietly from behind the family kitchen table. Through the din, Suzanne had almost forgotten that her taciturn husband had not yet left for work. But there he was, methodically eating his breakfast of oatmeal and grapefruit, just like he did every morning.

Myles was tall and slender, with hair fitting the exact description of what Suzanne's mother called "a rat's nest." Suzanne wondered why her husband always looked disheveled. Even first thing in the morning, she imagined he could have managed to tame a few rooster tails after his morning shower. But no matter what the time of day, he always looked like he needed a shave and a haircut, and his shirttail was inevitably untucked. Suzanne had come to excuse Myles' appearance, rationalizing that his artistic mind could not be bothered with such trivialities as appearance. That defense was getting a little stale though since Myles had not done anything remotely artistic in years. She remembered a time when she thought the hurried-little-genius aspect of Myles' personality was fascinating, even sexy. Now it was just another annoying aspect of her moody and distracted husband.

"What for?" Suzanne replied absently. She had enough on her mind in the morning without Myles adding to it.

"For your uncle's funeral, of course," he said, with typical quiet arrogance.

"Mom, I cannot go to school today," announced the teenage girl who flounced into the kitchen, pretty despite the fact she was still wearing pajamas and had not put a brush to her long snarled blond hair. Leigh, the eldest Gardner child at sixteen, had a new and different crisis each and every day of her life. Leigh wanted to be an actress when she grew up, and Suzanne recognized she was a natural given her passion for melodrama. Suzanne knew there was no way she could avoid Leigh's emergency of the hour.

"What's wrong, Leigh?"

"I cannot find my black jeans anywhere."

"You do remember that today is Donald Bowen's funeral, don't you, Suzanne," continued Myles.

"Of course, I do, Myles."

"What am I gonna do, Mom?"

"Leigh, can't you wear something else today?" Suzanne said in exasperation.

"No, I can't. Darcy Nelson is going to ask me to the dance today, I just know it, and I need those black jeans."

"Didn't you put the jeans in the mending basket? Didn't they lose a button?"

"Mom, isn't that button fixed yet?" Leigh said, grey eyes wide and hands waving in exasperation

"Unless of course you don't want to go," Myles said. "It is your family after all."

"Of course I want to go, Myles," Suzanne said, irritated at being forced to deal with two issues at once. "I just---"

"Mom!" called the bawling voice of another child, bursting into the kitchen. "Morgan took my slingshot!"

"Morgan, give Zane back his slingshot!" Suzanne called wearily.

"Mom, my jeans!"

Suzanne glanced at her watch. Once again the morning had escaped her: only ten minutes until the bus came to take the kids to school.

"Leigh, bring me those jeans right now if you expect it to be fixed. Zane, get in here and eat your breakfast. Morgan, where is Belle?"

Morgan looked up from her cereal innocently. "She was in the living room last I saw her," she said.

Suzanne darted into the living room to check on her ten year old daughter, the quiet and completely inconspicuous Isabelle. Suzanne never had to fuss over little Belle. She was always ready, always on time, always behaved. Suzanne often worried though about completely forgetting Belle in the clamor that was life in the Gardner home. She saw her daughter sitting in the armchair in the living room, dressed and combed and completely prepared, as usual.

"Belle, are you ready?" Suzanne asked the same redundant question she asked every morning.

"Almost. I need three dollars for art supplies."

"Suzanne," Myles spoke from the front entry where he now stood, lunchbox in one hand, hard hat in the other. "Are you sure you want to go to this funeral?"

"Of course, Myles. Why do you keep asking me that?"

"Wishful thinking," he said. "I was hoping you would decide to sit this one out. I expect that Beatrice will be there," he added with disdain, as if the name left a foul taste in his mouth.

Myles' words circled in Suzanne's head like an annoying song. The notion had not once entered her mind, until now. But now that the words had been spoken, Suzanne could not get rid of them. It was painfully obvious that what Myles had said was true. Beatrice would most certainly be there.

The routine of rummaging three dollars from her purse for Belle, sewing the button on Leigh's jeans, and refereeing another squabble between Morgan and Zane only half occupied Suzanne's consciousness. It was a cold expectant silence that met Suzanne after the children were shooed out the door and she had nothing to distract her from her thoughts. Her thoughts of Beatrice.

* * *

The only thing that Suzanne enjoyed more than watching a thunderstorm was standing out in the middle of one. The sensation of being pelted by huge wet nuggets of rain, and the accompanying symphony of lightning all around her, was a delight. It was a familiar family anecdote that a young Suzanne often ran out into the most frightening storm, arms reaching upward, hair and clothes pasted to her skin. She would continue her private rain dance until her frantic mother dragged her back inside.

Today, there was no time for frivolous immature rain dances; today was Uncle Donald's funeral. This day, the grownup Suzanne would settle for watching the storm from the dry sanctuary of the porch, quiet and alone, patiently waiting for Myles to pick her up. She shivered in the cool April morning and pulled her sweater closer around her body. As much as she would love to run through the torrent, her arms flung up to the sky in oblivious ecstasy, she had other more important matters to ponder today. She had to think about church and sober-faced relatives and townspeople. There was no time in her day to scamper in the rain like a six year old child.

In actual fact, Suzanne had no memory of any of this reckless abandon of the youngster Suzanne Duncan. Her mother had told the stories of Suzy standing out in the thunderstorms many, many times, and Suzanne had often tried to squeeze at least one of these incidents out of her stubborn memory. To no avail. Her childhood memories were oddly as porous as a sieve, diminished to confused flashes of faces and settings, like odd snapshots dropped from a shoebox in complete disarray.

Her childhood home at Thunder Ridge, the old farmhouse, the barn and the tattered sheds she had covered with countless coats of paint that would only be stripped by another summer of rain.

Chasing her dirty-faced brothers RJ and Charley around the yard, barefoot.

The institutional flashes of her classmates from Thunder Elementary and Headline School: Connie Sullivan, Jennifer McRae, Maureen Bowen, Sophie Andrews, Frances Parker and the unforgettable Beatrice...

Suzanne was startled. This blast of recollection was so real, so vivid. And so unusual. Memories rarely opened their eyes for Suzanne and when they did, she quickly pushed them away, frightened of some unspeakable unknown. So why was this happening now? Why had Suzanne been flooded with these vivid memories for the first time in years? It had all stemmed from an innocent thought of a young Suzanne who used run in the rain. Why were these scattered recollections pouring out with the rain?

Suzanne had been experiencing flashes of past memories all morning long. She had been ever since Myles had left for work. She had been flung into a long forgotten world of years gone by, a time so completely different from today that Suzanne could scarcely recognize it as her own life. But as painful as it was to remember those muddled and confused years of youth, it was much better than looking ahead to the Dreaded Task at hand: Uncle Donald's funeral.

It wasn't that Suzanne dreaded funerals. Lord knows she had attended enough of them over the years. She had thought nothing of going to this one either, that is until Myles' oh-so casual remark. Of course she knew the comment had not been casual either. It had been well-planned and perfectly timed to hit its mark with deadly accuracy. And now, as much as she had tried to avoid the thought, she could think of nothing else. Like a fly buzzing in her ear, it was there. The Dreaded Task.

All the time she had been dressing in that same old navy blue dress that she wore to funerals all the time. Navy blue. Not black.

You're supposed to wear black to funerals. But what's the big deal anyway. You go to funerals constantly, Suzanne. You've probably worn this same plain navy blue dress to half of them and it never bothered you before.

During her futile attempt to put some style in her mousy limp hair, Suzanne could not get her mind off...

Beatrice...

Suzanne was not even sad about the death of Uncle Donald. Sure, it was a terrible tragedy the way that drunk Terry Carruthers swerved right in front of him, killing them both. But Suzanne had not participated in a civil conversation with her uncle once in her life (unless you count the time she applied for a job at his newspaper and he had flatly turned her down). She only knew him because he was such an important man in Headline, publisher of the Headline Mail and president of the school board.

And of course because he was Beatrice's father.

Uncle Donald had always been distant. Every time Suzanne saw him he was silent and stern and distracted, as if he had too many important things on his mind. For all she knew, he probably did. Funny though, how he could be so serious and humorless, the exact opposite of his very own daughter.

Beatrice...

Beatrice Bowen was the bubbliest most upbeat person Suzanne had ever met. Beatrice had always managed to have a good time, whether she sniffed it out somewhere in Headline - The Most Boring Town in the Entire Dominion of Canada, or whether she created it herself. In every memory Suzanne had of Beatrice, they were either laughing or singing or crying. Suzanne felt tears gather in her eyes as she thought about the years with her dear friend. It had been so long since she had allowed herself to reminisce about Beatrice. The thoughts always caused a big lump to swell in Suzanne's throat and tears to sting her eyes. God damn it, I miss her!

Beatrice is going to be there...

So why the hell are you so scared about seeing her today? Admit it, Suzanne! That's the reason why you've been on so distracted all morning. That's probably why you're having childhood flashbacks. That's why you're worried about wearing this plain old navy blue dress to yet another funeral. You know Beatrice is wealthy and successful and you don't want her to know how wealthy and successful you are not! You remember telling Beatrice that you were going to be different, you were going to escape Headline and do something important. No one else knows how badly you betrayed your dreams, Suzanne, no one except Beatrice. Face it, Suzanne, you're embarrassed to see her again! After all these long years of yearning to see your old friend, the day has finally arrived and you're scared out of your mind!

Beatrice is going to be there!

So what if Beatrice is going to be there! And so what if Beatrice has lots of money and a big important job in Vancouver! Beatrice is still Beatrice! You can be sure she still has that infectious laugh that you have no choice but to join right in. I'll bet she can still mesmerize a room full of strangers in five minutes flat with her wit and humor. And Beatrice won't give a damn whether you're Headline Housewife 1995 or the richest person in the world. You know, Suzanne, that despite the fact that you haven't laid eyes on her in twenty years, she is still the best friend you've ever had.

Beatrice is going to be there.

I know, I know. And that's why I am so petrified and so electrified all at the same time. Suzanne closed her eyes, trying to calm herself. She tried to forget where she was going in less than fifteen minutes. Beatrice won't even remember me and even if she did what would we have to say to each---

"Suzanne."

Suzanne snapped out of her spiral of skepticism. She opened her eyes. There was Myles, dark and brooding as always, leaning against the veranda post.

"Are you ready?"

"I guess so," Suzanne replied uncertainly. "How do I look?"

"Fine," Myles said without even looking at her. Typical Myles. Myles Gardner could never be accused to throwing insults - or compliments for that matter. A man of few words, they said of Myles. Besides, there was no one left on the porch to be irritated with. Myles was gone, probably already in the car waiting.

Suzanne sighed. She picked up her purse and coat and followed her husband. As she stepped off the porch, she felt raindrops pelting down upon her. Just then, a jagged flash of lightning ripped across the sky, with a crash of thunder immediately following. Suzanne managed a weak smile.

Chapter 4

September 1, 1968

I scratch my head with the lightning and purr myself to sleep with the thunder.

"Life On the Mississippi"
- Mark Twain

Whenever Suzanne heard her parents begin to fight, she made her escape. She would not move an inch physically, but she would transport herself so far away from their cursing and screaming, she might as well be in Ottawa, Ontario. And today was no exception.

Even though she now sat scarcely four feet away from them, she heard not a word, not a scream, not a slap.

"How many times do I have to tell you? Jesus, Isabelle, you're so goddamn stupid, I dunno why I keep you around, woman!"

"Don't say that, Ray!"

"What woulda happened to your sad ass if I hadn'ta felt sorry for you."

"Ray, please," the feeble reply was cut short by a loud thump. Isabelle's frenzied wail rose and the blows fell.

Suzanne heard nothing, just as she had heard scarcely a cross word between her parents in all of her eleven years. And that was something pretty difficult to miss. Ray Duncan always found ample reason to screech biting assaults on his weak-spirited wife, or to simply beat her senseless.

Ray didn't want to be the bad guy. He didn't like having to battle this poor dense woman into submission time and time again. It was her repeated stupidity despite previous punishments that drove him to these rampages. If only she didn't pull such asinine blunders: blurt out embarrassing things in front of his friends, disagree with his decisions, burn the supper. If she could only stop making him angry, life would be so much easier for Ray Duncan.

Not to mention Isabelle. Or the children. But Ray Duncan's three children were the last thing on his mind anyway. Childhood was a black fog in Ray's own memory, a fog conveniently placed there to obscure some rather grim incidents. With no childhood to draw upon, he placed no importance on the age whatsoever. Let the little buggers run around and howl at the moon for all he cared, until they're old enough and big enough to be of some good to him, you know, chop kindling, hoe the garden, shovel the barn, whatever. In the meantime, just stay the hell out of Ray Duncan's path. And that's exactly what they did.

All three of the Duncan children could sense when a confrontation was about to spark between Ray and Isabelle. Before a harsh word was even spoken, before a hand was raised, Suzanne, RJ and Charley would all stash themselves away in their own private sanctuaries. RJ managed by putting as much physical distance between himself and his battling parents. At home, he would high tail it to the barn, dragging Charley behind him when his little brother was too young to fend for himself.

Suzanne, though, did nothing to run away from it all. Maybe because she was the oldest, Suzanne had experienced more screaming and swatting than her brothers and was simply immune. She had endured every possible stinging insult spit from her father's tongue and countless sobs of physical pain from her mother, only to witness business as usual in the clear morning's light. Mama and Dad both went back to work, cooperating in the operation of their subsistence dirt farm. It was that type of hypocrisy that could drive anyone to mental paralysis. But that was not the full story of Suzanne. She was a sensitive child who would never be able to bear any abuse inflicted on another living soul. Suzanne could never turn her back on anyone crying out for help. RJ and Charley would have to agree that they had the most kind-hearted, protective big sister in Headline, no, in the whole wide world.

Whenever that certain type of electricity hit the air though, the very specific kind that could be detected only by the children of Ray and Isabelle Duncan, the kind that sent RJ and Charley scattering, Suzanne would simply slip away. No matter where she was physically, she would drift off into a waking sleep, a slumber possessed by the thunder.

From an early age, Suzanne had learned to take shelter from the terrible things that her father did to his family. She did so by hiding in the thunder. The loud booms of thunderstorms that so often shook the Duncan home, drowned out the thumps and the screams in the kitchen or in her parents' bedroom on many a night. It was only a matter of time before Suzanne heard the thunder all the time, day and night, summer and winter, every time there was a fight. Whether there was a storm outside or not, Suzanne could feel the torrential rain pouring down upon her, soaking her clothes and hair to the skin. She could see the sharp swords of lightning streaking across the leaden sky. She could hear the booming cannons of the thunder.

Today was no exception.

Suzanne sat on a tattered lawn chair outside her family's tent, just one of a myriad of tents, trailers and campers clustered all around her. There must have been over one hundred units in all. And no wonder. It was the biggest event of the summer for the Headline area: the 49th Annual Labor Day Thunder River Campout. Rich and poor, friends and enemies, happy and miserable, everyone participated in what was affectionately known as the Long Weekend: a celebration of the close to another summer, a prayer for a successful harvest, a last chance to kick up their collective heels before another long northern Alberta winter. It was a "must attend" for everyone in Thunder Ridge and Headline, but especially the First Families of the area: the Gardners, the Bowens, the Abbotts, the Carruthers, the Edwards, the Foxes and yes, even the Duncans. These were the families that descended from the original pioneers of the Thunder River area, those that first laid eyes on this bountiful country, only to create colorful headlines and glorious stories of this land of milk and honey to the cities in the south. It was these near-fables of wheat growing as high as a man's chest and of tall and endless stands of timber that brought many more hearty settlers to the area. It was on this September Long Weekend that everyone got together to rejoice in their rich land and their own tenacity to endure the harsh climate: snow to the waist in the winter, and alternating extremes of sweltering heat and torrential rain in the summer. The Long Weekend had never been rained out yet though, which was "damn near a miracle," to quote old Jake Edwards, since there was no other dates on the calendar between April 13th and September 29th that had been given grace from the Headline storms. Of course there was one solitary person that was experiencing a brisk thunderstorm this day, and that was Suzanne Duncan.

Dressed in faded denim shorts and a sleeveless blouse, the scorching midday sun streamed down on Suzanne's scrawny brown arms and legs. She did not see the littered campsite around her, nor did she see her two year old brother, Charley, playing in the dust with a toy truck with only three wheels, sputtering and growling truck sounds as he played. Little Charley was completely grey with dust, except for the few streaks where he had sweated dust into mud. Suzanne's other brother, RJ, tossing a baseball back and forth to his best friend, Murray Hawkins. But of this, Suzanne saw nothing. She heard nothing.

"If you don't shut your stupid trap, Isabelle, I'll give you another one!"

"No, please, don't..."

"Suzanne."

"Oh, quit your whinin'. You're pathetic."

"Ray..."

"Suzanne!"

"I warned you!"

"SUZANNE!"

It was only when RJ bellowed mere inches from her ear that Suzanne finally heard her name being called. She returned from the storm to her family's campsite beside Thunder River.

"What, RJ?" she said with annoyance. She could not understand why her brother had to yell.

"I threw my ball too hard, and it's way over there in those people's campsite," RJ explained, his six year old face betraying not only immense concern over the lost ball, but worry over the racket coming from the tent. It was this distressed look that melted Suzanne, as it always did. Suzanne would never let anything bad happen to either of her brothers, not even a lost ball.

"I'll get it for you, RJ," she assured.

"But, Suzanne," RJ protested. "It landed by that big trailer over there." He pointed a pudgy finger at the shiny new holiday trailer across the clearing.

"That far?" Suzanne exclaimed. "You've got a strong arm, RJ." Despite his troubles, RJ beamed at the compliment. Suzanne looked across to the trailer. Now that she had made her promise to RJ, she wondered how she could possibly return her brother's ball to him.

"You stay here and watch Charley," she instructed as she marched across the campground. RJ crouched down beside his brother and put his hand protectively on Charley's back. As usual, Charley was oblivious to what was going on around him, both in the tent and between his brother and sister. At his brother's touch, Charley looked up at RJ with a frown. He clutched his broken red truck to his dirty chest, convinced that RJ was about to take it away from him.

Suzanne crossed the campground at a quick clip. Before her, resting on four sturdy jacks, was a shiny new holiday trailer, the latest model for 1968, she guessed. A brilliant green awning stuck out from the side, hung with numerous multicolored patio lanterns. Under the awning rested a picnic table laden with amazing food. Upon the checkered table cloth there was fresh baking, a bowl of fruit, and on the camp stove, what looked to be a simmering pot of chili con carne. Suzanne stared dreamily at the idyllic little world in front of her, amazed. She looked back at her own campsite and stared at the tattered tent and mismatched lawn chairs.

Suddenly voices rose from inside the trailer, and Suzanne stiffened, fear chasing away her bleak comparisons. What if they heard her snooping around out here? They would surely drag her back to her parents, where without RJ's ball she would have to face her father.

Suzanne refused to even imagine that scenario any further. She knew she had to collect RJ's ball and get out of here before she was discovered. She gazed around the camping area, beside trees, under the picnic table and the trailer itself.

Hey, there it was!

Suzanne saw RJ's dusty scuffed baseball, the very ball that her father had given him for his second birthday, resting innocently between the back wheels of the trailer. She groaned inside. She would have to get down on her belly and slither like a snake in order to get it back. And Suzanne knew that was exactly what she was going to do. Not only because going back empty-handed would break RJ's heart, it would also mean big trouble for her little brother. She knew her father would tear a sizable chunk of hide off RJ for losing that special ball. With that image in her mind, Suzanne got down in the dust and began squirming towards her mark. Her movement was slow in the cramped space under the trailer, but Suzanne could feel her inch-by-inch progress. She was unmindful of the grubby mess she was making of her clothes as she shuffled along. The ball was mere inches from her outstretched grasp when suddenly she felt a tremendous pull on her feet. With one brisk movement, Suzanne was yanked from the dark cool beneath the trailer back into the blinding afternoon sun.

"Hey!" she yelled as she emerged. She rolled over from her stomach to her back and faced whomever it was that had wrenched her out from under the trailer. Suzanne saw a girl, disheveled, redheaded and freckled and much bigger than herself. She recognized the girl, but since she went to school in Headline instead of Thunder Ridge, Suzanne did not know her name.

"Hey, you're not Connie Sullivan!" the redhead yelled.

"No, I'm sure not!"

"I thought that oddball was nosing around my trailer again! I can't stand that geeky Connie Sullivan, and you know what? She thinks she's my best friend. Now why would I be friends with that four-eyed idiot, snot running out of her nose every time you see her." As this bizarre red-head rambled on, Suzanne wondered whether the girl was going to get around to asking what Suzanne was doing under said trailer. Suddenly, her monologue stopped. "Hey, what are you doing under my trailer?"

"My brother's ball rolled under it." Suzanne explained feebly, attempting to sound less frightened than she really was. "I was just trying to get it back."

"Yeah right."

"It's true!" Suzanne exclaimed. "Just look and see!"

"Do you think I was born yesterday? I'm not getting down there to look for a ball that's not even there!"

"But it's there!"

"What's your name, you prowler, you?"

"I'm not a prowler---"

"WHAT'S YOUR NAME?"

"Suzanne."

"Well Miss Suzanne, you just wait until your parents find out what you've been up to. I'll bet they'll tan your ass---"

Before Suzanne even knew what she was doing, she began sobbing hysterically. "Please, please, don't tell my parents! I'm begging you! Just don't tell them! I just came over here to get my brother's ball."

"Whoa! Whoa! Whoa!" the redhead said. "Are you saying that there really is a ball under my trailer?"

"Y-yes!"

The girl bent and peered under the trailer. "What do you know? There is a goddamn ball under there!" Without a word, she dove under and came back a few seconds later, ball in hand. She tossed it to Suzanne.

"Gee, thanks!" Suzanne exclaimed with glee. She was sure that she was happier to see that ball than RJ could ever be. Suzanne imagined that her brother was peering over in this direction from his safe vantage point at this very moment, wondering if he would ever pitch his treasured ball again.

"No problem," the redhead said. "Oh, by the way, I'm Beatrice. I'm twelve." Suzanne was surprised that this girl was only a year older than she was. She was a full head taller than Suzanne and probably outweighed her by thirty pounds.

"My name is Suzanne. But I guess I already told you that," Suzanne stuttered. "I'm eleven and I'm going into the sixth grade." As soon as she said it, Suzanne knew that the sixth grade would not impress this Beatrice girl too much. She was probably in seventh grade. Maybe even eighth. Lord knows she looked it.

"Nice to meet you," Beatrice said politely. Suzanne was puzzled by this brash rumpled odd-looking girl who at the same time seemed to have at least a faint gleam of culture and breeding. But that sophistication didn't last long. "What school do you go to?"

"I was going to Thunder Ridge School 'cause we live out there. But I'll be going to Oscar Nelson School in Headline this year 'cause Thunder Ridge only goes to Grade Five."

"I'll be in Grade Six at Oscar Nelson too! I should be in Grade Seven, but I failed Grade One. My teachers say that I'm not 'academically minded,' whatever that means." As Suzanne listened to Beatrice's jabbering, inside she was thrilled. Even though she had just met this extraordinary girl, she seemed to be the type of person you would like to have on your side in a new school. Especially Oscar Nelson. There were some pretty uppity girls at that school. Girls whose fathers worked for the oil companies or owned big farms.

"Beatrice!" a voice called from across the campground. Both Beatrice and Suzanne looked.

"Oh, no!" Beatrice moaned.

"Who's that?"

"That idiot Connie Sullivan."

"I know her. She rides the same bus as me."

"Does she stink on the bus too?"

"Sure she does," Suzanne replied, wrinkling her nose. "She smells like sweat and bum." Suzanne could not believe what was happening here. She was actually gossiping with a girl who had been going to kill her only a couple of minutes before.

"Oh, shit," Beatrice cursed. "Here she comes. She thinks I'm her partner in the three-legged race."

"Why does she think that?"

"Because the sneaky thing picked me in front of the parents. What was I gonna do? Tell them all to go to hell?" Before Suzanne could answer, Connie was upon them.

"Hi, Beatrice," Connie sang, her voice dripping as much as her nose was. Suzanne saw her blotchy face and greasy hair, and didn't know whether to be revolted or feel sorry for the girl. For the sake of her new friend Beatrice, she decided upon revulsion.

"Hi," Beatrice replied shortly.

"Let's go! Three-legged race starts in ten minutes." It was immediately obvious that Suzanne was not a part of this conversation. In Connie's world, she simply did not exist. Suzanne was eternally relieved.

"Gee, Connie, I'd really love to, but..."

"What?" Connie looked alarmed. She looked as if a prized possession was about to be stripped from her very hands.

"Well, you see, Connie," Suzanne burst in. "Beatrice is my partner in the three-legged race."

"What?!"

"That's right," Beatrice said quickly. "I didn't want to tell you because I thought it might hurt your feelings."

"But you and me are partners," Connie persisted.

"Our mothers forced Beatrice and me to be partners," Suzanne piped up.

"Yeah," Beatrice said, with false resignation in her voice. "We had no choice."

"Aw…" Connie's shoulders slumped. She knew she was licked.

"But you know, Jennifer McRae is still looking for a partner," Beatrice said.

"Really?" Connie said, with newfound hope.

"Yeah," Beatrice said. You should head on down there right away and catch her."

"I sure will," Connie said. "Thanks!" She began to jog off.

"Does Jennifer really need a partner?" Suzanne asked.

"Of course not!" Beatrice howled. "The most popular girl in school? What I wouldn't give to see the look on Jennifer's face when creepy old Connie asks to be her partner!"

The girls laughed again.

"Hey, thanks," Beatrice said when the giggles subsided. "You have a good imagination. I coulda never thought that whopper up so fast."

"Yeah well, I owed you," Suzanne said. There was a short pause in the conversation, and Suzanne knew that the fun was over. "I guess I better be going."

"Going?" Beatrice said. "Going where?"

"Back to camp."

"What about the three-legged race?"

"But I thought it was all just a story to get rid of Connie," Suzanne sputtered.

"Are you crazy?" Beatrice grinned. "Of course we're gonna do it. We're a great team! And besides, how could I ever face Connie Sullivan if we didn't race together. Come on, we better get down there before the race starts."

"I don't know…" Suzanne wasn't sure whether she should be running off. After all, what would her parents say?

"Come on," Beatrice coaxed. "It'll be fun! Maybe we can still see Connie asking Jennifer to be her partner!" Suzanne couldn't say no. Not only was the whole scheme irresistible, but so was Beatrice.

"Oh, okay!"

"All right!" Beatrice yelped and started to run. Suzanne bolted to join her, noticing that she still had RJ's ball in her hand.

"Wait!" she called to Beatrice as she detoured in the direction of her own camp. Beatrice braked and looked back to see Suzanne jogging over to RJ, still hovering near Charley and his crippled truck. She wordlessly approached the worried-looking boy, and saw his face light up when she placed the ball in his tiny fist.

* * *

The only clue that the afternoon was growing late was the lengthening shadows. The lateness of the day could certainly not be discerned by the temperature. This first of September, 1968, was only growing more sweltering as the day grew older. It was probably this lack of afternoon chill that caused the campground children to play much longer than they realized. In fact, it was only when Beatrice and Suzanne were turning the final curve in the dusty road before their adjacent campsites that they realized just how much time had expired.

"I still can't believe it," Beatrice said, shaking her head. "Connie and Jennifer won the three legged race."

"Jennifer had the most shocked look on her face when they hit the ribbon at the finish line first," said Suzanne.

"Because they actually won?" Beatrice snorted, "Or because Connie farted at the very instant they snapped the ribbon?"

"Both!" Suzanne exploded into laughter. Beatrice joined in what must have been the twentieth fit of laughter between the two. As the hysterics calmed, Suzanne saw her own family campsite ahead.

"I guess we're back," she said. They stopped just beside the awning of Beatrice's family trailer.

"I guess so." Beatrice replied. Suzanne thought that she almost sounded disappointed. Suzanne felt disappointment herself. She had just had about the most fun day of her whole life. But she was positive that this type of frivolity was daily routine for a hoot like Beatrice.

"I should get back to my camp," Suzanne said, suddenly sobered. "My parents are gonna kill me."

They both looked up with a start though, when the trailer door swung open.

"Beatrice," said the lady at the trailer doorway. Suzanne thought she was beautiful, with carefully styled auburn hair and sharp green eyes. The resemblance to Beatrice told her that this was certainly her mother.

"Hi, Mama," Beatrice said.

"Where have you been?" Beatrice's mother said coolly.

"At the Games Day down by the lake," Beatrice said. "You remember they had all kinds of events planned. It was a lot of fun and we---"

"Come inside," Beatrice's mother said. "And bring your little friend in too. I'm sure your father would like to see who you've been running around with all day." Suzanne knew Beatrice's mother was not pleased with her daughter's shabby companion.

Beatrice shot Suzanne an apologetic look. She obviously did not relish sharing this moment of discipline. Suzanne was terrified. She was suddenly reminded that people who camp in beautiful brand new trailers probably don't want their children scampering around the countryside with any old hillbilly runt from across the campground. Especially a Duncan. Suzanne crept inside the trailer behind Beatrice and her mother.

The trailer was exquisite. The wood-grain cupboards and flowered curtains, the harvest gold stove top and plush carpeting. Making the Norman Rockwell picture complete was the perfect family sitting at the table. There was a distinguished-looking gentleman with his jet-black hair slicked straight back on his head. His clothes were casual, but still very expensive looking. A clean-cut teenage boy who looked a lot like Beatrice was sitting beside the man. This must be her brother Jeremy, the lumberjack. Taking her place at the table was Beatrice's mother. All three of them were looking at Suzanne and Beatrice with very stern eyes.

"Beatrice," said the man with the jet-black hair. "Where were you?"

"I was just telling Mama all about it. It was Games Day, so we had three-legged races and relays and sack races and there were the most incredible prizes---"

"All right, Beatrice," her father said slowly. "That's enough."

"Okay, Daddy." There was a long silence before anyone spoke again.

"Who is your little friend?" Beatrice's father finally said, with a heavy emphasis on the word "friend." Suzanne felt the spotlight fall on her and she felt very small and insignificant and very, very bad. She had obviously been the one responsible for taking Beatrice away all day. After all, Suzanne knew that she was a dirty Duncan, and Beatrice was obviously from a very sophisticated family. She wanted the world to swallow her up at this very second.

"This is Suzanne," Beatrice chirped.

"Suzanne who?" said Beatrice's mother, speaking for the first time since they had come into the trailer.

Beatrice looked at Suzanne incredulously. They had never exchanged last names. "Uh..." Beatrice fumbled.

Suzanne decided that she had better bite the bullet. Maybe Beatrice wouldn't get in as much trouble if her parents realized that she didn't know that Suzanne was a... well, a member of the most disgraced family in the whole area.

"Duncan," Suzanne said, looking at her feet. "My name is Suzanne Duncan."

"Duncan?" Beatrice's mother said, with a note of surprise in her voice. Suzanne looked up, startled. She had expected to hear disgust in this fancy lady's voice, not astonishment. Suzanne saw that there was even a hint of a smile on the face of Beatrice's mother. "Isabelle Duncan's daughter."

"Y-yes," Suzanne managed to stutter.

"Ray Duncan is your father?" Beatrice's father added harshly.

Suzanne's eyes fell to her feet immediately. "Yes," she mumbled.

"Isabelle Duncan is Donald's---" Beatrice's mother began, before Beatrice's father, whose name was obviously Donald, interrupted.

"Anna!" He said harshly.

"Sister!" Beatrice exclaimed, suddenly jumping up and down and clapping. "Isabelle Duncan is Daddy's sister! I know that because you mention her all the time whenever you talk about when you were just a kid, Daddy! You told me that Auntie Isabelle is a Duncan now but she used to be a Bowen like us! You told me about teaching Auntie Isabelle how to ride her bike and how you saved her from drowning in the river and how she ran away with a drunk---"

"Beatrice, that is just about enough!" Donald exclaimed, his face fire engine red. It was not as red as Suzanne's though. She was so overwhelmed with emotion, happiness at meeting some of her mother's family and mortification at what Beatrice had said about her father, the Drunk. The blood was rushing in Suzanne's ears so loudly that she was sure that her wish of the earth swallowing her up was coming true.

"But, Daddy!" Beatrice was not to be subdued just yet. Her parents, Donald and Anna looked simply overwhelmed. They were obviously accustomed to Beatrice's high energy. "If Suzanne is Auntie Isabelle's daughter, then that means we're cousins!"

"I guess it does, Beatrice," Anna said. Beatrice was completely beside herself. She grabbed Suzanne and hugged her with all her strength. Suzanne was forced out of her pit of shame into the arms of her newfound loving cousin. It was all too much to be borne!

"Suzanne!" Beatrice exclaimed. "Did you hear that? We're cousins! We're cousins!"

"Yeah," Suzanne smiled. She couldn't help but smile. She had been counting her blessings all day at finding a friend like Beatrice. Now that she knew that Beatrice was actually her cousin, that meant that they were blood, they were family. Maybe, just maybe they were meant to be together!

"How is your mother, Suzanne?" said Anna. Auntie Anna, Suzanne whispered in her mind, though she would not dare to say such a phrase out loud.

"Fine," Suzanne said quietly. She was still too overwhelmed to feel comfortable in this situation. After all, even though she was in the presence of family, she was still a Duncan.

"Anna..." said Donald with a warning tone. Suzanne was suddenly aware of some unspoken communication happening between her mother's brother and his wife. She did not understand what they were saying to each other with their penetrating eye contact and sharp one word phrases.

"And your brothers?" Anna continued, obviously ignoring her husband's signal.

"RJ and Charley?" Suzanne said with surprise. She was startled that this stranger knew so much about her. "They're good. You know how boys are, always playing in the dirt."

Anna let out a melodic laugh, a sound that served to diminish some of the tension that had built up within the confines of the holiday trailer. Except for Donald, that is. Suzanne noticed that the scowl had not budged from his face.

"I think it's time that Beatrice's little playmate went to her own camp," Donald Bowen said. No one offered a word of protest. Obviously no one dared. But Suzanne noticed a difference in the reverence that this family gave to the man of the house. They did not bow to the demands of this man because he was strong and would do hurtful things if he did not get his own way. They did as he said because they respected him.

Suzanne moved towards the door of the trailer. She realized that she did not want to leave. She wanted to stay with this nice normal family of Bowens. She did not want to go back to being a Duncan. But wait! If her mother was a Bowen, that meant that Suzanne was half Bowen too! Maybe the Bowen half of her could drown out the Duncan half and she didn't have to be a disappointment like everyone in Headline and Thunder Ridge expected her to be.

As Suzanne stepped out of the trailer she did not feel quite so bad. She felt a strange unknown emotion that if she could have recognized it, she would have called it Hope. She was not all-Duncan, but only half-Duncan. That meant that she was half-Bowen. And being half-Bowen was better than anything she had ever been before. A nagging voice inside her head kept whispering that her mother was all-Bowen and that hadn't helped her at all. Before Suzanne even heard the voice though, she heard Beatrice's happy call.

"See you soon, Suzanne," she yelled from the trailer door. "I'll see you at school. Cousin!" Suzanne turned back and beamed. That's right! Beatrice Bowen was not only her friend, but her cousin! And they would be going to school together in a few short days!

"Say hello to your mother for us, will you, Suzanne," said Anna, poking her head out the trailer door.

"I will!" Suzanne said, waving and walking backwards towards her own camp. "See you later!" She didn't know until she bumped into something as solid and as unyielding as a big black poplar tree that someone was standing behind her. She spun around, only to see a very familiar chest. She looked up into the face of none other than the terror of Thunder Ridge, Ray Duncan. Her father.

Ray Duncan was not a big man, but even first glance assured he was a powerful man. His wiry arms and legs looked ready for action at any moment, whether in a barroom brawl or domestic dispute. His face was cragged with lines, betraying each second of rough life behind him. His grown-out brush cut was streaked with grey and his eyes pierced a hard blue stare. The sight of Ray Duncan made the toughest Indian from the reservation or rig pig in the bar nervous and was enough to make any small child tremble with fear.

Suzanne's throat clenched and went bone dry. She tried to speak, but found that she had no voice. Her lips flapped uselessly.

"Where the hell were you?" Ray Duncan spit. Suzanne forced her voice to return and managed to whimper a reply.

"I was...um, I..." As Suzanne babbled, she frantically tried to think of something to say. She finally managed a lame excuse. "I was looking for firewood."

"I don't see any wood."

"I was looking and looking and there just wasn't any..." Suzanne was so frightened of the licking she was going to get for this transgression; she was totally oblivious of what she was saying.

"Get your lazy ass back to camp!" Ray Duncan exploded.

"Yes, Daddy," Suzanne said, nearing tears. She stumbled towards her family's faded army tent. Suzanne looked back at the Bowen trailer. From where she was, it looked so homey, with its awning and patio lanterns. She could see Beatrice still standing in the doorway, watching the exchange between Suzanne and her father with a worried look on her face. For an instant, Suzanne forgot the terror at the licking she was about to receive, and was flush with shame. She so badly wanted to hide her miserable existence from Beatrice. Suzanne knew that Beatrice would never want to see her again after this. But just as she was about to turn away and face her father's rage head on, Suzanne caught movement out of the corner of her eye. It was Beatrice, waving. Suzanne smiled, not with her mouth, but with her heart. She almost felt she could face her father now. As she turned and entered her family's camp, she heard the rumble of thunder in the back of her mind. She looked up into the clear blue sky and knew everything was going to be all right. Everything would be okay because now she had Hope.

Chapter 5

April 19, 1995

When shall we three meet again
In thunder, lightning, or in rain?

- "Macbeth"
William Shakespeare

Every cell of Suzanne's anatomy was focused on the aura of Beatrice, just eight short feet away from her. All that separated the two of them was the coffin of Donald Bowen and a six foot hole in the ground. But Suzanne's mind was nowhere near her dead uncle, or the misting rain, or the crowd of damp mourners all around her. Beatrice was the only entity that Suzanne was aware of.

Suzanne couldn't believe her eyes. She had looked at Beatrice again and again during the church service, blinking each time, as she was sure that her eyes were only playing tricks on her, that it was not really Beatrice after all. But there was no mistaking the vision before her. Beatrice had come back. She looked very much the same as she had twenty years ago. Her red hair had darkened to a beautiful auburn. She had grown into her height and large bones, coming across very elegant and stately.

Even now Suzanne could not help but stare, tingling everywhere at the nearness of her friend. She jumped only slightly when Myles reached over and took her hand in his. She was suddenly sure that Myles had noticed that she was staring. Guilt washed over her like a down pouring of rain, for she knew she was somehow wrong in gawking at her old friend. Especially after that horrible scolding she had taken from Myles in the car on the way from the church to the cemetery. Suzanne shuttered at the memory of what had transpired only moments ago between herself and her husband. She was overwrought with shame.

Myles had been angry about something. Suzanne was sure of that as soon as she got in the car. Over the rumble of the car's non-muffled engine, Suzanne could feel her husband's wrath. It was nothing that he said or did. It never was. But by the silent vibes she absorbed from him, Suzanne was certain Myles was angry, very angry, and she felt her stomach knot with familiar tension. Not that Myles' anger was loud or violent. Rather, it was deep and seething. When he did get around to expressing what was on his mind (which usually came only after long tedious prodding from Suzanne), it was always something that at first glance would appear small and petty. But Myles would take the time to carefully explain his disdain. For the benefit of Suzanne, this explanation was usually done slowly and methodically so that she would never cause it to happen again. And after Myles was finished, Suzanne would agree that his anger was justified and real and gigantic, bigger than anything that she could ever have going on in her own life. Myles' quandaries were always more important than hers. Even today. Even the day she was burying her dead uncle and seeing her very best friend for the first time in twenty years. Obviously in her distraction, Suzanne had neglected Myles' needs in some vital way. Now this critical slip was about to take center stage over this rare milestone in Suzanne's usually boring life. She knew it. She knew it because she knew Myles so well. It had been this way through nineteen years of marriage.

Despite her fear, Suzanne knew that she was going to have to face Myles' anger sooner or later. And if it was later, it was always much worse. So it may as well be sooner. Before they reached the cemetery.

"Myles," Suzanne crashed through the plate glass of silence that separated them. "What's wrong?" She knew right away that her voice sounded too resigned, too exasperated. She hoped for her sake that Myles did not hear it.

"What?" He said innocently. He had heard her defeated tone, and therefore he was not going to get to the heart of the matter. He was going to play the game instead. Suzanne knew this game very well. He played it exactly the same way every time. If she ever decided that she was going to be smarter than Myles and skip a few spaces ahead on the board, Myles would only penalize her by sending her back to start. She knew she would have to play each slow ruthless step of Myles' game.

"What's wrong?" she repeated slowly.

"Nothing," Myles looked over at Suzanne and blinked his wide grey eyes. "Why would you think that something is wrong?" Myles was so good at this game.

"Myles, come on..."

"I mean, have you done anything that would make something wrong?"

"Probably," Suzanne mumbled to herself.

"Excuse me?" Myles replied, tipping his head to her, as if trying to catch whatever it was he had not heard. The tone of his voice meant only one thing. Back two spaces for making a sarcastic comment under your breath.

"No, Myles," Suzanne said, repeating the correct standard response. "I can't think of anything that I may have done."

"So what could be wrong then?"

"You tell me." Another snippy response. Back another space.

Suzanne was playing this game very poorly today. Her mind was just not on it, she supposed.

Myles turned and gave her a long disapproving look. She knew that the game went a lot faster if she would only follow the rules. She was only making it more difficult on herself by stretching it out. She succumbed.

"Myles, please," she said, this time really meaning it. She did not want Myles to be mad at her. And more than anything, she wanted to know what on earth she had done wrong this time. "Tell me what's bothering you. I know something is. I can always tell." That was a correct move, one that usually got a response. By the look on Myles' face, he was pleased that she was back in the game.

"Suzanne, we have gone through this in the past," he said patiently. Suzanne recognized this as the part of the game where he moves from playing dumb to chastising her for not knowing to begin with: the "You Should Know Better" phase.

"What?" In her curiosity over what she had done wrong, Suzanne was on the verge of jumping ahead in the game.

"Back at the church..." Myles would only divulge his deep felt scorn in small pieces. Suzanne would have to work for each bit. It was like burping a baby.

"Yes?" Suzanne replied appropriately.

"You know I didn't even want to go to this funeral to begin with, Suzanne," he said accusingly.

"I know," Suzanne said, resigned. She knew she had screwed up big time. The problem was, she had no idea how.

"That's why I don't understand why you had to be so inconsiderate," Myles continued. He was moving along a little quicker now. He was entering the stage where he dumped a huge pile of shit on Suzanne's head.

"I sure didn't mean to be inconsiderate," Suzanne said.

"You never do," Myles smiled condescendingly. Anger rose in Suzanne's throat, but she dare not let it surface. It would only send her a dozen spaces back on the game board. They would probably have to start the game all over again.

"What did I do, Myles?" Suzanne knew as soon as the words came out of her mouth that he had done it again. He had got her to admit guilt to a yet unidentified crime. Suzanne remembered why she hated this game so much. Myles always won.

Myles took a deep breath. Suzanne knew this part of the game well. She cringed, waiting for the shit to fall. "You abandoned me, Suzanne. You took off and left me all alone to fend for myself with all your uppity Bowen relatives. You were off chatting with your dear widowed Auntie Anna and your cousin Wayne. Why I truly expected you to walk right up to that traitor Beatrice Edwards and start up a conversation with her---"

"Myles!"

"What?" Myles' tone was a warning. Watch out or this game will be set back a very long way.

Suzanne knew too well that her next move was a vital one. "Don't talk that way about Beatrice. She's my best friend in the whole world." Wrong move.

"Thanks."

"Myles..."

"I thought I was your best friend."

"You know what I mean..." Suzanne was jumping around between yelling and whining, neither of which were acceptable at this stage in the game. Whining was allowed only at the very end, yelling never.

"Oh, I know what you mean. You know, I never did see what you saw in her anyway. All those years you were friends, you were total opposites. She was always trying to mold you into something you weren't. I warned you not to trust her. The best thing that ever happened was when poor abandoned Beatrice bawled her way out of town."

"Myles..."

"Loyal to the bitter end, eh, Suzanne? I'm disappointed in you. I thought you had outgrown that childishness. I mean, you probably would have talked to that loud-mouthed pig at the church if she hadn't been so busy chatting it up with all the rest of those tight-ass Bowens. Obviously she's in no rush to talk to you. Best friend. I guess she's not so devoted to you anymore. And no wonder. She looks like all that Bowen money has been put to good use. You know as well as I do that she's like all the rest of them, just waiting for a chance to put everyone else down and brag about all their big money. She doesn't give a damn about you."

"Myles, it's been twenty years."

"That's right and not one word from her."

"We lost touch."

Myles said nothing in return. He just shrugged knowingly. Suzanne could never understand how he could twist her words around so that she was fighting against herself.

"Just promise me one thing," Myles said. "Promise me one thing and I'll forgive you for abandoning me at the church."

Here was a clincher. Just make one little promise and your sin will be forgiven. Suzanne had no idea how things had got to this point. She did not think that she had done anything to be forgiven for, but she was not so sure anymore. And the promise. It was always a doozy. This was the part of the game Suzanne hated most. The loser pays up.

"What?" She said.

"Promise me you won't talk to that bitch at the grave site."

"What?"

"You heard me."

"I can't promise you that, Myles," Suzanne pleaded. "You know I've been looking forward to seeing Beatrice for a long time."

"I knew no such thing."

"Myles, come on. She is, er, was my best friend. Besides, she's my cousin. Her father just died." Suzanne felt that she had stated her case very well, perhaps had earned a few consolation points.

"So does that mean you're not going to make your promise?" Your promise. How come all of a sudden it was Suzanne's promise.

Suzanne knew no way out of this horrible maze Myles had lead her into. She looked like such a fool defending Beatrice, because everything Myles said about her was more or less correct. She just hated giving in to him. "All right."

Husband and wife fell silent as they turned into the cemetery. Suzanne put on her gloves and reached for her umbrella. Despite the relief at having settled the conflict between herself and her husband, Suzanne did not feel very good at it all. No, she felt downright sick.

* * *

"Ashes to ashes, dust to dust..." Reverend Stephens' monologue began. His words brought Suzanne back to the cemetery. She tried hard to listen, but Suzanne knew that her mind was too full of clutter to be able to digest one single word she was about to hear. She even tried to feel guilty for not listening to the sermon over the grave of her uncle, but that did not work either. Her mind was racing with too many emotions already to add another one. Suzanne felt her gaze lift from her clenched hands to the blackened group closed in around her. On her left side was Myles, still holding her hand, the kind doting husband. She had a sudden desire to push his clutching hands away. But of course she wouldn't. She was stunned that such a horrible thought could even cross her mind. Especially here, now, during a funeral service.

Suzanne glanced to her right and saw RJ and his wife Michelle. Her sister-in-law appeared to be taking in every word of what the minister was saying. Suzanne was sure she probably was. Michelle was the only person that Suzanne could possibly describe as completely good. She had to be to put up with RJ in the early years of their marriage when he was busy sowing oats. Lord knows he was nothing like his father and namesake, Ray Duncan, but RJ had had his demons. Suzanne knew that conquering those demons had a lot to do with being married to Michelle.

Suzanne shot a glance ahead. Across from her, on the other side of the flower-laden casket stood Beatrice. Her head was bowed in grief; tears ran in rivers down her cheeks. All the worry that Suzanne had experienced all afternoon of not living up to Beatrice's expectations was now full blown terror. Suzanne had her own trepidations about her old friend that were only compounded by the cynical doubts Myles had planted in her brain. Suzanne was now completely convinced that she was an utter failure compared to Beatrice who was dressed so immaculately and still as school-girl fresh as the day she had left Headline all those years ago. Suzanne was so ashamed of her plain clothes and housewife haircut and the crow's feet around her eyes, she could barely face Beatrice. But more than anything, Suzanne was ashamed to be here. Not here at the funeral, though that was certainly torture enough. Suzanne was ashamed to be here in Headline, still living in this dead end town after publicly vocalizing her disdain for the place for so many years, proclaiming to anyone who would listen that she was getting out of this shithole as soon as she had high school diploma in hand. Her failure to escape had not bothered her so much in the past. After all, who was going to scorn her about not leaving Headline? Someone else who didn't get out either? Beatrice though. Beatrice was different.

Suzanne couldn't take her eyes off Beatrice despite her shame, despite the fact that she was enraging Myles by doing so. Maybe she was trying to will some of Beatrice's success and youthful appearance onto herself. Suzanne remembered how Beatrice's exuberance and positive attitude had transferred into her very being during their youth together. It was Beatrice's influence in the first place that had filled her head with silly notions of leaving Headline and becoming a world famous writer. Suzanne almost smiled at the thought of her and Beatrice together as young girls, frolicking through the countryside like puppies.

Just then, as if she could read Suzanne's thoughts, Beatrice looked up from her wet handkerchief. She looked straight over at Suzanne. Suzanne turned her eyes down instantly. She felt even more foolish than ever. Hadn't her mother, Isabelle Bowen Duncan, a true lady through any difficult situation, taught her that it was not polite to stare? Suzanne closed her eyes tight in disgrace and wished she had never come here today. After a very long time, once she was sure that Beatrice was not looking at her any more, she looked up. Straight into the deep green eyes of Beatrice. And this time she could not escape their magnetic attraction.

* * *

"Let's go," Myles muttered under his breath. His hand was on Suzanne's elbow, and he was plainly trying to steer her away as quickly as possible. The graveside service was over. Mourning family and friends wandered off to their cars in twos and threes. Suzanne, numb, allowed herself to be guided by her husband. She was too confused by the gloom of the day and marital squabbling and Beatrice's presence to protest. Suddenly she just felt tired, and wanted to go home where she could be safe and alone.

"Suzanne," a familiar voice called behind her. Suzanne felt Myles' pace quicken. "Suzanne, wait!" The voice did not relent. In a cloud, she turned and looked over her shoulder in the direction of the voice. She knew who she was going to see.

"Beatrice..." Suzanne stopped in her tracks, with Myles too paralyzed to do anything but stand beside her.

"Suzanne!" Beatrice stepped quickly up to her. "I'm so glad I caught you before you left." Suzanne smiled and said nothing. Her tongue was latched tightly to the roof of her mouth. She could not think of one intelligent word to say.

"Thank you for coming. It means so much to me to have you here today." Beatrice's gaze did not leave that of Suzanne's once.

"You're welcome," Suzanne managed.

"I was hoping that you would come over to the house for the open house," Beatrice continued. Suzanne had forgotten that there was no such thing as an uncomfortable lull in the conversation when Beatrice was around. She would fill any silence herself. "Everyone will be there."

"I don't know," Suzanne managed to choke out. She was really only stalling. She knew she would not go, promise to Myles or not. At this moment, she was so ashamed of her lifeless existence; she did not want to visit with Beatrice. She would only find out about how miserable Suzanne's life is, how empty and lonely and boring. More than anything, she did not want to disappoint Beatrice. Besides, Suzanne knew there was no way that she could drag Myles over to the Bowen house.

"Oh, please," Beatrice begged. "We have so much to catch up on. I want to hear everything about you and Myles and the children." On that sentence, her eyes lifted to Myles for the first time. Their cool green intensity did not betray any emotion whatsoever. Suzanne had recognized that look immediately as Beatrice's polite look. It had come to her as part of the Bowen breeding. Myles was very skilled at presenting good appearances too, for he returned her stare with one identical. His grey eyes were clear and cordial.

"Hello Beatrice," Myles said smoothly.

"Nice to see you again, Myles," Beatrice replied with equal persuasiveness. They were equally good at this game. "Can you and Suzanne come to the house?"

"I'm not so sure," Myles smiled. "I know Suzanne was anxious to get home. The children will be home for lunch soon..." He squeezed Suzanne's arm until it hurt.

"That's right," Suzanne said, wincing. "Belle is sure to try to make grilled cheese sandwiches if I'm not there. She may burn the house down since she's only ten."

"Ten!" Beatrice exclaimed. "Why the last time Mama showed me a picture of your family, they were all just babies!"

"Leigh and Morgan are sixteen and fourteen now. And of course there's little Zane. He's seven," Suzanne felt her tongue slip away on a familiar path. It seemed that the only thing Suzanne could talk about with ease was her children, and again, she felt shame. Before she could get too carried away, Suzanne locked her mouth shut. But she had already said too much, judging from Myles' glare of admonition.

"That's amazing!" Beatrice said. "You must be so proud!"

"We are," Suzanne said shortly.

"Is Leigh graduating next year then?"

"How's Annabelle?" Myles interrupted, before Suzanne could reply. "I noticed she didn't come up with you."

"Annabelle's fine. Very busy with her studies," Beatrice said shortly. It was instantly apparent to Suzanne that Beatrice did not wish to discuss her own child. Suzanne wondered what was wrong, for Annabelle was the only person Beatrice had in her life to love; she had never remarried or even had a boyfriend as far as Suzanne ever heard. For the first time, Suzanne wondered whether Beatrice's world was so perfect after all.

Beatrice continued, "But, hey, why are we standing out here in the rain? Please, come over so we can talk more."

"Well..." Suzanne found herself almost tempted by Beatrice's offer. She seemed so nice, so much like the old Beatrice, so very different from Myles' cutting depiction.

"You can tell me all about your writing and Myles' music and the construction business. I would be fascinated to find out all about your life, Suzanne." Those words were enough to send Suzanne reeling backwards away from her temptation to go over to the Bowen home. Myles was right as always. All Beatrice wanted was to find out about how awful everyone else was doing so she could tell them how wonderful her life was. And Suzanne had plenty of dreadful things to tell her.

Suzanne shuttered. "No, Beatrice, we have to go."

Suzanne turned away. She had known better than to talk to Beatrice, but no, her childlike faith had got her into a horrible mess. It could have been so much worse if common sense hadn't taken over. Myles was so right about staying away from her. Myles was always right, and Suzanne had to learn to listen to him.

"Myles, please, talk her into..." Beatrice stopped, realizing who she was trying to ally herself with. Myles turned and shrugged, as if the whole thing was completely out of his hands. And even though he didn't know it, it was.

Chapter 6

December 20, 1968

Whare sits our sulky sullen dame,
Gathering her brows like gathered storm,
Nursing her wrath to keep it warm.

- "Tam O'Shanter"
Robert Burns

"That was Miss Forsyth's Grade One Class singing 'Jingle Bells,'" Mr. Goff said. His mouth was too close to the microphone. Suzanne knew that because all his S's and F's boomed in the speakers like tiny explosions. The rest of the student body of Oscar Nelson Elementary School did not appear to notice. They simply applauded dispassionately as the group of tiny six year old singers was herded off the stage. Suzanne sat in the row of sixth graders, hidden amongst the crowd. She watched the small students impatiently. Admittedly, they were cute, but they sang terribly.

"And now students and guests," Mr. Goff continued to spit into the microphone. "I have a very special treat for you. As you all know, this holiday season, I asked the students of Oscar Nelson to compose an essay or poem about what Christmas means to you. I read each and every one of the poems and essays that you handed in, and I must say, I was very impressed. I was pleasantly surprised at the caliber of writing coming out of our talented students. Tonight though, I would like to have the writer of one of these compositions come up and read their work. There were so many excellent pieces that I will not say that this was the very best of the compositions. Instead I will say that this is my personal favorite, the piece of work that describes Christmas best to me. I'm sure you will agree that this essay really does give you the true meaning of Christmas. Please welcome, from Miss Wright's Grade Six class, Maureen Bowen."

Suzanne applauded, dumbfounded. The pounding together of her hands did not manage to jar her out of her sense of shock. Maureen Bowen! That girl barely has enough writing talent to spell her own name. And now she writes the best essay in the school! Excuse me, the <u>favorite</u> essay in the school. What could Maureen Bowen have to say about Christmas except it's just another excuse to get expensive presents from her indulging parents? Or maybe she will explain why Santa can only afford to give skis and doll houses to a select few very good children (usually with last names like Bowen or Abbott or Gardner) while the remainder of very good children only received rag dolls and wooden blocks.

Suzanne snatched a glance down the row of Grade Sixers at Beatrice. Her eager anticipation of going to the same school as Beatrice had only been slightly dampened when she found out that she and Beatrice had not been placed in the same class. Instead, Suzanne had found herself in the same class as her other Bowen cousin, Maureen (not that Maureen would ever acknowledge that she and Suzanne were even distantly related!). Suzanne noticed that Beatrice was watching Maureen with the same skeptical curiosity that Suzanne felt. Once again, Suzanne wished whole-heartedly that she was Beatrice's best friend, huddled next to her, giggling their shared secrets. The reality was that being in separate classes meant little time shared together. Recesses were short and Suzanne had to catch the bus home to Thunder Ridge right after school. Suzanne was stuck with the only other friend she had managed to make, a morose quiet girl with thick horn-rimmed glasses named Sophie Andrews. Their mothers were close friends, and had introduced the girls when it appeared they both had the same problem in school: unpopularity. Sophie was a nice enough companion, though she said very little and did poorly in school, comparing badly to Suzanne's perennial good grades. Much to Suzanne's surprise, Beatrice fared just as badly as Sophie and Suzanne in popularity circles. When Suzanne arrived at Oscar Nelson School, she expected to find Beatrice surrounded by friends, all attracted by the same bubbly personality that had drawn Suzanne so skillfully. But obviously, the rest of the Grade Six population did not agree with Suzanne's assessment. Beatrice was perceived as geeky, a head taller than the rest of the girls, and all arms and legs to boot. Her loud voice carried too far, her hearty laugh was embarrassing and abrasive, and she often said the wrong things. And though she did well athletically, Beatrice was not a good student. The only girl in Beatrice's class who would talk to her was her eternal fan, Connie Sullivan. Suzanne cringed as she watched Connie saddle up next to Beatrice on the gymnasium floor as everyone watched the stage.

Maureen Bowen made her way to the microphone. Her hair was done up in intricate ringlets and she was wearing a dress that Suzanne scarcely believed could even exist outside of picture books. The only way that she knew that such a dress was real was the fact that Suzanne had stared longingly at this very dress in the window of Barbara's Fashions downtown. It was a beautiful mauve, with yards of eyelet lace and silk ribbons. Suzanne guessed that it cost about as much as all the homemade dresses that her mother could ever make for Suzanne in a lifetime. She looked down at the brown corduroy jumper she wore today. Her mother had bought an entire bolt of this ugly brown material on sale, and it was enough for plenty of pants for her brothers and father, plus a few dresses for herself. Suzanne supposed she should be grateful that she had clothes at all, but she wasn't after looking at Maureen Bowen standing on stage like a princess. Suzanne thought that fancy mauve dress should only to be worn to a wedding or some other formal affair.

Only Maureen Bowen could get away with wearing such a dress to the school Christmas concert.

"Thank you, students, teachers, special guests," Maureen said into the microphone after Mr. Goff had lowered it to the height of her face. Her voice quavered a bit, but at least her mouth was not too close to the microphone. There was no annoying popping and crackling. Suzanne could hear every word Maureen said with perfect clarity.

"I have been asked today to read you an essay that I recently wrote. It is titled 'A Family Christmas.'"

At that instant, an odd fear gripped Suzanne's heart, a terror at what Maureen was about to say. It was ridiculous to tremble at anything that came out of the pen of a bubblehead like Maureen, but her mouth? That was a different matter. Suzanne could now not escape the dread. Inside her head, a voice warned Suzanne about Maureen Bowen, telling her of the mean cutting tricks she was capable of. She was no stranger to Maureen's biting tongue, even though it had yet to strike her. Suzanne had always been too far beneath Maureen to deserve comment but feared her time had come though.

"Christmas is a very special time of year for me, because it is a holiday to be shared with your family. It has become a tradition in my family to share the season with the rest of the Bowens." Maureen's eyes moved through the crowd throughout this early part of the speech. Now though, they stopped. Suzanne sat paralyzed in fear. Maureen stared down at Suzanne, her eyes laughing, mocking. She didn't know how Maureen had managed to find her in the throng of faces, but somehow she had. Of course she had. Suzanne suddenly knew that the entire speech was directed right at her. As far as Maureen Bowen was concerned, there was no one else in the auditorium. And Suzanne knew why. She guessed she should have known all along what Maureen was going to say about Christmas. Maybe deep down she had. After all, that Horrible Experience had only happened one short week ago. The dreadful embarrassing evening that would have been bad enough if Maureen Bowen had not witnessed it. But of course, she had. As much as Suzanne had tried to forget about it, the nightmare was never far from her consciousness. And as much as Maureen had never spoken of it, Suzanne knew she was carrying the Horrible Experience around like a weapon, waiting for the right time to strike. She stared up into Maureen's taunting eyes, pleading. Maureen's eyes stared back coldly. Are you listening? Can you hear what I'm saying? Suzanne heard every word, and with each flashed a snapshot in her mind from that Horrible Experience.

"Some time during the month of December," Maureen said sweetly, "one of the three Bowen brothers plans a special family Christmas evening and all the rest of us are invited. The reason that it is so special is that it is just for us. We enjoy spending time with the rest of the community during the rest of the holidays, but on that one night a year, our doors open to Bowens and no one else."

SNAPSHOT: Auntie Olive standing with her hand on the knob of the wreath-encrusted door to her expansive east Headline home, looking out onto the doorstep as if Jack the Ripper had come calling. Rather she was faced with the sight of the pathetic Duncan brood: a staggering Ray, a bleary-eyed Isabelle packing a howling Charley, a sullen Suzanne, and RJ who was already in the house digging in the snack trays.

Suzanne had felt completely mortified as she straggled inside the house. Even worse though, she felt responsible. All this was her fault. It was this inescapable fact that made the entire situation even more unbearable. She knew that she would have to take the humiliation of her father's drunkenness in front of the entire Bowen family. She was physically ill at the knowledge that Maureen Bowen was indeed here, and that she would most likely destroy her by blabbing the gory details to all the goody-goodies in school.

If only she hadn't listened to Beatrice's overjoyed descriptions of gaily decorated Christmas trees and stockings on the fireplace, eggnog and joyous family celebration. It had all sounded so wonderful though, so different from any Christmas she had experienced in her own sterile house. If only she had just laughed at Beatrice's suggestion that she join in this family tradition. "After all, you're family too!" If only Suzanne hadn't mentioned this Bowen Family Christmas to Mama in front of Daddy, especially when he was in that particularly rambunctious mood. Sometimes Ray Duncan was a happy drunk, content to sit in from of the TV, plastered out of his mind, loudly shouting racist comments at the news announcer. Sometimes he was a cranky drunk, picking an argument with whoever was handy, usually Mama. But on rare occasions, Ray Duncan was a sociable drunk, looking for a crowd of people to shower with crude jokes and shameful family secrets. If only Suzanne had known he was in one of those rare jolly moods. She would never have suggested that she be allowed to join her cousins at the Bowen Family Christmas. In actual fact, she was not interested in the least with her cousins, just one cousin, Beatrice. Because of the slivers of time she was allotted to spend with her cousin at school, Suzanne wanted to see Beatrice so badly, and she knew this party was the way to do so. Oh, sure, Mama and the boys could come too. They would have a good time; they deserve it. In the scenario she had concocted in her mind, Daddy had been left at home with a bottle of whisky, muttering under his breath about not being caught dead under the same roof as those phony Bowens. If only she had known! If only she had known!

When Daddy had caught wind of what Suzanne was pestering her mother about, well, he thought that was one helluva good idea.

"Let's head on over to brother Gerald's place," he had said. "Let's have us some Christmas cheer!"

Suzanne, instantly sensing a disaster in the making, did some quick back-peddling to get out of the mess, but to no avail. Ray Duncan was adamant. The whole family was going over to celebrate with the Bowens. Mama went as white as Suzanne at the prospect, but she knew better than to protest. She knew that would only make Ray more headstrong. Before Suzanne knew what happened, she was in the backseat of the family Oldsmobile with only one functioning headlight, swerving down the highway with Ray Duncan at the wheel.

"My favorite part of this Bowen family Christmas," Maureen continued, "is when we all gather around the fireplace. There is eggnog for the adults and hot chocolate for the children, and plenty of pleasant conversation shared by everyone."

SNAPSHOT: The Bowen family sitting around the fireplace, surrounded by Christmas festivity.

The massive fireplace was adorned with multi-colored stockings. The glittering Christmas tree stretched as high as the peaked ceiling, reaching its long branches in all directions. Under the tree rested dozens and dozens of brightly wrapping gifts. Suzanne was sure that she had never seen so many presents in all her life, and could not imagine that they were all for just six people. The entire room was decked with wreaths and holly and mistletoe. Sitting throughout the bright room was the Bowen family. Mama's brother Uncle Stanley and Auntie Eleanor plus their grownup children Laura, Dwight and Buck, Mama's other brother Uncle Gerald and Auntie Olive along with their daughter, snotty Maureen, Mama's only sister Auntie Amelia and Uncle Patrick along with their children Blake, Adam and Christina, and of course Uncle Donald and Auntie Anna, with Beatrice and Jeremy nestled between them. They were all seated in the neat ring of couches and chairs that circled the fireplace.

Suzanne sat in a large overstuffed armchair in a corner of the large festively decorated living room, trying as hard as she could to make herself invisible. She didn't think it would be too difficult to be inconspicuous in this showy display of Christmas cheer. Suzanne hoped that no one would see her, or worse yet, connect her with that hateful man who was slurring out some half intelligible tale. He had had the floor for the past half hour. The bristly-faced drunkard sitting next to the eggnog bowl swearing and laughing like a fool was Ray Duncan.

Abhorrence buzzed through Suzanne's head as she heard her father let loose a wonderful story about the time Suzanne and RJ had decided to play in the car. He guffawed as he told how they knocked the car into gear and crashed the poor old Oldsmobile smack into the chicken coop! Suzanne knew she would never live down the humiliation. Now everyone in school will know why Mama drives around Headline in a car that is smashed in on the passenger side and only has one headlight that works.

Suzanne's mother had given up more than an hour ago on trying to get the most out of this rare visit with her own flesh and blood. Now she just sat across the living room from her husband, pale and staring down at her hands. Suzanne watched her without emotion. She did not feel sorry for her mother, mainly because Suzanne was using all the pity in her system right now on herself.

Suzanne was convinced that she would have been dead of humiliation hours ago had it not been for Beatrice. Beatrice was with her all the way. Suzanne could feel the sympathy radiating from Beatrice's pained face across the room. Every time Suzanne managed to steal a glance across the room to her treasured friend, she was met with those unshakable green eyes, gazing at Suzanne as if this agonizing experiencing was hurting her as much as it was hurting her troubled cousin. Suzanne knew she had a friend in the room, and that was the only thing that kept her sane.

Suzanne found herself fantasizing about dashing out the big oak front door of Uncle Gerald's fancy house and running all those long twenty miles home. But it was cold and snowy and the winter wind whipped fast and fierce across the prairie fields this time of year. Nope, Christmas was not a good time to get flattened by a thundering semi or freeze to death on the shoulder of Highway 65. Instead, praying for invisibility in the corner was the best Suzanne could manage. But as hard as she tried, she knew everyone could see her. She knew that because Maureen Bowen was glaring at her with pure hate. Suzanne could almost hear Maureen's thoughts, for they were probably very near her own. Why is this drunken fool wrecking our perfectly wonderful family Christmas party? Maureen's evil glare never left Suzanne's blanched face. She crunched tighter into herself, making another valiant attempt at swallowing her body within itself.

"In conclusion, I must say that Christmas is a holiday that is well-protected by our family because it means so much to us. I truly pity anyone who does not know or understand this kind of special family togetherness." Maureen's eyes pierced fire on these final words. Suzanne looked away. She was nearly crying in shame. Maureen had done it. She had managed to humiliate her in front of the whole school without anyone knowing it. No one except Maureen and Suzanne. And Beatrice. Suzanne knew that Beatrice understood very well the coded message in Maureen's speech. She dared not look in Beatrice's direction for fear of what she may read on her face.

The Christmas concert went on, though Suzanne remembered none of it. She stared blankly at the performances. She applauded numbly when the others applauded and laughed when the others laughed. When it was finally over, and the crowd began to drift into the hallway, Suzanne worked her way through the throng. She felt nauseous and weepy all at the same time and she knew she had to get out of here. Pushing her way through the masses of parents and teachers and students, Suzanne received many looks of irritation, none of which she saw. It was only when she felt a hard tug on her arm that she pulled herself out of her inner torment. The last time Suzanne had been grabbed that hard had been this past summer when she was under a trailer getting RJ's ball. It was the memory of that tug that revealed the identity of today's tugger, the only individual capable of such strength.

Suzanne allowed Beatrice to lead her out of the crowded hallway. She did not know where they were going, nor did she care. Now that someone was taking care of her, she was able to let go, to allow herself to feel the pain that was blinding her vision and numbing her heart. With the hurt came the tears, but Suzanne simply did not care. As soon as Beatrice had dragged her to privacy, Suzanne could no longer hold back. The tears flowed as if they would never stop. She sobbed in Beatrice's arms for a very long time. There was much more to cry about than her anger at Maureen. There was all the humiliation linked to that Horrible Experience at the Bowen Christmas party. She had been carrying the disgrace around like a boulder for days, unable to allow herself to feel anything. She also cried for the shame of her father, the whole hidden part of her life that was Ray Duncan.

"There, there," Beatrice soothed, as the tears began to slow down, and sobs turned into choked hiccups.

"Beatrice..." Suzanne began. But she could say no more. There were no words for what she was feeling.

"Ssh," Beatrice said, understanding. "Don't talk." Suzanne obeyed. She allowed herself to calm down in the arms of her friend.

Chapter 7

April 28, 1995

There came a burst of thunder sound;
The boy - oh! where was he?

"Casabianca"
Felicia Dorothea Hemans

Only one more mile to go.

Ryan Gass knew this for a fact because he could see the turnoff to Mr. Fowler's place through the steadily beating windshield wipers of the school bus. And Ryan could hardly wait. For these last few seconds, he almost became deaf to the maelstrom of voices around him. Almost.

"Hey, Ryan, how come you get a whole seat to yourself?"

"Leave Ryan alone."

"Yeah, you know he's a big-boned boy."

"Is that what this is?" sneered another voice. "Bones?" Ryan felt fingers grab at his upper arm, gripping deep into the flesh. Or should he say, fat. Because that's what it was. This kid behind him, probably Melvin Mitchell, was grabbing the flab on his arm, not the flesh.

"Stop it," Ryan mewled, pushing the pinching hand away. He wanted his voice to sound threatening and angry, but it only sounded weak and sniveling and on the verge of tears.

"Oooh," called a chorus of voices.

"Did you hear that, Melvin? Ryan told you to stop it."

"Yeah, I better watch it, eh?" laughed Melvin, a large fireplug of a boy with a scattering of freckles. There was no other conclusion except that he was a very ugly kid, though no one would ever say that to Melvin's face. His tongue and temper were even uglier than his angry mug.

"You wouldn't want him to sit on you, would you, Melvin?"

Ryan wished with all his might that they all disappear. And soon they would. It was now less than a half a mile to home. To freedom. He knew better than any of them that he was fat. "Slightly overweight" was the way his mother described it. "Needing to go on a good diet" were his father's words. Gross, bloated, whale, tank, plow, fatty-fatty-two-by-four-couldn't-get-through-the-bathroom-door, were just a few ways that the kids at school put it.

Ryan was at his wits end trying to figure out what he could do to help himself. As desperate as he was to be thin, he was alone in his plight. Ryan's parents tried only sporadically to save him from his own appetite, and that meant a strict regimen of celery and diet shakes for a week or so, followed by a month of fats and sugars as usual once his parents got bored and discouraged with their efforts. Margo and Reggie Gass were never home to keep an eye on the fridge anyway. They both worked long hours, Margo as a secretary for Sureway Construction and Reggie as a trucker. When they weren't working, Margo was at bingo and Reg was watching the hockey game. Ryan's older sister Laurie was lost in the pubescent world of boys and clothes and music and talking on the phone. It was all too simple for Ryan to smuggle chocolate bars and doughnuts into the privacy of his bedroom.

Once a month or so, Ryan would have to put up with a tirade from his parents, demanding him to put some effort into losing some weight, getting in shape. Through the entire diatribe, Ryan would find strength in thoughts about the bag of cheese snacks under his bed, the very same one that he would devour as soon as his parents ran out of insults and shame tactics. Ryan knew that very soon his parents would quit yelling, and he would be safe for another few weeks.

Reggie and Margo were easy to satiate compared to the kids of school, though. Ryan's schoolmates refused to acknowledge any lame excuse such as Ryan's long-held conviction that his weight problem was simply glands, that he had no control over his ballooning body size. The odd snack that he ate behind closed doors was simply an indulgence he allowed himself due to the tremendous stress he was under. These treats didn't amount to anything anyway. After all, he was a growing boy.

"Hey, he's a growing boy!" came another voice from the very back of the bus. Ryan pushed the voices from his head. He could see the driveway to his own place now. It was mere seconds to freedom. His whole evening loomed ahead. He pictured reading Superman comics, playing Nintendo, making a batch of chocolate chip cookies while his parents were out and eating all the evidence before anyone got home. Ryan held onto pleasant thoughts; he knew that the pain inside his heart and the bile that was swirling in his stomach was going to end in only a few seconds once he stepped off the bus.

The school bus began slowing down.

"See ya, Lard Ass Gass!"

Ryan heard the familiar squeak of the bus's brakes, followed by the clunk of the opening door. He looked over his shoulder to see Laurie get out of her seat at the back of the bus. Her face was flushed too. He knew that Laurie was embarrassed by her younger brother, a fact that was proven by Laurie's actions, or rather, inaction. She rarely spoke to her brother, but rather glowered at him with contempt. She pushed passed Ryan, heading for the door of the bus without even a glance at him. She covered her head with her book bag and stepped out into the rain.

Ryan didn't care that it was pouring rain, that he was going to get soaking wet on his walk in to the house. All he cared about was getting off the bus, away from the constant prattle of haranguing voices. Ryan's thoughts were of nothing but escape as he stepped out of the bus. He lumbered off, for the first time in hours feeling a bounce and actual lightness in his step. He rounded the front of the bus, and began to cross the highway to the driveway.

He didn't see a thing; he probably didn't even feel a thing. One second he was waddling across the rain-swept road, daydreaming about freedom ahead. The next, he was smashed down by a streak of red.

Youngster killed on way home from school
(Headline Mail - Tuesday, May 2, 1995)

As his sister and a horrified bus load of children watched, a 12 year old rural Headline youngster was killed last Friday as he walked across the highway after getting off the school bus.

Ryan Gass, son of Reg and Margo Gass was struck by a 3/4 ton truck driven by Darren Savage of Headline.

The accident took place about 6 miles south of Headline at 4:05 p.m.

The southbound school bus was stopped on the right hand side of the road at the time of the accident.

The youngster was hit as he walked across the highway after getting off the bus. Reports indicated the Savage truck was also southbound.

Police said this morning investigation is continuing and no charges have yet been laid.

Chapter 8

September 16, 1972

Under an oak, in stormy weather,
I joined this rogue and whore together;
And none but he who rules the thunder
Can put this rogue and whore asunder.

- Jonathan Swift

The night on Opal Pond was black, with the only light for miles coming from the bare bulb of the farm house in the far-off distance. And of course there was the brightness of the moon, full and round and yellow as cheese. The only sounds were those of crickets chirping lazily in the pond and mosquitoes buzzing busily in the night. And sometimes, when the scant night breeze blew just the right way, there was the sound of far-off laughter. The jingle of giggling floated from the farm house, where life was clearly visible on the front porch. From this distance it was impossible to make out faces or even numbers of individuals. All that could be ascertained was movement and laughter bursting intermittently, followed by silence, and then full scale side-splitting laughter. It was only when the house was closely approached that one could make out what was going on.

On the porch were four young women, really not much more than girls. They were surrounded by mounds of wrapping paper and ribbons, and on the table next to the railing were trays and plates of food: sandwiches and squares and bits of fruit, all badly picked over. By the stairs were an enormous pile of household items - small appliances, utensils, towels and more, all still in their original boxes.

Suzanne could not believe that she was actually sitting on her own front porch, laughing hysterically with her friends. She could not ever remember being this happy in her own home before. But it really was happening, and as usual, it was all because of Beatrice. Tonight was Beatrice's wedding shower, an event that Suzanne felt compelled to host, despite the inherent risks, namely Ray Duncan. And as expected, it had not been easy. Suzanne had never asked to have friends over before because she simply had too much to hide at home. But this time, she felt relatively safe from any embarrassing incident with her father since it was harvest time on the farm. For these few short weeks in September, Ray Duncan was actually a conscientious worker, putting in long days on the swather and combine. It would be long after dark before Ray would stagger into the house, this time from exhaustion not booze. He would drink a solitary beer, then fall into bed. But this would not happen until long after the guests had left. As of right now, there were only two girls left, Sophie and Frances, plus Beatrice, of course, the guest of honor.

"Oh, Suzanne, look at this!" called out Sophie, still a rather unattractive girl with shoulder length brown hair hanging in her face. Sophie Andrews probably wore her hair that way to hide her plain looks and the red eruption of pubescent acne that perpetually dotted her face. Suzanne looked over, but she didn't even see Sophie's looks.

Sophie was a very special friend to Suzanne and Beatrice, had been since the sixth grade. But as close as their friendship had become, Sophie still held back from her friends. Where most of the times she laughed and cried, ate and drank like any other fifteen year old, she often turned quiet and reserved, as if she were holding some dark secret inside. And Suzanne was one of the rare few who knew what that dark secret happened to be. The story passed through the community was that Sophie's mother Monica had mysteriously taken ill a few years ago.

Sophie was extremely tight-lipped about this obscure "disease" that gripped her mother, a mystery condition that kept Monica Andrews from public eye nearly all of the time. Suzanne had heard all the dreadful details from her own mother, Monica's closest friend in the world. Sophie might have even been aware that Suzanne was privy to her family skeletons, but she said nothing. And neither did Suzanne. She knew all about family secrets, and the need to keep them that way. And Sophie had a humdinger of a family secret.

While Suzanne's miserable home life stemmed from an alcoholic and abusive father, Sophie's problem was very different: her house was inhabited by a lunatic. Monica Andrews was slowly slipping further and further into madness - a fact that was only known by the other occupants of the house and a few very close friends.

Monica Edwards Andrews had not always been crazy. In 1953, at the delicate age of eighteen, she was young and beautiful and the new bride of Glenn Andrews, the heir to the Andrew's Plumbing and Heating empire. She was a model wife and mother all through the fifties and into the sixties as she and Glenn raised an exemplary family: Bridget, born in 1955, Sophie in 1957 and Dale in 1962.

It was Christmas 1965 (Sophie, though she had never discussed the incident afterwards, remembered the day as if it were yesterday) that Monica began to crack, and with that, so did the ideal Andrews family.

As Glenn carved the turkey and grinned merrily down at his little family, Monica began to sob hysterically. The children and Glenn rushed to her with concern, but there was nothing they could do to console her. She bawled relentlessly, babbling about Thomas, a pet turkey she had had as a child.

Eventually, Glenn was able to get Monica off to bed, sedated with a couple of his prescription back pain pills. Bridget and Sophie soothed a wide-eyed Dale, as the half-carved Tom turkey lay ignored on the festive Christmas table, naked and cold and guilty.

After that day, Monica became detached and mute, spending more and more time in bed. The children continually tried to coax her out, which she eventually did, reemerging into the real world, emotionally bruised and blinking as if the harsh lights of reality hurt her eyes. Life began to inch towards normalcy, and the "Christmas Incident," as the event was forevermore referred to as, was unmentioned, supposedly forgotten. Until six months later when another seemingly insignificant event sent Monica into a frenzy. This time, a toad that Bridget and Sophie had captured from a pond near the house was responsible for a tirade about Clarence, a long forgotten schoolmate who had once dropped such a repulsive reptile on Monica's foot. After the fit, there was the same period of isolation before Monica finally emerged. The pattern was set and though no one knew it yet, it was a pattern that would monopolize the family routine from that day forward.

After Monica's first breakdown, things went downhill quickly in the Andrews home. Glenn's plumbing business (his alone since his father Marvin's death in 1961) had to be ignored more and more often as Glenn was forced to rush home in the middle of the day, summoned by Monica's hysterical cries on the other end of the telephone. After finding his wife crumpled in the corner of the laundry room or cutting old dresses into strips in the attic, Glenn would give Monica her "medicine," then try to salvage his plumbing contract left high and dry an hour before.

For as much as Suzanne knew all the sad details of Sophie's home life, she was sure that Sophie knew about hers too. Isabelle Duncan was sure to have leaked out the horrors of her own existence while listening to Monica's story. So while the two girls both had heavy burdens of secrecy to carry around, they also knew each other's burden, and shouldered them for each other. It all meant for a strong common bond between Sophie and Suzanne. It meant that Sophie didn't see Suzanne's scrawny build, and thin limp hair and Suzanne no longer saw Sophie's pocked complexion and her tiny too-close-together eyes behind thick glasses. All Suzanne saw tonight was her friend, squealing in laughter, pointing to a picture in an old yearbook.

"Oh, my God!" Suzanne guffawed as she saw the picture that Sophie was pointing to.

"Who's that?" asked Fran, the pretty blond girl seated between the two girls.

"Frannie, don't you recognize her?" Beatrice asked incredulously.

Fran took another long look at the picture. As easy as it was to forget about Sophie's unattractiveness, it was not so simple to ignore Frannie's enchanting looks. Every time Suzanne looked at her friend, she was simultaneously overwhelmed with pride and jealousy.

Frances Parker was a new girl in this tight circle of friends, having only moved to Headline a year ago. She was spunky, vivacious and funny, though no one could ever be quite as hilarious as Beatrice. For all her good humor though, there was something mysterious about Fran. She never talked about her family and her life before Headline. With her stunning looks, Fran Parker could have fallen into any clique she wanted to in school. Rather though, she gravitated into a small group of friends, associating only with the nerdy trio of Suzanne, Beatrice and Sophie. Though the boys continually asked Frances out to movies and dances, she always refused.

"I don't know who that is," Fran said, shaking her head. "But she sure does look familiar."

"Frannie, it's Jennifer!" Sophie bubbled. "Jennifer McRae!"

"No way!" Fran howled, only to be joined in by the other three girls.

"She looks so geeky!"

"It was Grade seven. We all looked geeky then. We all thought she looked pretty good at the time," Suzanne said.

"Obviously she did too!"

"The only one who never gave Jennifer McRae the time of day was Myles Gardner, and she always has had a huge crush on him," confided Beatrice.

"Myles Gardner!" gushed Fran. "He is so cute! I get chemistry lab with him."

"Uh-oh," Beatrice said. "I guess that's tough luck for you Sue."

"What do you mean, Bea?" Fran said, frowning.

"Sue's had a crush on Myles Gardner for years, ever since the Grade seven class picnic when he---"

"Oh, shut up, Beatrice," Suzanne interrupted. Her face was already bright red with humiliation. Beatrice knew no such thing as discretion. Imagine mentioning about her crush on Myles to Frances! It was true though: Suzanne was smitten by the brooding Mr. Gardner. He always had such fascinating things to say in English class. He had already read all the classics, and was brimming with insight on them all. He was so mysterious too, like an iceberg with much more going on below the surface than above.

"Gee, I'm sorry, Suzanne," Fran said. "I didn't realize you and Myles were going out---"

"We're not going out," Suzanne said shortly. She turned her face away from the light of the single bare light bulb hanging in the porch, hoping no one would see her incredibly red face. "I just, you know, like him..."

"I know what you mean," Fran grinned.

"He won't even notice me now, though," Suzanne said. "Not when a model right off the cover of Seventeen magazine is in his chem class." She had tried to make her statement sound good-natured, but it emerged from her mouth sounding bitter.

"Don't worry about me, Sue," Fran said. "I have no intentions for Myles Gardner." Fran's statement sounded so final, so sure. Suzanne was convinced that her friend's words meant so much more than what they had actually said. That was often the case with Frances though. She was definitely an enigma.

"You girls can fight over Myles all you want. I have Wade," Beatrice said smugly.

"Oh, didn't I tell you?" Sophie said. "Wade and I eloped last weekend." She held up her left hand displaying an invisible golden band.

"You die, girl!" Beatrice cackled. Another eruption of laughter lifted from the porch.

Wade Edwards was actually Sophie Andrews' uncle, a younger half-brother of poor deranged Monica. Everyone in Headline knew Wade Edwards. Not only was Wade the product of the most talked-about marriage in decades, that between the widow Peggy Carruthers Wilkins and the confirmed bachelor Jake Edwards, but he was also a character in his own right. Wade was the never-say-die adventurer, the risk-taker, the life of the party. No one ever presented Wade with a dare or attempted to place a wager, because he was always ready and willing to take up any challenge. The clucking tongues of Headline declared that Wade Edwards was simply spoiled, a late child to a couple who simply worshipped the child into overindulgence. Whether he was a two year old piling blocks to the ceiling, a ten year old attempting to standing on a moving bicycle, a sixteen year old out to break the record for chugging beer, Wade was always the center of attention. If there was a serious side to him, no one ever claimed to have seen it. Wade only worked when he ran out of money, and had no qualms about borrowing money from whoever was handy. It never stopped the ever-growing ring of friends that surrounded Wade, both male and female, always egging him on, always vying for his attention. It was only fitting then that Wade caused the second most shocking marriage in Headline when he proposed to Beatrice Bowen. As much as the broken-hearted young women and the beer-guzzling young men of Headline could not believe, Wade Edwards was Beatrice's husband-to-be, it was true. The infamous Wade was going to make a married woman out of Beatrice at the ripe old age of sixteen. Wade himself was a mature twenty one. Even though Beatrice and Wade had been an item since she was thirteen and he was eighteen, no one ever thought it would last. The relationship had been condemned in the beginning by both sides of the family. The Bowens wanted nothing to do with the crazy son of that whacky old Jake Edwards who nearly killed himself looking for gold in the Thunder Hills. They knew that Wade would never be able to provide for Beatrice in the style she was accustomed, and in a couple of months, she would come crying home to mother. The Edwards, on the other hand, thought that the Bowens were much too uppity for their precious boy, that they would suck all the spirit out of a genuine free thinker. The whole affair was finally tolerated after it grew apparent that those two crazy kids weren't going to get over each other. Beatrice had been telling Suzanne since Grade eight that she and Wade were going to get married someday, and Suzanne, for one, did not doubt it. Beatrice had no interest in staying in school. As witty as she was, Beatrice's marks were consistently low and her attention in class was always distracted. She simply put up with the whole education process for the socializing as she bided her time until Wade took her away from it all. Suzanne had no doubt in the true love that existed between Wade and Beatrice. Despite their differences, they had two vital things in common. They shared an indomitable free spirit and an unwavering commitment to each other.

"You don't have to worry about me, Bea," Sophie said. "I've got my eyes on Joe Mooney."

"Joe Mooney?" Beatrice squealed.

"Joe the biker?" Suzanne echoed.

"Joe's not a biker," Sophie defended.

"What's that two wheel contraption that he cruises up and down Main Street on then?" Beatrice persisted.

"Just because he rides a motorcycle, doesn't mean he's a biker."

"How did you ever meet up with this Joe guy, Sophie?" Fran asked innocently. Having only been in Headline for a year, Fran often lacked in knowledge of local history. This was one more piece of the Sophie puzzle she was about to put into place.

"I met him through my sister," Sophie said, muted.

"Your sister?" Fran said. "I didn't know you had a sister."

Suzanne looked down at her hands, wordless. A couple of years ago, Sophie's older sister Bridget began hanging around with a leather-clad gang of hoodlums and ended up following them to Edmonton. According to Suzanne's mother, the Andrews' rarely heard from their eldest daughter after that, except for the odd frantic drug-deprived phone call pleading for money. Heartsick, Glenn Andrews would usually send it. He had too many problems at home. He was afraid that saying no to Bridget might just bring one more problem home. But despite all the trouble that Bridget had caused for an already desperate family, Sophie could not stop missing her sister, remaining loyal and hopeful to the end. She never spoke badly of Bridget, and she always looked forward to the day she would return.

"Bridget doesn't live in Headline anymore," Sophie said softly. "She moved to Edmonton." An awkward silence fell over the group, one that Fran certainly did not understand.

"So has Joe Mooney ever taken you for a ride on that motorcycle?" Beatrice cooed, skillfully changing the subject away from Bridget.

"Sure, a couple of times..." Sophie admitted.

"Yeah, sure," Beatrice was at it again. Teasing was Beatrice's favorite pastime. "He probably took you out to the gravel pit." The gravel pit was Headline's northern town version of lover's lane.

"He did not!" Sophie objected zealously. The girls all laughed heartily. "What about you, Beatrice? I'm sure that you haven't been able to keep Wade's hands to himself all these years. Besides, you're practically married now."

"Wade and I have made a promise that we will wait until we are married. Though not a single snoopy bitty in town would believe that. They'll all be counting on their fingers for at least nine months after the wedding. I mean, why else would I be getting married at sixteen, except that I'm knocked up? I'd surprise the hell out of them all by declaring my virginity here and now."

"I wonder what it's like," Sophie grinned.

"What?" Suzanne said.

"You know," Sophie said. "It."

"Oh!" Suzanne said, comprehending.

"Yeah, I wonder," Beatrice said.

"Amy Johnstone said that her sister told her it hurts like hell," Sophie whispered, as if someone might actually overhear her startling revelation.

"Oh, how would Becky Johnstone know! No guy would touch her!" Beatrice said.

"I don't think it's supposed to hurt," Suzanne said. "Especially if you do it with the guy you love."

"When it happened to me, it did hurt, I guess," said a voice so soft, it could barely be heard. The girls couldn't even recognize who the voice belonged to at first. It was only then that they realized Fran had sunk quietly back in the porch swing, becoming a faceless shadow. She was only a quiet voice out of the darkness.

"He came into my bedroom one night after everyone else was sleeping," the voice in the dark continued. "I didn't know what to do when he started touching me, fondling me. I struggled, tried to push him away, to tell him to stop. He just shushed me, told me to be quiet or else I would wake up everyone in the house, as if that was something I <u>didn't</u> want to have happen. I didn't fight quite so hard after that. He made me feel like I was guilty of something, something I shouldn't get caught at. I wanted him to stop though, even though some of the touches almost felt good. I was so overcome with shame at this horrible thing I allowed to happen to me. I never once considered that I didn't have any choice." The soft monologue was interrupted by a muted choke. Suzanne realized that Fran was crying.

"He got on top of me and started kissing me. I guess by that time I was crying. I didn't realize it until he began kissing the tears off my cheeks and saying soft little words like, 'Don't cry, baby, everything is all right.' When it happened, it was so fast. It felt like a bolt of heat prodding between my legs, pushing harder and deeper until I felt like I was going to split right in half. By this time, I was biting his shoulder, fighting and crying out in pain. After he was inside, it was over really fast, less than a minute. Then he got up and got his clothes back into place. He looked back at me, lying on the bed, my nightgown twisted up around my neck and tears smeared all over my face. I didn't understand the look on his face. It was almost like disgust. He didn't say another word. He just left and closed the door behind him."

There was a long silence after Fran finished her tale. Even Beatrice was speechless after this numbing confession. It was Sophie who finally crashed the quiet.

"Who?" she croaked in an unsure frightened voice. "Who was it, Fran?"

"It was my father," Fran whispered in a voice almost too quiet to hear. "Daddy, it was Daddy." This time her tears could not be contained. Huge bubbly sobs erupted from her throat, but they did not stop Fran. She still had more to say. "I told my mother the very next day what had happened. She just gave me the same look Daddy had given me the night before, as if I had done something terribly wrong. And I guess I had. I existed. I lived under the same roof as a man who could not stand the sight of his own little girl growing up."

"Fran," Beatrice said. "Fran, I don't know how you stood it."

"Within a week, my parents shipped me off to Headline to live with my Aunt Babs. Mom had obviously decided who she believed, or who it was easier to believe. I never mentioned that night again to anyone, until tonight."

"You can trust us, Frannie," Suzanne choked.

"I don't even know why I mentioned all this to you guys," Fran began sobbing again. "You're the best friends I ever had, and tonight was just the greatest. Now I go and wreck it all by laying this on you." In a flash, Fran was up out of the swing, off the porch, out into the darkness. The remaining three girls looked at each other, startled, for a moment, before Sophie spoke up.

"I better go after her." She vanished into the night, leaving Suzanne and Beatrice alone.

"Holy shit," Beatrice whistled. Suzanne had never seen Beatrice speechless.

"I don't know what to say," Suzanne replied.

"Poor Frannie."

"I feel so sorry for her, cast out of her own home for something she had no control over."

Again, a silence fell over the porch. Neither girl could even comprehend what they had just heard, let alone comment. Finally, Beatrice spoke.

"I suddenly feel so lucky," she said. Suzanne almost opened her mouth to voice agreement, but when she remembered her own mess at home, she stopped short.

"Do you think she'll be okay?"

"Actually, the best thing that could have happened to Fran was for her to get out of that house, away from that animal."

"You're not kidding."

"Fran is a smart girl, a little scared and unsure, but she'll be okay."

"You think so?" Suzanne said. She could not imagine anyone ever recovering from such a horrific experience.

"In a couple of years, she'll be on her own and controlling her own destiny. I know one thing for sure. She won't go near dear old Mom and Daddy for a while."

"That's scary."

"What?" Beatrice said. "Going home to Mom and Daddy?"

"That too, sure. But no, I was talking about being on your own. I guess I didn't realize it was coming up so fast for all of us. You're just the first one."

"Hey, if there is one person in Headline who is ready to fly the coop, it's Suzanne Duncan. You've been planning your escape to university for years."

"I know. I get excited even thinking about it. But I get scared too. I mean, do you think that I could actually make it? I've been dreaming for so long, I think that if I ever really try, I'll just wake up disappointed."

"You'll do it, Sue. You're determined and smart and you have your whole life ahead of you. Nothing can stop you for attaining anything you want."

"I'm still scared."

"I know what you mean. I'm not going nearly as far as you are. The house Wade and I are going to live in is only a few blocks away from my parents' house. But the whole change of lifestyle is a little intimidating."

"That's really what you want, isn't it?" Suzanne said. "You really want to be Wade's wife and have a dozen kids."

"Maybe not a dozen, but yeah, that's pretty much the picture. I was never a brain like you, Sue. I could never make it with a career. There are too many rules and clocks to punch. I love Wade and I love kids and that's all I ever wanted out of life."

"Then I'm happy for you."

"And I'm happy for you, my soon to be famous journalist best friend."

"Best friends forever."

"Baby I love you, Suzie Q," Beatrice sang the line from the famous Creedence Clearwater Revival song. It was the line she always sang to Suzanne when they were confirming their best friendship. The two girls laughed and hugged affectionately. Suzanne didn't know what she would do without Beatrice.

Just then, Suzanne heard footsteps on the porch stairs.

"Hey, what's going on in here?" said a booming male voice. Suzanne's heart lurched. Her first thought was that her father had come in from the field before the shower was over.

"Wade!" Beatrice exclaimed, bounding into her fiancé's arms. And Suzanne's heart landed back in her chest.

"I thought I heard singing up here. Some pretty awful singing at that." Wade grinned.

The couple spent a few moments admiring their new acquisitions, and then Wade began loading the gifts into his little red Valiant. Every time Wade and Beatrice got within three feet of each other, they were drawn together, exchanging small touches and squeezes like a secret code.

Suzanne, if she hadn't known herself better, would have felt jealous at the closeness that existed between her best friend and her man. But rather than identifying those pangs in her stomach as envy, Suzanne decided that she was anxious to start her own life, just as Beatrice was doing. And she was so happy. Suzanne supposed that she was indeed envious of Beatrice in some small way, and she swore to find a way to attain Beatrice's satisfaction. She had some time to wait though. Having just started the tenth grade, she still had almost three years before she would be leaving home and Headline.

As Wade carried the last box of shower presents away and Beatrice helped Suzanne clean the mess of dirty plates and torn wrapping paper, Sophie crept quietly up the steps of the porch. Fran was a few feet behind her, standing just barely inside the circle of light around the porch. Her face was streaked with tears.

"We saw Wade drive up. I guess it's time to go home," Sophie said.

"How is she?" Beatrice said with concern.

"She had a good cry and talked some more about her dad," Sophie paused, momentarily speechless. "She'll be all right. Tonight did her a world of good," she concluded.

Just then, Fran walked up the steps behind Sophie.

"Fran..." Suzanne managed to say, before she simply walked up to her friend and hugged her.

"Thanks for the nice time," Fran said. "Despite my horrible appearance and the nasty scene I made, I had a great time. With my friends." She reached out and took a hand from Sophie and Beatrice. For a silent moment, the four stood in a circle, holding hands. Suzanne realized at that instant that this was the last stand of this group of four friends as they were. From now on, they were going to be five. Or three. But not four, no, not ever again. Beatrice had managed to change it forever, not for any reason other than she was the first to take flight in this passage into adulthood.

Fran and Sophie made their way to the car where Wade was waiting.

Alone, Suzanne realized this was the moment she had been dreading all night. It was time for goodbye. As if possessing the same thoughts, Beatrice turned her clear green eyes on Suzanne.

"Suzie Q," she said.

"Bea..."

"I gotta tell you something, and I mean this with all my heart. You're the best friend I have in the whole world, and no husband, no kids, nothing, will ever change that."

Suzanne felt her lips moving, though she had no idea what they were trying to say. No matter, as Beatrice put her hand to Suzanne's mouth.

"Don't say it. I know a lot of best friends say these things when they move on with their lives, when they grow up. But I'm different, <u>we're</u> different. We're best friends <u>forever</u>."

Long after Suzanne and Beatrice had shared one more embrace, long after Wade's headlights pulled out of the driveway, long after Suzanne had finished cleaning up and had quietly snuck up to bed, Beatrice's words echoed in her head. Suzanne lay awake for a long time, thinking about the past, the present and the future, Beatrice and Wade, Mama and Daddy, Fran and Sophie. It was only when she heard her father's tractor pull into the yard and his heavy work boots climb the porch steps, that Suzanne's mind swung back to her own bed, her own now.

As sleep finally took her away from all the unanswerable questions that swam in her head, there was but one thing that Suzanne was sure of: Beatrice had been right. They were best friends forever.

Chapter 9

May 2, 1995

Here comes the rain again
Falling on my head like a memory
Falling on my head like a new emotion.

"Here Comes the Rain Again"
Annie Lennox and Dave Stewart

The two oldest buildings in Headline stood at opposite ends of Thunder Avenue. Even though Suzanne drove by these historical structures on almost a daily basis, she was always in awe of their antiquity and splendor.

On the south end of town, just off the turn from Highway 65 was the historic train station. Built with the arrival of the railroad in 1910, the solid pine building had accommodated Canadian Pacific offices and housing until the 1960's when bigger and more modern facilities were built a half a block to the east. Since then the building housed the Headline Train Station Museum, a treasure trove of local history and an actual tourist attraction. Suzanne loved Headline's little museum, and the irony of that fact did not escape her. As much as she resented her hometown, she was a true scholar of its history. Perhaps it was the hard work and steely eyed vision of the pioneers of the region that she seemed to have no trouble romanticizing. She loved visualizing the determination and diligence that it must have taken to stake out and settle this part of the country almost a century ago, all against brutal elements and an even harsher environment. Every time Suzanne visited the exhibits at the old train station, she was transported deep into Headline's colorful history.

At the other end of Thunder Avenue, on the far north side of town sat the second oldest building in the town, St. Peter's United Church, another wonder of early architectural design that Suzanne loved and admired. Built by pioneers back in 1915, the building's solid brick framework, its majestic spire, and fabulous grounds were the pride of the entire region. The Duncans had never been a church going lot by any stretch of the imagination, but every time that Suzanne attended a wedding or a yet another funeral at this amazing place of worship, she agreed with the consensus: St. Peter's was truly a magnificent church. She was awed by its exquisite stained glass and colorful tapestries every time she went inside the church's heavy wooden doors.

Unfortunately, Suzanne was back at St. Peter's. It had been little more than two weeks since the funeral of her uncle, and now she was here for another memorial service. Yet another person had been killed in an accident on Highway 65. This time, poor young Ryan Gass was the victim, the son of Margo, Myles' secretary at Sureway Construction. Myles could not get away from the job site for the services, but Suzanne felt she just had to come and show her respects to the family. She caught sight of the grieving family in the front pew, Margo, hunched and sobbing, Reg, rigid and stoic, and Ryan's sister Laurie who simply looked shell-shocked. For all her troubles, Suzanne realized that there were people with so many more reasons to be miserable.

She blinked back tears and turned her glance around the large expanse of the church. The first thing that she saw as she gazed across the pews was an auburn head that she instantly recognized. Beatrice!

Before Suzanne could decide how to react to seeing her old friend, she overheard two familiar voices directly behind her.

"If you ask me, she's here to stay," said the first voice.

"But she's been gone for twenty years," the second chipped in. "Not once coming back for a visit or anything."

Suzanne realized that she was not the only one who had noticed Bea's presence in the church. It had not occurred to her until this moment that others in town might be fascinated by her sudden return to Headline.

"Mark my words; now that Daddy's business needs tending to, Beatrice Edwards is gonna stick around. She's just been honing her skills in Vancouver, running that little restaurant of hers. She was always the type to take advantage of a situation. Trust me, I know the people in this town."

Suzanne didn't have to turn and look over her shoulder to recognize the voices of the two gossipy mourners behind her. The yappy know-it-all was Coreen Carruthers, a plump blue haired old bitty who worked at the drug store further down Main Street. She was a tough old bird who knew everything about everybody in Headline. She wore the crown of the town gossip proudly. Her young protégé was Joanna Geary, the police chief's wife who worked at the drug store part time.

"Beatrice is a city girl now," Joanna said.

"I'm not so convinced she ever was a city girl at heart. You were too young to remember her when she was growing up. There was no one who was more of a hometown girl than young Beatrice Bowen. All she ever wanted to do was get married and have babies. And that's exactly what she was doing up until that whole fiasco in the summer of 1975. You must have heard all about that mess. Not too long after that, couldn't have been more than three months or so, she packed up her things and headed on down the highway. Her parents were sick about the whole ordeal. I always said that she went a little nuts that summer and taking off that way was just Beatrice being crazy. I knew someday she'd regain her senses and come high-tailin' it back. It took two decades, but she's back."

Joanna was silent throughout Coreen's monologue. That's about all anyone could do when Coreen got on a roll. She was a walking history book of Headline, with plenty of scandal and hearsay to spread upon any ear, willing or otherwise.

By this time though, Suzanne was no longer relishing her clandestine eavesdropping. What had started out as some small secret glee in overhearing Coreen's opinions on the newest Headline returnee was now turning into a bitter ache. She looked down at her feet, jolted by a rush of memories that Coreen's crude history lesson had thrust upon her. It was difficult listening to what old lady Carruthers had to say, mostly because it was all true. Suzanne found herself reliving that horrible summer of twenty years ago.

"Anna Bowen can't manage that paper alone," Coreen continued without missing a beat. "And with both Donald and Jeremy gone now."

"Shh!" Joanna cut in sharply.

Suzanne immediately saw why Joanna was shushing Coreen. Beatrice was coming down the church aisle, straight towards them. Suzanne felt the sadness of the moment slip away, replaced by the heat of rage. How dare these two talk about Beatrice's misfortunes and tragedies like some kind of soap opera plot? Suzanne could not stand the thought of what would happen as soon as Bea was out of earshot. Coreen would dig deeper into the wounds of the past, most particularly, the summer of 1975. She had to do something to stop that from happening.

"Beatrice!" Suzanne heard herself saying. Bea looked over at her with a look of shock and pleasure.

"Hi, Sue!" she replied.

"Are you sitting with anyone? Want to join me?" Suzanne said.

Beatrice did not even miss a beat. She certainly had no clue why the frost had thawed in Suzanne's demeanor, but at this place and time, she was not going to second guess. She sashayed into the pew and plopped down next to her friend. As she settled in, she said, "Well hello, Mrs. Carruthers. Joanna. Nice to see you. Such a tragedy about poor Ryan."

Suzanne looked over her shoulder. There was no way she was going to miss this exchange.

"I know, we are all just devastated for the poor family," said Joanna.

"It's awfully nice to have you back in town, Beatrice," Coreen clucked. "It's just too bad your return had to be under such tragic circumstances of your own."

"Yes, Daddy's passing was a terrible shock to us all," Beatrice said.

"Of course it was, my dear," Coreen cooed. "How is your mother?"

"She's fine, though she is really quite lost right now. She depended completely on Daddy, and now that he is gone, she's really all alone. Uncle Gerald is still alive, but he's living up in Sunset Manor."

"What's she going to do?" Coreen asked, her voice dripping with concern. Suzanne could not believe the hypocrisy. She doubted if Beatrice was fooled by it for a minute either.

"I don't know. I told her I would stay on for as long as she needs me."

Coreen gave Joanna a knowing look, and Suzanne was angry all over again. She pulled her eyes away from the pair behind her, only to see Beatrice's green eyes on her. Instead of matching her own fury, Beatrice's eyes were full of mirth and warmth. She was not offended by the gossips of Headline. She was amused, as of course she would be. Suzanne was suddenly reminded of what a calming and soothing presence Bea always had been in the face of the wagging tongues of the town.

"It's great to see you again, Sue," Beatrice said with misty eyes as she took hold of her friend's hand. She did not let go of the glance or the fingers, both held tightly.

"You too, Bea," Suzanne said. Her gaze returned to her lap. An uncomfortable silence fell between the two.

"Suzanne, I've been thinking about something," Beatrice began.

Just then the side door at the front of the church opened, and the minister stepped in. The service was about to begin.

* * *

"Was blind, but now I see," the congregation sang the final line of the old funeral standard, signaling the end of yet another Headline farewell. In twos and threes, the people packed into the pews began filing out of the church. Suzanne sat. She knew that she should get up off the hard wooden bench of the pew and leave. But it felt so wonderful to be sitting here next to Beatrice. She did not want to moment to end.

"Thank you for asking me to sit with you," Beatrice said quietly from her side.

"I had to do something to get that horrible Carruthers woman to stop talking about you."

Bea snickered quietly in the church silence. "I figured she was up to her old tricks."

"It made me so mad to hear her talk about you like today's biggest headline. It just wasn't right."

"Well, thanks again."

Suzanne let the silence blanket them again. She finally tried to stand, but Beatrice took her hand again.

"Don't go," she said. "This feels too good and too right."

"I know. I am sorry I ran off at your father's funeral. That was a terrible thing for me to do. It was just…you know."

"I know," Bea replied. "Myles."

"No, Suzanne said. "It wasn't Myles. Well, yes, it was Myles bullying me, but really there was more to it than that. I was just so ashamed and I didn't want you to find out what a tiny and terrible existence I am living. I am so ashamed of my life, Beatrice. I guess over the years I just got used to it, but seeing you again, well, it brought it all back. I wanted so badly to be a great writer. I wanted so badly to say important things that people would read and remember and carry with them. And you. You're a big successful restaurant owner, a magnificent career. You have everything I ever wanted."

"Suzanne…" Beatrice said. "If you remember so clearly what your dreams were, then you have some distant memory of what my most important goals were."

Suzanne looked up, staring deeply into her friend's eyes. She did remember, and she was listening.

"All I ever wanted was a husband and a house full of kids. And just like you, I was well on my way to achieving my goal. But in one fell swoop, it all vanished. It vanished somewhere on the highway." Beatrice's voice broke. Suzanne wondered how often Bea even thought about this part of her life, let alone speak about it. How long had it been that she had spoken about the house of cards that was her former life in Headline, and how it had all come tumbling down?

Beatrice continued. "So I had to try to do something with my life. I went away because it was too painful living here, seeing all the things that reminded me of what I lost. I got a job and I had my baby, and I never once went back to my dream. Oh, sure I am successful in my career, probably because I buried myself in it to get through the rough times. But I'm a failure as a mother."

"I'm sure that's not true," Suzanne said immediately.

Beatrice tried harder to explain. "Suzanne, I am so ashamed of myself. I was so crushed by losing everything, my happy little life and my home. I wasn't capable of loving after that, the ultimate betrayal, and Annabelle, she suffered so much. I was a stranger to her all her life"

"Beatrice, you're too hard on yourself," Suzanne said, unconvinced. "I know you're a perfect mother because that's all you ever wanted to do. And at least you had a chance at it. At least you tasted your dream, even if it was for a short period of time. But me, I never had it. I went straight from Mama to Myles and I was never my own person for one single day. And that's what I so wanted."

"That is what I was trying to say before the service. I think I can help you. The fact is, I need your help."

"Me? You need my help?" Suzanne laughed ruefully. "What, do you have some blinds that need dusting?"

"No, I need your help at the newspaper."

"Please, don't patronize me."

"I'm not patronizing you, Suzanne," Beatrice pleaded. "And if you'll just listen to me for a minute, I can explain it all to you."

Suzanne relented.

"I seem to have found myself running a newspaper since I came back. Mama never did have much to do with it, and Daddy's siblings are in no shape to help out. But, I don't know anything about the newspaper business. I can't even spell; you know that from all the spelling tests you helped me cheat on. I need someone who knows what they're doing. I need you, Sue."

"This is very nice of you to think of me, but I don't know anything about running a newspaper."

"I didn't say anything about running it. I know enough about business to be able to handle that. It's the writing that's throwing me for a loop. Daddy never had an editor on staff because he did it himself. Now the reporters are running wild. I'm working eighteen hour days trying to stay on top of things. I need an editor, Suzanne. Badly."

"And you think I'm that editor," Suzanne said skeptically.

"I know you are."

"Beatrice, you're as crazy as you were twenty years ago. I have never worked for a newspaper. I haven't written a published word in fifteen years."

"But I bet you've written plenty. Unpublished."

"Oh, sure. Stories for the kids. My diary," Suzanne scoffed. "Some resume, eh?"

"I think there is much more than that," Bea said with that familiar glint in her eye. "If I know you, and yes, indeed, I do know you, there are drawers and filing cabinets full of your writing at that house of yours. Nothing you are willing to show or even admit to in Myles' presence, but I know it's there."

Suzanne said nothing. She was stunned at how well her old friend knew her, even after two decades apart.

"So I am right?"

Suzanne ignored the question. "Beatrice, forget it. It was a nice gesture, but there is no way I could do it."

"What are you scared of? Failure?"

"Yeah, you're right. I am scared of failing because that's all I've ever done. You know the whole sad story. You wrung it out of me already."

"Or is it Myles you are scared of?"

"Pardon me?" Suzanne looked angry for the first time in the conversation.

"You won't do it because Myles would go nuts." She blurted it out in statement form, as if there was no arguing the truth of her words. And there wasn't. Both of them knew it.

"I'm going home now," Suzanne said, pulling free of Beatrice's grasp.

"Oh, sure," Beatrice said, her voice rising. "Go. Walk out on me and all the hope that I am offering you. You want to rot for the rest of your life in this safe little cocoon you have built for yourself. But it's a cocoon of unhappiness, Suzanne, can't you see it? All I want is for you to do something for yourself. I know it's what you want." Beatrice was crying by now, and the few heads that were still in the church were now craning.

"Beatrice, please," Suzanne hushed her. "Keep your voice down."

"I can't stand to see you like this, Suzanne. I have a genuine need for someone of your talent, but you're so caught up in your feelings of self-loathing that you won't even see this at face value. I need you, Suzanne, and damn it, you need me."

Again there was silence. The craned necks around the church went back to their own business.

"Okay," Suzanne said. She had never been able to say no to Bea and today was no different. The bottom line though was that she didn't want to say no. She really did want to take this job!

"Okay, what?"

"Yes, I will do it!" Suzanne nodded her head like a marionette on strings. There were tears running down her cheeks now, and a big grin on her face. It was the first legitimate smile Beatrice had seen on Suzanne's face in a long, long time.

"What about failure?"

"I've already done that. I guess it's time for something new."

"What about Myles?" Beatrice said with a note of gravity that told Suzanne she understood what size of a hurdle her husband would be.

"I don't know what I'm going to do about Myles," Suzanne admitted. "But maybe it's about time Mr. Myles Gardner didn't get his own way."

Beatrice inhaled and exhaled. "Are you sure? If I've bullied you into something, you can back out anytime."

"No, Beatrice," Suzanne said, her eyes clear. "I'm sure. Maybe I wasn't when I said yes. But I'm sure now. I know this is what I need, and right now, what I need is more important than anything that Myles and the kids need. I can recognize that."

"All right," Beatrice said, hugging Suzanne close.

"So," Suzanne smiled. "Are you going to take me to work and show me around?"

Chapter 10

May 4, 1995

The second before the sun went out we saw a wall of dark shadow come speeding at us. We no sooner saw it than it was upon us, like thunder. ...It was as if an enormous, loping god had reached down and slapped the earth's face.

- "Teaching a Stone to Talk"
Annie Dillard

    Suzanne knew she was going to die. Strange though, there was no fear in that knowledge, just a certainty as strong as the headlights barreling down on her. She had expected something more, her life to flash before her eyes or something. Just one thought, a ridiculous thought really, flicked through her mind. Suzanne was suddenly very sorry she had argued with her mother earlier in the day.

    "You know you really should come. I baked Roberta's favorite cake," Isabelle Duncan had said enthusiastically over the phone line. "And did you hear? Walter is giving her a brand new car." Isabelle's words breathed with all the excitement that pulsed through her veins. "It is a very special anniversary you know. Roberta and Walter have been married four years now."

Suzanne tried very hard to get excited about her only sister's wedding anniversary, but she simply couldn't muster it. Not only did she have absolutely nothing in common with Roberta, but she knew that even if she did yearn to trek all the way out to Roberta and Walter's ponderosa for a slice of angel food cake and Neapolitan ice cream, Myles would never consent. Myles hated all family get-togethers. He refused to even socialize with members of his own family, let alone the Duncans. His hard and fast rule was to attend only public family gatherings, when members of the Headline Chamber of Commerce (and therefore potential customers of Sureway Construction) might be present. That limited him to weddings and funerals and the odd christening. Besides, Suzanne was trying to bank some goodwill with Myles right now. She still hadn't broken the news to him that she was going to start her new job at the Headline Mail on Monday morning.

"I'll try, Mama," Suzanne said, trying to sound hopeful. She did not want to disappoint her mother, but it seemed she always did in spite of herself. The whole reason that Roberta was Mama's obvious favorite and focus of so much attention was that Roberta hadn't disappointed Mama. In Mama's eyes, Roberta had married very well, hitching up with the affluent Walter Fox. She lived at the most beautiful and well-known ranch in the area, the prestigious Abbott House, all before the tender age of twenty. Suzanne, meanwhile, pushing forty, was stuck in a ramshackle old shack in the poor end of Headline with an antisocial husband who could barely keep food on the table. Suzanne did not have the heart to break it to her mother that in reality, Roberta and Walter weren't doing much better than she and Myles. Walt worked inhumanly long hours running that enormous farm, all to pay the immense mortgage and taxes involved in keeping Abbott House and that all important Fox image afloat.

"Try? What do you mean, try?"

"I just don't know whether we can make it," Suzanne replied. You know tonight's a school night."

"Well, Nina and Cookie have preschool tomorrow morning, and Skipper is always in bed by eight, so you won't be late," Isabelle said brightly. "Oh, say you'll come. Roberta and Walter and everyone would be so thrilled to have you. We haven't seen you since Uncle Donald's funeral and then you didn't even come to the house afterwards---"

"Look, Mama, I'll do my best," Suzanne said, exasperated. "It's a busy time of year for Myles, and the kids all have their own things going. You know Morgan and Leigh are writing exams."

"Well, I would hope that you could get them all together for an important occasion like this." Isabelle's tone was turning to nearly a whimper. Suzanne bit her tongue as a flurry of retorts shot up her throat. She wanted so badly to ask her mother what was so important about Roberta and Walter's fourth anniversary when none of Isabelle's other children warranted such a special celebration. But she didn't, because she knew the answer. This was Roberta and no one was more special than Isabelle's lastborn. Mama simply could not see reality. Roberta was nothing spectacular at all: plain looking, unambitious and as thick as the cream skimmed off the fresh milk she extracted from the farm cows every day at five a.m. "You can't miss it. The rest of the family will be there."

"Even Charley?" Suzanne said cunningly.

"Suzanne, that's not fair," Isabelle replied in a tone that betrayed the true hurt of just speaking that name out loud.

"I'm sorry, Mama." Suzanne regretted it as soon as the words came out of her mouth. She knew darn well that just mentioning Charley's name caused Isabelle great pain. Suzanne really didn't want to hurt her mother; she just wanted Mama to quit hurting her.

"Roberta was saying just the other day that she was hoping she could spend more time with you," Isabelle said. "You haven't even seen her new dining room furniture yet." By this point in the conversation, Suzanne was beyond arguing. Just put up with one night of Green Acres and you can go back to your own thrilling existence. She is your only sister, after all. Suzanne knew that she wouldn't even bother asking Myles to come. She would gather up as many of the children as she could, and make the best of an evening of Roberta's showing off and Mama's crisp comments about Suzanne's numerous shortfalls.

Disheartened, Suzanne mumbled something about trying her best to be there. She asked what time and what to bring and hung up, dejected.

Suzanne winced as the conversation played itself over and over in her head all the eight miles out to Abbott House. In the back seat of the car, Zane was trying to pester Belle into a fight, to no avail. Suzanne's youngest two were the only members of her family that agreed to attend the momentous celebration of four years of marital bliss for Walter and Roberta Duncan Fox. The only reason Zane and Belle agreed to accompany her was that they adored Roberta's children: the twins Nina and Cookie and toddler Skipper. Suzanne agreed that the three girls were delightful, but even that depressed her. She felt the little girls had no real future either, that they were all doomed to be bumpkins just like their mother, farmwife Roberta, and their clodhopper father, Walter Fox.

Suzanne was on the verge of turning around and going home, sparing herself the torture of the evening. Her foot hovered over the brake pedal, when a pair of bright headlights emerged to her right, lighting the entire highway. A car was coming up to the highway off of Johnson Road, and it was not stopping. No, it was not even slowing down. Suzanne stared into the lights like a deer blinded in the middle of the highway. All she could distinguish was the shape of a small car with two heads looking straight ahead out the windshield. After that, she saw ink black.

Inquest ordered into highway deaths
(Headline Mail - May 9, 1995)

An inquest has been ordered into the deaths of Barry Linden, 32 and his 8 year old daughter Kimberly, of the Thunder area who died in Headline Hospital last Thursday from injuries received in a 2 car collision 7 miles south of Headline on Highway 65.

The girl was a passenger in a car driven by her father, when it was in collision with a car driven by Suzanne Gardner, 38, of Headline at the intersection of Highway 65 and Johnson Road. Mrs. Gardner's 2 children, Isabelle, 10 and Zane, 7 were also in the car.

Impact of the collision rolled the Linden car completely over, landing it right side up in an 8 foot washout on the south side of the road.

With Mr. Linden in the car were his wife Carol, and 4 small daughters, Angela, 9, Kimberly, 8, Heather, 6 and Tracy, 3.

Mrs. Linden was hospitalized for spinal injuries and shock. The youngest girl, Tracy, was thrown 15 feet when the car rolled and suffered extensive bruises along with 2 other sisters.

Barry and Kimberly Linden were rushed to hospital. Mr. Linden was pronounced dead on arrival. Kimberly did not recover consciousness.

Driver of the other car, Mrs. Gardner is currently in hospital with minor back and neck injuries. The two Gardner children were uninjured.

PART 2
August 31, 1975

Chapter 11

> Probable nor'east to sou'west winds, varying to the southard and westard and eastard and points between' high and low barometer, sweeping round from place to place; probable areas of rain, snow, hail, and drought, succeeded or preceded by earthquakes with thunder and lightning.
>
> - Mark Twain

Only after that unforgettable horrid day was over, did Suzanne come to understand that life as she knew it was over as well. In the days and weeks of grief and confusion that followed, she learned how much she had to be thankful for in her former apparent pitiful existence. It was oh, so much better than what she had after. Astonishingly, Suzanne found herself looking back fondly to that pre-Labor Day life. She even searched her memory to discern the very last moment of what she what she came to call the days before August 31, 1975: her Old Life. She became obsessed to know what was happening in that very last instant in her final gasp of breath of naive carefree childhood, before the painful rebirth of the new adult Suzanne Duncan. Eventually, after long and patient searching, she found that last playful instant of youth, stored safely in her memory. In times of unhappiness, she would take that memory off its shelf and fondle it, touch its gentle surfaces, and experience all of its dulcet pleasures. It seemed so long ago.

Suzanne had been almost alone on the long white sand bar of the Thunder River. Except for a few couples walking hand in hand and the odd child frolicking in the waves, there was no one else along the entire shore. This was a truly rare accomplishment, one that Suzanne found herself relishing. It was, after all, the 56th Annual Labor Day Thunder River Campout, and as it happened every year, <u>everyone</u> was there. The entire campsite at Thunder River was crammed with campers, tents and motorhomes camped side by each, melding the wealthiest Headline merchants and oilmen and business people with the poorest of Thunder Ridge dirt farmers. No one seemed to care who their neighbors were, at least for this one weekend a year.

But on this particular Saturday afternoon, the campground was nearly deserted. A large chunk of the weekend's population was nowhere to be seen. Some had gone fishing for the bountiful walleye and perch that inhabited the river. Others were enjoying a mid-afternoon siesta, escaping the heat of the day inside their trailers and tents. A few had gone into Headline or Thunder Ridge for supplies. The group of young campers that Suzanne was tenting with had gone on a lengthy hike. It was a perfect day to enjoy the sunshine, for like every Labor Day weekend in the history of the Campout, the weather was sunny and hot.

Suzanne had decided not to accompany her friends though. She used Beatrice as an excuse, but if the truth be known, she simply wanted some calm and some privacy, rather than the strenuous effort and boisterous company of a long walk.

Suzanne had just finished a milestone school year, having graduated as valedictorian from Headline High School. She was also the recipient to a full scholarship to the arts faculty at the University of Alberta. Suzanne had worked very hard to get where she was, and after graduation was over, she found herself very, very tired. During the final two months left in this hellhole named Headline, she found herself physically exhausted from her summer job of laying sod, but mentally rested, and all the while counting down the days to her new life as a student in the big city of Edmonton. It was all going to be very overwhelming and a tremendous amount of work. But Suzanne was ready and very restless. It was only a couple of days until she left! There were many times Suzanne almost caught herself running south down Highway 65 in eager anticipation. But she was able to control her urge to high tail it out of town. The final days would only go slower than all the rest leading up to it. For now, she had to be content to skip rocks in the water, taking odd glances over in the direction of Beatrice who was sleeping soundly in the shade.

Suzanne smiled at the sight of her friend. Beatrice looked less like a nineteen year old girl than a large mound of gingham with a shock of red hair. She wondered where in the world Beatrice found such an utterly ugly maternity dress. In fact, every single mom-to-be outfit she wore was an outrageous explosion of bright color and bizarre pattern. Suzanne supposed that being a fashion statement was not a concern when you're packing forty extra pounds on your stomach. Of course, Beatrice should be used to this condition by now. After all, she was now in her third trimester.

Suzanne stumbled, quickly turning her glance from Beatrice to her throbbing toe. There by her foot was a stick, about two feet long, washed smooth and grey by the pounding waves. She picked it up absently and continued her stroll along the edge of the water. Her thoughts returned to herself and her own excitement over the future. She thrilled at the prospect of fleeing Headline for good, of leaving that horrible little house that she had lived in all of her life. But more than anything, she longed for the prospect of discovering who Suzanne really was. All her life, she had only been identified by her attachments to other people: Ray's daughter, Beatrice's friend, and most recently, Myles' girlfriend. Now though, she wanted to be known simply as Suzanne. Period.

Without even realizing what she was doing, Suzanne plunged the end of the stick into the sand, and began printing in big, bold, capital letters.

S...U...Z...A...N...N...E

There it was, in letters a full four feet high, the name of the person who was about to conquer on the world. Suzanne stood back with her hands on her hips, admiring her handiwork. It seemed an appropriate, almost necessary statement, as if thinking and believing was not quite enough. The rest of the world had to know Suzanne's dreams too.

A few odd drops of water began dotting her creation. Suzanne looked up into the sky, frowning. It couldn't be raining! It never rained on the Labor Day weekend! But indeed, that is exactly what it was doing. While Suzanne had been busy with her own thoughts of the future, the clear blue sky had clouded in, and the scattered beads turned into steady raindrops. Suzanne dropped her writing stick and ran up the beach to the shady birch tree which sheltered Beatrice.

"Beatrice! Beatrice!" she called. "Wake up!"

"Huh?" Beatrice croaked, lifting her head heavily. Everything she did lately seemed to be such an effort. Not that Beatrice would ever complain. She seemed to thrive on pregnancy, adoring every moment of the process. "Is Wade back with the ice cream?"

Suzanne smiled. Beatrice had sent her husband to Headline for ice cream only about fifteen minutes earlier. There was no way he could be back yet, especially since he had taken their quaint little red Valiant, scarcely capable of reaching the speed limit.

In the three years since Beatrice and Wade had married, they had miraculously been able to shush all the naysayers in Headline and Thunder Ridge. All the clucking tongues who had said Wade wouldn't be able to keep a job and Beatrice wouldn't be able to keep a clean house or cook an edible meal were stunned into begrudging silence after less than a year of marital bliss for the newlywed Edwards. Wade had managed to get a job. Not a very profitable one, but a job nonetheless: Wade Edwards drove for Peace Trucking. Beatrice was equally surprising, turning from a rich little brat into a competent housewife. The only blemish in the Edwards marriage was the fact that Beatrice was not able to get pregnant right away as she had hoped. It was an elated young couple that announced to the entire world that their first child would be born in early December 1975. True to her commitment to her well-loved career, Beatrice dove into pregnancy with enthusiasm. She did everything by the book, except that she took her ice cream without pickles. Her true craving was Fudgsicles.

"No, Wade's not back yet, Bea," Suzanne said. "But it's raining. We had better get inside."

"Raining?" Beatrice raised her head a little higher. She frowned fiercely. "It never rains on the Long Weekend."

"It is this year," Suzanne said, motioning inanely at the sky.

"Well, I'll be damned." Beatrice pulled herself to her feet slowly and the two began piling their arms with blankets and bags. Suzanne sent Beatrice ahead while she picked up the last of their belongings scattered along the beach. She then followed Beatrice in the direction of their camp.

Camp consisted of a cluster of five or six tents in various stages of disrepair. There was the huge wall tent belonging to Bruce Armstrong, shared by about six or eight different people. Next to that was the tiny bright orange pup tent shared by Lee Gardner and his girlfriend Mary Ellen Young. Lee's little sister Kelly was supposed to be bunking with him too, while Mary Ellen was supposed to be in the Armstrong tent. Unbeknownst to the Gardner parents, Irwin and Mildred, Kelly's sleeping bag was actually next to that of Bruce Armstrong in the wall tent. Suzanne shared her tent with her old friend Frannie. Suzanne was pleased to be sharing a tent with Fran for the weekend, though she was slightly disappointed that she hadn't been able to convince her boyfriend to share this romp in the woods. The instant that Myles found out that Lee and Kelly Gardner were camping with the group though, he adamantly refused to go.

Myles Gardner got along with very few members of his family, citing the big money snobbishness of the rest of the Gardners as reason enough to stay clear. That was just Myles though: highly principled and stubborn once his mind was made up. Suzanne wished she could be so disciplined in her standards. But she sometimes wondered whether there was something more to Myles' boycott of his family. Was it high standards that led Myles to this stand with his family, or was there just a hint of jealousy? Myles was one of the very few Gardners who had not gone on to money. While uncles and aunts and cousins were all doing quite well, thank you very much, in business or professions alike, Myles was still pouring concrete. Suzanne was sure that good fortune was looming on the horizon for Myles though. He was a very talented musician, and would soon be making a bundle as a professional entertainer. Suzanne was actually quite proud of Myles and his prospects. In the meanwhile though, it would be nice if Myles could be a trifle more tolerant of those who seemed to have hit their stride a little earlier than he.

Pegged immediately next to Suzanne's tent was the bigger and somewhat newer tent inhabited by Mr. and Mrs. Wade Edwards. Beatrice's parents had insisted that she and Wade take the family motorhome, but Beatrice would have nothing to do with that notion. She was certainly not going to camp in luxury while her friends romped in the dust. So Wade and the massively pregnant Beatrice slept in a tent like everyone else. Beatrice would have it no other way.

Juggling magazines and pillows, Suzanne managed to slide under the flap of Beatrice's tent. She half dropped, half set down her armful of items, then looked around to find Beatrice. Her friend was at the other end of the tent, rearranging the blankets and pillows back into a bed for the evening.

"I wish Wade would get back with that ice cream," Beatrice said, almost crossly.

"Patience," Suzanne smiled. "Patience."

"That's easy for you to say."

"I have yet to meet a pregnant woman quite the likes of you," Suzanne grinned.

"How many pregnant woman do you know other than me?"

"There's Sophie," Suzanne continued, suddenly sobered.

"Poor Sophie," Beatrice shook her head with despair.

After Beatrice quit school and got married at the start of the tenth grade, Suzanne had been left with the companionship of Frannie and Sophie. But it was only a little more than a year before Sophie found herself in desperate straits. By the middle of the eleventh grade Sophie was pregnant, and good old Joe Mooney vanished from the face of the earth. Nowadays, Sophie was living at home, miserable and lonely, caring for her little son Nathanial and her ever-failing mother.

"I always knew that Joe Mooney was good for nothing," Suzanne added.

"Poor Sophie," Beatrice repeated, as if those were the only words that could express her feelings about her longtime friend who was experiencing pregnancy and motherhood at a one hundred and eighty degree difference to herself. Suzanne wondered whether Beatrice could truly fathom how difficult life had become for Sophie.

"At least you and Sophie are not pregnant in your old age," Suzanne said, her tone verging on repugnance.

"Oh come on, Sue, you should be happy," Beatrice said. "You're going to be a big sister again soon."

"Yeah," Suzanne said with no enthusiasm.

"It's a big deal! You should be excited."

"Oh, yeah, I am thrilled all right," Suzanne could not help but betray her lack of excitement on the impending birth. Even after Sophie's undesirable experience, it was unfathomable for Beatrice to look upon a new life as anything but a blessed event. Suzanne had tried to get excited last fall when her mother had broken the news to then seventeen year old Suzanne, twelve year old RJ and eight year old Charley that

Isabelle was expecting again. What was Mama doing pregnant at her age anyway? She should be looking forward to spoiling grandchildren, not raising yet another child. Suzanne could not comprehend bringing another human being into that house of horror. She knew only too well how Ray Duncan had managed to twist the minds and souls of his three existing children and she shuttered at the thought of yet another child falling victim to his abusive rampages. Mama, you should know better!

"I know one thing for sure," Beatrice smiled, patting her own enlarged girth. "If there is one thing that can put life in a whole new perspective, it's a baby."

Chapter 12

Loud roar'd the dreadful thunder,
The rain a deluge show'red.

"The Bay of Biscay"
- Andrew Cherry

From inside the dank chicken house, Isabelle did not hear the rain when it started. It wasn't until the light sprinkles turned into pelting raindrops banging down upon the metal roof that Isabelle finally noticed the storm. As soon as she heard the rain, she turned away from gathering the eggs from the nests. Even though she was alone (except for thirty odd clucking hens, strutting and cocking their heads) Isabelle smiled with satisfaction. She moved to the door of the chicken house and went outside. She stood under the eaves, staring out into the plummeting rain. She had been right.

Isabelle had known as soon as she woke up that morning that it was going to storm. She could not even say how she knew, but it was a certainty in her mind. Ray, of course had laughed at her prediction.

"Rain!" he chortled. "It never rains on Labor Day weekend. Bein' knocked up has started to fuck up your mind now, hasn't it, woman?"

But Isabelle had stuck to her guns on this one. She knew as sure as the rising and setting of the sun that there was going to be a storm today, and from what she could figure, an immense storm at that. There was electricity in the air that seemed to send a current through her blood; it could only mean one thing.

After Ray finished eating breakfast and belittling her prophesy, he hobbled out into the yard. "Gonna chop some kindlin'," he announced as the screen door slammed behind him. Isabelle knew better than to believe that this chore would keep Ray busy for long. This prediction was just as sure as her first too. Within an hour, he would be back, sweaty and dirty and above all, thirsty. From there, Isabelle was not quite so certain. It was always questionable whether Ray would then decide to crack open a beer and put his feet up on the porch, or whether he would head into town, to his stool at the tavern in the Headline Hotel.

Isabelle went back inside the chicken house to finish her task. Hopefully by the time all the eggs were gathered, the rain would let up a bit so she wouldn't get drenched to the skin on her way back to the house. Isabelle made her way through the hens, each pecking at her shoes and singing their song of chicken contentment. Back at the nests, she reached under the warm down of a nesting hen, feeling for a warm smooth egg. Isabelle felt safe and calm, listening to the pounding of the rain on the roof and the cackling of the hens. She had always enjoyed taking care of the chickens, and today, the task was even more gratifying.

Isabelle found herself again thinking back to the sight of her husband earlier that morning. She remembered watching out the kitchen window at his wiry form, tackling blocks of wood with intense strength and energy. Strangely, as she watched, Isabelle felt a stirring inside her that she initially took to be movement of the baby. But then she realized it was not a motion in her body, but in her soul. Her heart swelled with what she could only recognize as love. She wasn't sure though; it had been a long time since she had experienced anything even similar to affection, especially when it came to Ray Duncan.

Isabelle knew Ray better than anyone else in Headline and Thunder Ridge, she reckoned, and she knew there was a lot of good in the man. She knew all too well the infamous bad side of her husband, but she alone understood his passion. She knew about the powerful emotion that coursed through his veins, the sensation that often led to an explosion of rage. But it was a zeal that always meant well, an emotion that only yearned that the lives of Ray and the people he cared for to be better than what he had.

Everyone in Headline knew the stories of Ray's grandfather, Abe Duncan, who raised his two sons Sam and Jack on his own after his wife Celia ran off in fear. It was common knowledge how Abe had abused and mistreated his sons, probably with the same intensity that he had tormented poor Celia. Though it was never brought to a court of law, there were few who doubted that Abe was responsible for the death of young Jack who was found battered and bruised at the bottom of the cellar stairs in 1923. Years later, Abe Duncan was finally thrown behind bars for the savage rape of Peggy Carruthers. Sam Duncan, Ray's father was all alone, all by the age of sixteen. Sam attempted a gold mining partnership with Jake Edwards, only to have the entire partnership disintegrate after a vicious argument left Sam in hospital with a gunshot wound to his leg. Sam vanished for a few years, returning with a taciturn homely wife named Audrey McKenzie. They settled on a homestead near Thunder Ridge that remained the Duncan farm to this day, establishing a domestic scene that Isabelle would readily recognize. Audrey finally left Sam Duncan, taking with her the two youngest children, daughters Felicia and Fiona. The oldest child, Ray, stayed on with his father, weathering the storm of Sam Duncan's violent temper on his own. Ray had often told Isabelle how much he hated his father, and how badly he wanted his life to be different from that of the past two generations of Duncans. But alas, the hard times of farming and generations of breeding for hard drinking and quick temper, Ray was only slightly less brutal than his father and grandfather. It was a fact that troubled Ray, a reality that often sent him into deep depression. And depression is not a good state of mind for positive family relations and sobriety. Isabelle nursed Ray through all of his ups and downs, unthanked and unappreciated, but loyal to the end.

Isabelle Duncan was a believer in fate, that everything happened for a reason. She had long ago accepted her lot as the wife of Ray Duncan and all the castigation that went with it. It was simply meant to be. She knew that Ray was not pure evil, and if the rest of the world was too closed minded to figure that out, then it was their loss. Of course, there were only a handful of people who knew the debt that Isabelle owed to Ray, one that she was willing to pay every day of her life.

Isabelle had put her palm against her swollen abdomen as she watched Ray chop wood. She found herself almost smiling at the sight of this narrow window of normalcy, at this possibility of what could have been, if only Ray had been a little stronger than the ghosts that haunted him.

Just then, she had seen a small figure running up to Ray. It was Charley, their youngest son. Charley caught Ray's attention between blocks of wood, and the two talked briefly before Charley ran off towards the house. Isabelle heard the screen door slam as Charley burst into the kitchen.

"Mama! Mama!" Charley bellowed.

"What, son?" Isabelle smiled.

"Daddy said that we're gonna go over to Thunder River later this afternoon," Charley beamed. Isabelle knew how badly Charley wanted to go to the river. After all, it was the Long Weekend, and everyone from Headline and Thunder Ridge and all points in between was over there enjoying the holiday, including Charley's older sister and brother, Suzanne and RJ.

"When did he say we were going?" Isabelle asked. "After he's done choppin' wood?"

"No," Charley replied. "He's pretty much done chopping wood, but he's planning on going in to town for a while. We're gonna go when he gets back."

"Okay," Isabelle said, her expression remaining blank, not betraying her knowledge of the truth behind Ray's words. She knew what Ray really meant. He was going to the bar for the afternoon, and that meant he would be gone for the entire evening too. Charley would not be going to the Thunder River at all today, of that Isabelle was certain. She wished Ray wouldn't get the boy's hopes up, only to dash them every time.

Now, five hours later, as Isabelle filled her tin bucket with eggs, she knew she had been right. As right as she had been about the coming of the rain, she was right about Ray not coming home until the wee hours of the morning.

As Isabelle made her way through her memories and the long row of nests, a crash interrupted her thoughts. She rushed to the door of the chicken house, only to see a large branch fall to the ground, right on top of the brightly painted wooden rabbit that was perched on the lawn beside the house. Charley had made it for her only last winter, and even though the painting was rather uneven, Isabelle loved her son's effort just the same. From where Isabelle was, she could tell the rabbit was crushed under the large branch. Charley would be crushed as well.

Suddenly, a flash of lightning lit the darkened afternoon sky. It was followed by the booming retort of thunder. Isabelle gazed out the chicken house door as the storm bore down. The clouds burst open, setting free their entire massive weight of rain. Yes indeed, Isabelle could not have been more correct in her prediction. There was going to be a very violent storm today. More lightning lit the purple sky and more thunder pounded, each strike closer than the one before.

"Mama! Mama!" a thin voice called through the maelstrom.

"Charley!" Isabelle called back. She couldn't see him, but she wanted him to know she was nearby. "I'm in the chicken house. Where are you?"

"Mama..." Charley called. "I'm up here."

Isabelle's eyes searched for her son, until they finally scanned across the boy, looking very small and fragile, in the loft of the barn.

"Stay there, Charley," Isabelle called. "I'm coming over to the barn." She carefully set the pail of eggs down under the safety of the chicken house eaves. She didn't dare leave them inside with the chickens. Those mild-mannered little hens would cannibalize their own unborn without giving it a second thought and that would never do. Isabelle knew that

Ray would call her everything under the sun if a day's worth of eggs were lost. The eggs safe, Isabelle stepped into the tempest, soaked to the skin in an instant. She splashed across the muddy barnyard as briskly as was possible with her cumbersome weight. As she stepped inside the barn, Charley emerged from the rafters.

"It's really storming out there!" he exclaimed.

"It sure it, son." Isabelle smiled, wet and proud. Charley was the most passionate of her children, feeling everything with massive intensity. Ironically, it was Charley who reminded her most of Ray, and Charley who suffered the most from her tumultuous marriage.

"Do you think it's raining at Thunder River?"

"I expect it is, Charley."

"Oh." His single word reply betrayed all of his disappointment. Isabelle was only relieved by the fact that the weather was disappointing her son today, not Ray Duncan. Another clap of lightning lit the darkened room, followed immediately by a loud eruption of thunder. Charley's eyes grew with wonder and what was verging on fear.

"Don't worry, son," Isabelle said. "We're dry and safe inside---" Before she could even finish her reassurances, Isabelle was cut off by an explosion of light and sound, of lightning followed so closely by thunder that they were simultaneous. The ground shook as if they were sitting directly on an earthquake fault line. Before the shuddering even finished, Isabelle heard a sound that she recognized to be the cracking of fire. Her heart leapt with panic, and she ran to the barn door. Terror gripped Isabelle when she saw what that explosion had been. Her house had been struck by lightning, and was now being eaten by flames. Isabelle's thoughts turned to pails and water and working to save the forlorn little shack that had nonetheless been home to her for eighteen years. But her thoughts went no further than that. She felt a tight pain in her back and stomach that she recognized immediately. She should know it, having gone through it thrice before: Isabelle was in labor.

Chapter 13

Hast thou given the horse strength? hast thou clothed his neck with thunder?

Job 39:19

"We better get out of here, gang," Kelly Gardner called, eying the sky worriedly. "It's gonna rain." Thunder had been rumbling ominously in the south for a while now, and the sky was looking more and more bruise purple.

"Ah, Kelly, quit yer frettin'," called her big brother, Lee. Without another word, he took a long graceful dive from the top of a monstrous mound of what would appear at first glance to be sand. As Lee landed fifteen feet below in a splash of brown, it was obvious that this was not sand. It was too soft, too frothy, with fragments much too large to be grains of sand. It was a sawdust pile, one of dozens that dotted the back-woods of the Headline area. Sawmills had been a major local industry in the forties and fifties, only recently dying out during the oil boom. The legacy of what had once been booming little communities of sawmill workers and their families were mountains of sawdust, the remnants of sawing countless trees into planks that built the homes in the area and many a house in far-off Edmonton and Calgary and Vancouver. Lee and Kelly Gardner and their group of friends had stumbled across this island of wood chips during their hike, and were enjoying a few thrills, leaping from the top into the soft cushion below. Everyone, that is, except Kelly.

Kelly Gardner had never been much of an adventurer. She had always been the type who was content to stay behind within the safe confines of home, quietly sewing or reading or playing Scrabble with her grandmother. Both she and Grandma Gardner were what her grandmother called "house cats." Kelly would not have even accompanied her friends on this outing, if her brawny boyfriend, Bruce Armstrong had not insisted. If she had had her druthers, Kelly would have stayed behind with Suzanne and Beatrice.

"Bruce, come on," Kelly called out as she watched her boyfriend climb up to the top of the sawdust pile for yet another dive. She was feeling sprinkles of rain on her arms and legs now. The storm was upon them. "We're gonna get soaked." As if in agreement, the sky flashed with lightning.

"She's right, guys," called a girl with short curly dark hair. She stood on the top of the pile with one sock in each hand, shaking them viciously to remove the sticky sawdust.

"Thanks Maddie," Kelly said gratefully. Finally some support. Madeline Fox, Kelly's best friend, was a girl that could only be described as wiry. She was skinny to the point of looking anorexic, with a head topped off with the tightest curls imaginable. She had an energy that matched her looks too; Madeline never ran out of stamina.

The group exchanged glances with each other and the sky, and the unspoken consensus appeared to be that play time was over. It was time to hike back to camp. As the group came down the hill in pairs or on their own, it soon became obvious that they had heeded Kelly's alarm too late. The clouds burst, soaking them almost instantaneously. Lightning crisscrossed the sky and the ground seemed to shake from the responding thunder. Everyone began moving a little faster, if only to get out of the clearing and into the relative shelter of the trees. They found themselves trudging along the path towards camp, wet and disheveled and covered from head to toe in sawdust.

"Okay, Kelly, say it," said a well-built young man with a shock of red hair.

"Say what?" Kelly answered innocently. She knew very well what he was after.

"Say it," Jeremy Bowen grinned through clenched teeth. "Say I told you so."

"I don't have to," Kelly said. "You just said it for me."

"Yeah, thanks, Jeremy," added a pretty girl with long blond hair nearly to her waist.

"You're welcome, Mary Ellen," Jeremy said. Mary Ellen turned and stuck out her tongue back at Jeremy. She then raced up to catch up to Lee. She grabbed him around the waist from behind, giggling. Lee and Mary Ellen had only recently become engaged, and were sickeningly inseparable.

"If you want my opinion," piped in a tall willowy girl with a sloppy bun on the back of her head. Several chunks of sawdust still clung to her dark tangled locks. "This is the best part of the adventure. What is more exciting than getting caught in a storm?" The girl, Jessica Bowen, reached out and grabbed the hand of her husband, Jeremy who was marching directly in front of her.

"How far back to camp?" came the distant voice of Frannie Parker from the back of the line of hikers. It seemed strange Frannie would be lagging behind; she was the best athlete of the group. But there was good reason for her positioning, and that was the lanky dark-haired fellow in front of her by the name of Blake Abbott. For the first time, Frannie had discovered romance.

After Beatrice quit school to marry Wade Bowen and Sophie left to raise Joe Mooney's son on her own, Suzanne and Fran found themselves alone to complete Grade twelve together. There was little doubt that both would accomplish that feat. Suzanne had always been an honor student, and even after she began dating Myles Gardner several months ago, her marks remained high. And as much as Suzanne encouraged Fran to get out and have a little bit of fun, she remained aloof to all advances from the opposite sex. Suzanne found herself feeling very sad for Fran, banished from her family and scarred with a memory that refused to leave her. Not that Fran ever let on. After her confession at Beatrice's wedding shower three years before, Fran never spoke of her ordeal again. She gradually worked through the experience, allowing time to heal her wounds. Fran began to smile, then laugh on a regular basis. After years of remaining reserved and aloof, Frances blossomed into what could almost be called confident. She was still shy, but thanks to the unwavering friendship of Suzanne, Beatrice and Sophie, she was healing. The greatest catalyst for Fran's stirring though was the company of Blake Abbott. Fran was convinced that Blake thought of her as merely a friend, but she did allow herself to hope for more. Most certainly it was Blake's laid-back approach that let Frannie feel comfortable with his company and to develop affection for him. Only a few days before the Long Weekend, she had confided in Suzanne. She was madly in love with Blake Abbott.

"Only another mile," called Lee from the front of the line. Lee was always the leader of any group endeavor, always first, always directing.

"Aww," groaned everyone at once, including Fran.

"Are you tired, Frannie?" Blake said over his shoulder. Fran nearly blushed at the attention. She hadn't really been trying to attract the sympathy of Blake, but now that she had it, she melted like sugar in the rain.

"No," she admitted, stepping surefootedly over a fallen log. "Just wet."

"Yeah," Bruce grinned through a wet lock of hair dripping between his eyes. "I know what you mean."

The rain was now pouring in buckets. Even under the umbrella of the tall forest, the group was feeling the full force of the storm. Lightning flashed hair-raisingly close, and the thunder boomed so loudly, they could not hear each other speak. Frannie looked up the trail, past the eight people in front of her. All she could see was bush. Endless bush.

As Fran gazed ahead, she witnessed something that struck her completely with awe. Never before had she seen the full force of nature so vividly. A bolt of lightning struck a tree not twenty feet from the trail, splintering it in an explosion of sparks and slivers of wood. The break happened about ten feet off the ground, severing the tree into two distinct pieces: the solid bottom half, still firmly rooted in the ground, and the fractured top half, now falling heavily to the spongy earth below. Fran wrestled to regain her voice when she realized where the tree was falling.

"Look out!" she called, panicked. Incredibly, her voice could not be heard above the clamber of the thunder and the combustion of the tree. From her vantage point, Fran was sure that the tree was going to fall directly onto the front people of the line. Lee and Mary Ellen and Bruce and Kelly all appeared to be in mortal danger. Some of the group were looking up, and getting clear of the falling tree. Some still had not seen what was coming down upon them. Fran was not sure who had run clear and who had not when the tree finally smashed to earth in an explosion of branches and leaves. All this, from the strike of the lightning to the final resting of the tree had taken less than three seconds. Fran stood transfixed for yet another couple vital seconds before she found her legs and rushed to the tree. She joined her friends, who were hurriedly digging through the tangle of branches.

"Is everyone all right?" Fran called loudly, still finding it hard to be heard through the storm.

"I don't know," called back Madeline, pulling branches. "I don't know whether everyone made it!"

Fran could scarcely believe what was happening. She could not fathom the thought of her friends being crushed under these branches, or even more tragically, under the trunk of this once mighty poplar tree. She joined Madeline in her mad struggle through the foliage.

"Kelly! Kelly!" Fran could hear from the other side of the tree. It was Bruce, calling for his fiancé.

"Bruce!" Fran called. "Where's Kelly?" She dreaded Bruce's reply.

"I think she's under here," Bruce called. "I saw that tree knock her down, and then she disappeared."

"Oh, my God!" a voice spoke in surrender. Fran recognized it to be Lee.

"What?" Bruce asked, alarmed to the point of shock.

"It's Kelly," Lee replied in anguish. "I see her leg."

Bruce said nothing. He only dove below to where Lee was situated amongst crushed branches and leaves. He disappeared beneath the fallen tree, desperate to find his love all right.

"She's still alive," he called from beneath the tree. "Give me a hand to lift this tree off of her." The entire group moved to positions on either side of the long poplar's trunk. Fran wondered if eight people could even hope to budge this unwieldy tree. Lee directed the group as they all lifted as one, straining and heaving with every ounce of strength in their being.

"Lift!" Lee called, and they all did so, though there was no sign of their efforts in the position of the tree. It remained motionless, still settled, unyielding in its captor of Kelly. "Lift," Lee yelled again desperately. Amazingly, the eight lifted with even more strength, and held their push for a longer duration. Each felt their muscles retort, ignoring the pain. At the last instant, the tree budged.

"Keep going," Bruce called. "Don't let 'er go." No one needed the command though, as each dug even deeper into their fiber for strength to not only maintain the effort they were already exerting, but to add that little bit of extra strength. Fran noticed a minuscule movement in the tree, as it inched its way upward.

"Okay," Lee directed. "Let's move it away now, towards me." Everyone obeyed Lee's charge, adding to the strain by pushing and pulling the log off to the side. Fran was on the opposite side of the tree as Lee, so was pushing towards him. As she worked her way forward, she felt something under her foot as she stepped, something like a branch. She glanced down to see Kelly's wrist, lifeless and white. Fran shifted her step frantically, barely missing crushing her friend's arm beneath her step. She nearly stumbled in the endeavor, pushing the weight of the tree forward and losing her portion of the weight. Lee and Jessica on the other side of the tree caught her panicked look and juggled the extra weight. Fran quickly regained her footing and her hold, taking the weight back from the overburdened arms of her rescuers. She could see in both Lee and Jessica's eyes the relief as the weight returned to her.

"Okay, I think we're clear of her," Bruce called from beside Lee. "Let's put this thing down, slowly." Fran wanted so badly to just let the tree go, freeing her muscles from the unbearable strain. But she knew that was foolhardy, likely to leave yet another member of her party crushed under the poplar's massive weight. She allowed her arms to straighten and lower slowly, as her muscles cried out in agony.

"Okay, when I count to three," Lee instructed. "Everyone let go and back up." Fran didn't know whether she could last the full count. "One... two...three." The immense poplar crashed the final few inches to earth, sending up another splash of branches and leaves. The eight rescuers jumped clear. Each was rushing to the side of Kelly, lying frighteningly motionless in the foliage. As soon as Fran saw her, she was sure she was dead.

Bruce was the first to Kelly's side, feeling her wrist for a pulse and checking for even faint breathing. "She's alive," he panted. "But she won't be for long if we don't get her to a doctor." Bruce and Lee lifted Kelly's limp form from the ground. "I'll run ahead," Fran suggested. "I'll get help."

"Good idea," Bruce said. "We won't be able to go nearly as fast as you."

"Hurry!" Mary Ellen said hysterically. Fran turned and ran through the woods as fast as her weary legs could travel. Only once she tripped over a fallen log. She barely noticed her bleeding hands as she returned to her frenzied gait.

Chapter 14

When that I was and a little tiny boy,
With a hey, ho, the wind and the rain
A foolish thing was but a toy,
For the rain, it raineth every day.

- "Twelfth Night"
William Shakespeare

    Charley stared out the wide open doorway of the barn, his eyes wide in disbelief. Even though he could see it with his own eyes and smell it with his own nose, he could not quite comprehend what was happening. His house was in flames. The windows were exploding in the heat and the wood was disintegrating into fiery red. What really confused him was the fact that the torrential rain was pounding down on the fire, but the flames refused to subside. The fire only hissed with annoyance at the rain, turning it into useless steam. The sight that truly brought the cruel reality home to the boy was the sight of the tattered blue sailboat curtains in his bedroom incinerating in the fury. In all of his nine years, he had never seen anything so immense and so uncontrollable and so terrifying all at the same time. He was watching the only home he had ever known, literally his whole world collapse into itself, and there was nothing he could do about it. There was nothing anyone could do about it, especially since there was only he and his mother here watching the house burn. He was only a little boy and Mama wasn't well.

Charley did not know what was happening to his mother, but he knew very well that something was wrong. As hastily as she had managed to reunite herself with him in the barn, she had begun acting very strangely. Now Mama was laying down on her back over in the hay, panting and sweating and looking like she was in pain. There was a puddle of water forming on the barn floor between her legs.

"Charley..." Charley heard his mother call out weakly. He reluctantly pulled his eyes away from the blaze.

"I'm right here, Mama," he said obediently. He was very worried about his mother and would do anything she said to make things better.

"Charley---" Isabelle said again, stopping as a sharp pain appeared to cut through her. Once the hurt had passed, she spoke again. "Charley, come here to Mama."

Charley walked over to his mother, and knelt at her side as she softly spoke. "Charley, you have to do something for Mama. Something very important."

"Sure..." Charley said uncertainly. He would do anything for his mother, but he was also very frightened. His house was being destroyed by flames and there was a terrible storm raging outside and Mama was in trouble. It seemed like the whole world was crashing down around him.

"Is it still raining?" Isabelle asked.

"Yes, Mama." Charley was astounded that his mother had to ask such a question. The rain was beating on the tin roof of the barn like a tom-tom. The sound of the thunder was only magnified by the large hollow of the barn. But Isabelle Duncan was unaware of it all; she seemed only partially conscious of what was happening around her. Charley felt another stab of fear run through him.

"Do you know where Suzanne is, Charley?" Isabelle said slowly and deliberately, as if each word were an enormous effort.

"Suzanne?"

"Yes, son," Isabelle strained. "Do you know where she is?"

"She's at Thunder River," Charley was almost afraid of where this conversation was going. Suzanne was so far removed from this present situation. Or was she?

"That's right," Isabelle managed a smile. "Do you know how to get to the campsite from here?"

"Yeah..." Charley admitted reluctantly.

"Tell me how to get to the campground where Suzanne is," Isabelle said patiently.

"You go out to the main road," Charley began. "Goldmine Road." He added quickly. Charley recognized the need to be exact in his explanation. He had the feeling that a lot was riding on his ability to find Suzanne.

"That's right," Isabelle said. She almost seemed to relax at Charley's knowledge of the facts, and that made Charley calm down somewhat too. "Then where?"

"Then you turn right," he said, holding up his right hand for reassurance. Charley was concentrating very hard on his directions as he watched the route in his mind. "You go down that road for a long way, past the creek. Then you turn left," Charley put up his left hand, "and go down the hill through the trees. The campsite is right down there."

"Very good," Isabelle smiled. "Do you think you could go there all by yourself?"

"And find Suzanne?" Charley said meekly. He had figured out the plan without his mother coming right out and telling him. He knew he was going to be going out in that storm all alone and he was going to get Suzanne to help Mama. Mama needed help bad.

"Yes," Isabelle said simply. "And find Suzanne."

"Okay, Mama," Charley said. "What do I do when I find her?"

"Tell Suzanne to go to the Thunder Store," Isabelle said weakly. Charley thought she looked like she was going to go to sleep, except for the pain that seemed to keep her awake. "Tell her to call the fire department and the doctor."

"The doctor?" Charley said, alarmed by his mother's candor. As much as he knew something was wrong, he didn't like hearing it spoken out loud by his mother.

"Yes," Isabelle said. "I need a doctor because I am going to have the baby."

"Oh," Charley said. He was partially relieved by the revelation. He knew that having a baby was a normal thing, something that ladies did all the time. At least he could be comforted that Mama was not dying as he had earlier expected. But still, she looked so helpless. Charley had never thought of his mother as a person who could ever be sick.

"Charley, there's one more thing," Isabelle continued, her voice no more than a whisper. Charley leaned closer to hear her soft voice. "Tell Suzanne to call your father."

Chapter 15

*Into each life some rain must fall,
Some days must be dark and dreary.*

*- "The Rainy Day"
Henry Wadsworth Longfellow*

Standing behind the till at the Thunder Store, Kathy Atkinson had a clear view of the gas pumps out front. Right now she could see Old Man Edwards filling up his battered old green Chevy pickup. It was actually her job to go out and pump gas for customers, but she rarely managed to get outside to do it. The locals had generally all been trained to do it themselves if they were in any kind of a hurry.

That old fool Jake Edwards appeared to be in a bit of a rush today. Even though he was puttering around as usual, washing his windshield and checking his oil, Kathy could tell he was tottering around at a slightly quicker pace. The mere sight of Jake Edwards disgusted Kathy. He was grimy and unshaven; she was sure he had not bathed in weeks. Kathy remembered when she was a little girl, when Jake's wife Peggy was still alive; he had been as neat and tidy as any respectable Headline gentleman. But since Peggy's death two years ago, Jake had gone back to his old ways, back to living in that grubby old two room shack on his gold claim that he had abandoned upon marrying Peggy back in the 40's. It was the life that Jake Edwards obviously loved best, even though he had managed to give it up for Peggy for the thirty two years of their marriage. Jake didn't leave his place too often nowadays. He stopped by the Thunder Store every couple of weeks for bacon, canned beans and toilet paper. He rarely went to Headline, seldom visited with family or friends. Today though, it looked like Jake was heading out. More than likely, he was going to the Labor Day Thunder River Campout.

Jake Edwards and everyone else in the whole stinking world was going to the Long Weekend, Kathy thought bitterly, everyone except Kathy herself. She always missed all the fun because she had to work. Kathy could not understand the justice of a world that forced a talented artist like herself to work as a store clerk instead of painting resplendent landscapes as she should be doing. Somehow in her father's attempt to create a perfect resume, she had ended up here in Thunder Ridge, the armpit of Canada, daughter of the local elementary school principal. Big deal. Les Atkinson's assurances that his tour of duty in northern Alberta would be short, profitable and would lead to better things had been enough to get Kathy to agree to move here. But the promises stopped right around the time Kathy was in the tenth grade. Soon after that, the Atkinsons built their dream home on a beautiful river front lot, just out of Thunder Ridge. Kathy knew then she would have to get herself out of this shithole. But even though she had graduated from high school two years ago, she had not yet managed to leave Thunder Ridge. Her father had readily offered to put her through university, but of course it would mean going to the Faculty of Education. Kathy could not bear the thought of devoting her life to the molding of small unwilling minds. She had much better gifts to offer the world. Besides, Kathy's marks had been barely good enough to graduate. Her high school academic ambitions had only been a prelude to her university aspirations: non-existent. Academia was useless, an utter waste of time. The only thing Kathy had ever excelled at had been a natural gift, something that could never have been taught. She had always been able to paint and draw exquisite landscapes. And that was not just Kathy's opinion; many around town admired her work. So it was her art that Kathy was determined to make a vocation out of. Working at Thunder Store was simply passing time until the right moment arrived.

Kathy saw that Old Man Edwards was finishing up with his truck. It was about time. This could turn into a perfect opportunity for what Kathy called Making a Profit, perfect because the store was now completely empty and Jake Edwards was about to come in to pay for his gas.

Making a Profit was Kathy's way of supplementing her pitiful two dollar an hour wage and, if the truth be known, it was a very simple procedure: Kathy simply neglected to punch certain purchases into the till and pocketed the money. It was quick and easy. Too easy, really, thanks entirely to the store owner, Colin Funk.

Even though Colin owned one of the most lucrative businesses in the area, Thunder Store was not his claim to fame and fortune. Rather, he was renowned for his lightning strength moonshine, which sold for top dollar, nearly as much as liquor store booze. Colin had a still, well hidden in the bush behind the store, and when he wasn't out there stewing his latest batch, he was drunker than a skunk from sampling his next-to-latest batch. It was this not so secret enterprise that kept Colin away from the store most of the time and cerebrally unaware of what was happening all the time. It was the 'shining than made Kathy's Making a Profit possible.

It had started out small: penny candy and the odd bottle of Coca Cola. Over the months though, Kathy realized how little attention Colin paid to his business, and how much more she could get away with, if only she had the guts to do it. Now, she did daily personal deposits of gas fill-ups, the easiest and most lucrative of all her schemes. It was particularly simple because Colin Funk was constantly staggering up to the pumps, filling up his own beat up pickup for deliveries of moonshine to customers all the way in Headline and even Grande Prairie, never once keeping track of his own consumption. He never missed the gas profits, never once even questioning the deposits Kathy made daily at the Bank of Montreal in Headline, in both the Thunder Store account and her own personal account.

Jake Edwards screwed the gas cap back into his truck. He reached for his tattered wallet as he made his way into the store. Kathy smiled smugly and turned away, pretending to arrange some cigarettes on the shelves behind the till. She heard the bell tinkle as the front door opened.

"Well, hello there, Mr. Edwards," she smiled as she turned to greet her customer.

It was only when she had turned completely back towards the door that she saw that it had not been Jake Edwards that came in through the door. Instead, it was two other people who had run into the store in front of him, a teenage girl and a young boy. Kathy recognized them immediately as those loathsome Duncan children, Suzanne and Charley. They headed straight for the public telephone which hung on the wall right beside the front counter. They were a mere three feet away from Kathy as Jake Edwards ambled through the door.

Kathy was heartsick as she took a five dollar bill from Jake Edwards. He didn't require any change: his purchase had been exactly five dollars. He started walking away before Kathy even reached for the till. A perfect opportunity. Well almost. It would have been so easy to put that money in her pocket. But she couldn't. Not with Suzanne and Charley Duncan standing right beside her. Kathy was not going to Make a Profit on this transaction today. She was so enraged by her fouled up plot, she barely saw what was happening at the telephone.

Suzanne had already pumped a nickel into the telephone, and had quickly dialed the hospital number. She spoke quickly and sharply to the person on the other end of the line, explaining exactly what the situation was out at the Duncan home. She didn't even hang up the phone, rather she pushed the button, deposited another coin and dialed again. This time she was connected with the Headline Volunteer Fire Department. After hanging up this time, she put one final nickel into the telephone and dialed the number of the Headline Hotel. She knew the number off by heart. She had reached her father there many times before. It was this phone call that bothered her more than any. Mama had given her strict instructions to call her father, but Suzanne knew Ray Duncan, and he would not take well to finding out his house was burning to the ground, let alone that Mama was giving birth in the barn. Suzanne could stomach her father's sharp tongue if she knew it would do any good, but she knew better. Ray Duncan could do nothing to make this bad situation better. If anything he would only make it worse.

"Can I speak to Ray Duncan? I think he's in the---" She didn't have to finish her sentence. The desk clerk knew exactly where Ray Duncan was. "Thank you." Suzanne said meekly to a telephone line already hooked onto "Hold." She looked down at Charley as she waited. He looked as though he were in shock. She could only imagine what the young boy had gone through, watching his house burn to the ground and nursing his mother through labor, then walking three miles through torrential rain to find her at Thunder River.

"Hi, Dad?" Suzanne said quickly to the slurring voice on the other end of the line. She knew that Ray would be extremely perturbed at being interrupted and she would have to talk fast. She would have to get across the seriousness of the situation before he started chastising her for the intrusion. Within forty five seconds, Suzanne had rattled off the entire story, leaving Ray Duncan with no doubt as to the grave state of affairs at home. He hung up with phone without even saying goodbye. Suzanne knew he would be in his car and flying down the highway in mere seconds. That thought left no reassurance in her mind, rather giving her more to dread.

As Suzanne and Charley left the store, they did not notice a sly smile appear on the face of the girl behind the counter. Another vehicle had just pulled up to the gas pumps.

Chapter 16

> Time has no divisions to mark its passage,
> there is never a thunderstorm or blare of
> trumpets to announce the beginning of
> a new month of year.
>
> - "The Magic Mountain"
> Thomas Mann

It was a Labor Day weekend tradition for Alfred Fox to paint his cabin. After all, the weather was always perfect on Labor Day, always clear and blue and hot. At sunrise on the clear morning of August 31, Alf had risen from his small hard bunk as was his routine. On any normal day, Alf would linger over black coffee and runny eggs, before starting his day of chores. Today though, with a special purpose in mind, he had gone straight to task.

Against the cabin Alf leaned a decaying ladder, the wood split and weathered to a lifeless grey. He then opened a gallon of white paint he had purchased the day before from Thunder Ridge Dry Goods. He stirred the paint thoroughly and jerkily climbed the ladder. Even with a bum leg he still got around pretty good, if Alf did say so himself. Once positioned comfortably at the top with his paint and brush, he set contentedly to work. If anyone would have seen Alf Fox on the top of that ladder, they would have sworn they saw a smile on the man's face.

Alf Fox lived a solitary existence out in his cabin on the banks of the Thunder River that he would only begrudgingly admit was a happy one. He had lived this isolated lifestyle for about seven years now, each year adding to his reputation for being a crazy old hermit. And even though Alf didn't mind the supposition, since it kept people away, in actual fact, he was anything but deranged. He was simply a very bitter man. And in Alf Fox's mind, he had plenty of reason to be. As if a tragic farming accident that left him partially paralyzed and a drowning that killed his ten year old son weren't enough, Alf had even more reason to want to distance himself from society.

Fifteen years ago, he had got into yet another screaming match with his wife Caroline. Another, because violent arguments were commonplace between the Foxes. Some said that neither of the two had ever come to grips with the death of their son, Gordon, and were blaming each other for the accident. Others said it was Caroline's nonstop tongue that always got her into trouble. Whatever the cause of that infamous row of May 1960, Alf had to have been called the victor. And the loser. In a fit of anger he later could not even recall, Alf took his Caroline by the shoulders and shook her and shook her and then started banging her head against the wall. When the police answered the neighbors' complaints of screaming at the Fox residence, again, they found a bloody mess in the Fox kitchen, and Alf sitting in the living room watching television. Alf Fox served eight years for his part in his wife's death, but only because his lawyer was smart enough to know winning this case was hopeless. He talked Alf into taking a plea deal.

Alf Fox had plenty of time to think during the long hours of incarceration in his cell. He decided that he was a bit sorry for killing Caroline, though he had not really missed her since her death. He reasoned that any sane man would have done the same thing under similar circumstances; Caroline Fox's mouth could drive any man to murder. He had been forced by family into marrying that woman to begin with, that being the first of many tragedies in his pathetic life. And none of these misfortunes were ever his fault! Alf Fox ascertained that the world had done him very, very wrong, and if he gave them another chance, it would do it to him again.

When Alf was released from prison in 1968, he sold the house he had shared with Caroline in Headline and bought a bush quarter of land out by the Thunder River. And there he remained, bitter and sometimes just plain lonely. He had made it very clear he wanted nothing to do with human beings once and for all; they had been the ruin of all his happiness and weren't going to do him in the rest of the way. But sometimes, just sometimes, Alf wished someone would come and visit, share a pot of coffee. But Alf had not a friend in Headline after his sensational trial, no one depending on him, and no family to speak of beside a high-falutin' businessman brother Freddie with his nose too high in the air and a spinster librarian sister who got no pleasure out of life that was not in a book. It had made it easy for Alf to pack up his few belongings and move out to the river.

Most of the time, Alf liked his simple life on the homestead. He farmed very little, sowing only enough to pay the bills. He hunted wild game in the autumn and trapped in the winter, eking out a modest living from the land. He was governed by the seasons and the rise and fall of the sun and moon, living by no time clock and no calendar, only the natural routine he had fallen into over the past seven years. That routine said that the Labor Day weekend was cabin painting day.

The paint brushed on in smooth wide strokes, obliterating all sign of the peeling cracked paint applied a year ago. Alf was pleased with the fresh look of the cabin, emerging with new life in its clean coat of whiteness. Alf came to the meticulous window trim, concentrating carefully on not getting any paint on the glass. Alf had never bothered with masking tape in his paint jobs. It was an unnecessary expense; all a man had to do was take the time, work slow and painstaking with a steady hand. Alf was pleased at the smooth straight line of paint that ended at the precise edge of the wood.

"Hey!," shouted a frantic voice from directly below his feet. Alf started, jerking the brush across the window in a white line that looked like the top of an exclamation point. He mentally cursed the smear. But when he looked down into the panicked face of a pretty young woman standing at the bottom of the ladder, panting like a dog, he knew something was wrong.

The girl recovered her breath enough to finally speak again. "You got a phone, mister?"

"Yeah, sure," Alf said sulkily. "In the cabin."

"Could I use it, sir?" the girl said, pushing a long lock of wheat-colored hair out of her eyes. "There's been a terrible accident."

"Yeah, go ahead," Alf replied cautiously. He wiped the paint off the window with a rag from his back pocket, and then began to make his descent from the ladder. Before he even made it down two steps, the girl had vanished inside the cabin. By the time Alf walked through the porch into the living room/kitchen/bedroom of the cabin, she had already dialed and was waiting for the line to be picked up on the other end.

"Hello," the girl said, responding frantically to the voice coming through the receiver. "This is Frances Parker. There's been an accident out in the woods by the Thunder River. A tree was hit by lightning and it fell on my friend, Kelly Gardner---" The girl, Frances, stopped her rapid fire narration, listening momentarily. "Yes, we moved her. We had to. It was a mile or so out, no roads," She paused again, her blue eyes darting as she listened. "I ran ahead for help. The others are bringing her out."

Pause.

"Yeah, I'm at a cabin. It's---" Frances looked over at Alf for the first time since he entered the cabin. "Where am I?" she demanded. "Whose place is this?"

"This is my place. I'm Alfred Fox. Everyone knows---" Alf wasn't able even able to complete his sentence. This frightened girl, Frances, was back talking on the phone.

"I'm at Alfred Fox's place," she repeated her host's name into the receiver carefully as if to make no mistake. "Do you know where that is?"

Pause.

"Oh, good," Frances said, relief showing on her face for the very first time. "Can you send an ambulance out here right away? I know they're not too far behind me and Kelly has to get to a hospital right---" This time the pause was accompanied by a look of horror on Fran's face.

"What?" she finally choked. "What do you mean there's no ambulance? Where's the ambulance?"

Pause.

"Oh," was her terse reply. "Mrs. Duncan's baby. I see." Frances paused for a few seconds, obviously thinking very hard, very rapidly. She was a young girl dealing with a difficult life and death situation. "We have to get Kelly to the hospital. We'll drive her in ourselves. Be ready. We'll be there in fifteen minutes. Or less."

Frances hung up the phone quickly. She stared out the grimy window of Alf's cabin for a few seconds, carefully pondering. Alf suddenly felt uncomfortable, out of place in his own home. He figured it had to do with the fact that this pretty little lady was the first person who had been inside his cabin in ages, years really. It seemed strange to have someone in here with him, especially someone who was so oblivious of Alf's very existence. Her entire focus was on the plight of her friend.

Alf moved toward the stove. He decided, really out of lack of any idea what he should do, to pour himself a cup of coffee. His movement startled the girl out of her muse. She suddenly took flight running out the cabin door as quickly as she came in. It was then that Alf found his thoughts and his tongue.

"Where you goin' little lady?" he called after the girl, Frances was her name though he didn't feel right in calling her that.

"I'm going to camp to get my car," she sputtered. "I have to get Kelly to the hospital."

"Don't be a fool, girl," Alf said. "Use my truck. It's parked right outside the door." Frances stared at Alf wide-eyed and speechless.

"Thank you, mister," she finally blurted when she recovered her tongue. "Thank you so much!"

"Oh, don't thank me," Alf said. "Just let's get out there and get 'er running. You'll be on the road as soon as your friends get here."

"'You'll?'" Frances repeated. "Aren't you driving? It is your truck, after all."

"Oh, hell, no," Alf said. "You young people know how to drive a hell of a lot faster than I do. And I ain't worried about you stealin' the old Fargo. You wouldn't want to."

Frances managed a short smile. Alf grabbed the keys off a nail by the door, and the two went outside. Frances watched nervously as Alf started a tired rusting old truck. She was glad that Jeremy was an experienced driver of old jalopies. As the blue truck roared to life, Frances saw her friends emerging from the trees in the distance. She ran to meet them, to tell them about the substitute for an ambulance ride ahead of them.

Chapter 17

Oh, what did you hear, my blue-eyed son?
And what did you hear, my darling young one?
I heard the sound of a thunder that roared out a warnin',
Heard the roar of a wave that could drown the whole world,
I heard one hundred drummers whose hands were a-blazin',
I heard ten thousand whisperin' and nobody listenin',
I heard one person starve, I heard many people laughin',
Heard the song of a poet who died in the gutter,
I heard the sound of a clown who cried in the alley,
And it's a hard, it's a hard, it's a hard, it's a hard,
It's a hard rain's a-gonna fall.

A Hard Rain's A-Gonna Fall
- Bob Dylan

The instant Ray Duncan burst through the front doors of the Headline Hotel, he was blinded by the light of mid-afternoon. Even though it was cloudy and threatening to rain, the brilliance was enough to overload his wide open pupils which had had several hours to adjust to the dim smoky bar inside. Unable to see a single thing and more than a little lightheaded from the rum, Ray's first step was aimed for the concrete in front of him, but actually hit the open space above the gravel of the hotel parking lot. Ray tumbled to the ground in an explosion of pebbles and profanity.

"God damn it!" Ray blasted through the pain that shot through his head and his left knee. "Whoever put that fuckin' step there..."

"Whoa, Ray," slurred a familiar voice, as an arm grabbed him, helping Ray to his feet. "Dat was some kinda tumble, eh?"

Ray looked up, this time able to see, though his vision was blurred by stars that were flashing in front of his eyes. He was able to make out the whisky-weathered face of that ignorant deadbeat, Paulie Dubois, his thick black hair sticking out in a dozen different rooster tails. It looked like he had just woke up, and Lord knows where that could have been.

Paulie Dubois was the only man in Headline who had a worse reputation than Ray Duncan, and that was reason enough for Ray to dislike him. While Ray half-assed managed to keep up a farm and still had a family, Paulie was completely destitute, living in culverts and under bridges in the summer, and in the Peace River Minimum Security Prison in the winter. For as long as anyone had known him, he was always looking for either money or liquor or both. It really didn't matter what he was able to mooch, because it all ended up as booze anyway. Vivian Dubois had left Paulie in 1960 via the Headline Hospital. Ray had no respect for any man who would put a woman in the hospital.

"Paulie, get outa my fuckin' way," Ray growled, pushing him off his arm. When he let go, Ray, still wobbly on his feet, fell flat on his behind. Even though it was probably not good for his health, Paulie couldn't help but laugh.

"Let me give you a hand," Paulie said. "Me dere, I've taken dat step de wrong way myself a few times, me. It's even trickier after a few belts of whisky. I remember one time---"

"Paulie," Ray said, finally standing without any support. "I gotta go." He took a few strides, then looked around the deserted hotel parking lot. Where was that god damn car anyway?

"Where yeah headin', Ray?" Paulie asked, chasing Ray as fast as his short legs could carry him. "You goin' to a party, eh?" he said hopefully. You had to hand it to him, Paulie Dubois had a one track mind.

"No, I'm goin' home," Ray said, spying his battered brown Chrysler parked at an odd angle just to his left.

"Home?" Paulie was disappointed in Ray. It wasn't even sundown. Why would Ray be heading home so early? "Why would you wanna go dere?"

"The house is on fire," Ray said as he swung into the car. He wanted to get to hell out of here and that idiot Paulie Dubois was slowing him down.

"Holy shit!" Paulie said.

"And Isabelle's havin' her baby," Ray added, almost as an afterthought. He swung the car door shut and started digging for his keys.

"Dat's rough," Paulie said, leaning on his forearms and sticking his head into the window. "That's why I don't bother wid a house or a family, me. Dey always seem to get in de way, don't you find dat, Ray..."

Ray couldn't seem to maneuver his fingers around his keys. He felt like he was wearing thick work gloves that couldn't get a hold of the right key. Ray knew it wasn't the liquor that was screwing up his coordination, rather just the shock of the news. He knew he wasn't so very drunk. He'd only been in the bar for an hour or so by his calculations. He had arrived at shortly after one, and it was only... What! Ray looked at his watch and saw the time to be a quarter past four. Where had the afternoon gone? Ray was filled with a new sense of panic. His clumsy fingers finally grasped the car key, and he jammed it into the ignition. The car started with a blast, drowning out Paulie Dubois' monologue.

"...me, I useta always tell Viv---" Paulie was saying as Ray forced the car into reverse, and hit the gas. His comfortable position in the car window was instantly interrupted and he went tumbling to the ground in a cloud of gravel.

"Hey, you god damn asshole!" Paulie bellowed from a seated position. Ray didn't hear a word. He just put the car into drive and swung into the street. Ray gunned the engine, drowning out the honks of the car he had cut off. It was none other than Nancy Abbott, proudly driving her newest grey Cadillac home from the car lot.

Chapter 18

Still falls the Rain--
Dark as the world of man, black as our loss--

- "Street Songs"
C.H. Sisson

"How's she doin'?" Jeremy Bowen said, glancing away from the highway only for a moment. He had Alf Fox's old blue Fargo pushing eighty miles an hour, which was a real challenge without power steering and with four people crammed in the cab.

"I don't know," Bruce said helplessly. "She's still bleeding quite a bit, and she's awfully pale."

"Can't you go a little faster?" Lee urged Jeremy. "I don't know whether we're gonna make it in time."

"I'm going as fast as I can without crackin' this heap up," Jeremy replied. Despite his own caution, Jeremy pushed the gas pedal down a little further.

The only reason Jeremy was even a part of this emergency sprint into Headline was that he was the best driver in the group. Jeremy had been driving since he could see over the steering wheel, and had been racing stock cars since he was fourteen. If there was anyone who could get you somewhere fast, even in an old battered Fargo, it was Jeremy Bowen. These reassurances came from his friends as they pushed him into the driver's seat, but it didn't make Jeremy feel any better. He liked to drive fast, just over the edge, but only when his neck was on the line. This was so much more serious, too serious. Kelly's life depended on Jeremy getting her to the hospital right away.

"Hang in there, baby," Bruce coaxed his unconscious sweetheart. He hugged Kelly close and kissed her pale cheeks again and again. "We're gonna get you help right away. Jeremy's driving so you know you're in good hands, sugar."

Lee simply stared down into his sister's face, his own nearly as white as hers. The twenty three miles to Headline were taking much, much too long. Lee looked up and out the cracked front window of the truck and saw the farmhouse of Aron Chester. That meant they were still ten miles from Headline. Ten miles! That meant at least ten agonizing minutes, ten minutes that he didn't think Kelly could survive without a doctor. Why had that stupid ambulance been on a call when Fran had telephoned the hospital? The Headline ambulance service was barely used, just often enough to keep the battery in the ambulance charged. Sometimes the ambulance didn't turn a wheel for weeks on end. So why two calls in the same day? At the same hour? All these thoughts about ambulances, Lee began to hear sirens in his mind. He shook his head, clearing his mind from useless "what ifs" and "why me's". There were more important matters at hand, like getting Kelly some help---

Help...

Help was on its way. Lee was sure of it. He wasn't just imagining it, he could really hear sirens, and up ahead on the breast of the highway, was, yes, it was an ambulance, heading straight for them at break neck speed.

"Jeremy, pull over," Lee screamed. "It's the ambulance." Jeremy pounded down on the brakes and skidded the Fargo onto the shoulder of the road in a shower of gravel. Before the truck was even stopped, Lee and Jeremy piled out either door of the truck, waving their hands frantically at the approaching ambulance, which they could now see was closely followed by a fire truck. The sirens were blending together into an eerie high pitched wail, getting louder with each second.

"Stop, stop!" Lee bellowed. "We have a life and death emergency." But Lee's pleas were drowned out by the shriek of the sirens as both the ambulance and fire truck passed the waving boys at break neck speed. Lee and Jeremy looked into the wind of the passing vehicles in dismay, dumbfounded, listening to the fading sirens. The ambulance had not even slowed down. The great feeling of Hope slipped from Lee's heart.

"Come on, you guys!" Bruce called from inside the cab of the truck where he still cradled Kelly's comatose form. "Quit standing there like idiots! Let's get moving."

It was enough to send Jeremy and Lee bolting from their spots at the same instant, immediately abandoning their feeling of doom. They still had Kelly to take care of. Jeremy popped the clutch and gunned the Fargo's engine. In a spray of rocks, the truck was off again, rushing headlong in the direction of Headline. More than ever, there was panic in the air, and Jeremy held nothing back.

Chapter 19

Blow, winds, and crack your cheeks!
...ingrateful man!

- "King Lear"
William Shakespeare

"I don' know what that woman is tryin' to prove," Ray slurred under his sour breath, "but there's gonna be hell to pay." With that thought, he pushed the gas pedal a little closer to the floor mat.

What Ray Duncan could not figure out for the life of him, was how Isabelle had managed to set the house on fire? Was she cooking doughnuts in hot grease over the wood stove again? Ray had told that woman time and time again that those spoiled kids don't need none of that baking. It's bad for their teeth and turns them into little butterballs.

Ray gritted his teeth. His body and mind were pulsating with annoyance, and with each moment he was getting more and more pissed off, and at more than just Isabelle. He was annoyed that all these emergencies like house fires and wives giving birth in the barn always seemed to happen to him. Why was Ray Duncan always picked on?

Ray was also irritated by the alcohol haze that continued to grip his faculties, despite his frantic attempts to shake the booze off. When he had come to a rolling stop at the stop sign on the edge of town, Ray had actually slapped his face three sharp times in order to clear his head.

All that had managed to do was give him a colossal headache of the hangover variety.

Most of all, Ray was irritated by pouring rain that the tattering windshield wipers of the family car could not even keep up with. The rain had started just as he got out of Headline and it made visibility with his alcohol-hazed eyes even more difficult. Ray remembered Isabelle's premonition of that morning and cursed her once more under his breath. Why hadn't Isabelle predicted that the baby was going to be born instead giving him a useless weather forecast? He swore at Isabelle again because she hadn't started having this damn baby before he left. He's not that big of a dick that he would take off for town and leave his laboring wife alone. Why hadn't her water just broken a little earlier?

His head began to throb even harder as he peered bleary-eyed out the front windshield. He could not believe he was going to have to fight this goddamn storm all the long stretch between himself and his house, presently burning to the ground, taking with it his scant worldly possessions. Thankfully, the traffic was light. Everyone in Headline and Thunder Ridge was at the Long Weekend.

As Ray sped headlong into the open road ahead of him, his thoughts wandered off to a day a very long time ago that had been so much like today it was uncanny. Unnerving. He had started out in the same place then had been forced to race home for the very same reason: an impending birth. He had driven down this same road in the middle of a tremendous thunderstorm. Ray just prayed that was where the similarities ended.

It must have been the fall of 1946, because Ray knew he had been eleven years old at the time. He remembered it like it was yesterday because that very day he had been placed on the PeeWee All Star hockey team, and was proudly wearing his new red, white and blue jersey, the proud colors of both the Montreal Canadiens and the Abbott Motors Dynamos. He remembered because the blood stains were never completely washed out of his prized jersey. It was a stark legacy of an unforgettable night.

It had been a Friday night, and Ray was in his usual Friday night spot: the front seat of the family station wagon parked behind the Headline Hotel. He had been there for three or four hours now, ever since hockey practice had ended at eight. But instead of heading straight home like all the other boys and their fathers had done, Sam Duncan and his son had headed directly to the Headline Hotel and Sam's favorite bar stool. Ray was lost in thought in the car, not sleeping, not really thinking about anything, just daydreaming the way only eleven year olds can.

Suddenly, without any warning, the passenger door that he was slumped against flew open. The first thing that crossed Ray's mind was that some drunk from the bar had found the wrong ride home. But as he tumbled to the mud, Ray looked up into the face of his father. Ray was surprised; he hadn't expected Sam Duncan to emerge from the bar until at least one in the morning.

"Get up, you little shit," Sam Duncan slurred. Ray scrambled to his feet. He knew what would happen if he didn't jump to his father's commands instantly. In his father's words, he would see stars.

"Dad, what are---" Ray started.

"Shut up, and get in the fuckin' car," Sam babbled. Ray started getting back in the passenger door, but his behind wasn't even on the vinyl when Sam grabbed his skinny arm savagely.

"Not there, ya dummy," Sam garbled. "Get in the driver's seat."

"Wha--?"

"You're drivin', so shut your mouth or you're gonna see stars," Sam said. He pushed Ray out of the way and collapsed onto the seat.

Ray ran around to the other side of the car, opened the door, and sat down behind the steering wheel. He could barely see over the dash. Sam Duncan was digging in his pockets for the keys, which he eventually unearthed. Ray took them reluctantly and put the key in the ignition. When the car roared to life, Ray was frightened by the power of the engine, a power he was now controlling. He hesitated in pure terror. He was only eleven years old! How was he supposed to drive a car?

"Get a move on, boy," Sam growled from below Ray's head. He was nearly lying on the seat beside him. "We gotta get home right away. Your mother's havin' a baby and the doctor might not make it in time." The speech was almost too much for Ray's inebriated father. He rested his head against the back of the seat, his mouth slightly open and panting.

Ray was startled by his father's news. Mother was going to have a baby! He and his little sisters Felicia and Fiona had been waiting with eager anticipation for this event for months. He could hardly believe it was finally happening. Ray was also pushed into action by his father's words. If Mama was in labor, and the doctor might not be there, then she could be in danger. He had to get there right away!

Ray never forgot the sensation of pushing the car into gear, and feeling it slip into motion. It took only a few moments of apprehension though before Ray forgot his fears, and sped out of Headline. It was the longest twenty miles of his life. The entire trip was a blur of headlights that seemed to be coming straight for him, vicious bullying and commands from the slobbering Sam Duncan, and the deep rooted certainty that he was going to die in a fiery car crash on Highway 65.

Now, twenty nine years later, Ray was not nearly so petrified by the drive to a woman in labor. He was more annoyed. Maybe that was the way his father had felt during his drunken drive to the side of his wife. Of course, what his father had felt really didn't matter in the long run. Audrey Duncan's labor and delivery was a difficult one, one that required a doctor long before she finally got to one. By the time Ray had driven his mother all that long agonizing distance back into Headline, she was screaming from the pain. There was blood everywhere. Something was terribly wrong. Sam Duncan screamed and rampaged unceasingly. Once at the hospital, there was nothing the doctor could do. The baby was breach, and now, dead. Casey Samuel Duncan died on that dreadful rainy October night, and so did the marriage of Sam and Audrey Duncan. Audrey had been so disgusted by the behavior of her husband that night that she left him immediately, heading straight from the hospital to the safe haven of the police station. That dark fall night had been pivotal indeed. Ray thought about his own present situation, a laboring wife and a burning house, and wondered if this day of birth would be equally pivotal.

Another car, idling at a mere fifty miles per hour, appeared out of the storm, directly in front of Ray. He scowled miserably. Ray glanced out the side window and saw that he was presently cruising past Johansen Creek, a measly seven miles out of Headline. Dead ahead was Abbott House and the Carruthers farm. At this rate he was never going to get home or at least what was left of home. As he and the red Valiant in front of him began to climb the hill out of the creek, he hit the gas of the tired old Chrysler and started to pass. He was not going to wait all goddamn day.

Chapter 20

> Tempt me no more; for I
> Have known the lightning's hour
> The poet's inward pride,
> The certainty of power.
>
> - "Magnetic Mountain"
> C. Day-Lewis

Dean West was in no condition to be driving. But because the mixture of hallucinogenics and Jack Daniels that coursed through his abused veins was marginally less than that of the other passengers of the band's bus, Dean had been given the assignment of driving the long trip from Edmonton to a hicksville by the name of Headline strictly by default. And even though he was less stoned than the rest of the guys, Dean wasn't so sure he should be behind the wheel. The road in front of him was blurred at the best of times, non-existent at others as his eyes slid nearly shut, lulled to a doze by the rhythmic beating of the wipers as they pushed the torrents of rain aside.

Then there were the images that kept playing in his mind that made it difficult to keep his mind on the road. First, there was that piece of jailbait with the butterfly tattoo on her thigh that Dean had had his way with in the back of the bus after the show last night in Edmonton. Then there was the new song that was circling in his head, a rhythm and a melody that wouldn't go away. That was the way songs were usually conceived for Dean, and this one was catchier than most. He was almost at the point where he was going to have to pick up a guitar and a piece of paper and write this one down.

 Dean felt a pull on the right side of the bus, and realize that he had allowed the bus to drift towards the ditch. He jerked the steering wheel to the left, pulling the vehicle out of the gravel in the nick of time. Through the buzzing in his head, Dean was able to comprehend the close call he had just allayed. He forced his eyes wide open, taking a long swig of Jack Daniels to perk himself up. He gaped ahead, blinking like an owl.

 When Dean saw the fire ahead of him, he reasoned it to be the sun glinting off the hood of an oncoming car. But even in his inebriated state, he knew something wasn't quite right with that deduction. It was the beating of the wipers that finally jarred his brain into realizing that the sun wasn't going to flash off anything in a downpour like this. The thick grey cloud cover made sure of that. So what was that bright spot on the road he was now presently bearing down on much too quickly? The speedometer caught Dean's eye long enough for him to realize he was travelling at a pretty speedy clip (110 miles per hour!), and he had better slow down if he didn't want to rush right into the center of that glow on the highway. Dean's foot found the brake and he felt the bus rushing to a stop, though he was wondering whether it was going to be in time. He now saw that the glow ahead of him on the road was a roaring fire, and he was heading straight for it. As near as Dean could tell, his foot was down as far as it could go, and he would have to hope he was going to stop soon enough. When the bus finally skidded to a standstill, there were a mere ten feet between it and the red-hot blaze. Dean punched the bus into reverse and backed up before it had a chance to add fuel to the bonfire. Far enough back, Dean shut the engine down and opened the bus door with the large control handle to his right. He tumbled out of the bus, landing on his knees in the muddy ditch. Dizzy with fright and relief, Dean felt his stomach lurch its retort. He had no strength to fight it. He unceremoniously puked a yellow puddle in the weedy gravel in front of him. Once the convulsions in his belly stopped and his head began to clear, Dean looked up.

The fire in the middle of the rain-soaked highway looked as though it actually used to be two vehicles. The old blue pickup truck and the big rusty brown sedan were now welded together by the heat, and were only recognizable by the rear ends of the vehicles. Whoever was inside the two automobiles had not lived long enough to smell the combusting fuel.

There was no sound, except for the constant downpour, the roar of the fire, and the occasional boom of thunder. Dean suddenly felt overcome with grief and desperation, kneeling in his own sick, his long dirty hair hanging in his face.

"Hey, Dean," called a smoky voice from inside the bus. "Why the fuck did we stop? Are we there yet?"

Dean looked back to see his drummer, Lonnie Haley, stumble out the door of the bus. Dean didn't answer. He just looked in the direction of the fire. Lonnie stared into the flames with drug-ravaged eyes, hypnotized by the bright light and heat. It was the sight of Lonnie's stoned gaze that tripped Dean into reality. This was no time to gaze in awestruck wonder at highway travel gone terribly wrong. It was time to do something, anything, if not to help the poor unfortunate souls inside the burning wrecks, then at least the oncoming traffic, now careening unknowingly towards disaster. Dean knew how close he and his band mates had come to such a fate.

He stumbled to his feet, and ran back to the bus. He grabbed Lonnie by the shoulder and shook him violently.

"Hey, man," Dean said. "We gotta get some fuckin' help here."

"There ain't nobody survived that," Lonnie replied, his eyes locked on the inferno.

"I know, I know," Dean said. "But I damn near crashed right into that. We gotta get the cops and fire department or whatever fuckin' emergency hay wagon they have out here in the sticks to put the fire out and clear this off the road."

"Oh shit, man, this is terrible," Lonnie said, stepping down from the bus.

"Go use a phone at a farmhouse. I'm gonna go see if anyone possibly survived."

Lonnie wandered off, looking first east, then west, obviously trying to decide which of the two farm roads he was going to traverse for a phone. West led up a long drive to a huge ranch style house with a massive veranda. East led to a modest little farmhouse tucked amongst a cluster of granaries and a big red barn. He chose east, but only because the walk look shorter. Lonnie put his lethargic feet into motion, turning his back to the sign which read "Abbott House" and heading up the driveway to the farm with the named "Carruthers" on the gate.

Dean walked towards the crash, putting his hands up to his face to fend off the heat. He peered into the burning mass of melted metal, looking for any sign of movement that would signal life within. There was none. Dean backed up, glad to be distancing himself from the heat, but reluctant to surrender the accident's victims to the eternal fire.

He saw the same things Lonnie had: two farmhouses, one on each side of the highway. He also noticed on the west side, right next to the road, was a large pond, a dugout he supposed these hicks called it. Probably dingy drinking water for these hillbillies. Dean turned away in disgust. Why had he ever consented to playing up here anyway? It was only when he moved his hypnotized gaze from the dugout back to the wreck that he noticed movement, not in the burning vehicles, but on the other side of the crash. His eyes grew as he watched in disbelief. What he saw could not possibly be real, but he was seeing it right now with his own bloodshot eyes. Later, Dean would blame the drugs and the Jack Daniels for what he came to call his "Mother Fuckin' Hallucination." But at that moment, as he stared into the netherworld, he knew in every cell in his being that this was no illusion, this was very, very real. He broke into a run, and clambered into the bus, screaming himself hoarse.

Rod Fender, one of four other passed-out band members, was roused from his delirium by a voice that at first he thought belonged to a crazy person. Rod was surprised when he sat up to see it was not some lunatic standing over his hallucinogenic-inert form. It was just a pale and wide-eyed Dean West. Rod wondered what kind of bad acid his buddy had gotten himself into. But once he actually forced his ears to listen, Rod made out enough of Dean's insane babble to realize that the bus was stopped because of a wreck on the highway. At least that's what he made out of Dean's hysterical babble about people screaming out to him from burning car windows. He got off the bus unsteadily, and watched the remains of what used to be a truck and a car burn into one mass of metal. He was unnerved by Dean, who skittishly jumped at the rumble of the thunder and whose eyes darted uncertainly over the wreck and the surrounding highway, talking to unseen people on all sides. Rod could see there was nothing here, nothing but farmers' fields and trees and a couple of homesteads. He didn't understand why Dean was so nervous; there obviously were no survivors.

Just then, sirens could be heard in the distance. Rod was relieved that help was on the way, but Dean looked more than abated. He looked saved.

"Lonnie musta got help," Dean said.

"Looks that way."

As if on cue, Lonnie's skinny-legged form could be seen ambling back down the drive of the Carruthers farm. As soon as he was close enough to be heard, he called to his band mates.

"The fire truck is out on a call. The police will be here as soon as they can to direct traffic."

"Wow, they're awfully quick. We can hear them now," Rod said.

"Shit, that's not the police," Dean said, peering to the south. "That's an ambulance and a fire truck, and they're coming from the opposite direction than Headline."

"What the hell is going on here?" Lonnie said, approaching Dean and Rod. "Where did they come from?"

Both emergency vehicles appeared to have seen the obstruction in front of them, if not the burning vehicles, then the multicolored psychedelic bus parked at a precarious angle in front of it. The ambulance that led the way, pulled up beside what looked like a group of drug-ravaged hippies, which in actuality it was. A paramedic jumped out of the ambulance and scrambled to the wreck. When he was convinced that no one survived, he roared the ambulance siren back to life, and swung the vehicle around the wreckage through a narrow passageway on what would be the passing lane to northbound traffic like himself. It was only then that Dean realized that the collision had taken place in the northbound lane, that the brown car was obviously in the wrong lane.

His deductions were interrupted by the sound of a large spray of water hitting the rubble of the crash. The tiny Headline fire truck which had pulled up after the ambulance hosed down the blaze in a cloud of steam in less than a minute.

The ensuing hours of police interrogation and signing of reports was all strictly a blur to Dean. His mind was filled with recurring images of inconceivable sights he forced himself to believe he hadn't seen. He was inundated with shadowy sensations of dread that led him to maintain with every ounce of his being that he could not stay in this town any longer than he had to. Dean had seen something on that highway that had scared the shit out of him, and he was getting the hell out of this freaky little one horse town. Now. It all added up to Dean West cancelling his weeklong gig at the Headline Hotel, despite the bitter protest from his band members who insisted they needed the money a hell of a lot more than he needed to escape his own drug-induced ghosts.

August 31, 1975 became a date etched in local history for the tragic deaths of Bruce Armstrong, Lee Gardner, Kelly Gardner, Jeremy Bowen and Ray Duncan, but to those scant few who were not personally affected by these untimely deaths, it was a memorable day for another reason. It was also The Day Dean West Almost Played In Headline. Thanks to a catchy and somewhat naughty ditty about oral sex with an underage tattooed groupie entitled, "The Back of the Bus," Dean West exploded on the Canadian and international music scenes only months after he nearly played in Headline. He went on to be a major influence in the international rock and roll scene, a path that many in Headline would attempt to mimic. Not unlikely considering the town's close call with greatness.

Chapter 21

*That's a good question.
Why am I standing out here alone?
I guess I don't know enough to come in from the rain.*

- "Watching You"
Melissa Etheridge

My scholarship check was in the glove compartment of the car.

Despite the fact that her house was a smoking mound of ashes, her father and four close friends were dead in a fiery car crash, and she had a newborn baby sister, Suzanne could not get this one nagging thought out of her mind and it was nearly driving her crazy. She was irritated to distraction by the fact that this one insignificant piece of mental driftwood kept surfacing in the rapids of life-shaping events that were spilling through her brain.

Suzanne rushed around the darkening campsite, in and out of the small tent, doing more running around in circles than gathering up items for this abrupt exodus from the 56th Annual Labor Day Thunder River Campout. Her mind darted from one frenzied thought to the next.

Everything I own is in this campground...

Dad is dead...

Can I still go to university now that my check burned in the crash...

Mama's baby...
Where are we all going to live now...
Lee and Kelly and Bruce and Jeremy...
I'll call the dean...
Where's my hairbrush. I just had it this morning...
"Suzanne, it's time to go."

A serene smooth voice pulled Suzanne out of her mental ping pong match, bringing her back to the spot where she now stood in the middle of a muddy campground, rain spitting her clothes against her skin. She looked up through wet strings of bangs into a calm face, shadowed by the lateness of the day. Myles. Suzanne was filled with relief at the sight of his familiar placid face and that relief surprised Suzanne. The attraction that had brought Myles and her together had been one of mutual admiration, since they had never known each other well enough to call themselves friends. Myles had a reputation of being a pensive poet, a somewhat romantic fellow if a little too much to himself. Since Suzanne was a writer herself, she was thrilled at the potential, and obviously so was he. It was only after they were officially a couple that Suzanne got to really know her boyfriend. And frankly, she admitted secretly to Beatrice, she was somewhat disappointed. Suzanne found the reality behind the myth to be a non-communicative workaholic, obsessed with his music, having little time for his new gal, except to verbalize for hours with ruthless judgment on society. But despite the disappointment, Suzanne did not see Myles a total waste of time, and continued to see him. After all, he was a distraction from her dysfunctional home life and offered some kind of a constant Suzanne could count on, for better or worse, until she was off to university anyway.

But now, everything was suddenly different in her life, everything that is, except Myles. Now, when she needed stability most, Myles was there, and Suzanne was sure that all of his calm theorizing would somehow add some sanity to her life at a time when there was no meaning or sense at all. Suzanne wanted to rush into Myles' arms and sob all of her fears and grief away. But Myles was not big on open displays of emotion.

And besides, now was not the time. Myles had driven all the way out to Thunder River to drive her and RJ to the hospital where her mother and new sister rested, where poor frightened Charley waited, where her father lay in the morgue.

"Okay," she said, grabbing a few more items from the picnic table.

"We'll come back later and get everything," Myles said smoothly. "Just take what you need."

"I know," Suzanne said, distracted

Myles said nothing. He was very good at providing the silence that speaks volumes, so much more logical that grasping for words. Suzanne could almost feel what he was trying to say to her. His hush was telling her that right now was not the time to understand the incomprehensible, but rather a time to survive. At least that is what Suzanne supposed he was wordlessly saying. Maybe she was reading too much into his silent stare, but at this moment of helplessness, she doubted it.

"My friends are dead, my father is dead, my house has burned down and my family, including a newborn baby sister has no place to go. I---"

"You're strong though, Suzanne. You'll survive," Myles said softly. "There's no need for you to be afraid."

Suzanne looked over at him with a start. How had he known how she was feeling? She was just about to say how terribly frightened she was at all the uncertainly in her life. After all her previous doubts, Myles was proving to be a true enigma.

All Suzanne could see was the darkened silhouette of Myles' head, bent in the moonlight. Sitting on a large rock, hunched and reflective, he looked like a pondering James Dean, a comparison that would have pleased Myles very much if she had shared it with him. He always tried very hard to give the desired effect.

"How can I not be afraid, Myles? My life has gone completely out of control in a matter of hours," she replied with a note of alarm.

"And what was so exceptional about your life to begin with?" Myles said simply. The crushing truth of that statement was overpowering. It was not only the bare honesty of his words that startled Suzanne. It was the finality of Myles' tone. Suzanne understood that her former life was now over. That horrible old farmhouse was gone, and even more significant, the oppressor father was dead. But what would fill the void?

"I don't know, Myles," Suzanne knew that she wasn't making any sense. But her thoughts just wouldn't fit together in any logical order. "Everything is just happening so fast."

"You'll catch up. You have the rest of your life to heal." Myles always said such philosophical things. Suzanne had learned to accept Myles' eccentricities and expect the unexpected, but these poignant remarks caught her totally off guard. Tonight, he was so right about her feelings and emotions, he may as well be reading her mind. Most of the time, Suzanne only half-listened to Myles' philosophical babbling. She wondered now if she had been missing something important.

Myles joined Suzanne in loading her belongings into his car. They were both silent through the entire task. When they were done, she looked at Myles for some kind of hope, some guidance, anything. His eyes, deep and clear, stared at her with unwavering certainty. His conviction in his beliefs was as pure as snow. Suzanne longed deeply for that kind of resolve. Suddenly, she could not find it in herself to be angry at Myles for not dragging her safely from her emotions. Myles was only being Myles, reflective and unerringly objective about collisions amongst humanity. She could only envision Myles' insight and that very special way that only he saw the world. For that, she was jealous.

At that moment, in the quiet dusk on the Thunder River, Suzanne felt something she did not recognize right away. It was a strange kind of affection towards Myles, a desire for possession, for closeness, for more. She could scarcely believe she was capable of such emotion, especially with a poor pathetic local dreamer by the name of Myles Gardner. Her thoughts had been so focused on escaping Headline for so long, she had not truly seen the potential. She had been oblivious of the warm sensitive person standing right beside her all along. Her relationship with Myles had been one of purely killing time, not real feelings. Until now. Now she felt something move inside her heart for the very first time. She wondered if this was what it felt like to be in love with someone. The thought frightened her. There was no place for these kinds of emotions now. She had too much to think about.

"I have to get Beatrice," Suzanne said, breaking the spell of emotion that now gripped her. Without another word, she slipped past the shadow that was Myles and padded down to the beach.

Beatrice stood alone on the shore, her arms folded on her chest in a gesture that made it look as though she was cold. She was staring blankly into the river.

"Bea..." Suzanne said as she approached her friend.

"Sue..." Beatrice said, reaching back and taking one of Suzanne's hands. The two stood hand in hand for a few seconds, appreciating each other's closeness at this heart wrenching moment.

"I'm so sorry about Jeremy," Suzanne finally managed to say.

"And your dad..." Beatrice said. Suzanne was glad that she didn't finish her sentence. Any attempt at remorse at the death of Ray Duncan would be a lie on Beatrice's part, and Suzanne did not want her to attempt to deceive.

"Myles is here to take RJ and Charley and me to Headline," Suzanne nodded back towards camp. "Mama is in the hospital."

"Of course," Beatrice said. "You go on ahead with Myles."

"Well, what about you?" Suzanne asked, surprised at Beatrice's answer. "Just about everyone has left now because of the accident. I can't leave you here alone."

"Well, I want to wait a little bit longer for Wade," Beatrice said.

Suzanne frowned to herself. In all the bedlam of the past few hours, she had completely forgotten about Wade Edwards. Where could he be? He had left for ice cream hours ago, and still had not turned up. Suzanne could not believe the insensitivity of Wade, leaving Beatrice here to worry, especially now that she had the horror of her brother's death to deal with. Wade was going to have an awful lot of explaining to do when he got back.

"What about your parents? Jeremy was---" Suzanne began.

"No, Suzanne," Beatrice said in a tone that made it very clear she had made up her mind. "I'm going to wait for Wade."

"Okay."

"Give my best to your mother," Beatrice said. The conversation was over, Beatrice had made that clear too. She obviously wanted to be alone.

As Suzanne began to turn away from the beach, she noticed the spot where she had scrawled her name, those few short hours ago, that lifetime ago. The tall letters that spelled her name were now barely legible, pounded away by the rainstorm of the afternoon. It was an image that would stay with Suzanne for a very long time: the setting sun, Beatrice alone on the beach waiting patiently for Wade, and her very identity pounded away by the thunder.

PART III
Headline

Chapter 22

May 5, 1995

Love comforteth like sunshine after rain.

- "Venus and Adonis"
William Shakespeare

"You should be struck down on the spot for saying something like that!" said the girl with the long dirty blonde hair. Even though she was prominently pregnant, there was something about her that made it impossible to think of her as anything but a girl.

"Strike me down, Roberta. I just said it," said a husky red-haired man in cowboy boots and blue jeans, seated casually in a chair across the room. Between the two, there was a hospital bed occupied by a pale unconscious woman. It was Suzanne.

Roberta sniffed and turned her back on the red-haired man. She looked out of the window, staring blankly down onto the grounds of the

Headline Hospital, presently in the transition stage of spring that is not really brown and not really green. The grounds were completely empty of patients and staff today. It was damp and cold, with a frigid wind blowing in from the north. Roberta shivered, as if the wind penetrated her frail form through two panes of glass.

"It's just wrong, RJ," she said, turning to face him again. "It's wrong to speak in such a manner about the dead."

"Oh, dead, smed," said RJ. "Barry Linden was a good-for-nothing, just like the rest of his bunch. He damn near killed my sister last night. As far as I'm concerned, good riddance to bad rubbish."

"RJ!" Roberta exclaimed. "She's my sister too, but that doesn't make it right to say horrible things like...like..." Roberta began sniffing. She gingerly pulled a tissue out of her pocket and patted her eyes and nose delicately.

"That enough, RJ," said a gangly dark-haired man hidden in the shadows beside Roberta. "You're upsetting my wife."

"Walt, the sight of me cleanin' fish upsets your wife," RJ drawled as he lifted his meaty hands and clasped them behind his head. He picked up one hefty booted foot and rested it across his knee. "Why don't the two of you meander on over and visit reality once in a while?"

Walt got clumsily to his feet and pointed an accusing finger. "Now that's enough RJ!"

Walt stopped as the door to the hospital room swung open, and a plump but pretty woman of about thirty wearing a faded blouse and tight polyester pants sashayed in. Walt looked at her guiltily.

"I left Little Ray in the cafeteria with Belle and Morgan," the woman bubbled as she made her way over to the woman in the bed. "Any sign of improvement?" she asked with concern.

"No, none," Roberta whispered, still wiping her eyes. "No improvement at all, Michelle."

Michelle looked at Roberta with a frown. Her gaze wandered to the faces of Walt and RJ. "What's going on here?" she asked suspiciously.

"Nothing," Walt said too quickly.

"What is going on?" Michelle repeated deliberately, eying her husband suspiciously. RJ met her frown with a look of virtue. No one spoke.

"Roberta?" she demanded.

As if the very vocalization of her name compelled her to confess when she did not want to, Roberta spoke. "RJ was talking about Barry." Roberta whimpered, as though the sin had been her own. "He was saying it was a good thing he was gone."

Michelle turned to RJ and scolded him. "Are you on that again?"

"It's just terrible for him to talk that way, especially since Barry is, was your second cousin and all." Roberta seemed intent on confessing all now that she had started.

"Oh, don't remind me," Michelle grimaced. "Barry was a loser and he was doomed to an early grave." RJ's expression changed to one of triumph. Michelle saw the look and added quickly, "But that doesn't make it right to insult his name before he's even in the ground." It was talk like that that always upset Roberta. As if on cue, she began to sob again. Walt crossed the room over to his wife and put a thin arm around her shoulder uncomfortably. RJ glared at them, and then turned away in disgust.

"I hope those kids are all right with that ice cream!" he brayed, changing the subject.

"Oh, Morgan will watch them," Michelle assured.

"I don't know whether I trust them down there," RJ pursued.

"Why don't I go down with you, Michelle, and we'll check on them?" Roberta said, looking for an escape from her brother's cutting tongue. He called it honesty, but she saw it as out-and-out blasphemy. "I have to phone Polly anyway and check on my girls."

"Say hi to Polly the Parrot for me, will ya, Roberta?" RJ laughed.

"RJ," Michelle disciplined light-heartedly. "That's Walt's mother."

"I know," RJ guffawed. "I know a Fox from a mile away. If there's a handout or a free ride, they're right there, bushy tail high in the air." RJ's booming tones faded in Michelle's ears as she approached the woman lying in the bed. She was just going to take one more quick check before going back downstairs, when she noticed something strange. Movement. It was such small movement, she barely noticed. But now that she saw it, she knew it was definitely there. The pale woman in the bed was moving her lips. Michelle moved closer, hoping she would be able to hear any words that may be spoken.

"...If there ever was a bunch of freeloaders, it's those Foxes!" RJ continued. Michelle heard not one word her husband said.

"Shut your mouth, RJ," Walt said in a tone that was unusually harsh for him. "First you run down your wife's poor dead cousin, and then you start in on my family---"

"If it weren't for Ben Abbott's will, you Foxes would all still be livin' in tarpaper shacks down by the grain elevators." By this time, Roberta was sobbing uncontrollably.

"Why don't you clean up your own family problems before you start diggin' into other people's lives?" bellowed Walt. "You and your sisters and brother are barely speakin'! Your mother lives all alone, broke and miserable and your father was the biggest drunk in Headline."

"Don't you say one word about my father!" RJ roared, getting to his feet.

"RJ!" Michelle said with urgency. RJ sensed he was in deep trouble now. He could rant and rave and scare the biggest and toughest men in Headline, but his tough talk had no effect on Michelle. Except to annoy her immensely. And if there was anything RJ could not handle, it was riling Michelle.

"Aw, Michelle," he began. "He was askin' for it!"

"It's Suzanne!" Michelle interrupted.

RJ realized that his wife's acerbic tone had nothing to do with his little spat with Walt "the Weasel" Fox, his least favorite in-law. He suddenly doubted if Michelle had even heard one word of that ugly exchange.

"She's trying to say something," Michelle called, pointing a terrified finger down at Suzanne's still form.

RJ stepped closer to the hospital bed and saw it. Sure enough. His sister's lips seemed to be moving, mouthing something. No audible words could be picked up though. Walt and a tear-streaked Roberta traversed to the bed beside RJ and Michelle, family feuds and children smearing ice cream in hospital cafeterias completely forgotten.

"What's she sayin'?" Walt asked.

"Nothin'" RJ replied, his eyes never leaving Suzanne's face. He noticed that her lips seemed to be moving faster and faster and that a look of deep concern had washed across her face. Then a whisper of audible phrases began to rise from her frantic lips.

"**...don't he'll only hurt you and blame you for everything whatever you do don't take Charley with you...**"

"Did she say 'Charley'?" Roberta asked sharply.

"Sh!" RJ hushed her briskly. Roberta fell silent instantly. She didn't have time for her customary pout, as Suzanne's voice continued to rise.

"**...stop no please don't phone him he's going to do it all over again just like all those other times he can't do anything for Mother anyway...**"

By this time, Suzanne's voice was clear and loud.

"She must be dreamin'" Walt said.

"Get the doctor," RJ said abruptly, nudging Michelle into motion. She scooted out the door without a word.

"**...get the doctor,**" Suzanne seemed to repeat. "**...from down in Headline because he knows it's time anyway...**"

RJ and Roberta glanced at each other uneasily. They were both beginning to understand what Suzanne was talking about and why she was so upset.

"**...he's had way too much to drink sittin' in the bar all day and the first thing he's gonna wanna do is rush home to Mama and that will only make it worse and no DON'T don't do it DON'T LET HIM BEHIND THE WHEEL HE CAN'T DRIVE IN THIS CONDITION PLEASE STOP DON'T GO DADDY!**"

At that instant, a white coated doctor burst into the room, a concerned Michelle on his heel.

"What's happening?" he asked, pushing to the bedside of Suzanne, still yelling uncontrollably.

"She just started talkin' in her sleep, Dr. Powell," RJ said, "and then next thing we knew she was yellin' and screamin'."

"Yeah, she's delirious," Walter said, "talking all kinds of nonsense about doctors and drinkin' in the bar."

"Shaddup, Fox!" RJ snapped. Walt did as he was told, oblivious of what he could have possibly said this time to upset RJ so.

Dr. Powell paid no attention to RJ and Walt's bickering. His attention was focused on his distraught patient, as he and a nurse prepared a syringe and injected her arm with a harmless-looking clear liquid. Within moments, Suzanne was calm.

Chapter 23

May 20, 1995

Thunder always happens when it's raining.

"Dreams"
- Fleetwood Mac

There was never a day that Jake Edwards actually wanted to go into Headline, but today, more than most, it truly pained the eighty-six year old trailblazer to make that twenty mile journey into civilization. Unfortunately, he had put off the visit as long as possible, and now he had no choice.

Jake had to buy a few groceries, some rubber boots, a few miscellaneous tools and supplies. None of these items warranted a trip all the way to Headline though. Jake was able to buy nearly everything in groceries and hardware and rubber boots at the Thunder Store, owned and operated by his good friend Peter Carlson. Peter always gave Jake a few deals too; on account of Jake's long time gold mining partnership with Peter's father, Rod Carlson back in the 30's. Rod had long since passed on back in 1977, but Peter was a good kid, loyal to the old-timers. That was a rare thing in youngsters these days. Not that Peter was much of a youngster anymore; he must be pushing fifty himself.

Peter had a good head on his shoulders though. He was smart enough to see the goldmine of a different variety when the "For Sale" sign appeared in front of Thunder Store back in the late '70's. Everyone in Thunder and Headline knew that Colin Funk was running that store on borrowed time. He was never there, always running around the countryside 'shining and hiding from the cops. He did not manage that store of his properly, and it was only by accident that he discovered how that conniving little bitch Kathy Atkinson, the high school principal's daughter, was robbing him blind, had been for years. Of course Kathy was fired and charged quicker than lightning, much to the delight of every single Thunder Store customer; no one had ever liked that girl. But getting rid of Kathy didn't solve Colin Funk's problems. He investigated his bank accounts, only to find he didn't have enough money to pay for the next shipment of stock that would be arriving later in the week. Colin didn't even put up a fight when he saw the writing on the wall. He listed the store for sale as soon as he could get the real estate agent out with the sign, and disappeared into the woods with his still. Jake and the rest of Thunder Ridge wondered why Colin Funk had ever bothered with the store to begin with. He made plenty enough money selling his bottled lightning, without any of the headaches of running a store.

No one saw much of Colin Funk these days, no one except his regular moonshine customers, of which Jake Edwards was one. He had been drinking home brew since he was a boy, and Colin's product was as good as any he had ever tasted. Jake Edwards was one of Colin Funk's better patrons, but that didn't stop Jake from publicly stating that Peter Carlson was the much better man for running Thunder Store, side bargains notwithstanding.

Peter would special order just about anything for Jake, eliminating at least three quarters of his trips into Headline. But this time Peter couldn't help Jake. Peter was almost magical in what he could conjure up for his father's old goldmining buddy, but he could not set up a car dealership for him.

Jake had to go into Headline to buy a truck. Not a new truck, mind you, but a used one. Jake knew how those salesmen robbed you when they sold brand new vehicles, tacking on all those extras like warranty and scotch guarding the seats. Nope, Jake was buying a 1990 Dodge that he had seen sitting at Abbott Motors for a few months now. He had even been talking to Garry Miller down at the lot and had managed to swing a deal. Today was the day he would drive his old truck into Headline and trade it in on the Dodge. And even though it was a big thing for Jake Edwards to make a major purchase like this, he still dreaded it. He dreaded the drive to Headline, and he dreaded the streets and stores and people. Especially the people. But the old truck just wasn't going to last much longer. And Jake was getting just a little too old for monkeying around under the hood of that old truck anymore.

Jake Edwards had been driving the same 1968 Ford four by four since he had bought it new. He had never bought a new vehicle before or since. He had only bought it because Peggy wanted it so badly. Wade had just turned seventeen, and needed a vehicle, Peggy reasoned. They could give him their old truck, and they would get a new one. Jake protested, but he knew he was licked. He could never say "no" to Peggy and Wade. Jake felt his heart clench at the memory of his son. He was surprised that it still hurt so badly after all these years. Even the thought of Peggy being gone didn't bother him so much. At least he knew where Peggy was: peacefully waiting for him in the Headline Cemetery. He had loved that woman more than any other person on earth. He was not ashamed to admit that he would have done anything for Peggy. And he had. He had given up life on the claim for life on the farm, the Wilkins homestead a mile out of Headline that Peggy had inherited from her first husband. He had surrendered the existence he loved, that of digging in the rocks for the mother lode, in exchange for the life of parenthood, becoming a father for Peggy's twins from her marriage to Leroy Wilkins, Morley and Monica. Of course, he and Peggy eventually had a child of their own. But at the time of the marriage, Jake didn't give a second thought to what he was giving up. He only looked to what he was gaining: the love of his life, Peggy Carruthers. It was no shock that Jake had gone against everything he believed in and bought that brand new Ford four wheel drive in the fall of 1968.

The old '68 had accompanied him throughout the next twenty seven years. It carried him through a lot of heartache and sadness. Like the death of Peggy in 1973. The '68 had carried all his belongings away from the house on the farm where he and Peggy and Wade and Morley and Monica had lived for more than twenty years. But the kids had all married and moved out, and now that Peggy was gone, so there was no reason for him to be banging around that big old farmhouse. Besides, Jake hated the farm. He always had, though he would have never admitted it to Peggy. He only lived there for Peggy and the kids. On the day the old '68 carried away his possessions, he never looked back. Since he left the farm back in 1974, he had been back to Headline maybe three or four times a year. Once Wade disappeared in 1975, he made it into town even less often.

It was enough for him to be able to notice the changes that were happening in the town. Changes he didn't like. Jake could not put his finger on it, but there was something very wrong in Headline. Something bad was happening there, and he didn't want to even come close to the taint. Jake didn't have a name for what he felt was amiss with Headline, but he knew the smell of it. It was the smell of a big bad secret and the name of the secret was death.

The old '68 was running better than ever today. It was behaving just like old Black Jack, the old hound dog Jake had had to put down a few years ago. Just like old BJ, his canine companion for seventeen years, this damn old cantankerous truck was acting more rambunctious than any time in recent memory. Just like the morning Jake took Black Jack into the woods with the shotgun, the ol' truck seemed to know it was on its last journey. The engine hardly missed at all today and the gears didn't grind nearly so bad. Even that old tattered windshield wiper on the passenger's side seemed to be sweeping more of the rain away than usual. It all served to make Jake all the more antsy.

If this truck is going to run this good, I'll wait till winter to trade it in. No need in wasting good money when this truck gets me around just fine.

But before Jake could change his mind and turn around, the truck engine died. It didn't sputter or cough or give any kind of warning. The old '68 was running like a top one minute, and then silent the next. Jake pulled over on the shoulder, cursing under his breath. He knew he didn't want to go to Headline today. A voice had warned him to stay home today, and he had ignored it, and look where he ended up. Broke down half way between Thunder Ridge and Headline in the middle of a god damn rain storm. It didn't take much more than a good hard look under the hood for Jake to decide that this was a problem bigger than his own mechanical skills.

"Damn it to hell," Jake muttered under his breath as he began hoofing it down the highway, already soaked to the skin. "If only that no good piece of shit had made it until after the trade." He found himself walking north, in the direction of Headline. Not for any love of the place. No, Christ, no. He wasn't going this way because Headline was a few miles closer than Thunder Ridge either, because Thunder was actually only eight miles behind him and Headline was still twelve miles down the road. The way Jake figured though, he was only a couple of miles south of Abbott House, and across the road, the homestead of Ernest Carruthers.

Jake's first hope was that someone would come along and give him a lift. But after a half a mile of drenched ambling, Jake began to lose hope. It was eight o'clock in the morning on a Saturday: no one was up this time of the day, except old buggers wanting to get an early start on their errands in town. And farmers.

Jake had nearly forgotten. The only other traffic he had seen on the highway this morning was that German bastard, Gunther Fischer. He had been driving his tractor down the highway, heading slowly north. Now, as he felt the rain drip off the end of his whiskered chin, Jake actually hoped that Fischer would catch up to him right quick and give him a ride. It was still a good mile and a half to the homes of Walter Fox and Ernest Carruthers who lived right across from each other. Given his druthers, Jake would prefer to impose on Ernie Carruthers (his own brother-in-law through Jake's marriage to Peggy) than that good-for-nothing Fox. But Walter Fox was even better than Gunther Fischer. There was only one advantage to Fischer, that being that he may be Jake's first opportunity to get dry, if only he would pick up the speed on that old rusted-out Massey Ferguson and get his ass over here. Jake sneezed. He knew damn well he was going to get a cold if he didn't get out of this cold May rain pretty quick. And a cold was the last thing his bones needed when they were getting near ninety years old.

There was only one thing that stopped Jake from doing an about face and start walking in the direction he came from, going back to meet Fischer. That one thing was that Jake wasn't so sure where Fischer was heading. He was probably heading over to that Herman Schultz's place over north of Headline. Those krauts always stick together, trading machinery back and forth. But Fischer could also have been heading to Clive Morrow's place. Fischer's daughter and Morrow's son were getting married, or so said an announcement in the Headline Mail a few weeks back (which Jake faithfully subscribed to despite his aversion to the town). Jake knew how families stuck together once their offspring started getting on. So, despite the pouring rain and his certainty that his ride would be coming up behind him any minute now, Jake continued trudging towards Headline, half hoping he made it to Ernie's place before that idiot Gunther Fischer found him wet and cold and disgusted.

The storm was getting worse too. The rain was coming down like sheets hanging on the clothesline, and the thunder was crashing way off in the Thunder Hills. Jake barely heard the thunder though. Seven decades in the region had made Jake Edwards more than accustomed to the thunder than most. He found himself falling back into his thoughts. Of Headline. Of Peggy. And of course, of Wade. Between the storm and Jake's ruminating, he was truly in his own world. He didn't see or hear a thing, particularly the rumbling Massey Ferguson tractor coming right up behind him. By the time the roar of the engine brought Jake out of his daydream, it was too late. The tractor was only thirty feet behind Jake when he looked over his shoulder and saw it coming down upon him. Jake didn't have a chance either, since the Massey was moving at nearly forty miles an hour.

The tractor roared down on Jake, not even slowing to his screams. In one rumbling push, the Massey Ferguson obliterated Jake Edwards, wiping the look of shock and horrible recognition off his face.

TRACTOR KILLS THUNDER OLDTIMER
(Headline Mail - Tuesday, May 23, 1995)

Jake Edwards, 86, a longtime resident of the Thunder Ridge region, was killed Saturday morning when he was struck by a passing tractor on Highway 65, eleven miles south of Headline.

The accident, which occurred at approximately 7 a.m. involved a tractor driven by Gunther Fischer of the area. Police say Edwards was walking in a northerly direction when Fischer apparently swerved directly into the man. His abandoned and broken down truck was discovered approximately a mile south of the accident. Fischer is recovering in hospital with minor injuries.

An inquiry will be held into the death.

Jake Edwards is survived by his stepson Morley (Fiona) Edwards and stepdaughter Monica (Glenn) Andrews, both of Headline, his daughter-in-law, Beatrice Edwards of Vancouver, plus grandchildren Gloria Edwards, Kenneth Edwards, Bridget Andrews, Sophie Andrews, Dale Andrews and Annabelle Edwards. He was predeceased by his wife Peggy Carruthers Edwards in 1973.

Chapter 24

June 8, 1995

And now in age I bud again,
After so many deaths I live and write;
I once more smell dew and rain.

- "The Temple"
George Herbert

On any other night, Suzanne would shudder at the first snore that erupted from the lump beside her known as Myles. Every night was a race for Suzanne, as she forced her breathing and heart rate to slow down in an attempt to get to sleep before Myles. If she didn't succeed, well, then she was forced to give him curt kicks under the blankets and try to fall asleep before he began grunting again. For most years of their marriage, Suzanne had usually won the initial race, finding sleep a welcome solace from the day to day routine. It was a rare night that Suzanne found herself suffering a fitful sleep, usually only after a fight with Myles or her mother.

That is until three weeks ago.

Suzanne was amazed that since she had started work at the Headline Mail, she felt more awake and alive than she had been in years. She truly felt like Rip Van Winkle, having just woken up from a long slumber. And being so rested from years of wakeful sleep, Suzanne was suddenly annoyed at the idea of having to sleep at all now. Night after night, she found herself wide-eyed in the dark, alternating between tossing and turning, and staring up at the unseen ceiling, her mind racing with ideas and plans for the newspaper. Myles would sometimes awaken to the heat of her tireless vitality beside him and slur some grumble about her keeping the whole house awake. But Myles' griping was well-known in the Gardner household, having only become more intensified since Suzanne went to work.

Suzanne had been prepared for a fight when she told Myles she had taken the job that Beatrice had offered her: Editor-in-Chief of the Headline Mail. She had come armed with a long list of reasons why it was a good idea: they needed the money; the kids were all in school and didn't need her at home all day; she was bored wandering around the house all day. She knew that none of these arguments would have any potency against Myles' one and only contention: he did not want her to work. He never had given any reasoning behind his decree, and in the past, Suzanne had never fought it. But this time, Suzanne was prepared to stick to her guns, and fight off any attempt at bullying, sniveling or down right demanding on Myles' part. It was a long hard battle, but Suzanne dug in her heels and finally won, only by wearing Myles down. She would go to work, and Myles began his bid for the World's Record in Most Consecutive Days of Pouting. It was nothing Suzanne wasn't used to, and besides, now she didn't have time to notice Myles' sour disposition. Indeed, Suzanne found her husband was not nearly so annoying when she had something else to occupy her time. He was good for at least an hour long tirade each night telling her all the reasons why she was wasting her time at that paper, how Beatrice Bowen was taking advantage of her, and how her family was suffering at this little self-indulgent ego trip she was on. But Suzanne barely heard what Myles was saying. She had never been as happy as when she was at work, and Myles could talk until he was hoarse. She would never quit, of that she was certain.

Tonight though, Myles was annoying her. For once, his heavy snores seemed a long time in coming. Of course it was only because she was impatiently waiting for him to fall asleep. Once it finally came, she wondered how long she should stay in bed, how deep of a sleep she should allow before she took flight. Her entire plan would be thwarted if Myles should happen to wake up and catch her tiptoeing out of the room. It was an unending five minutes before Suzanne could not stand it any longer. She rolled out of the bed without disturbing the blankets, grabbed her pile of clothes she had left conveniently by the bed and crept out of the room. For good measure, she closed the bedroom door behind her, hoping to muffle any noise she should happen to make. Not that she planned to make any kind of a commotion that would alert Myles to her antics.

Suzanne had lived in this tumbledown house for thirteen years, plenty enough time to be able to make her way through it in the pitch dark. In the darkened hallway she dressed quickly in jogging pants and a sweatshirt, discarding her nightgown in a guilty heap. She then made her way to the back door. Once she was at the back stairs, she felt safe to switch on a light. It was a bit of a necessity too: she surely didn't want to tackle putting her shoes and jacket on in darkness. The glaring bulb blinded Suzanne's wide eyes, in full gear for night vision. After a moment, her eyes adjusted, and she fumbled her outerwear on. Suzanne took a deep breath and opened the back door.

It was a warm June night, but still early enough in the year to demand a coat. Gardens were known to freeze in late May and early June in Headline, living proof of the harsh climate at this high latitude. Suzanne stepped outside, snapped the entry light off behind her and closed the door. She was back in total darkness, again blinded by the suddenness of the blackout. After a moment, she gathered her courage and began to walk.

It was a short two blocks to the Headline Mail office. Suzanne knew that for a fact because she walked it every day to work. She was forced to walk everywhere now that Myles refused help her get some new wheels to replace the car she had crashed up. As long as she thought she was such an important working woman, she could fend for herself, Myles said. That meant no new car to replace the one that had been totaled in the accident. It also meant no credit card, no joint checking account, nothing. Suzanne didn't mind too much. The job paid her well enough she didn't need Myles' money. She smugly clung to the hidden truth that her checks would be larger than Myles' take home pay more often than not. Plus the job kept her so busy she didn't have time to tootle around town, wasting money. But Myles' sanctions were an awful nuisance when it came to running errands for the kids and shopping. Beatrice had come to the rescue so far, lending Suzanne her huge Buick whenever she needed it. Suzanne told her that the insurance was slow in paying out for the car, and prayed Beatrice wouldn't suspect what was really going on in the Gardner household. Beatrice had a sixth sense about Myles and his tricks.

Suzanne walked briskly through the night. She felt overly conspicuous walking the Headline streets at ten minutes before midnight. Within five minutes though, she let herself in to the back door of the Headline Mail. This time she was not so shy in turning on the lights.

Suzanne went straight to the basement, to the large vault where the archives of the Headline Mail were stored. With the turn of a key, she was inside, staring at three walls lined with shelves. Upon each shelf were chronologically arranged newspapers, crisp and yellow with age. Suzanne breathed in the air of millions upon millions of journalistic words, of authentic history.

In the center of the room, there was a single wooden chair and a table, bare except for a file folder and a notebook. They were in the exact same spot that Suzanne had left them just a few hours ago. Suzanne took a seat at the table and opened the file. There staring at her was an article clipped from a newspaper, prominent in its difference from the remainder of the newspapers in this room because it was current: white and clean and pliable. It was also different because it came from the Grande Prairie newspaper, the Daily Herald Tribune. The June 7, 1995 issue to be exact. Suzanne lifted the clipping from the file and read it for what must have been the tenth time in that day.

CARNAGE ON HIGHWAY 65
Human error main factor in 15 deaths since 1992

Since 1992, 15 people have died in 13 separate traffic accidents on a 30 kilometer stretch of Highway 65 between Headline and Thunder Ridge.

There is no easy explanation for the carnage.

Alcohol, heavy traffic and carelessness are some of the reasons cited by police and area rescue workers.

"It's not the highway itself," says Headline RCMP Constable Stuart Paulson, a collision analyst. "In less than 2% of accidents, the highway's design is a contributing factor. Most commonly you find it's human error, and it's something the drivers themselves could avoid."

Lucas Simon, a statistician for Alberta Transportation, says 2 or 3 fatal accidents would be considered normal on that stretch over 3 years.

But between 1992 and 1994, 11 people were killed and 11 injured in 11 fatal accidents. So far in 1995, 4 people, Donald Bowen, Terrence Carruthers, Jake Edwards and just 2 days ago, Lorraine Templeton, have been killed in 3 separate accidents.

Paulson says he sees people driving too fast and passing and turning when it's unsafe. Often the defensive driver pays for someone else's mistake.

It had all started so innocently, when Beatrice placed this very clipping upon Suzanne's desk earlier today, or actually yesterday, Suzanne thought ruefully as she looked at her watch. It was now a couple of minutes past midnight.

Suzanne thought back to that moment, when Beatrice had marched into her office, full of excitement and eagerness. The sound of Beatrice's footsteps snapping into her office, followed by Beatrice's sharp excited words, all echoed in her memory. At the mere recollection of it, Suzanne's blood coursed through her veins, just as it had when Beatrice had spoken to her over her heavily piled desk.

"Read this," Beatrice had said abruptly. Obediently, Suzanne picked up the newspaper article and read it for the first time of many. It was an interesting piece, but nothing that really grabbed Suzanne. At least at first.

"Uh huh," Suzanne said vaguely as she sat the article down on her desk. She assumed that there had to be a reason for Beatrice bringing this to her attention, but she had no idea what it was.

"What do you think of that?"

"Statistics," Suzanne replied. The facts of Headline's high accident fatality rate were well known, just as it's higher than average occurrence of thunder storms. Maybe it was a big deal to Beatrice who had been gone for so long, but to a lifelong resident like Suzanne, it meant next to nothing.

"I know it's just statistics," Beatrice said impatiently. "But what about the story behind the god damn statistics?"

"Like the officer said, human error. That pretty well sums it up."

"Bullshit," Beatrice said. Suzanne thought she had grown accustomed to Beatrice's foul mouth, but right now it was getting on her nerves. Suzanne had a lot of work to do - a community events column to write and the entire paper still to proof by the end of the day. Though she usually had patience for Beatrice's self-admitted lack of newspaper savvy, today Suzanne was not in the mood for one of Beatrice's wild goose chases.

"Bullshit?" Suzanne raised her eyebrows.

"Bullshit," Beatrice stated firmly. "There are too many accidents around here to be ignored, but I think it's just a whitewash on the part of the media and the authorities who can't think of any better reason than human error. I think there is more to this than Joe Citizen drifting off and crossing the center line. What about the fact that most of these accidents happen in the summer time, not during the winter when the roads are icy and visibility is non-existent? What about the fact that these accidents are getting more frequent instead of less, despite public awareness and strict drunk driving laws? What about all that?"

"It's all true, Beatrice," Suzanne admitted.

"Yes, it's true! But no one in this town seems to give a damn about any of the truth. I thought if anyone would care about the facts it would be you, Suzanne!"

For the first time in the conversation Suzanne found herself truly interested in what Beatrice was chattering about. She was talking about real journalism. Digging into the real story behind the statistics and the pat answers given in scheduled interviews. This is what had been Suzanne's ambition when she was young. And the thought of getting involved in some real investigative journalism made Suzanne feel eighteen all over again.

"What do you want to do?" Suzanne asked.

"What do you think we should do? Accept this lame article by the media of the paper from the big city down the road, or do it right ourselves?"

"I guess I could do some research, talk to some people, and find the story."

"Good girl!" And with that, Beatrice was off and running, babbling an endless stream of possible story leads and ideas and excited theories on how a story like this would set Headline on its ear. Five minutes later, Beatrice was gone, and Suzanne was alone with a newspaper clipping and the seed for one great story idea.

As soon as Suzanne had been able to get her day's work out of the way, she had gone straight to the archives for some research material. It was already nearly three o'clock when she went down to the basement, so that didn't give her much time down there. She could get away with working until five thirty at the latest. After that Myles would be getting hungry and thus crankier than usual.

She started with the first edition of the Mail from January 15, 1915, published and edited by her grandfather James Bowen. He was also Beatrice's grandfather, giving them equal lineage to journalistic instincts. For the first time since coming to work for the Mail, she realized that she had just as much right to be here as any of her Bowen relatives. The Bowen part of Suzanne had always been played down by the community. They preferred to think of her as the daughter of that drunk Ray Duncan or the wife of that shiftless Myles Gardner. Now she was able to come into her own as Suzanne, just plain old Suzanne.

The pages of the old newspapers were brittle and crackled in her touch. Suzanne was sure the sheets of newsprint were going to turn to dust right in her fingertips. But they managed to survive her careful study as Suzanne found herself lost in the timeless world of Headline town history. She drank in the stories of exploration and discovery, of daily routine and happenstance, like champagne. Most of the narratives were filled with information she already knew. Headline had a rich history, much of which was the basis for all kinds of myths and tall tales. Reading the facts on which the legends were based was fascinating to Suzanne. Never before in her thirty eight years had Suzanne felt any kind of pride in her home town of Headline. But after reading these publications, each giving a weekly update to the growing population on what was happening in their little town, Suzanne could almost feel her heart swell with the intricate overlapping of happenstance that was Headline.

March 22, 1921. This week, Abbott House, a roadside cafe and general store opened 8 miles south of Headline...

February 6, 1923. Sam Duncan, 10 and Jack Duncan, 7 were arrested last night for stealing food from the Thunder Store. RCMP say...

February 13, 1923. The death of 7 year old Jack Duncan is reported. The authorities say that the apparent cause of death was massive head injuries as the result of a fall down the cellar stairs...

July 15, 1924. Anyone interested in working as a miner in the Thunder Hills should contact Jake Edwards at...

January 3, 1928. A recent government census shows the population of Headline as 1134 and that of Thunder Ridge as 207...

April 16, 1929. Richard and Erica Gardner are pleased to announce the engagement of their daughter, Carmen to Andrew Abbott, son of Phillip and Sarah Abbott...

July 30, 1929. Abe Duncan was arrested overnight for the assault and rape of 19 year old Peggy Carruthers...

December 10, 1929. The community is saddened to hear of Jennie Abbott Fox's passing during the recent delivery of her son Floyd. Jennie's husband, Freddie is...

August 12, 1930. Sam Duncan was rushed to hospital after being shot in the leg during an alleged fight with Jake Edwards over the claim of their goldmine which has yet to strike any ore...

September 8, 1931. The community has rallied around the family of Justin Carruthers who drowned on the weekend in the dugout at Abbott House directly across the road from the Carruthers farm. He leaves to mourn his parents, Frank and Nora Carruthers, 3 sisters, 2 brothers and...

January 8, 1935. The New Year's baby of 1935 is a son born to Sam and Audrey Duncan. The bouncing baby boy is named Raymond after...

September 8, 1936. Leroy Wilkins has been killed in a farming accident, leaving to mourn his wife Peggy (nee Carruthers) along with their twins, Monica and Morley. His widow has yet to say what will be done with the family farm...

July 13, 1937. Former Headline resident Abe Duncan, 41, has died in the Peace River Minimum Security Prison...

November 15, 1938. Phillip Abbott of Abbott Industries died Wednesday at the age of 72. The entire Abbott estate, estimated to be worth millions of dollars, is said to have been willed to his eldest son, Andrew...

April 23, 1940. Jake Edwards, 31, has been critically injured when his mine collapsed. His long-time partner, Freddie Fox dragged Mr. Edwards out of the rubble, in an effort that doctors say saved his life. Mr. Edwards' injuries are such that he is not expected to return to his claim.

August 19, 1941. Jake Edwards and Peggy Carruthers Wilkins married on Saturday at the office of the Justice of the Peace. Mrs. Wilkins, the widow of Leroy Wilkins...

September 16, 1941. In a stunning double ceremony, David Phelps married Anita Abbott and Douglas Phelps married Julia Abbott. The two couples of brothers married to sisters plan to run Abbott House along with the store owner and father to the girls, Ben Abbott.

October 27, 1942. A bankruptcy sale for Abbott Farm Implements, formerly owned by Andrew Abbott will take place at the dealership on...

May 4, 1943. Martin Gardner, 33, has announced the acquisition of the Abbott property, Abbott Dry Goods. Gardner states that the store will be renamed Gardner Store, and will be managed by local men, Rod and Roger Carlson, both 37. Gardner is brother-in-law to the former owner of Abbott Dry Goods, Andrew Abbott. In less than 2 years, Abbott has lost control of two of his family businesses. All that remains is Abbott Fine Cars. Another Abbott, Ben, owns Abbott House, a cafe, gas station and general store, 10 miles south of Headline...

October 8, 1946. Casey Duncan, son of Sam and Audrey Duncan, passed away at Headline Hospital at the age of one day. The baby is survived by his parents, his brother, Raymond, his sisters, Felicia and Fiona...

July 3, 1951. Anita Phelps, 32 and Julia Phelps, 31, both daughters of Ben and Ruby Abbott, were killed when a car in a weekend wedding party went over a bridge on the Thunder River. Investigators have released information that the brakes on the Phelps car were faulty. The Phelps girls' father, Ben Abbott, has stated that he blames the deaths on his brother Andrew Abbott, since the car in the crash belonged to Andrew and was being lent to the Phelps girls for the wedding. The Phelps girls, married to brothers David and Douglas who were injured in the crash, worked at Abbott House with their husbands and father. The investigation continues.

August 10, 1954. Floyd Fox and Polly Williams are pleased to announce their marriage which took place over the weekend. Mr. Fox is manager of the Fox Den diner, while Mrs. Fox is a waitress at the same cafe.

July 17, 1956. James and Belinda Bowen announce the marriage of their daughter Isabelle to Ray Duncan of Thunder Ridge...

November 27, 1956. Vernon and Nadine Gardner are pleased to announce the birth of a son, Myles Chester, born November 22 at the family home...

January 6, 1957. Ray and Isabelle Duncan are pleased to announce the birth of their first child, a daughter, named Suzanne Marie born January 2 at Headline Hospital...

March 28, 1961. In the wake of the death of Headline pioneer, Benjamin Abbott, the Abbott and Fox families have become embroiled in a bitter dispute over Mr. Abbott's will. According to the will, the entire estate of Ben Abbott has been given to Floyd Fox, only son of his sister, the late Jennifer Abbott Fox. Nothing has been left to Ben's brother, Andrew, who is taking the legality of the will to court. Floyd Fox is nephew of well-known Headline restaurateurs, Johnny and Mable Fox, owners of the Fox Den.

September 19, 1961. Floyd and Polly Fox have reopened a Headline tradition. Abbott House will cater to...

August 11, 1964. James Bowen, founder of the Headline Mail, has died. His widow, Belinda Bowen, has stated that she will continue to run the paper with the help of her son, Donald.

It was only at this point that a bleary eyed Suzanne finally looked at her watch: 5:45 p.m. Her heart leapt. She could not believe that the time could possibly have gone by so quickly. She knew she was going to be in trouble when she got home to Myles. None of it seemed to matter though; Suzanne was so excited by what she was reading she could barely stop. And why should she stop? For an instant, Suzanne considered bringing the newspapers home with her. She could read them tonight, after Myles and the kids are all sleeping. But after only a second's consideration, she knew that would be impossible. There were still shelves and shelves of papers for Suzanne to read, too many for her to cart home. No, she would not be able to lug all these valuable pieces of archival material to her house. But Suzanne knew very well what she would do: she would come back here tonight.

Suzanne threw on her jacket and raced home, Myles' expected tirade echoing in her ears. When she did slam headlong into Myles in the doorway, she did not hear a word he bitched. She was thinking about the newspapers.

Back in the vault after midnight, Suzanne resumed her study of the archives. She was now up to the section of newspapers from the late 1960's and into the 70's. For the first time in her reading, she actually remembered some of the events that were taking place. Births, deaths, openings and closings of businesses, awards, accomplishments of all sorts, all details in the lives of people she knew during her adolescence. It had been a time when Suzanne had paid little attention to what was going on in Headline and Thunder Ridge, what with the goings on at home and her hell-bent desire to get out of town. But she recollected a surprising amount of the town happenings as she read them, despite her lack of interest at the time.

But keeping in mind her original reason for all this research, Suzanne was astonished by the lack of deadly accidents on the yellowed pages. There was the odd fiery car crash or deadly head-on collision, but not anything like the record numbers that Headline had seen in recent years. Suzanne was puzzled. After all, the highway wasn't even paved until 1958. Surely it would be logical to assume there would be more accidents in those dusty days of a graveled Highway 65 than now, when it had smoothly polished hardtop.

Suzanne read and read, and as she plowed her way into the mid-seventies, she found herself feeling apprehensive. At first she could not understand these strange sensations. Maybe she was getting tired; after all it was now after one in the morning. But as she came to the headlines of September 2, 1975, she came to the headline she had been dreading all along.

FIVE KILLED IN TWO CAR PILE UP

Suzanne's stomach lurched. She did not want to read any further. It was late and she had read so much by now that her mind was swimming with images of lines of print and grainy photographs. But her eyes were drawn to the headline and the grisly photos. It all seemed so recent, so fresh, but the age of the newspaper forced Suzanne to realize how long ago that fateful accident had taken place. A lifetime ago. Suzanne thought about the Suzanne Duncan of 1975 and how, through all her suffering, she had been able to retain one thing: Hope. She thought of the intervening years, and then of the Suzanne Gardner of today, the Suzanne trying so desperately to regain some of that Hope, despite objections from her family and careful scrutiny of the community. Suzanne knew then she had no choice. She had to read on.

She read the story of the death of her father and all her dear friends. The tears welled in her eyes, even twenty years after the fact. But they did not fall. Suzanne blinked them back and turned to the next newspaper. And the next. Suzanne was spellbound by what she was reading, but in a way so different from before. Suddenly stories jumped out of the page at her, daring her to see the horrible truth of their words. She had read all of this before, she remembered it so well. But somehow the true force of the words had not sunk in. She had been witness to the assassination of a town on a single ribbon of asphalt and had not even batted an eye.

It was after four thirty when Suzanne turned the final page of the final newspaper: Tuesday, June 6, 1995. She was paralyzed with an overwhelming fear. She now knew so much, or rather, now comprehended what she had known all along. Something was terribly wrong in Headline. She didn't know what it was yet, but she had to find out.

For now, she was alone and terrified in the basement of an old downtown building in the middle of the night. As much as she knew Myles would be livid in the morning, she knew she could not go back home tonight. Suzanne could not face darkness in the little town she was only now beginning to understand. She would stay here, among the safe white newspapers and call Myles at the time he would be getting up, tell a tall tale about coming to work early to meet some deadline. Facing Myles' wrath in the morning though would be much easier than the alternative. Suzanne knew she could not walk through this horrible secretive little town in the middle of the night, especially since it had so many ghosts that could no longer stay buried.

Chapter 25

June 9, 1995

Scholars' pens carry farther, and give a louder report than thunder.

- "Religio Medici"
Sir Thomas Browne

"Suzanne, you look terrible!"

Suzanne looked up into the bright well-rested face of Beatrice and managed a feeble smile. Suzanne knew how horrible she felt after grabbing two measly hours of sleep on the floor of the vault. She could only guess at how that ordeal showed on her face.

"I love you too, Bea," Suzanne said. Despite her lack of sleep, or maybe because of it, Suzanne was giddy. The light of day chased away most of the spooks that had rested in her heart during the deepest part of the night. Now all that remained of her four a.m. epiphany was the sheer excitement of finding something to investigate that had all the right ingredients: mystery, death, secrets, and some great characters. She could hardly contain herself. She wanted to tell Beatrice everything she had discovered in her all-night reading marathon in the vault.

"Sorry, hon," Beatrice said sympathetically. "You look rough though. What happened? Did you and Myles have a row?"

"Not yet," Suzanne said cryptically.

"Something's going on here," Beatrice said, grabbing a chair and sitting down in front of Suzanne's desk. She was never one to be in the dark on any goings on. "Tell me what you're up to. If you and Myles have split, don't worry about a thing. You and the kids can come and stay with me---"

"Relax, Bea, relax. This has nothing to do with Myles. Yet."

"You're doing it again!"

"It's simple, Beatrice. The reason why I look so dreadful is that I worked here all night, researching your too-many-accidents-on-Highway-65 story."

"And Myles hasn't killed you?"

"He hasn't had a chance to yet. I slipped out of the house last night after he was asleep. It got so late I decided to sleep here. I called this morning and talked to Leigh, told her I had come in early."

"You were here all night!" Beatrice exclaimed. "Are you crazy?"

"It was your idea."

"It was my idea to follow up on that article, not to pull an all-nighter."

"Beatrice, you're not going to believe what I found out," Suzanne could no longer contain her fervor. "You were right! Something weird is going on here, but it's even weirder than you thought!"

"What are you talking about?"

"I'll show you," Suzanne bubbled. She opened the file that used to contain the single clipped article from the Grande Prairie paper. Now though, it was filled to stuffing with photocopies of dozens of articles. They were copies of articles she had found in the archives last night, articles that opened a previously unexplored door in Headline history.

"What's this?" Beatrice said, puzzled. She was obviously overwhelmed by the amount of thought and work Suzanne had put into this story. If she would have known that this is all it took to pull Suzanne Duncan out of her shell, she would have faxed her some scandalous story ideas a decade ago.

"Accidents," Suzanne said, stating the obvious. "Did you know there have been over 120 fatalities on Highway 65 since 1975, Beatrice? That is four times the national average. Of those, 112 were local residents, 8 were travelers from outside the area. In most usual cases, fatalities run closer to two to one, locals to tourists. The percentage here is way out of whack. Plus, there's---"

"But, Suzanne," Beatrice was confused. "This is all since 1975? Why didn't you go back further?"

"That's the most interesting part of this, Bea. I did go back. I went back to the first edition of the Mail in January 1915. From the time when the first automobile owned by Richard Gardner scared the hell out of Ernie Carruthers' horse, until 1975, Headline's stats are the same as any other small town in northern Alberta, if not a little lower. The accidents didn't start to pile up until 1975," Suzanne paused. "August to be exact."

"August?" Beatrice said sharply. She may have been away for a long time, but she knew the significance of that month and year. Her stomach dropped into her intestines.

"That's right." Suzanne was pleased with herself. Beatrice looked scared, as scared as she herself had been when the truth was dealt out to her in black and white. She had had time now to digest the information. It was a relief to see someone else react to the news as she had in the wee hours of the morning.

"Are you sure, Sue?" Beatrice said in a small worried voice.

"Look at this."

Suzanne handed Beatrice the first photocopy on the pile, a large article with a huge blaring headline and a horrifying photo.

FIVE KILLED IN TWO CAR PILE UP
(Headline Mail - September 2, 1975)

Trip to deliver a critically injured woman to hospital took a tragic turn Saturday afternoon when a 2 car collision 8 miles south of Headline claimed the lives of 5 local people. According to authorities, the station wagon driven by Raymond Duncan was on the wrong side of the road when the collision occurred. Mr. Duncan was apparently travelling to Thunder Ridge where his house was on fire.

Dead as a result of the crash are Mr. Duncan of Thunder Ridge, Jeremy Bowen, Lee Gardner, Kelly Gardner and Bruce Armstrong, all of Headline. The three young males were transporting an injured Miss Gardner after she had been crushed under a falling tree hit by lightning. The vehicle they were driving was a pickup borrowed from Mr. Alfred Fox.

According to witnesses, Mr. Duncan had spent several hours that Saturday afternoon in the Headline Hotel bar.

Alcohol is suspected to have been a factor in the accident. The RCMP investigation continues.

"Suzanne, why are you digging this up..." Beatrice shuttered. She pushed the article away in disgust. "I didn't bring this up to have you pulling this type of skeleton out of the closet."

"Bea, I had no intention of making an issue out of this particular accident. It's as painful for you as me. You lost your only brother in that crash, but I lost my father. And he was to blame for it all. I have to deal with grief as well as guilt. But it seems to be the starting point."

"Starting point?"

"There was only one fatal accident in 1974. A car caught some ice during a freezing rain storm in late October. There were no crashes in '75 until August 31. Five killed. But then the flood gates open. September 10. One man killed when he missed an approach. September 17. A woman killed, her son injured in a two car collision. September 22. Two dead---"

"Okay, okay, Suzanne," Beatrice interrupted. "You don't have to go on."

"No, I don't. After the September 22 crash, that was it. No more accidents for the remainder of 1975."

Beatrice frowned.

"But it started again in 1976. April 20. A semi flips in the ditch and the driver is killed. By the end of September, seven more fatalities."

"That's what I was saying yesterday and it doesn't make any sense. The roads are a mess during the winter. Vehicles are skidding all over the place."

"There are a few accidents in the October to March period." Suzanne referred to her file again. "A total of six between 1975 and 1995."

"Six?"

"Six," Suzanne repeated. "Out of a total---"

"One hundred and twenty," Beatrice recited the statistic Suzanne had fed her earlier. As grisly as this whole discussion was, Suzanne could feel Beatrice was hooked. And Beatrice knew it as well as she did. Something was going on here.

"And that's not all," Suzanne said, her eyes gleaming.

"There's more?"

"I got to thinking," Suzanne said. "My accident happened during a thunderstorm. I'll never forget that - the headlights coming right at me through the windshield wipers and the rain. I know that Jake Edwards was killed during a storm too. So was your father and so was Lorraine Templeton on Monday. I looked it up. It seemed like an awful lot of accidents in the rain, so I checked the others. Out of those one hundred and fourteen summer time accidents on Highway 65 between Headline and Thunder Ridge, one hundred and two happened during a rain storm."

"You didn't sleep at all last night, did you?" Beatrice said incredulously.

"How could I, Bea?" Suzanne said. "I can't believe I didn't see it before. I guess when you're not looking for anything peculiar, living your own life, minding your own business, you don't see what's happening under your own nose. The point is: something is going on here."

"What?" Beatrice said. "What is it?"

"I have no idea," Suzanne said, mystified. "I am not one for conspiracy theories, but something is causing people to smash up their vehicles during thunder storms on Highway 65."

"Local people too," Beatrice mused. "It's like a force that only attacks residents of Headline and Thunder Ridge.

"Tell me about it," Suzanne said. "I had no idea how many of my friends, relatives and acquaintances have died horrible deaths over the years. I thought it was just my imagination when I felt like I was going to an excessive number of funerals. Take a look, Bea. You in particular will be shocked, being gone for so long."

Suzanne passed the open file to Beatrice and she began leafing through the articles.

TRUCK DRIVER KILLED ON HIGHWAY 65
(Headline Mail - August 30, 1980)

The owner of an oil transport was killed when the vehicle rolled into a ditch on Highway 65, 6 miles north of Thunder Ridge, Sunday morning en route to Peace River. He was Adam Abbott, 22, of Edmonton, a former Headline resident.

His assistant was uninjured.

Mr. Abbott, owner of Twilight Transport, was proceeding 6 miles north of Thunder Ridge at approximately 6 p.m. Sunday when the right wheels of his truck and semi-trailer loaded with oil struck a soft shoulder on the road.

The truck rolled into the ditch, fatally injuring the driver.

Jimmy Hunter of Fort Saskatchewan, who had been driving until the pair stopped for coffee at Thunder Store, just 6 miles before the accident, was asleep in the cab. He was not injured.

Cause of the accident was not known.

Hospital authorities' examination indicated Mr. Abbott had suffered severe head and internal injuries.

A Headline resident until 1977, Mr. Abbott is survived by...

Beatrice couldn't continue. She had never been close to her cousin Adam, but they had only been two years apart in age, good enough to be seated together at the children's table at dozens of Thanksgivings and Christmases. Adam had been a good kid, as near as Beatrice remembered. What bothered her most though, was that she hadn't even known he was dead.

She was wary to read further, but she flipped through the pages Suzanne had so patiently photocopied.

EXHAUST FUMES CLAIM 4 LIVES
(Headline Mail - April 25, 1985)

Carbon monoxide fumes pouring into a stalled car caught in a muddy ditch on Highway 65 claimed two lives Monday morning.

The car which police assume had skidded on the slick wet road was stuck in axle deep mud for over 3 hours with outside temperatures between 32 and 35 degrees Fahrenheit. A passing traveller from Whitehorse, Dan Harley found the bodies at 3:20 Monday morning.

Dead are Connie Sullivan, 28, and Jan Davidson, 25.

The accident is believed to have occurred around midnight. Although police report that road conditions "were not bad," it is assumed that the car slid on water on the road.

"Connie Sullivan..." Beatrice whispered.

"I know," Suzanne replied softly. "She turned out to be not a bad person you know. She learned to blow her nose and got rid of those ugly glasses. She worked at the bank at the time..."

"I don't believe it," Beatrice said. She turned back to the pages in front of her in shock. What next?

INQUEST SLATED IN PLAYER'S DEATH
(Headline Mail - September 28, 1992)

Inquest will be held in the death of 17 year old Nathanial Andrews of Headline, killed Thursday morning when the car he was driving smashed into the rear of a parked trailer transport.

Accident happened about 2 miles south of Headline on Highway 65.

Young Andrews was driving to work at the Goldmine gas plant outside of Headline shortly after 7 a.m. Thursday when his car, a 1986 Toyota, burrowed its way under the rear end of a large Western Freightways tandem trailer parked on the shoulder of Highway 65 just south of town.

Nathanial Andrews was killed instantly.

Driver of the large truck, Mack O'Brien was uninjured.

Highway at the scene of the fatality is straight and unobscured. However, Andrews, travelling south, had just come over the brow of a hill leading down into town.

RCMP said today that an inquest would certainly be held.

Nathanial Andrews was a star forward with the Thunder Valley Hockey League's Headline Headhunters. He was a Grade twelve student and worked part time for Amoco Resources. He is survived by...

"Nathanial Andrews!" Beatrice exclaimed. "That's Sophie's boy!"

"Yes," Suzanne said.

"She must have been devastated," Beatrice said, obviously overwhelmed herself. "Suzanne, I can't read anymore. I had no idea this was going on. How could you stand it?"

"You don't see them all piled on top of each other in a manila file when they happen. As each tragedy happens, you grieve and get over it and hope there's no more where that came from."

"Good God," Beatrice said.

"Bea," Suzanne said, shuffling through the file. "There's another one you really should read. I don't think you knew..."

Beatrice reluctantly took the paper from her hand. Her heart was pounding so loudly, she could barely concentrate.

5 IN FAMILY DIE AS CAR, TRUCK CRASH
(Headline Mail - July 17, 1994)

5 persons representing 3 generations of one family had their lives snuffed out almost instantly early Monday afternoon in one of the most tragic highway crashes ever to occur in the Thunder region.

Dead are Carlton Raines and his wife Marsha of Calgary, both 70, their son Merle of Headline, 41, the latter's wife Frances, 36, and their 3 year old daughter Nadine.

Travelling north on Highway 65, about 2/3 miles north of Abbott House at approximately 1:30 p.m., the light European car carrying the family group was in a head-on collision with a freight truck. Apparently Frances Raines was the driver at the time of the accident.

Few details of events surrounding the crash have been released by RCMP.

Truck driver has been identified as Gilbert Smith. He was uninjured in the crash.

"Carlton Raines, Gilbert Smith," Beatrice said, confused. "I don't know any of these people."

"Frances Raines," Suzanne said softly. "That's Frannie. Frannie Parker."

"No," was all that Beatrice managed to croak. It was a revelation that cut her to the bone. Fran Parker had been one of Beatrice's very best friends. Beatrice would never forget Fran's shocking confession at her own wedding shower so many years ago. Fran was such a good person, and deserved the best. After a moment, Beatrice found her tongue again.

"Frannie married this Merle Raines guy?" she said. "What happened to Blake Abbott? I thought they were pretty sweet on each other."

"Oh, they had the wedding date set," Suzanne said. "But then Blake went out on the highway one stormy night..." She couldn't finish. She didn't have to. Beatrice saw the rest of the story on Suzanne's face.

"Oh, no," Beatrice said. "Not Blake too." She was now completely overwhelmed by the immenseness of the havoc that hit Headline. "Is there anybody left, Suzanne?"

"Well, me and you, anyway," she said sheepishly.

"And it's a miracle you're still alive," Beatrice shuddered. "You just about got killed in one of those all-too-common killer storms."

"Don't think I haven't pondered on that one."

"That's a good starting place, though, Suzanne. You were out there, driving on a stormy night. A car smashed right into you, and those poor people were killed. Did you see anything out of the ordinary? I mean, did UFO's come out of the sky and pour green ooze all over the highway?"

"No," Suzanne said as she searched her badly damaged memory. "Nothing that I can think of... No, wait," she exclaimed. "There was something. I remember because it was one of the first things that I talked about after I came to in the hospital. I remember thinking that I must have hit my head too hard and wasn't recollecting things clearly. I was pretty sure of what I saw. But then RJ told me what the police said."

"What?"

"RJ was showing me all the clippings in the paper about the accident. I missed all the excitement since I was out cold. He told me that the police said the only thing that saved all the rest of the people in the car, Mrs. Linden and three of the four little girls was that they were all fast asleep. Mrs. Linden and one little girl were lying down in the front seat and the other three girls in the back."

"So?"

"So, that's not what I saw. When that car was careening towards me, I did have a fraction of a second to take a good look. I felt like a deer in the headlights, witnessing my own massacre. But as that car came right for the passenger's side of the car, I got a good look at the driver. And the person sitting in the seat next to him."

"But there wasn't anyone sitting next to him. His wife and kids were sleeping," Beatrice argued.

"So the police say," Suzanne replied. "But I distinctly remember seeing someone sitting next to Mr. Linden."

"His wife? Maybe the police were mistaken---"

"I can't say who it was. It was more just silhouettes, not distinct features that I saw. All I know is that I saw two people sitting in the front seat of that car. It's not something I would forget, considering I thought it was my last instant on earth at the time."

"Don't even talk that way," Beatrice shivered. "So what did RJ say about this?"

"I didn't tell him," Suzanne said. "I was pretty out of it at the time, and, like I said, I thought I was just remembering things wrong. I figured my head would clear in a few days and I would recall things just the way the police said it happened. But it never came out that way. I didn't tell anyone until now."

"What do you think it means?" Beatrice asked with trepidation.

"I don't honestly know," Suzanne said. "I could come up with some pretty far out theories, but that's all it would be."

"What do we do now?"

"Well, the way I see it," Suzanne said, "if I remember something a little odd about my accident, then maybe someone else will too. Despite these clippings, not everyone involved in these accidents died. Surprisingly, a high percentage did. A lot of the survivors aren't around anymore either, moved away, died from natural causes, whatever. But there are a few people around town I should talk to."

"You don't sound very enthusiastic."

"You know me, Bea. I always was a little on the shy side. I find it hard to ask for service at the hardware store. Plus I've lived here a long time. People know me. They know Myles. They gossip. I know for a fact people are laying bets on how long it will be until Myles makes me quit my job." Suzanne was startled at her own sudden candor on the topic of Myles. She was so ashamed of Myles and his shoddy treatment of her, and went by the unspoken rule not to discuss him. This breach in protocol seemed fitting though. She felt she could trust Beatrice.

"And who's going to win the pool?"

"I don't know. Was anyone allowed to lay money on never?"

"Good girl. You know, Sue, despite what I think of Myles, I'm awfully proud of you, standing up to him on this point," Beatrice confided.

"Thanks, Bea."

"Seriously," Beatrice continued. "If W--, my husband had asked me not to do something, I would have had a really tough time saying no to him."

"If I was married to your husband, I would have a hard time saying no too. Myles is nothing like that."

Beatrice was silent. Suzanne wondered what she was thinking. What was there to think about a husband who had vanished twenty years ago, never to be seen again? She supposed it would put your life in ruins.

"I have an idea, Beatrice," Suzanne said, changing the subject. "Why don't you interview the local townsfolk? You always did have a way with people. You're anything but shy."

"But I'm not an insider anymore, Suzanne. You must have noticed it. No one treats me like a local girl anymore. I'm the big city bitch.

No. Everyone would clam up tighter than a nun's legs when I started asking questions. You're the only one for the job. It's your story anyway, Sue."

"Thanks," Suzanne said without enthusiasm.

* * *

After Beatrice was gone, Suzanne was again swamped with her unrelenting thoughts. Who should she talk to first? Law enforcement, accident victims, witnesses, family members, the list was lengthy. But unfortunately she didn't have the time to ponder very long on the Story of the Decade. She had other fish to fry. Today was going to be a long day on two hours sleep. There were community picnic and grammar school concert stories to be written for the upcoming issue. And of course, always lurking in her thoughts was Myles, who was probably sharpening his claws at this very moment. And then there was the other story she was working on, the one she had neglected to tell Beatrice about.

Suzanne pulled out a different file from her desk and placed it upon the one marked "ACCIDENTS." This one was marked "WADE'S DISAPPEARANCE." Suzanne felt a little ashamed for not telling Beatrice that last night she had gotten another great idea for a story. After reading the half dozen articles about the long-lost Wade Edwards, Suzanne decided it was time to find out what really happened to Beatrice's husband. Suzanne planned on contacting the authorities for a summary of the investigation and an update on a person and vehicle matching the description of Wade and his little red car, but expected to find out nothing new. Still, it was worth a try, despite what Beatrice would say if she found out what Suzanne was up to. Suzanne knew Beatrice; she knew that Beatrice would nix the entire idea of finding Wade without a moment's hesitation. As much as Beatrice seemed to thrill at the idea of uncovering old buried secrets, there was one she was just as happy to leave where it was. Maybe the pain of not knowing was sufferable, where knowing the truth would be too much for poor Beatrice to bear.

There was one thing Suzanne was sure of. Beatrice had forced Suzanne out of hiding and into the light of day, bringing her back into the land of the living. And despite the fact that Suzanne had come in kicking and screaming, now she could not be happier. Beatrice needed to stop hiding from the past too, and if it helped her only half as much as Suzanne had been helped, well, then it would all be worth it. For that reason, Suzanne would be hell-bent to find out the whereabouts of Wade Edwards.

Chapter 26

June 9, 1995

The thunder of your words has soured the milk
of human kindness in my heart.

- "The Rivals"
Richard Brinsley Sheridan

Just as eight o'clock in the morning always sent Suzanne's spirits souring with optimism of the possibilities of a new day, five o'clock in the afternoon brought her soul back down into black despair.

Suzanne came through the back door to find a house still and hushed and tense.

"Hello?" she called, testing the waters. There was no reply. She could hear the television yakking in the distance, but nothing else. There was life in the house to be sure, just none that was about to make itself known. Suzanne was suddenly riddled with guilt. Her sleepover at the paper office may have been innocent enough, but it was sufficient to send Myles into a fury that he was sure to have taken out on the children. Myles would be the first to agree: this job was doing more than just taking her away from her children's needs; it was putting them under undue stress. There the agreement ended. Myles felt the strain on the children was not having their mother available to their beck and call; Suzanne knew it had to endure Myles' rampages.

Suzanne kicked off her shoes and walked into the kitchen. From here she could see directly into the living room. There sat Myles and Zane, side by side in identical poses: feet on the coffee table, arms folded across their chests. Suzanne hated to admit it, but Zane was a chip off the old block. That was probably why Myles quarreled with Zane so much more than the girls: they were so much alike in their black and white image of the world. She certainly didn't begrudge her husband his one and only son, especially since he had insisted on trying again and again, through three daughters. She just wasn't sure that a Myles Junior was the best thing for society.

"Hi guys," Suzanne said as she neared the living room doorway. Myles ignored her completely. Zane acknowledged her presence with a worried glance and a quiet nod. Suzanne could see the concern in the young boy's eyes, and her stomach clenched again. She and the children lived in constant fear of Myles' whims. Though he never struck out with a fist or even raised his voice, Myles knew exactly how to make his family behave the way he wanted. At this moment, more than anything else in life, she wanted Myles' dictatorship to end.

"Supper will be ready soon," she managed to say through her terror, though she had no idea what supper was going to be. She was tired and hungry and wanted a warm bath. Why hadn't Myles at least started supper? She knew he had probably been home since three o'clock. It was a stupid question because the answer was too simple. Myles would do nothing to help her, just as he had decreed at the start of their marriage. He had never helped around the house when she was a loyal housewife, and now that she was striking out against his wishes, it was only worse.

Suzanne was so busy digging through the freezer for some meat, she didn't even notice that Myles had entered the kitchen. She saw him only when she closed the freezer door, a package of solidified pork chops in her hand. He was leaning against the kitchen table with his arms folded across his chest. Suzanne observed that Zane had vanished from the living room. He was probably hiding out in his bedroom like the girls.

"Oh, Myles," Suzanne said. "I didn't see you there."

"Yeah."

"Sorry about this morning," she said, deciding to get this stupid confrontation started. There was no use for a bunch of tense foreplay. "I had a lot to do and needed to get in---"

"Yeah, sure."

"What do you mean, 'yeah, sure'?" Suzanne came back. She was too tired to play any games tonight. She just wanted Myles off her back. As far as she could figure, the best way to do that would be to lay the truth on the line for him.

"I mean, sure, if that's the way you're gonna be," Myles said with a matter-of-fact air.

"It is the way I'm gonna be," Suzanne said. She made her way over to the microwave and put the pork chops on defrost. "Besides, it didn't hurt any of you that I wasn't here this morning."

"If that's what you believe," Myles said. He always tried to make her think he was so much smarter than her. Maybe he had been for all those years he had kept her under his control, but not anymore. Suzanne had been wondering for days why she had allowed Myles to brainwash her into giving up her entire life for him. Even though she thought she loved him at the time of their marriage, Suzanne pondered now if she had ever really loved Myles, any more than he loved her. He had never given her any kind of a great life, boring the spirit out of himself with a business that he hated and saddling them with baby after baby until finally a precious son was born. It was only after careful contemplation that Suzanne came upon the answer. She gave up her dreams for Myles because Myles had given up his.

After the accident that left her mother a widow, it only took Suzanne a couple of days to realize that she was not going anywhere near university, at least for the first semester. There were so many things to be done and classes were starting in the next few days. The family had no home, no income, not even a car. They needed her guidance and financial support, whatever pittance she would be able to contribute. Of course Myles came out of his pout as soon as he found out Suzanne was staying, and promptly began courting her like the dickens. Promises of a wonderful career in music paired up her journalism career sounded truly spectacular, and ended with a Christmas wedding. But the dreams were crushed by reality. Myles started a construction company to pay the bills until the rock and roll career got rolling. Suzanne worked in the hardware store to help run her own and her mother's households, until she found out she was pregnant in the spring of 1978. It was just as well, Myles had gushed. You should be at home writing, not weighing nails for all the dirt farmers in the country. Besides, Suzanne's mother had begun working in her brother's law office, and the Bowens had kindly put together enough money to buy Isabelle, RJ, Charley and baby Roberta a little house in Headline. Before she knew it, Suzanne was a stay-at-home writing mom, and surprisingly, she was very good at both.

Every time Myles came home from pounding nails on the job site, dirty and hungry and cold, Suzanne was waiting for him with a hot supper and another acceptance letter. But it was just too much for him to handle. Myles wouldn't say a word outright, but he had a hard time being enthusiastic about Suzanne's successes. Suzanne knew he was bitter and angry that she still had her dream and he didn't. He didn't even have time to play his guitar anymore, let alone compose new songs. Seeing the hurt in his eyes deepen with each published article, Suzanne found it harder and harder to maintain interest in publishing her writing. Eventually she couldn't even mail out the completed manuscripts, with visions of Myles' dejected face in her mind. Officially, she told family and friends that she was much too busy to write, what with the two little girls, Leigh and Morgan and another baby on the way. But in reality, quite the opposite was true. With no curious onlookers wondering about her latest project, Suzanne's writing flourished. She was able to create freely and her productivity increased. While the girls played or napped, she plucked happily away on her sturdy manual Olivetti typewriter. Just as Beatrice had guessed, Suzanne had been secretly writing for many years.

Myles never did acknowledge the fact that Suzanne had quit writing. The only time he ever mentioned it was once a year when he got out the guitar and tuned up for the annual local talent show. "Sue, you should dig out that old typewriter and bang out a story," Myles would say, his eyes sparkling as he carefully practiced his chords. "You used to be pretty good." Suzanne would only smile in return.

But it was time for the deception to end. Suzanne had had enough of the Myles way of doing things. She had given up her ambitions for him for twenty years, and that was enough. Just because he could find no happiness or accomplishment in life, didn't mean she should be forced to do the same thing. She had been writing for an audience of one for long enough. Now was the time to wake up and move forward.

"Myles, I think it's about time you began to believe a few things too," Suzanne said.

"Like what."

"Like none of your whining and bullying and trying to turn the kids against me is going to change things. I have a job and I will continue to have a job for the foreseeable future." Suzanne could not believe that she had actually found the courage to stand up to Myles. For years she had wanted more than anything to find enough guts to speak her mind to her husband. Now, it didn't seem so difficult. She wondered how much of this courage had to do with doing a good job at the paper. And Beatrice. Of course Beatrice.

"Don't say things you're going to regret, Suzanne," Myles warned. She should have known he would have some kind of a snappy retort. Threats were an all-time favorite of his.

"Don't try to intimidate me, Myles," Suzanne said, the fatigue beginning to show in her voice. She found the bag of potatoes in the cupboard, and dumped about eight in the sink. Suzanne began peeling the potatoes vigorously, while Myles continued to watch from his post at the kitchen table.

"It's not a threat," Myles said. "What you're doing is selfish, Suzanne, and you can't see it because you're too brainwashed by that bitch Beatrice Bowen..."

Suzanne attempted to interject, but could not get a word out between any of Myles'.

"...You won't see it either," Myles continued without missing a beat, "until you've completely destroyed your family."

"This is the best thing that has ever happened to you bunch of spoiled brats," Suzanne exploded. "You've had me as a personal slave for years. Those kids, even Zane, they're all capable of taking care of things around here, doing laundry, cooking meals. What favor am I doing them by waiting on them hand and foot?"

"That's fine," Myles said. "You keep up that attitude and you'll see what will come of all this foolishness."

"You really don't get it, do you Myles?" Suzanne said, bringing her voice down.

"What do you mean?"

"In all of this, in all of the years that finally led up to me making this decision, you never once thought of me and what I want. You say it's the kids, but you're just using them to make me feel guilty. It's always Myles, Myles, Myles. I am so sick and tired of you putting yourself before everyone else. How can you consider yourself so god damned important when you couldn't even write a song good enough to sell? You've been holding me back for years, just because you're too stupid or lazy or untalented to try for yourself." As soon as the words were out of her mouth, Suzanne wanted to reach out and grab them and put them back, safe and unspoken.

"You're going to regret that, Suzanne," Myles said, his voice cracking. And then he was gone.

Suzanne turned back to peeling the potatoes, collecting her thoughts, regretting everything she had said. How could she be so cruel? How could she expose Myles' faults so heartlessly, destroying all his dreams with one fell swoop? But then Suzanne remembered how Myles had dashed her dreams with twenty years of oppression. After a few more moments Suzanne had completely reconsidered. Spilling the truth to Myles was the best thing she could have ever done. The truth had only served to help Suzanne, and the truth would certainly help Beatrice and the entire town of Headline once her investigations were complete. Myles' encounter with the truth had been long overdue.

But even though she did feel somewhat better about her confrontation with Myles, Suzanne was still disconcerted. So much had happened so fast, and now, after twenty years of predictable routine, she realized she didn't have any idea what was going to happen next.

Chapter 27

June 13, 1995

> I've been down, but never on my knees
> I've seen the forest for the trees
> If it ever stops raining,
> If it ever stops raining
> If it ever stops raining
> We can dry our eyes
>
> If It Ever Stops Raining
> The Black Crowes

The last time Suzanne had been inside the Royal Canadian Mounted Police station in Headline was about fifteen, sixteen years ago. And it hadn't even been in the daylight.

Her last visit had resulted from a middle of the night telephone call from a frantic and very inebriated RJ, a common occurrence during that slice of time. "RJ's going through a difficult phase," Isabelle Duncan used to say. Suzanne didn't know whether she believed her mother or not. She wasn't sure whether it was a difficult phase, or RJ just falling into what was expected from a Duncan male. Following in the footsteps of his great-grandfather Abe, his grandfather Sam and his father Ray, RJ was quickly becoming a drunk, just like the whole town expected him to.

Suzanne had been the one who was called on to bail RJ out of trouble. In the years since her marriage, there had been numerous times she had found RJ passed out against her front door, finger triggering the doorbell. When the phone had rang in the middle of the night, her first thought was that it would be news that RJ was dead. That was until she had answered the phone, only to hear his sheepish drunk voice on the other end of the line, begging for money or a ride or the phone number of some girl who worked at the hardware store. Myles had never been pleased about Suzanne trying to save RJ from himself. He had been even more irate when she bailed him out from jail that night many years ago.

The memories made Suzanne shiver. She pulled her coat tighter around her as she waited in the reception area of the police station. She wasn't even really cold, but the day was cool for mid-June. It felt like rain. Did that mean there would be an accident on ol' 65 tonight? Suzanne instantly felt bad for even considering such a terrible thought. She felt at loose ends today, what with Myles constantly scorning her, the pressures of the job, the house, the kids, and most prominent in her mind, the grisly story she was covering. But that was why she was here today. She was waiting to see Constable Matt Geary.

Inside, the police station did not seem nearly so threatening today as it had the last time Suzanne was here. Of course, these were much different circumstances. She was no longer a young wife and mother coming to rescue her drunken brother. She was now a modern career woman of the 90's, a reporter covering a breaking story. It was daylight now, not the stormy night of a decade and a half ago. Matt Geary had been the officer on duty when Suzanne had come in to bail out RJ. He looked as though he felt sorry for Suzanne, saddled with such a sack of troubles as RJ, but Suzanne reassured him that she could handle her brother. Suzanne smiled at the irony of the situation though. Only five years or so after that night, RJ had married none other than Matt Geary's baby sister, Michelle. Suzanne imagined that Matt had been scandalized to have RJ Duncan as a brother-in-law, but Suzanne had to admit that marrying a saint like Michelle, sister and daughter of police officers, had been the best thing for RJ. He settled down considerably after his marriage, though it did take a few rough years for him to get it through his thick skull that Michelle wasn't going to put up with any of his childishness. It proved Suzanne's long held conviction that all it took to straighten a spoiled man out was a strong handed woman. It was only recently that she realized that many of her problems had resulted from not being very strong handed with her own husband.

"Hey, Suzanne!"

Suzanne pulled herself out of her thoughts and looked up into the wide smiling face of Matt Geary. Matt had always been the favored police officer in Headline. Suzanne had her own family reasons for liking the man, but it was a sentiment shared by the entire town. Matt's father, Stephen, had been constable in town for years, and when his eldest son went into the force, Headline shared the Geary's pride. Everyone especially popped their buttons when Matt decided to come back to Headline. He loved his home town, and told everyone who asked that he didn't want to live anywhere else. Not a sentiment shared by Suzanne, but nonetheless, she was glad Headline had Matt Geary.

A big man with a big voice, Matt kept his hair in a short brush cut. His severe appearance was never enough though to override his great smile when he turned it on.

"Hi, Matt," Suzanne grinned back as she got to her feet.

"Come on into my office," he said. Within a moment, Suzanne was seated in an aged wooden chair in a small plain office. Matt closed the door and took a seat behind his massive cluttered desk.

"I'm kinda surprised to see you, Sue," he said.

"Why, Matt?" Suzanne said, confused. "I made this appointment with you last week."

"I just didn't know whether you were still working at the paper. I heard you were only filling in for a little while to help Beatrice out."

Myles. Suzanne read his work all over that piece of local gossip. It was especially probable since Matt's brother Conrad worked for Myles.

It was on the tip of Suzanne's tongue to give Matt a little bit of her own gossip to spread back to Myles. But of course she wouldn't. Suzanne was never one to air her dirty laundry in public; her mother had taught her better than that. Besides, Matt was too good of a guy to burden with household bickering.

"I'll be there a little longer than expected," Suzanne managed to reply.

"Hope it's not too much of an inconvenience for you."

"I'm actually enjoying it, Matt. Which brings me to the reason for my visit," Suzanne said, anxious to change the topic. "The Wade Edwards case."

"Right, right, right," Matt said, digging through his desk, obviously knowing what he was looking for. Not too far down in the mess, he found a thin file. "Wade Edwards..." he mused as he opened the file. "That was a strange one."

"Really?" Suzanne said.

"Yeah, I remember it clearly because it was my first missing person's case after I started working in Headline. It's also the only one that remains unsolved."

"Oh," Suzanne said, disappointed. "Did you have any good leads?"

"The only lead we had was that there was no sign of Wade or Wade's car again."

"How can that be a lead?"

"In most of these cases, the missing vehicle turns up in some gas station parking lot or something within a week. But not in this case. For years we watched for the license plates and serial numbers out of that car, but nothing. That car was never registered again, never received a speeding ticket, nothing. It was as if Wade vanished from the planet."

"What do you think happened?"

"Well, the trail I followed for a while was that Wade was in some kind of an accident."

"Accident?" The word stuck in Suzanne's mind.

"You know, piled up on the interstate down in California or something."

"But couldn't a car accident be traced?"

"Not necessarily. Not if it was burned too badly and he was a long way from home."

"So what did you find on that lead?"

"Nothing. This accident would have had to happen shortly after he went missing. Otherwise the car would have been spotted along the way. For six months though I watched for fiery crashes all over North America. I didn't find Wade."

"And after that?"

"Well, not much. It seemed kind of strange to me. I wasn't getting a lot of pressure to find Wade Edwards."

"From who, the community?"

"The community only cares for a short while. After that it's the family that usually phones a couple of times a week to find out what's new. But Jake was getting old, and he had lost Peggy to cancer only a couple a years before. Morley and Monica had their own problems." Suzanne knew only too well about those problems. Monica's mental state not only kept her own family jumping, but she often dragged her brother into her hallucinations too.

"What about Beatrice?" Suzanne asked.

"That was the really strange part," Matt said. "Beatrice left town a month after Wade vanished, and she didn't contact me again. It seemed to me like she was scared to find out what happened to Wade. Everyone knew how much she loved him, and for him to up and leave like that with her pregnant and all, she musta just turned her love off after that. I don't think she could face the hurt of finding out where he was or even seeing him again."

"That sounds like Beatrice. Closing that book and opening a new one," Suzanne agreed.

"That's the way she wanted it to look on the surface. I'm pretty sure she went through hell. Which brings me to a question for you," Matt leaned forward.

"What is it, Matt?" Suzanne asked.

"Does Beatrice know you're doing this? Doing a story on the twentieth anniversary of her husband's disappearance?"

"Well, no," Suzanne admitted.

"I didn't think so."

"I would really appreciate it, Matt, if you wouldn't say anything to her."

Matt frowned, but he didn't ask any more questions. "Anything else you want to know?"

Suzanne did indeed have something else to talk to Matt about. She wanted to find out if Matt knew anything about all the accidents that had been occurring in Headline, but she knew she had to be careful. Suzanne had been attempting to discuss the topic of the Headline accidents with various locals in the know all week. But as innocently as she tried to introduce the topic, as subtle as her questions were, everyone would clam up. If anything, it made Suzanne even more curious, more eager to dig into the deep dark secret everyone seemed to be keeping. And it must be a good one for big mouths like Polly Fox and Coreen Carruthers to keep quiet. More than anything, Suzanne didn't want the pattern to repeat itself with Matt Geary. If there was anyone in town with some valid information, it would be Matt. He had been on the Headline force for over twenty years and had seen dozens of accidents.

"This is something on a more personal nature that I have to ask you, Matt. It has to do with my accident," Suzanne continued cautiously.

She had thought long and hard about which strategy to take with Matt, and this seemed the best route. She recounted the story she had confided to Beatrice, the one about the person sitting up on the seat next to Barry Linden. She tried to make herself sound less sure of what she saw, more likely to have been delirious than when she talked to Beatrice. Best play it safe before laying the whole theory out on the table. Not that she had gotten so far as having a theory.

"But the newspaper said that Barry's wife and daughters were all sleeping when the accident occurred. How could that be? Was I seeing things? This is really starting to bother me. I've even had dreams about it, the car heading towards me, each time a different person in the seat beside Barry Linden."

"That must be pretty disturbing," Matt said thoughtfully.

"It is, Matt," Suzanne said. "I just need to know if it's possible there could have been a mistake in the information the police gave the media. I need to know Mrs. Linden was sitting up in the car. It's really giving me the creeps."

Matt dug through the piles of files on his desk, and came up with another one. Suzanne noted it had "LINDEN/GARDNER" printed in large letters on the top of the file. Matt leafed through it for nearly a minute before he looked up at Suzanne.

"Here's what Mrs. Linden said in her statement, Sue," Matt said finally. "'We had been driving for a long time, having come all the way from Barry's folks' place that afternoon. The girls and I were all tired and before we even got out of the Thunder Hills, the girls were all asleep. I tried really hard to stay awake, to keep Barry company, but I just couldn't. My eyes were really heavy and I told Barry I was just going to lay down with Kimberly for a minute. The next thing I remember I was being pulled from the car by some paramedics.' It goes on."

"So it looks like I was seeing things," Suzanne said.

"Appears that way." Matt was suddenly very quiet, so unlike his gabby self. Suzanne knew he had more to say. She just had to find a way to get him to spill it.

"That's too bad," she said. "I was really hoping you could offer me some information that would put my mind to rest. Let me know I'm not going crazy."

"Well," Matt said slowly. "There is something I could tell you, something that happened to me at an accident site a few years ago. I don't know whether it's related to what happened to you, but I know it spooked the hell out of me. Maybe you'll feel better just knowing someone else had a freaky experience with a traffic accident."

"Sure," Suzanne managed to speak over the heavy beating of her heart. This was it, she was sure of it. The very first confirmation that something very strange was going on in Headline.

"It was, oh, late July about six or seven years ago, really hot and muggy for days. You know, the dog days of summer. But one night, I was on the night shift, and the skies opened up. You know Headline. You can't go long without some kind of thunder storm. Anyway, this was one mother of a storm. The thunder and lightning was rippin' up the sky, and the rain, well, it was coming down like cats and dogs and horses and cows, I'll tell you. It was shortly after eleven, I'd say, when the call came in. Some motorist called from Russell Mooney's place to say they'd just passed a pile up on the highway. A pickup truck flipped into the ditch.

"I was out there in fifteen minutes, me and Bud Collins, the ambulance driver back then. It seemed a pretty standard accident. It was when Vince Carlson finally did himself in, you remember?"

Suzanne certainly did. Vince had come to be known as the guy with nine lives. He had managed to survive falling out of the loft of the barn, being beaned on the head with a softball, getting pinned under a tractor that flipped over on top of him, plus various other misadventures. It was only when he crashed his souped-up monster truck into the ditch the year before Zane was born that Vince Carlson finally ran out of lives.

"It looked to me like Vince had been going way too fast when he took that bend in the road by Mooney's, and hit the ditch. The truck flipped over and landed upside down in a big bog of mud in the ditch. I was the one that waded in to the truck to see if he was alive. He wasn't wearing a seat belt and had been killed instantly. Open and shut case.

"But here's where things got a little weird. As I was pulling Vince out of the truck, I noticed another set of footprints beside mine. At first I thought that the passer-by who spotted the wreck must have walked up to the truck to check things out. But I remember the guy said he hadn't gone near, and his boots were clean. He would have had boots three feet wide after sloppin' around in that muck. You know Headline mud, Sue. They use that stuff to give concrete its strength. The really peculiar thing was that the tracks were only going one way: away from the truck. It looked to me as if someone had crawled through the driver's window and walked away. Pretty amazing since it was a killer accident. Pretty stupid because whoever it was crawled right over top of poor Vince instead of the other way, completely unobstructed out the passenger door. The driver's window was smashed too, big pieces of jagged glass all over the place. The guy would have cut himself to pieces going through that window. I checked to see if someone walked over top of their own tracks, but no way. It was a single set of tracks, no overprints. We found out right away where Vince had been coming from, where he was going. Apparently he had just been at the Thunder Store for a pack of cigarettes, and was telling the clerk he was heading straight home. Alone."

Here Matt stopped. Suzanne sat quiet for a long moment, digesting what he had just told her.

"Do you know what you're saying?"

"I'm not saying anything," Matt denied. "I'm just telling you the facts, like you told me the facts about your accident. The way I think about that Vince Carlson accident, not all the evidence is in yet. Therefore it's impossible to draw any conclusions."

"So what I told you today, is that some more evidence you can use?"

"Possibly," Matt said. Suzanne could tell Matt was not going to budge. He was not going to speculate on any kind of supernatural influence or anything.

"Thanks Matt," Suzanne said. "I don't feel quite so crazy now. You've been a big help."

"Well, Suzanne, I'd do anything to help the press get at the truth."

"What are you getting at, Matt?"

"I just think you have a very newsy interest in what happened to me on the highway with Vince Carlson's wrecked truck."

"Everything that I told you about my accident is true, Matt."

"I don't doubt it, Suzanne. I don't doubt that an experience like that is enough to get a curious girl like you nosing around for a story. If you're chasing a wild goose like Wade Edwards, I can't see why you wouldn't be chasing Headline's high accident rate and the few mystic experiences that surround them."

"Don't tell anyone, Matt," Suzanne said. "I'm having a hard enough time getting people to talk to me."

"I won't say a word," Matt said, "as long as you never repeat the story I just told you to anyone."

"So why did you tell me, if you knew what I was up to?" Suzanne asked.

"Because I'm just as curious as you as to what the hell is going on around here. Yours isn't the first such story I've heard you know."

"You've heard of others?"

"You bet."

"Can you tell me about them?" Suzanne was getting excited. She had hoped that Matt would shed some light on the situation, but this was more than she had dreamed.

"Well, I won't tell you anybody else's stories, but I can tell you where to look."

"Okay."

"I think you should look up an old suicide story in your archives there at the paper. One Jonah Belcourt who killed himself back in 1970 or 71."

"I remember that," Suzanne said. "But what does that have to do with car accidents."

"Check it out," Matt said mysteriously. "And while you're at it, you should talk to Dwight Bowen."

"Dwight Bowen?" Suzanne hadn't heard her cousin's name in years. Dwight had been paralyzed and brain damaged in a car accident a decade ago. He was confined to a wheelchair and lived in the long term care ward at the hospital. Dwight didn't talk much to anybody anymore, and when he did, it didn't make much sense. Dwight still lived in 1980.

"Dwight isn't quite as witless as he appears. I think he spends a lot of time not thinking about certain things. Like his accident. I talked to him in the hospital right after it happened. His memory was as clear as a bell."

"Is there more?" Suzanne asked, drinking in all that Matt would feed her.

"That's all I can think of right now, Sue."

"Thanks, Matt. You don't know how much I appreciate this."

"You have my best wishes, girl. There's a reason why no one will talk about these things and why no one wants to find out what's shakin', and that's because they're scared. I'll admit it, I'm scared too. I've heard too much and seen too much that put the hair up on the back of my neck."

Chapter 28

June 19, 1995

We heard the miniature thunder
where he fled.

"The Runaway"
-Robert Frost

Suzanne fell back onto the porch swing and stared up at the late evening sky. Clear and dark, the sky was dotted with a myriad of flickering stars. It was all very peaceful and quiet, exactly what Suzanne craved right now. All evening she had looked forward to this quiet time by herself, when she could finally get a chance to think things through. Now here it was.

As she looked up into the infinity of the night sky, Suzanne was struck with her own smallness, her own weakness, and she was ashamed at her recent bravado, rushing around town like she was the first female reporter in the world. She had been such a fool.

Myles was gone.

She should have noticed something was wrong as soon as she walked up the sidewalk after work. Myles' truck was not parked in its usual spot by the overgrown hedges. No bells rang in Suzanne's head though, despite the fact that Myles was always home before her. It wasn't until she walked into the house and found all four of her children seated in a row on the living room couch. With the television off.

"What's wrong?" she asked at once. Suzanne's heart was already pounding. It wasn't just the fact that her kids never sat down in the living room without a remote control or a Nintendo controller in their hands. It was the look on their faces. To a one, they were petrified.

Leigh, the eldest and always the leader spoke. "Dad's gone, Mom," she said.

"What do you mean, 'Dad's gone'?" Suzanne said, her mind racing. Myles never went anywhere.

"He left," said Belle.

"He came home about an hour ago, just after we got home from school," said Morgan. "He packed a few things in his gym bag and said, 'Tell your mother I won't be back.' He got in his truck and drove away."

Zane remained quiet, stunned into silence. If there was one person in the world who saw the good in Myles Gardner it was his only son. Zane would sit and listen to Myles' philosophizing for hours after his mother and sisters had wandered off. Suzanne always believed that there had to be a lot of devotion in a child who could love one person so unconditionally.

Suzanne was stunned by what her children had told her. As much as she would have never expected Myles to pull such a childish stunt as leaving to get her to quit her job, it all fit into the Myles pattern. Suzanne's mind was whirring with anger and betrayal. But there would be time later to think about the consequences this sudden turn of events would have on her life. Right now there were the children, Zane of course, who was devastated, but the girls also, who despite their maturity over young Zane and their distance from their father, were more than just bothered by this sudden change in their small world.

Suzanne talked with the four children for a long time, trying to explain the cold realities of marriage gone wrong to young romantic minds in terms that weren't too harsh. Suzanne knew she sounded foolish, but there was nothing else she could think of to do to ease her children's minds. As often as she asked them what they thought, if they had anything to say, any questions, they were uncommunicative. She was partially relieved. How could she respond to questions she did not know the answers to? The girls did have a few comments, some observations on Myles' unhappiness of late. Zane though, was dumbstruck and no amount of prodding could get him to express his feelings. Suzanne knew that he was deeply hurt and betrayed, left in a house full of women, deserted by the only man he trusted. Nothing she could say would suffice. Nothing she could offer would replace what Zane really wanted: his father. The girls wandered off to their respective rooms, citing homework as their excuse to escape this painful discussion that was turning into more of a repetitive monologue by their mother, desperately trying to fill the empty spaces. Zane went to his room too, though Suzanne didn't imagine he was going to accomplish much homework tonight. She decided to leave the four to themselves, to mull over this incident in their own minds. There was nothing more she could say.

It was nearly eleven o'clock, long after lights had been out and silence fell on the house when Suzanne heard the sounds. At first she thought there was a cat or a puppy lost in the dark. After inspection outside, Suzanne found no disoriented pet. She searched the inside until she came to the bedrooms. She opened Zane's bedroom door and in the beam of the hallway light, she saw her son, crying into his pillow.

Suzanne went to his side and sat on the edge of the bed. She said not one word. There was nothing left for her to say. Suzanne only petted Zane's soft brown hair, comforting her son, crying out to him in her nonverbal way that there was one parent that was there for him in his pain. After a few more minutes, Zane's sobs abated into jerky hiccups. Suzanne wiped his face dry with a tissue and got him to blow his sniffly nose. She pulled the blankets up to his chin and kissed him gently on the cheek.

"Goodnight, Zane," she said. "Everything is going to be all right."

It was this promise to her youngest child that rang through Suzanne's mind as she swung gently on the porch swing. The swing was notorious for squeaking, but Suzanne knew that small careful swings were safe. It was now well past midnight, and she wanted to wake neither the neighbors nor the children.

Suzanne knew well how easy it would be to make things right again. Right for Myles and Zane, anyway. All she had to do was call up Beatrice in the morning and tell her she was done with the job. Beatrice and the Headline Mail would survive. Myles would return, and Zane would meet him at the front door with a wicked grin and a strangling hug. The girls had learned to live with Myles' moods, and were all looking forward to their futures outside this house anyway. And Suzanne would go back to her old life.

That's where the fantasy blew up. As much as she wanted the people around her to be happy, there were certain things she was no longer willing to do for the sake of others. Going back to that old way of life was one of them. Maybe she was being self-indulgent like Myles said, greedy and inconsiderate of the needs of her family. But maybe he was being equally selfish in demanding she give up something that he knew was important to her. That was an old story with Myles though. He was an insatiable appetite for making demands on other people's lives, all for the sake of his own. Suzanne really shouldn't have been surprised at what lengths he would go to get what he wanted, especially since he had done so for many years now.

"I'm really sorry, Myles," Suzanne whispered to the stars overhead. "I can't give in to you this time. You can use the children as blackmail. You can spread rumors around town. You can try any of your little tricks, but you will not win this time."

Suzanne had never been one for talking to herself. Her mother had always told her that was the sign of a loose mind. But somehow speaking the words out loud gave them some validity they would have lacked just floating around in her head. She knew now that the words had been spoken, they could not be taken back. For the first time in hours, Suzanne felt happy and relieved. She had been right when she had told Zane everything would be all right.

She had made up her mind.

Chapter 29

July 5, 1995

He that has and a little tiny wit
With hey, ho, and the wind and the rain,
Must make content with his fortunes fit,
Though the rain it raineth every day.

- "King Lear"
William Shakespeare

    Starting when she was about twelve years old, Suzanne often found herself pulling a chair up to the bookcase in the living room in order to reach the Bible on the top shelf. She loved leafing through the thick pages embossed with big important words of the Lord. Each word rang in her head like thunder.

    But the real reason that she brought the Bible out in the first place was not to read scripture. She liked to bring down this book for what was written on the very last page. There, after all the scripture and psalms and prayers, her mother had neatly printed their family history over the years.

Raymond Charles Duncan - born January 1, 1935
Isabelle Belinda Bowen - born May 23, 1936
Ray Duncan and Isabelle Bowen married June 12, 1956

Suzanne Jean Duncan - born January 2, 1957
Raymond Samuel Duncan - born December 15, 1962
Charles James Duncan - born February 23, 1966

None of this information was startling or new to Suzanne. She knew her family's birthdates well enough and there had been no new entries for many years. But there was one word on that page that she was constantly drawn to, one word that she would not believe except for the fact that it was written on the page in the Bible. Twice.

Bowen.

Until her fateful meeting with Beatrice in the summer of 1968, Suzanne had been oblivious of her mother's parentage. Isabelle's family was never mentioned, therefore it was Suzanne's assumption that they lived far, far away. It was a shock not only to find out that her mother's relations lived right in Headline, but were also one of the more prominent families in the area. It was this startling revelation that gave Suzanne immense hope that her Bowen lineage could lift her above the dismal world that she had grown up in, the world that was Duncan. Constant taunting, Ray Duncan jokes by the score, kids ganging up on her and RJ in the playground. Indeed, her day to day existence was often so bleak, she needed the occasional reminder of the words in the Bible just to keep her spirits up.

Not that the Bowens of town helped matters either. Other than Beatrice's devoted friendship, Suzanne, along with her parents and her brothers, were completely ostracized by the rest of the Bowen family. Suzanne imagined that the marriage of the eldest Bowen daughter to a scallywag like Ray Duncan was probably a grave disappointment to the family, but she was troubled by the fact that they simply could not let the matter go. The Bowens held the very existence of Ray Duncan as an in-law against Isabelle and all three of her children.

Thanks to the constant nagging of Beatrice, the Duncans were invited to the odd family function, including that memorable Christmas of 1968. But without fail, these attempts at family unity were dismal messes. Suzanne would have stopped going to them altogether if not for Beatrice. And Dwight.

Dwight Bowen, Suzanne discovered, was a ray of sunlight in a dim Bowen world. Eight years Suzanne's senior, he was grown up and working as a mechanic in a local garage when she met him at some festive get-together or another. She was captivated with his carefree wit and easy going manner. She wondered how mutants like he and Beatrice managed to survive in such a stiff pretentious family.

Over the years, Dwight and Suzanne had occasion to enjoy each other's company. This irregular merriment was never enough for Suzanne though. Each time they got into a good-natured snowball fight or polkaed their way around the Thunder Ridge Hall, she realized what it would have been like to have had an older brother. Dwight taught Suzanne how to light a perfect campfire with one match, how to shoot a bow and arrow, how to drive. On her eighteenth birthday, he took Suzanne to the Headline Hotel and bought her first beer.

Suzanne had been about to leave to take Leigh to swimming lessons on that unforgettable July afternoon in 1985. Then she got a telephone call that there had been a terrible accident. Dwight Bowen was badly injured, and not expected to survive. Buck, Dwight's younger brother, was dead. Instead of driving for the Headline Recreation Center, Suzanne motored straight to the hospital.

Dwight Bowen, Suzanne's pal and cohort, did survive that terrible accident, but he would never be the same. He was paralyzed and brain damaged, fading in and out of awareness of his surroundings. Suzanne's visits of the first couple of years after his accident gradually dwindled to being occasional, then rare.

It was now nearly nine years since the accident, Suzanne noted as she drove into the parking lot at the long term care center at the Headline Hospital on this sunny early July day in 1995. She realized it had been three years since her last visit to Dwight. It only served to make her feel even more ashamed when she noted that the reason for her visit had nothing to do with checking up on her old dancing partner. It had to do with chasing her story.

"Hi there, Suzanne," smiled the chunky pock-faced woman behind the reception desk. "How you doin'?"

"Good, Laverne," Suzanne replied. She had known Laverne McCullough since childhood, plus through all the years their daughters Belle and Rebecca went to school together. Laverne had worked in this wing of the hospital ever since it had opened back in the late 70's. Suzanne could not figure out how Laverne managed to work in such a depressing place and stay so damned cheerful.

"You here to see Dwight?" Laverne asked.

"Yeah, I sure am," Suzanne said, turning a bit anxious. "How's he doing? I haven't been to see him in a dog's age and I feel real bad. It's just so hard to see him like this and---"

"Oh, don't worry about it, Sue," Laverne waved off her repentance. "Dwight is the same as always, living back in the Brian Mulroney years most of the time, but once in a blue moon, he comes in clear as a bell. Besides, you're here now."

"Can I go see him?"

"Sure," Laverne said. "You know the way."

* * *

Suzanne stood in the doorway of Dwight's room for a long while, watching her cousin. He was seated in his wheelchair, positioned to give him a direct view of the hospital grounds out the window below. His gaze appeared to be fixed intently on something happening outside. Suzanne envisioned him watching someone, a patient or nurse he knew maybe, laughing to himself at some funny antic or other. But what was more likely Suzanne realized, Dwight was probably enjoying some special moment that happened many years ago, with someone, unbeknownst to him, dead or long since moved on.

Suzanne was saddened by the world frozen in time that Dwight now existed in, all because of that dreadful accident all those years ago. Suzanne felt another rush of guilt, but this time for a different reason than avoiding regular visits. Who was she to barge back into his placid life with the wicked intention of taking him back to the day that destroyed his life? Such memories could be very devastating to Dwight. Before her nerve completely dissipated though, Suzanne forced herself to step forward into his room.

"Hey, Dwight," she called casually, surprised at her own ability to mask her discomfort.

"Hi there, Suzy," Dwight called back. He sounded just like the same old Dwight, only played on thirty three and a third speed instead of forty five. His speech was slow and slurred, but Suzanne was still cheered by the sound of his voice. She suddenly knew that despite everything that had happened to him, the Dwight she had grown to love was still under there somewhere and she ached from missing him, the old Dwight. She could see him back there, behind the glazed eyes.

"How you doin', cuz?" Suzanne asked as she pulled a chair across from him and took a seat.

"Oh, okay, I guess," Dwight said. "I have good days and bad days sometimes. They're nice to me here though."

"That's good."

"How 'bout you, Suzy?" Dwight grinned. "How are you makin' out? It's been a few weeks now since you came by to see me. You been busy?"

Suzanne sunk deep into herself. A few weeks? Her heart ached and a painful lump rose in her throat when she realized how time was truly standing still for poor Dwight. The sad state of his cognition reminded her of all those reasons why she continually stalled and delayed when it was time for a visit. "Yeah, I have been pretty busy," she said.

"You been havin' any more babies, Sue?" Dwight asked.

"No, no more babies for me, Dwight," Suzanne laughed. Entering Dwight's room at the hospital was a trip on a time machine back to 1986. "I have a job now," she added. She wondered how much of her friendly gossip would help out Dwight's spirits, and how much would only confuse him.

"A job?" Dwight exclaimed in his big lumbering voice. "Where you workin'?"

"At the Headline Mail," Suzanne said. "Beatrice is running the paper now, and she needed some help."

"Beatrice?" That name seemed to perplex Dwight.

"Yeah, you remember Beatrice, don't you, Dwight? Beatrice Edwards. Uncle Donald and Auntie Anna's daughter."

"Oh, right," Dwight said. The puzzled look did not completely leave his face though. "So she's running the paper now, eh?"

"Yeah."

"She's back in Headline then?"

"Right," Suzanne said. "She's been back for a couple of months now."

"That's good," he said. "It's about time Uncle Donald retired and took the chance to enjoy life. I always said Donald Bowen worked too hard." He stopped and got a look of careful concentration on his face.

"It's an interesting job," Suzanne chatted. "I get to go to a lot of awards ceremonies and---"

"Suzanne," Dwight interrupted. "Did Beatrice ever find that husband of hers?"

"Wade?"

"Yeah," Dwight agreed. "That bugger ran off on her a few years back."

"No," Suzanne said. "No one has seen Wade since 1975."

Dwight looked worried, as if he was about to say something, but he stopped himself. Suzanne was puzzled. She wondered why Dwight had honed in on the topic of Beatrice and Wade. As far as she knew, Dwight was not close to either of them, though Wade and Dwight had curled together for a couple of winters. Suzanne wondered if that was the way his brain worked now, travelling along as if on a narrow mountain road: no side roads and no way to turn around. Once you're on the trail, there's no choice but to follow it through.

"What is it, Dwight?" Suzanne said.

"Nothing."

"I was in an accident a couple of months ago, Dwight," Suzanne said. She decided to try to get a little closer to the topic she had come here to discuss, willing, no, almost eager to bail out at any moment that Dwight appeared unable to handle it.

"An accident?" Dwight looked concerned. Accidents were obviously a topic he could relate to. "Were you hurt bad, Sue?"

"Not too bad," she said. "I was in the hospital for a few days. But I'm okay now."

"I got hurt bad in my accident."

"Yeah, I know," she said. "We were all really worried about you." Dwight did not respond. He looked as if he were visited a cobwebbed corner of his mind that he hadn't seen in a long time. Suzanne had no idea what he was thinking. She wanted more than anything to stop here, not to ask that next question. But there was a curiosity that was burning inside her now, a curiosity stronger than her twenty year veneration to Myles, stronger than sympathy for a handicapped cousin. She simply had to know what was going on around Headline, though she had no idea why it was so urgent that she do so.

"Do you remember much about your accident, Dwight?" There. She said it. The question was out there now, hanging in the air like an icicle. Suzanne almost wished she could reach up and break it off and throw it to the ground, smashing it to bits.

"Buck died."

Suzanne was devastated by her cousin's thin memories. "I know, she said sadly. Then she tried to direct the loops of memories again. "Do you remember the day it happened? I know, my memory is bad about my accident," Suzanne coaxed. "It was storming like the dickens. The rain was coming down so fast my wipers could barely keep up and the thunder was booming. I saw the lights coming at me and the next thing---"

"No!" Dwight repeated. Suzanne had thought that negative reply meant that he remembered nothing, but now she wasn't so sure. It seemed to Suzanne that he was fighting off the memories, that the "No" was not directed at her at all.

"What's wrong, Dwight? Are you remembering something?"

"I didn't know he was so serious," Dwight interrupted. He was staring straight out the window, his eyes wide.

Suzanne sat in stunned silence.

"I didn't know what was going on. He just kept telling me to hurry up."

"Dwight, who?"

"I never saw him so damned upset. I thought he was going to rip the steering wheel right out of my hands."

"Did you and Buck have a fight?"

"No!" Dwight said, waving his hand at Suzanne with irritation. She was obviously not following what he was telling her and he was getting annoyed. "Buck didn't even see him. But he was there, right beside me. I ignored him for the longest time, but he just got more and more mad. When I finally answered him, started tellin' him to leave me alone and let me drive, I'm sure Buck thought I was crazy." Dwight giggled a nervous laugh. "Hell, I thought I was crazy."

"Dwight, please," Suzanne was getting frightened now. There was something terribly wrong with this story. Dwight and Buck had been the only two people in that wreck. Who was this third person Dwight kept referring to?

"I-if I'd've only known h-how serious he was," Dwight was getting excited now, trying to talk faster, but only stumbling over his own tongue in the process. "I th-thought he w-wasn't real, 'cause no one had seen him for so long. I h-hoped he would go away if I-I ignored him."

"Dwight," Suzanne said. "You don't have to talk about this anymore. It's upsetting you---"

"I t-told him to l-leave us alone, that h-he would c-cause an accident," Dwight was getting louder and louder and more agitated. If he would have had the use of his legs, he would have been up on his feet by now.

"But h-he kept insisting on us t-taking him back, and he k-kept talking about that g-god damn ice cream..."

Dwight broke down. He leaned forward and sobbed like a child. Suzanne took his hand and did her best to soothe him, whispering calming words and assurances, just as she did with her children. She was reminded that Dwight was, after all, not much more than a child himself.

After a long time, Dwight lifted his head.

"Excuse me, miss," he said, staring blankly into Suzanne's eyes without the least hint of recognition. "Could you please go get the nurse?"

Chapter 30

July 9, 1995

And the lightnin' strikes
Another love grows cold
On a sleepless night
As the storm blows on
Out of control
Deep in her heart
The thunder rolls

The Thunder Rolls
Garth Brooks

Zane Gardner may not have had the largest cheering section at the ball diamond, but he certainly had the most vocal.

"All right, you guys are in trouble now!"

"The home run king comes to bat!"

"Knock it down his throat, Zane!"

Zane clenched the bat tightly and stared straight ahead at the pitcher. He appeared to not hear a single word his rowdy sisters were shouting. Only Suzanne could tell how truly unnerved he was by this outspoken show of support and confidence. His ears, poked outward by his ball cap, were bright red. It was something only a mother would notice, a mother who knew that her son's ears blushed when he was embarrassed.

Suzanne wanted to tell her daughters to hush up, that they were going to jinx poor Zane, who was trying desperately hard to keep his team ahead in the game. The Headline Headhunters were leading the Thunder Bolts in the bottom of the sixth inning, but only by a score of six to four. Zane was an average player at best, certainly not the home run king, and definitely not capable to driving any ball down any pitcher's throat, but what he lacked in talent, he made up for in enthusiasm. And what he lacked in enthusiasm, well, Leigh, Morgan and Belle made up in spades.

The pitcher tossed the ball, and Zane swung with all his strength. Suzanne was thrilled when she heard the sound of the bat crack against the ball. But that was the last thing she heard. After that her eardrums were shattered with the hysterical screaming of her daughters. She was sure that it had to be a home run, the way the girls were carrying on. When she looked out on the field though, she saw Zane had hit an easy single. He was safe on first base, with a wide grin Suzanne could see from the stands. Suzanne wondered if the girls would have any voice left at the end of the game.

The next batter was Rocky Schultz, a big bruiser of a player, little more than a goon. He was great as catcher, intimidating and bullying anyone who dared to try to steal home. On the bat though, he was surprisingly inept. Today was no exception. Rocky struck out and Zane was left stranded on base. It was common courtesy not to "boo" one's own player, but Zane's sisters made no bones about their displeasure in Rocky's performance. Rocky scowled in their general direction. Dejected, Zane ran to the bench, grabbed his glove and headed out to center field.

Suzanne took the break in play as an opportunity to take a look around the stands. She was sitting on the second from the bottom row of seats, and hadn't had a chance to scan the crowd for familiar faces. Since starting work at the paper, Suzanne was constantly trying to meet up with people, potential contacts, for any story from a bake sale to her main interest, her breaking story on the accidents of Headline.

There was Polly Fox, probably here to watch her precious grandson, Nicholas, the star pitcher for the Thunder Bolts. Suzanne smiled to herself. It hadn't bothered her nearly as much as she expected when the gossiping biddies of the community, led by Polly the Parrot, began to whisper and click their tongues when they saw her. They had heard about the Myles and Suzanne Gardner Situation; for that matter everyone in Headline had learned the news within twenty four hours of Myles checking in to the Travel Inn. And the blue rinse set was off and running. The only thing Suzanne was curious about was which way the popular opinion leaned. Was Suzanne Gardner a selfish bra burning destroyer of the traditional family unit, or was she a courageous woman who finally stood up to that worthless oaf, Myles Gardner? It wouldn't have made any difference either way. She would stick to her guns against Myles, and the town would continue to prattle until something more interesting happened.

Suzanne's gaze continued through the crowd. Lots of familiar faces, all chatting together and enjoying the July evening sun. There was her old nemesis, Maureen Bowen, now Maureen Bowen-Gardner. Suzanne was sure that the only thing that had bothered Maureen more than being cousins with Suzanne Duncan, was ending up with the same last name. Maureen had married Myles' cousin Greg, the only surviving child of Irwin Gardner after his son, Lee and daughter, Kelly had been killed on Highway 65 on August 31, 1975. What more reason to hate Suzanne Duncan though, than to marry someone scarred for life by the drunken antics of her sot father, Ray? Oh, well, Suzanne thought, forget about Maureen. She has her own problems now. If Headline gossip was correct (and it usually was) Maureen was a hopeless addict, hooked on prescription pain killers that she had started using years ago after minor knee surgery.

There were other familiar faces in the crowd. Suzanne's sister-in-law Michelle, here to cheer on Little Ray.

Coreen Carruthers, the old biddy. Maggie Johns and Jennifer McRae, rumored to be lesbian lovers...

Oh, my, God, Suzanne panicked. There's Myles!

One side of her brain was racing with thoughts of how she could get to hell out of here without having to talk to that man, while the other side was spinning with warm cozy feelings towards the father of a lonesome son coming to see his boy play ball. Suzanne was riddled with indecision, before she realized she really had no choice. She would have to risk confrontation with Myles, if only for the sake of Zane. She wanted her son to know that Myles cared, that he was here today for him. She had dried too many of Zane's late night tears over the past three weeks not to know what this would mean to him.

The game had started again in front of her, and Leigh, Morgan and Belle were screaming loud enough for Zane to hear them in the outfield. Suzanne was buried in her thoughts of Myles, distracted only when a familiar figure walked across in front of her. Uncle Morley. It was enough to chase any ponderings on Myles out of her head, only to be replaced by more journalistic thoughts.

Suzanne had not seen Morley Edwards since the funeral of his step-father, Jake. She had only spoken to him briefly at the reception in the church basement after the burial, and she barely remembered the conversation. If her memory served, that had been the day she had been offered a job at the Headline Mail. Beatrice had singlehandedly succeeded in diverting Suzanne from any other thought but newspaper for a very long time. In fact, her mind had yet to stray far from the topic.

Morley Edwards had married Fiona Duncan, Ray Duncan's youngest sister, making him Suzanne's uncle by marriage. Suzanne loved her Uncle Morley immensely. She adored him for his quick smile and warm grizzly bear hug. Morley was irresistible to all children, especially his nieces and nephews. His pockets were always full of gum and he was constantly tramping through the bushes with the children, fabricating willow whistles and bows and arrows and crude spears. People said he had turned out just like Jake, which wasn't hard to fathom since Jake

Edwards had come into Morley's life when he was a young boy needing a father figure.

When Jake Edwards married Peggy Carruthers Wilkins in 1947, he had found himself with an instant family. Peggy's twins, Morley and Monica, had been the product of her short marriage to Leroy Wilkins. Twelve years old, still reeling from their father's untimely death, and not so sure about this new man in their lives, Morley and Monica were slow in taking to their new step-father. Any warming trends were expected to cool even further with the birth of a baby, Wade, in 1951. But in actuality, the new baby brother had the opposite effect. Finally, Jake, Peggy, Morley and Monica all had something in common: their adoration for this new little life. Wade became the focal point for the entire family. He was spoiled and doted on, commonly believed around the town to be the main reason why Wade turned out so wild in his adolescence and young adulthood.

When Wade married the strong-willed Beatrice Bowen, the community believed that he had finally settled down. No one said anything about those predictions now though. Not a soul in Headline would ever admit to believing anything but the worst about Wade Edwards after August 31, 1975.

As wide as the age difference was between Morley and Wade, Suzanne knew that they had been close. Suzanne was able to watch this closeness with her own eyes. Whenever Uncle Morley and Aunt Fiona came to visit, Wade was usually with them, his eyes firmly fixed on Morley, taking in every word he had to say. Along with Jake and Peggy and Beatrice, Suzanne was sure that Morley had taken Wade's disappearance pretty hard.

Suzanne wandered over to the spot where Morley leaned against the chain link fence. "Hi there, Uncle Morley," she said casually.

Morley looked over at her and beamed. "Hi there, Suzy. How ya doin'?"

"Good, really good," Suzanne grinned back.

"I've been hearin' stories about you 'round the coffee shop," Morley said with a laugh in his voice. He was the last person to take town gossip too seriously, but anything that had to do with one of his own, he was quick to find out the truth of the matter.

"Yeah," Suzanne replied. "The legend is probably much more interesting than the truth."

"Is it true?"

"About Myles? Yeah, we're separated."

"Uh-huh." Uncle Morley was not one to condone couples splitting up. He was of the old school that believed marriage was till death do you part. "What do you think's gonna happen?"

"I really don't know, Uncle Morley," Suzanne admitted. "I just know that I won't let Myles blackmail me into doing something I don't want to."

"Like quit your job?"

"That gossip mill is fairly detailed, eh?"

"Apparently so," Morley laughed, then he sobered. "Well, I'll tell you this only once, Suzy, and I don't want anyone else knowin' I said this either, but I think you're doin' the right thing. You stick to your guns on this one. That Gardner character never did right by you."

"Thanks, Uncle Morley."

"Myles is here today, you know."

"I know. He came to see Zane play," Suzanne said, then added. "I'm glad he did come. It means a lot to Zane."

"Fathers and sons always mean a lot to each other." Morley's words seemed to refer to much more than Zane and Myles.

"I'm really sorry about Jake," Suzanne said.

"So am I."

"After living such a long life, he didn't deserve to---" Suzanne didn't get a chance to finish.

"It really didn't matter, Suzanne," Morley said. "Dad hadn't had much desire to live lately. For years really, ever since Mom died. Then the heart was plum pulled out of him when Wade disappeared. After that, nothing seemed to matter much to him."

"Wade," Suzanne repeated the name thoughtfully. "What do you think ever happened to him, Morley?"

"That little shit got scared of fatherhood and commitment and headed for the hills, that's all," Morley said, quickly, maybe a little too quickly. He wouldn't look at Suzanne when he spoke.

"You don't really think that, do you, Uncle Morley?" Suzanne asked. "I saw a lot of Wade during that time, maybe even as much as you did. I saw how much Wade loved Beatrice, how much he looked forward to that baby. I always had a hard time believing that he would just up and leave like that, without a trace, never to be seen again."

"You never know what lies inside a man's heart," Morley said caustically.

"I just always thought there had to be another explanation. It was so easy for everyone to go back to those old conceptions of Wade, to forget the good things about him."

"You're a charitable girl, Suzanne," Morley said without a smile. "You always were."

"But didn't you ever wonder, Uncle Morley?" Suzanne dug a little deeper. "Didn't you ever just let your imagination run a little wild? You know, try to imagine a few less incriminating scenarios about what ever happened to Wade?"

"Like what?"

"Oh, I don't know. Like he was kidnapped or murdered or something, that he really wanted to be with Beatrice and the baby." The words appeared to strike a raw nerve with Morley. He looked down at her with dark deep eyes, surrounded by the wrinkles that only a lifetime on the land could produce. Suzanne stared into them, cautious of what she might see inside.

Fear. And maybe, just maybe, the truth.

"When Wade disappeared, I spent weeks looking for that little bastard. I drove from here to Edmonton and back. I covered every back road, every one of his old hideouts. I figured I would have the best chance to finding him, much better than the police. You know what

I found, Suzy? Nothing. I was the first one to go through his house, even before Beatrice got back home. There was nothing out of place. He didn't take a toothbrush or a pair of socks or a five dollar bill from the cookie jar. If I had found one single thing missing, one thing that indicated that Wade had picked up and ran, I would have had hope. But the lack of a missing suitcase put lead in my stomach right off the bat. I knew right then that Wade wasn't ever gonna come back."

"Why not? Where is he, Morley?" Suzanne asked.

"Wade's dead," Morley answered flatly. They were words that hit Suzanne like ice water, but words that she knew were true nonetheless.

"How do you know that?"

"I don't know it with any tangible piece of proof. I know it in my heart. I know it because of something that happened to me a few years back. At the time and for a long time afterward, I told myself it was all a bad dream, but after a while, after a couple of years distance, I knew that it wasn't a dream. It really did happen."

"What?" Suzanne asked.

Morley looked down at Suzanne for a long moment, apparently contemplating. In the background, she heard the sharp ring of the ball being hit off the bat and the ensuing cheers. The game seems much further away than just a few feet. Finally, her uncle spoke.

"You don't wanna know," he said, shaking his head.

"I do wanna know," Suzanne said clearly. "I want to know because I may have shared that same bad dream."

"You---"

"I was in that car accident a while back."

"Of course."

"Tell me," Suzanne implored. Morley just stared down at her. She could tell he wanted so badly to share his story.

"I was driving down the highway," he started out slowly, turning his eyes out on the ball diamond. "It was a stormy night in late June early July, about this time of year. Lots of thunder and lightning."

Suzanne felt the hair stand up on the back of her neck. She suddenly didn't want to hear any more of what Morley Edwards had to say. But he was already continuing into his story. Suzanne lost all awareness of the ball diamond around her, the cheering crowds, the hot dusty air. She was inside the car with Morley, listening to the rain pelt the roof.

"I was heading back to town from Dad's. He and I was workin' on some piece of machinery or something of his, and had quit 'bout eleven thirty when it finally got too dark. You know how late it gets dark this time of year." Suzanne nodded numbly. This far north, the sun went down close to midnight, only to come up again around three or four in the morning. It never did get completely dark around the time of the summer solstice.

"Anyway, I was bone tired, working on Dad's broken down piece of shit all day. I coulda even dozed off for a minute or two, but I don't think so. The next thing I remember though was hearin' Wade's voice. I knew it was Wade right away, 'cause he had such a bellowing voice.

"'Hey, Morley, you gotta help me out,' this Wade voice said. I couldn't figure out where it was comin' from. I thought I was just imaginin' things. I carried on complete conversations with Wade after he vanished, but this was different. The voice wasn't comin' from inside my head. It was comin' from the seat beside me. I didn't want to, but I looked, and sure as hell, there he was, sitting right next to me in the car. I tell you, Suzy, I damn near lost control of that vehicle right then and there." Suzanne wondered how many people wouldn't hit the ditch if Wade Edwards appeared in their vehicle out of nowhere.

"'Holy shit, Wade,' I said. 'How did you get in here?' My first thought was that he'd been hidin' in the backseat of the car when I left Dad's and had crawled up front without me noticing. But he looked really strange, Sue. He was white as a sheet, and his clothes were all wet and tore up and rotted away, like he had pulled them out of a sewer or something. That's when the smell hit me."

"The smell?" Suzanne was frozen with fear. Somehow she felt she knew where this tale was going, and she wanted desperately to put it all back, to push Morley's story in a different direction.

"There was a heavy rotting smell in the car," Morley said. "I can't really describe it, but it was the worst stench I ever smelled. I'll never forget it. It was like the smell of a roadkill moose left in the sun a coupla days, but only worse.

"Anyway, Wade wouldn't answer me when I asked him how the hell he got in the car. He was talkin' real fast, tryin' to talk me into helpin' him. I told him I'd do anything he wanted, if he'd just slow down.

"'You gotta get me out to Thunder River, Morley,' he said. I was almost surprised he even knew who I was. He looked really out of it, like he was drugged or something.

"'Why do you wanna go to the river, Wade?'" I asked. He looked at me like I was stupid or something and told me Beatrice was waiting for him."

"Beatrice..." Suzanne whispered. She knew how Beatrice had been waiting for Wade that stormy late August day so long ago. And she did wait. Beatrice had waited for hours and hours, but when Wade didn't show up, it was like she gave up on him forever.

"I tried to explain to him that Beatrice wasn't at Thunder River, that she had moved to Vancouver years ago, but he wouldn't get it through his head. It was when he started talking about taking her this ice cream before it melted that it finally sank into me. Wade wasn't living in 1981 like I was. Whatever had happened to him in the six years since he disappeared, he was still living in 1975. I figured right away he had amnesia or something, he didn't know anything about Beatrice moving away or anything that had happened in Headline. I figured I better humor him. I was pretty shook up. Wade appears out of nowhere all tattered and torn and smelling like yesterday's garbage and completely off his rocker. So I reached over to grab his hand. Lord knows, he was shaking like a leaf. But when I reached over, I didn't grab onto anything. My hand went straight through him, Sue. I could touch the vinyl of the seat under his rear end, but I couldn't feel Wade, not his skin or his ripped clothes, nothing. That's when I lost it. I couldn't see ten feet in front of the car 'cause of the rain, so I hit the brakes. The car skidded in a completely one eighty. Thank God there was no one in the other lane, or we would have all been dead. All except Wade, that it, since the way I figured, he was dead already. When the car finally stopped, my head hit the steering wheel and I saw stars for a long time. When I lifted my head up and looked around me, I was all alone. Wade was gone, if he had ever been there. I probably could have put it all to fatigue and overwork, except for one thing."

"What's that?" Suzanne asked.

"There was a wrapper on the seat where Wade had been sitting."

"What kind of wrapper?"

"A Fudgsicle wrapper."

"Beatrice's favorite ice cream," Suzanne said softly.

"I kinda figured that too," Morley said. He was looking down at his hands now. A long moment of silence passed between them.

"I guess you're probably right then," Suzanne finally said. "Wade's dead."

"He was dead before anyone even knew he was missing," Morley stated.

"Where's his car then? How come no one ever found any sign of the accident? There are no cliffs for him to go off of."

"Don't think I haven't wracked my brain on that one, Suzy."

"I can't believe it," Suzanne shook her head.

"It's a tough one to swallow."

"There have been a lot of accidents around town, Uncle Morley," Suzanne risked her theory. "Mostly during thunderstorms."

"I know."

"Do you think---"

"Wade?" Morley said. "Yep, I think it's him. I think he's desperate to get to Beatrice."

"My God," Suzanne said in a whisper. "What can we do?"

"What can we do, Suzanne?" Morley said. "I've been walkin' around for fourteen years knowin' that the ghost of Wade Edwards is haunting Highway 65. I even drive around on stormy nights, hopin' Wade will come back so that I can talk to him, explain to him what has happened, find out where his car is in case his body's still in it. Anything. But no use. Wade won't come back for me. Maybe he's mad at me because I wouldn't help him before."

"Why did you tell me about this?"

"You sounded like you needed to know. You had your own little accident and I suppose you saw something too."

"I sure did. But does that mean you and I are the only ones who saw Wade?"

"Oh, I think there have been plenty of others. A lot of them died. Some went crazy and killed themselves like that Belcourt fellow. Some, they can't talk about it too well."

"Dwight Bowen," Suzanne said.

"Yep," Morley agreed. "There's a few around town like me though, a few that met up with Wade Edwards on a dark and stormy night and lived to tell about it. Except no one will. Everyone's just too scared to talk about it."

"Scared of what?"

"Scared of getting laughed at, maybe," Morley said. "Or maybe, scared of not getting laughed at. Scared of finding out that it really was real, and that it wasn't a bad dream or bad drugs. I wanted Wade back so bad 'cause he's my brother. To the rest, he probably just scared the shit out of them and gave them nightmares for a coupla months. I think they would just as soon call it a hallucination."

"Do you know anybody else who saw Wade, Morley?" Suzanne said. "I'd like to talk to them, find out what they saw. Maybe I can figure out what happened to Wade and---"

"No, Suzanne," Morley said firmly. "You're not going to do any such thing. I know you're chasin' around town, tryin' to find out what's causin' all these accidents, but you're gettin' into something you shouldn't.

People have heard too many Wade Edwards rumors and they don't want to hear any more."

"But Uncle Morley---"

"Don't make me regret telling you what I just did," Morley said. "Please." Without another word, he walked away, leaving Suzanne alone, staring blankly through the chain link into the playing field.

It was only a bloodcurdling scream that she instantly recognized as belonging to one of her own that brought her out of her thoughts. Suzanne gaped wildly into the stands, only to see Belle screaming crazily and Morgan and Leigh standing and cheering. She followed their gaze back into the field where, to her astonishment, Zane was rounding the bases. He had hit a home run! Suzanne joined in the screaming at once.

The ensuing celebration was enough to drive her conversation with Uncle Morley out of her head. For the time being. But even through the celebratory carrying of the hero on the team's shoulders and festivities at Petie's Pizza after the game, Suzanne found herself shivering at the memory of Uncle Morley's low monotone narrative. She was staring out the window of the restaurant at Highway 65, filled with a million disjointed thoughts, when someone sat down in the booth right beside her. She looked over into the melancholy face of Myles.

"Hi, Myles," she said.

"Hi," he replied shortly, looking down at his gnawed fingernails.

"Thanks for coming today," Suzanne said.

"I did it for Zane."

"It meant a lot to him."

"So are you done?" Myles said.

"Done with what?" Suzanne's previous warm feelings for Myles were quickly evaporating. He was going to try to guilt her into submission, she knew it.

"Done with your little romp with Beatrice," he said. "Are you ready to be a wife again?"

Suzanne looked at her husband incredulously. He actually believed that the past three weeks without him had been hard on her. He truly thought that his absence would shock her into accepting his version of the perfect family. And while she had found four kids a bit of a handful on her own, she had managed quite well. Beatrice had lent her a car until she got a new one for herself, and all four kids had taken well to household responsibility. She knew that Myles could never face the reality that the Gardner household was functioning even better without his tantrums and manipulation.

"Myles," Suzanne said. "If you hadn't left your family without a word of explanation, I would have been able to clearly define to you my position. I am going to continue working indefinitely. The children are able to accept that reality, and I think you should grab together enough maturity to do the same. Your little game is not going to work. I am not going to submit to your selfish little---"

"Selfish!" Myles said. "You and I both know who is selfish here and---"

"Myles, I refuse to argue with you, especially in a public place," Suzanne said. "I am going to the washroom, and when I come back, I don't want you sitting at this table. But first, I want to give you something to think about. Are you angry with me for abandoning the family, or for abandoning your twenty year attempt to justify giving up your own dreams and goals. You made me give up writing once because I felt sorry for you. You won't succeed again. Why don't you try it my way, Myles? Sure, trying is scary because there is that chance you will fail. But it sure is a hell of a lot better than not trying at all."

Suzanne managed to make it to the washroom before the tears began to fall. She leaned against a sink, sobs jerking out of her tight throat, hoping no one would walk in and catch her in this moment of weakness. After a while, Suzanne had no idea how much time had gone by, she managed to gain her composure and mopped her tears away. When she returned to the table, Myles was gone.

Chapter 31

July 18, 1995

Do not say things. What you are stands over
you the while, and thunders so that I cannot
hear what you say to the contrary.

- Ralph Waldo Emerson

    Suzanne hated bologna sandwiches. She had for twelve years of bagged lunches as a schoolgirl, and she did now. There was no way in the world though that she would let on to Belle. Her youngest daughter, the first to jump at new responsibilities, had taken on the job of packing the lunches since Myles' departure. All through the last few weeks of school and even now during summer vacation, as Suzanne continued to take bag lunches to work, those Belle-prepared lunches always included the same thing: oatmeal raisin cookies, a naval orange, boxed grape juice and a bologna sandwich, all the favorites of the eleven year old. Suzanne nibbled at the oatmeal cookies after she had guiltily thrown Belle's prized bologna handiwork back inside the brown paper sack in front of her. Despite Suzanne's aversion to bologna, the lunch could not have been more perfect. To Suzanne, it represented how well her children were adjusting to the new responsibilities thrust upon them over the past couple of weeks.

Suzanne gazed up dreamily into the cobalt blue sky. It was a hot midday in Headline, not unseasonably warm for the middle of July, just something to be savored. Suzanne adored the sweltering weather, and drank in as much of it as she could. Today, for a change, she had decided to eat her lunch at the picnic table outside the office back door, rather than the Headline Mail coffee room. Summers were so short in Headline, every instant had to be savored, and that's exactly what Suzanne intended to do. Her office job kept her out of the sunshine eight hours a day, sending Suzanne into deep longings for the outdoors. She had often taken the children to the pool during the summer, but there was no time for such slothful activities nowadays. There was too much housework to be done once her day at the Mail was complete. Suzanne tried not to think of those nagging chores that always seemed to be undone of late: the laundry, the dishes, the vacuuming. The lawn badly needed to be mowed, but there just wasn't enough time to do it herself nor energy to nag the kids into pulling the lawnmower out of the garage. Mechanically incompetent, Suzanne was afraid of that greasy noisy machine, which always seemed to need gas or oil or a spark plug every time it was operated. Maybe she could hire some neighbor kids to come by and mow the grass for her.

"There you are!" The familiar voice pulled Suzanne out of meandering domestic thoughts. Beatrice had tracked her down. Suzanne groaned to herself. Beatrice was a darling, but sometimes, she was also a pain. As much as Suzanne ate, drank and slept the Headline Mail, Beatrice was somehow even more obsessed. It came from being owner, not just salaried employee, Suzanne supposed.

"Hi, Beatrice," Suzanne called out, lazy from the heat. "Want a bologna sandwich?"

"I can't believe you would do this to me!" Beatrice exclaimed angrily. She obviously did not hear Suzanne's offer of the sandwich. Beatrice's face was even redder than her hair, and she was mad enough to spit.

"What are you talking about, Bea?" Suzanne asked, only to have a single piece of paper thrust in her face. Suzanne recognized it instantly.

"This garbage!" Beatrice ranted.

The paper was filled with double spaced typed words, words Suzanne had pounded into the computer only the day before. It was a draft article for an upcoming issue of the Mail, a story recounting the nearly twenty years since Wade's disappearance.

"Bea, look," Suzanne started. "Let me explain."

"I don't need any explanations," Beatrice raved. "I thought you were my friend! How could you write something like this when you must know how it would hurt me?"

"I didn't do it to hurt you," Suzanne said. "I did it because it was important news. It has been twenty years, you know."

"I know damn well how long it's been, Suzanne," Beatrice cried. "Don't you think I'm aware of it every minute of every day of my life?"

"No, Beatrice," Suzanne said. "I didn't know that. As a matter of fact, the way you walk around, acting as if Wade Edwards never even existed, one would have to think that you had completely forgotten about all this." Suzanne waved the paper back under Beatrice's nose. She didn't want to be cruel to her friend, but she decided it was time to repay Beatrice the favor she owed her.

"That's not fair," Beatrice said, wounded. "You know more than anyone how much he meant to me."

"Wade."

"Yes, of course."

"No, I mean say it."

"Say what?"

"Say his name. Say Wade Edwards," Suzanne pursued. "You know you never have said your husband's name since you came back to town."

"Suzanne, why are you doing this to me?" Beatrice pleaded.

"Beatrice, do you remember when you first came to town? You forced me to look at myself in the mirror, regardless of how ugly the image was. Remember asking me to come to work, and making me admit that there was no damn good reason for me to say no, except for the fact that I was hiding from reality in a stale marriage?"

271

"Yeah..."

"Well, honey, I'm turning the mirror back on you. It's fine and dandy for you to force me to pull my head out of the sand, but I think if you looked at yourself clearly, you'd see some startling resemblance to an ostrich yourself. You have never come to grips with Wade's disappearance. You refuse to face any of the possibilities of what happened to him. It was so much easier, less hurtful to just accept what everyone had been telling you about him ever since you first started dating him. Wade Edwards is no good. He is lazy and self-centered and will do nothing but bring you heartache. Didn't you ever stop and wonder about the alternatives? Didn't you ever think that Wade Edwards was incapable of anything but loving you till the last breath was out of him, and beyond? Did you ever think that maybe, just maybe, Wade didn't just take the easy way out of responsibility, that something terrible happened to him that day that stopped him from returning to you with the ice cream?"

By this time, Beatrice was crying. Huge tears flooded down her flushed cheeks.

"Don't you think that even considering that possibility is even more abhorrent to me, Suzanne? At least if I can imagine that he ran off to Mexico with some bimbo, at least I can pretend he's still alive."

"Aren't you a little old for pretend, Beatrice?" Suzanne said. "You decided that I shouldn't pretend that I was a happy little housewife. I have now decided that you're not going to hide from Wade anymore."

"Thanks," Beatrice said glumly, but at least she almost smiled through her tears. Suzanne knew then that this had been the right thing to do, that Beatrice could handle this. Of course, there never was anything that Beatrice was unable to deal with.

"So," Suzanne said. "Say it." Beatrice looked confused for only a minute, then she knew what Suzanne meant. It was a long moment before she finally spoke.

"You know what, Sue," she said. "More than anything, I miss Wade. I think about him, er, about Wade every day. I talk to him too. But when I talk to him, I can say his name. I say, "Wade, how's it going wherever you are? Things are okay with me, I guess. I just wish you were here. I wish you were here to see your daughter grow, the daughter who doesn't know anything about Wade Edwards except the few bits and pieces I've told her. I have to admit, Wade, I haven't told her much. It's just so hard to talk about you to her. She looks just like you, Wade. I think that was the hardest part about having Annabelle. Every time I look into her face, I see Wade Edwards. Wade Edwards...Wade...Wade... Wade..." Beatrice could no longer continue. She was sobbing uncontrollably, with the utterances of her husband's name coming between weeping gasps.

Suzanne knew exactly how Beatrice felt. Sad and exposed and frightened. But free.

Headline Alberta

EDWARDS MISSING TWENTY YEARS
(Headline Mail - August 1, 1995)

The date of Saturday, August 31, 1975 is most often remembered as the date of a tragic highway accident which cost the lives of five Headline and Thunder residents. There is another terrible anniversary though which is marked on the very same day.

August 31, 1975 was the day that Headline resident Wade Edwards was last seen.

The last time that Edwards was seen alive was at the campground at the Thunder River where he was camping with a group of friends and his wife, Beatrice. He left the campground at approximately 3 p.m. heading northbound towards Headline. He was apparently going for ice cream. At approximately 3:30 p.m., Edwards was seen by several witnesses in the Quick Stop convenience store purchasing several grocery items, including ice cream. His red Valiant was seen leaving Headline, heading southbound shortly after that. Edwards has not been seen since.

Following the disappearance, there was a massive nationwide search for Edwards. RCMP were on the lookout for the Edwards car for over two years, but neither the car nor any vehicle bearing the Edwards' license plates ever surfaced. There were a few unconfirmed sightings of Edwards, none of which were taken seriously.

Local RCMP Constable Matt Geary offers few clues as to Edwards' whereabouts. The only thing Geary seems sure of is that Edwards is likely not alive today.

"If Wade were still alive, he would have returned to Headline by this time. He has family here that he would know is waiting for him."

Theories as to Edwards' whereabouts range from a hidden gold mine in the Yukon to alien abduction. The most common hypothesis though as to the reason for his disappearance is that Edwards is hiding out in a warm climate or that an accident took his life.

Where is Wade Edwards? We will likely never know.

Chapter 32

August 12, 1995

Long as I remember
The rain been comin' down
Clouds of mystery pourin'
Confusion on the ground
Goodness through the ages
Tryin' to find the sun
And I wonder, still I wonder
Who'll stop the rain.

- "Who'll Stop the Rain"
Creedence Clearwater Revival

As soon as Monica turned off the side road onto the highway, she could feel another spell coming on. She knew the signs so well: a fluttering in her heart that felt like she had drank too much coffee, roaring in her ears, oppressive heat, an overwhelming urge to run as fast as her legs could carry her. And most of all, shame.

Monica never knew when one of her spells was going to hit. It could happen in the middle of a joyous occasion, a difficult time, or like today, in the middle of a day that was so ordinary, it would be forgettable in the blur of other ordinary days. Except now, this day was no longer ordinary. It was to be marred by Monica making a scene. She would fight it as hard as she could, but Monica knew that, just like dozens of times in the past, she would not be able to fight off the anxiety and the overwhelming fear.

All the fuss and mess was going to happen soon, and Monica knew driving down the highway was not a good place for a spell. She pushed the gas pedal and sped the car up. It was a short ride home, but Monica had very little time. In knowing what was coming, Monica began to cry.

It had been a perfectly normal, yes, almost boring day. Monica started the day early when she drove the single mile from Headline to her brother's farm south of town. It was the homestead that her natural father Leroy Wilkins' grandfather had staked out back in the 1920's, the farm that was one of the most valuable in the area. Morley had moved out to the farm soon after he married Fiona Duncan in 1960, living in a trailer in the yard until Jake, Monica and Morley's second father, got fed up with farming and moved back out to the bush. To the mine, as Jake would say.

Fiona and Morley kept up the farm beautifully, Monica thought. And Fiona Edwards was known to have the most bountiful gardens in Headline. That was precisely the reason why Monica went to the farm on this bright early August morning: Fiona's garden. Fiona's pea patch to be exact. This particular day, Fiona caught Monica with nothing particularly exciting on her agenda. Both Sophie and Bridget were away for the day, Sophie working this Saturday at the hair salon, and Bridget gone babysitting her son Rick's new baby. With nothing else going on, it was the perfect day for picking peas.

All the hour or so it took Fiona and Monica to strip the pea plants of their plump pods, the sky grew darker and meaner. It was obviously going to storm, so they picked up their pace, trying to finish before the sky let loose its fury of rain. They made it, too, laughing as they raced to the house in the first sprinkles. After a cup of tea, Monica took her bag of unshelled peas to the car, telling Fiona she had to get back to make lunch for Glenn. It had all been so normal, so ordinary.

Now, passing the sign designating Headline town limits, Monica stared through her tears, hating herself for her sickness. As well hidden as her mental illness was from the community, she still felt like a leper in the community, constantly on guard for the warning signs, the telltale symptoms that sent her scrambling for home and her pills and her family. Her family. Another tear squeezed out the corner of Monica's eye at the mere thought of them. Glenn, Bridget, Sophie and Dale had all been so supportive of her over these horrible years. She wanted so badly to be well again, if only to give her poor family some relief. After each spell, she would pray that it would be the last. And at the onset of another one, she would curse herself for bringing such a tortured life to those she loved.

As of right now she felt fine, but that would not last for much longer. Pretty soon, something in her environment, something she saw or smelled or heard would pull some horrible long forgotten image from her subconscious, sending her into a fit of fear or sadness or despair. Immediately before and immediately after the spell, she would know that nothing she was reacting to was even real, but at the moment, it was very real.

Monica slowed down as she drove past the service stations and oil outfit offices that ran on both sides of the highway running into Headline. Highway 65 ran right through downtown Headline, before branching off towards Grande Prairie. Only a few more blocks now, Monica told herself, her hands trembling on the steering wheel. She began to think she was going to make it home in time. Only once had she ever had a spell away from home, once at Dale's house, and that was terrible enough. Having one behind the wheel of the car would be unthinkable.

"Monica..."

She frowned. Monica thought she had heard her name spoken, but that was impossible. There was no one in the car with her, and no one on the sidewalk outside her open car window.

"Monica, hey, I need a hand..."

There it was again. That same voice, so familiar she could almost place who it belonged to. And it was coming from right beside her, not the sidewalk. Monica looked to her right, and saw something that sent her into hysterics. The sane part of her brain vanished into the psyche of the insane.

"Monica, please, calm down," said the person beside her. "Please I just want to talk to you for a minute. I need your help."

Monica was not even listening. To the person beside her or the stream of words pouring out of her own mouth.

"Monica, what's wrong? It's Wade. Don't you recognize me?"

As Monica drove through downtown Headline, she responded to her brother's question with another blood-curdling scream. It would have been small consolation for her to find out that she was not hallucinating, that what she was now seeing was real. But Monica Edwards Andrews would never know that.

Chapter 33

August 14, 1995

Who can number the sand of the sea, and the drops of rain and the days of eternity?

- Ecclesiasticus 1:2

CAR SLAMS INTO LOCAL RESTAURANT
Local resident dies, Fox Den sustains thousands in damage
(Headline Mail - August 15, 1995)

While a dozen stunned witnesses looked on, local resident Monica Andrews sped her 1992 Ford Tempo down Main Street Headline, Saturday, reaching speeds of nearly 100 kilometers per hour, before finally crashing into the downtown restaurant, the Fox Den.

Mrs. Andrews was knocked unconscious in the accident. She failed to regain consciousness, and died at Headline Hospital late Sunday evening.

Witnesses from the street outside the restaurant report hearing Mrs. Andrews yelling from inside the car, though no one is sure who she was shouting to.

No witnesses were injured in the accident, though some damage was received by a car parked in the Fox Den parking lot. The car, owned by Roberta Fox, recei

Suzanne stopped typing midword. Without warning, she was spent of all energy to write. No, not just energy to write, energy to think, to breathe, to be. She was suddenly so tired that she wanted to put her head down on her desk and snooze. She wanted to sleep a dreamless sleep, and wake up refreshed into a world where people did not meet horrible bloody deaths on a long narrow strip of asphalt because they have just met up with the ghost of a long dead young man.

Suzanne was suddenly overcome with grief. Not just grief for poor Monica, dead after years of tortured existence, but for Monica's family, now motherless, and for Suzanne own mother, Isabelle, lost without her very best friend. But there was more grief than that too. There was grief for a whole town, a town Suzanne had stubbornly claimed to hate. But now that it was dying before her eyes, she knew that Headline was much more important to her than she had ever realized.

How could this go on for twenty years without someone coming forward with the truth? After asking herself this one question over and over again during the past few weeks, Suzanne finally knew the answer. Just thinking the truth about her own hometown, Headline, Alberta was totally inconceivable. Saying it out loud, telling one person, let alone the whole town was incomprehensible.

Suzanne was stunned by the cold facts that surrounded Highway 65; she had files full of cold hard facts, only to be made again thicker by the recent deaths of young Ryan Gass and now, Monica Andrews. The scope of the tragedy was only escalated though by Suzanne's realization of the growing list of people who also knew the truth of Headline, or at least knew enough to the truth to be too damned scared to want to know more and completely petrified of saying anything to anyone lest be thought insane. Uncle Morley, Dwight Bowen, even Matt Geary to an extent.

Over the past few weeks Suzanne had begun to piece together the reason why this mystery had gone apparently unsolved for so long. She now knew there were plenty of people who knew the truth, but none who were fearless enough to admit that what they knew was fact, not just a bad nightmare that haunted their sleep night after sleepless night. It would be almost possible to live with this reality, especially since it was so much easier to fool yourself into believing it was all in your mind, a bad dream, a hallucination, just as Suzanne had done for the first few weeks after her own accident. So therefore, no one talked about it. No one attempted to verify the facts. No one except Suzanne. And now because of her reporter's curiosity, she knew possibly more than anyone.

She knew there were many members in the Wade Edwards Club, all wanting to believe that nothing had ever happened, or if that was impossible, then that they were the sole member of the Club, all hiding their membership cards so not to attract the attention of any other Headline citizens, member or otherwise.

So the question facing Suzanne was a big one, one that kept her awake staring at the ceiling night after night. Should she do what the rest of the town was doing, hide from the truth? Or should she keep going, digging into this horrible festering secret until the truth was known to all, until Wade Edward's poor tormented soul could somehow be put to rest. Suzanne could barely stomach the thought of poor Wade, wandering through the nether world, desperately looking for a ride back to his precious pregnant Beatrice, so patiently waiting for ice cream. He must be so frustrated, trying for twenty years to find someone who can stay on the road long enough to get back to the Thunder River. He must be so tired of riding around in other people's cars. He must be so bored with the rain.

More than the thought of the rambling spirit of Wade, Suzanne's thoughts went back to his many victims. Dozens upon dozens of Headline and Thunder folks who found Wade in the passenger seat of their car on some stormy day or night: unlucky people who didn't live past that horrific vision and the even more unlucky few who did survive, who were never the same again. Looking back again and again through the archives over the past few weeks, Suzanne had found still more examples of Wade's influence. There was the story of Jonah Belcourt, a shirt-tail cousin of Wade through his Wilkins connection. Jonah killed his poor wife, Beverly, with his 30-06, then turned the gun on himself. The blood speckled note that he left behind mentioned a visit by Wade Edwards. Johan Belcourt had been injured in automobile accident only weeks before.

Then there were the other victims. The people who did not see Wade's transparent self, but were casualties nonetheless since they were innocent pedestrians or passengers in the vehicle. Little Ryan Gass, Jake Edwards, Beverly Wilkins. And then there was Beatrice. More than anyone else, Beatrice, who lost her husband to a merciless highway. She never knew that Wade had not abandoned her and their baby, that he continued to love her into the afterlife.

It was at that moment that Suzanne made her decision. She had to go on with her search. It had not been enough to finally see Beatrice face the reality of her husband's disappearance. There was no way that Suzanne could have told her about Wade's stormy hauntings, especially since there was really no proof, just a lot of similar stories and odd coincidences. But to save the future highway victims of the town, and to allow Beatrice to finally bury her husband, Suzanne had to go on. She had to find the final piece of this puzzle, the one that would complete the picture undeniably and conclusively. She had to find Wade.

Without even finishing the word on her computer screen, Suzanne pulled away from her desk. She grabbed her purse and her keys, and she was gone. She knew exactly where to go for the next part of her investigation.

* * *

"Look at your beans, Roberta. You're gonna have a bumper crop this year."

"They're gonna be early this year, too."

"Hopefully not too early. You're going to be busy with your peas for a while."

"No kidding."

Suzanne followed behind her mother and sister as they toured and inspected Roberta's half acre garden. Mama spent a lot of time out at Roberta's place. Suzanne was grateful that Roberta had both the time and patience to put up with Mama's dowdy ways, but at the same time she had to admit she was a little jealous. Today was no different, Suzanne thought ruefully. Mama was out here with Roberta again. It was nothing that Suzanne didn't expect. After all, Monica's death had hit Isabelle hard, and she needed to be with Roberta during this difficult time. Plus, it was her mother's inadvertent news tip that had brought Suzanne out here in the first place. Isabelle had likely just hung up the phone from Roberta when she called Suzanne to tell her the news: Roberta, plus poor little Nina, Cookie and Skipper had been walking into the front door of the Fox Den when Monica had slammed into it.

Suzanne had been shocked. For once, her mother called her with some real and valuable information, some gossip she could use in her ongoing investigation. And if the news was important enough for Suzanne to show up at Roberta's house, Mama would certainly be here with bells on. As soon as Suzanne arrived at Abbott House from the newspaper office, she had tried to quiz Roberta about her experience in front of the Fox Den on Saturday. But typically Roberta, she refused to even talk about the episode. She claimed it would be too upsetting to their mother to hear the grisly details of her best friend's death, but Suzanne knew better. Roberta was so completely squeamish, she found Monica's accident something that was totally impossible to think about, let alone discuss in graphic details. Suzanne was brutally disappointed by her sister's unwillingness to talk, but it was something she should have expected. For the time being, she would have to turn this dead end investigation into a family visit.

Suzanne followed her mother and sister back towards the house. They were going to take a look at Roberta's flower beds. From the garden, Suzanne had a gorgeous view of Abbott House and its spectacular grounds.

Abbott House had been built in 1921 by Benjamin Abbott as a hotel, cafe and general store for people negotiating the passage through the mud that would later become Highway 65. At the time called the Thunder Trail, this one and only route to the northern centers of Grande Prairie and Peace River was often impassable, slow and arduous the remainder of the time. For that reason, Abbott House became a godsend to weary travelers to whom the last ten miles to Headline may well have been a hundred. Back in the early years, Abbott House did a booming business. With cafe and store on the main floor and rooms for rent on the second and third, the massive house was always crowded with people. Ben Abbott and his wife Ruby had a staff of eight, but worked sunup to sundown themselves.

The Abbotts' two daughters, Anita and Julia were raised on Abbott House, brought up with their destiny sure in hand. They would run the House after their parents. But when the two girls were killed in a single auto accident in 1951, the heart went out of Ben Abbott and subsequently Abbott House. The House ran, business as usual, but everyone knew that the life had gone out of the most recognizable house in the area.

After Ben Abbott's death ten years later in 1961, Abbott House was not willed to his brother Andrew, a scandal that rocked Headline for many years after. Instead, the Ben Abbott fortune went to his renegade nephew Floyd Fox. Floyd was the eldest son of Ben and Andrew's younger sister, the favorite Jenny who died during childbirth at the tender age of twenty eight. Floyd Fox was the last man in Headline who should be taking on a small business. Though he tried his damnedest, Abbott House was forced to close down within a couple of years. Though supporters of Andrew Abbott blamed the failure on Floyd, the more realistic cause for the collapse of Abbott House was the gravelling of Highway 65 in 1951 and paving in 1956. There was simply no need for a stopping place along the way when the bright lights of Headline were just down the road. Abbott House's heyday was gone, and it became simply a lavish house, a grand and beautiful house, but no more the inn for weary travelers.

Floyd and his wife, Polly, remained in that monstrous house with their four children, but their real interest lay back in Headline. They found it more their cup of tea to invest the remainder of Uncle Ben's fortunes in real estate and small business deals around town. In 1990, Floyd and Polly finally gave up on taking care of the huge place, and moved into town. Their youngest son, Walter, remained out at Abbott House, not for the house, but for the farm. Walt was the first Fox to ever take an interest in agriculture, and he did it in a big way. Abbott House sat on a half section of some of the most fertile land in the area, land that had never been broke or cultivated. Within a couple of months, Walt wed young Roberta Duncan, fifteen years old and three months pregnant, and Suzanne's poor spoiled sister was given the biggest challenge in her life: keeping up Abbott House. It was a challenge that Roberta was never completely up to. She tried. Lord knows she tried. But Abbott House had fifteen rooms and six bathrooms. Suzanne knew that half the time her mother came out to visit Roberta, it was to help her with the house. Rumor around Headline had it that Walter and Roberta had tried to sell Abbott House several times, but there were no buyers for the place. Suzanne had thought more than once that the real reason why her sister was intent on having a big family was to fill up the bedrooms and to get some help in keeping the place clean. Lord knows she had a head start in the children department. Turning twenty on August thirty first, Roberta was expecting her fourth child.

Suzanne wandered over to the house twenty feet behind Roberta and her mother, who were now inspecting a lilac bush. She was rescued from taking a look herself by a chorus of little voices.

"Auntie Suzanne! Auntie Suzanne!" chirped three little girls, as they ran hell nell into her outstretched arms.

"Hi there, girls!" Suzanne grinned as she hugged her nieces, receiving a shower of kisses from the girls. Despite her feelings for her sister, Suzanne adored her nieces. "Where were you girls?"

"We were playing in the playhouse! I was 'tending to be the mom." Cookie replied. Cookie was the loudest and most outgoing of the twins. Even though they were identical in appearance, they were instantly distinguishable from each other as soon as they opened their mouths. Or at least as soon as Cookie talked. Nina rarely spoke.

"I'm the baby," Skipper said proudly.

"How about you, Nina?" Suzanne asked.

"I was the teacher," she replied, not betraying whether this was something that she enjoyed or not.

"Skipper!" Roberta interrupted. "What happened to your shirt?" Suzanne noticed a large spot of brown on the front of the toddler's clothes.

"Choc'late milk," Skipper replied.

"Girls, take her into the house and clean her up!" Roberta ordered. Nina took Skipper's hand and led her up the porch steps into the house. Cookie didn't move. This was obviously a regular routine. Nina was the caregiver. Cookie couldn't be bothered.

"Auntie Suzanne," Cookie said after her sisters were gone and her mother and grandmother were back admiring the flowers. "Grandma Monica died." she said with gravity dripping from her words.

"Yes, I heard," Suzanne replied.

"Monica wasn't feeling good."

"That's right. But she was a very nice lady."

"Auntie Suzanne?"

"Yes, Cookie?"

"I was sad."

"It was a terrible thing that happened. You saw Grandma Monica crash her car, right?"

"Yeah, she was driving really, really fast. She went through a stop sign without looking if anybody was coming," Cookie said. Suzanne could tell that she had gone through this story before, getting more articulate with each repetition to family and friends and police.

"Did you see her coming?" Suzanne asked.

"Yeah I saw her car and I heard the wheels screeching. And she was yelling real loud."

"Did you understand anything that she said?"

"I don't remember."

"Think, Cookie. Try to remember what she was shouting about."

Cookie pondered for a moment. Then she spoke. "I think she was yelling at a man."

"Who?"

"I don't know, but she was mad. She said a cuss word," Cookie said with disdain.

"What did she say?"

Cookie lowered her voice, "She said she didn't care if his God damn ice cream melted." She immediately looked in the direction of her mother to see if her profanity had been overheard.

Suzanne was speechless. As much as she had been hoping to squeeze some details out of Roberta, she had never imagined questioning her nieces, let alone hearing this kind of a story from a four year old. It only made it more difficult to hear. As much as she was desperate to solve this mystery, it was always difficult dealing with the gruesome demises of so many of her friends and family. This story from Cookie was yet another example of Wade Edwards desperately trying to get some help on his intrepid quest.

In another moment, Nina emerged from the house, holding the hand of a fresh and clean Skipper. Roberta and Isabelle were deciding to get a spade to dig up an extra plant to be taken home by Isabelle and put in her flower bed. The girls were all clambering for the chance to dig in the dirt for Grandma's plant. Suzanne found she had no more patience for this green thumbing, and made her excuses. She told them she had to get back to work and finish a story she had been working on, which was exactly what she was going to do.

Chapter 34

August 14, 1995

Here I am, an old man in a dry month
Being read to by a boy, waiting for rain.

- "Ara Vus Pruc"
T.S. Eliot

Suzanne's drive from Abbott House, back up the driveway to Highway 65 was filled with deep contemplation. Her mind again flashed with images of the dozens of people, strangers and friends, all victims of Wade Edwards. Now that she had almost all the pieces of the puzzle, it seemed like the terror had been going on all of her life. Lord knows how far back it went.

But wait, Suzanne thought. She knew how far back it went. She remembered the days that Wade was alive and well, jocular and happy and always smiling. And in love with Beatrice. Forever. But that all came to an end on August 31, 1975: the day Wade disappeared, also the day of that horrible crash between her father's car and Alf Fox's truck.

Suzanne was stung with a poignant thought. Ray Duncan was a drunk. He had been drunk at the time of the accident on Highway 65, the autopsy proved that. But maybe there was another reason for the crash. Maybe, just maybe, for once in his life, Ray Duncan was not the villain, but rather the victim. Wade Edward's first victim. After all, it had been raining at the time of her father's accident, just like all of Wade's other victims. Was Ray visited by a dead Wade before anyone else? The idea was so overpowering, Suzanne threw the car into park as it approached the highway. She got out of the car hurriedly, as if running away from the sheer magnitude of the idea.

What if it was true? What if Wade was already dead when Ray Duncan was spinning down the highway, heading home to a burning home and a birthing wife? What if Wade decided to get a ride with Ray back to the lake where his wife was waiting for ice cream?

Suzanne gazed at her surroundings. She was chilled by what she saw. This was the spot. This was the exact spot of the accident. Right now it was all so tranquil, so peaceful. Behind her, the drive into Abbott House, serenely settled behind some spruce trees. Off to Suzanne's left was the Abbott House dugout, just off the highway. It had been dug years ago to provide water to the house, but had been abandoned shortly thereafter when eleven year old Justin Carruthers drowned in it in 1931. In front of her was the short driveway into the Carruthers house across the highway. It was a scene straight off of a Norman Rockwell painting: white two story house, brick red barn, rolling green fields. There was even a dog on the front porch barking.

Frank and Nora Carruthers had settled this homestead in the early years of Headline, and raised their large family in the same house that stood today. Though a couple of their children died (young Justin who drowned and Dorothy who succumbed to polio), enough of them survived in the Headline area to make the Carruthers one of the most sprawling families in the area. It was often said that everyone in Headline and Thunder was related to a Carruthers in some way or another, and by in large, it was true. Today, the Carruthers homestead was inhabited by Frank and Nora's eldest son, Ernest Carruthers. His wife Rebecca had died in 1993, but eighty-nine year old Ernest remained on the farm, despite protests from his many family members. His sons farmed the place, all while living in town. Ernest Carruthers always said that he had lived in that house since he was a boy, and he intended to die in that house. Suzanne could not imagine living in the same house all her life. She supposed that Ernest must have been around on the day of the accident, since he wasn't out at the Long Weekend. He could very well have been sitting on the front porch as he so often did.

Suzanne wondered. Did Ernest Carruthers see anything that day? Did the police ever question him? She doubted it, since none of her research had ever unearthed any reference to Ernest Carruthers. She was hot and tired and had a pounding headache, but Suzanne knew that she had to find out. She had to talk to Ernest Carruthers and learn what he knew.

Suzanne reached inside the open driver's side window of her car and pulled out the keys. She then set out walking across the smooth asphalt of Highway 65, then down the bumpy gravel road up to the Carruthers house. Between two parallel tire tracks was a mixture of quack grass and dandelions.

As Suzanne neared the house, the black and white dog began to bark louder and more viciously. Suzanne saw the porch door open, and a grey heavy set man peered out. She was close enough now to be heard, so she called out.

"Hello, Mr. Carruthers," she said.

"Who's there?" he barked, verging somewhere between annoyed and alarmed.

"It's Suzanne Gardner. I used to be Suzanne Duncan, Ray Duncan's---"

"I know who you belong to."

Suzanne didn't know what to say to that. She walked the last few yards up to the railing of the porch.

"What do you want, Suzanne Duncan? Did you have vehicle trouble?"

Suzanne remembered her car parked conspicuously at the highway, and realized how stupid she looked, parking across the road and walking over for what? A visit and iced tea? She decided to take the less idiotic stance. She decided to lie.

"Yeah. I don't know what happened. It just quit."

"Why didn't you go back into your sister's place for help?" For an old codger, this Ernest Carruthers was a witty bugger. Suzanne hadn't seen old Ernest in probably fifteen years, back when Leigh was a baby and she and Myles had dragged her and diaper bags full of bottles out to one of the famous Carruthers' barn dances. That had been the last time she had gone to a barn dance, and Suzanne suddenly missed them immensely. She would go to the next one, she promised herself.

"There's nobody home there," Suzanne continued her fabrication. "I stopped by for a visit, but nobody's there."

"That's surprising."

"What, that there is nobody home?"

"No, that you came out for a visit with your sister." Suzanne was again stunned into silence for a moment.

"Could I use your phone?" Suzanne asked. "I'd like to get someone out here to take a look at my car."

"Your husband?" Ernest said with a gleam in his eyes. He obviously knew more than he was saying. For once he didn't say it all.

"No, my brother RJ," Suzanne said, ignoring the insinuation. "He's the mechanic in the family."

"Sure," Ernest said. "Come on in." Suzanne saw in the old man's eyes that he still was dubious about what she was saying. And rightfully so, she thought guiltily.

Ernest directed Suzanne to the telephone on the wall in the hallway. Suzanne caught a glimpse of the living room of the house Ernest shared with no one but the odd ghost from the past. It was immaculately clean, as if expecting company at any time. She thought of the weed overgrown driveway and was suddenly sad for what was obviously a very lonely man.

She dialed her mother's home number, and talked to the endlessly ringing phone on the other end. She felt guilty for pulling such a charade on this guileless old man, but at this point she had no choice. She had truly lied herself into a corner. When she hung up the phone, Ernest was leaning against the kitchen doorway, sipping a glass of lemonade.

"Is he comin' out?" he asked.

"Yeah," Suzanne replied. "He said he'd be here in fifteen minutes."

"Do you wanna sit on the porch while you wait? Have a glass of lemonade?"

"I'd love it," Suzanne beamed genuinely. All this duplicity was just adding to her headache, and she could really use a cool drink right now. Ernest poured her a tall glass, and they settled together on the porch.

"It's been a while since I seen you, girl," Ernest commented.

"I was just thinking that myself," Suzanne said. "I figured it was about fifteen years ago. Myles and I came out with our baby for a barn dance."

"You ain't been to one since?"

"No," Suzanne admitted. "I got busy having babies and you know..." She couldn't finish her sentence, since it was such a lame excuse.

"You'll have to come back out again. Now that you don't have that Myles fellow to drag along," Ernest looked deep into Suzanne's eyes with his own watery ones. She read volumes in those rheumy orbs. "We still have barn dances you know," he added.

"The longest running Headline tradition," she quoted. "Lasted even longer than the Labor Day Long Weekend."

"Hell, it's been a long time since the last campout."

"Twenty years," Suzanne said.

"That long?"

"Yep," she said. "1975."

Ernest whistled a long low tone.

"Did you ever go to the Long Weekends?" Suzanne ventured into the territory she had been steering the conversation into all along.

"No," Ernest guffawed. "I didn't bother with any of those. Those things were just excuses to get drunk. Mostly for the young kids and the boozers."

"Yeah," Suzanne smiled wanly. "I went to all of them."

"You probably didn't have much of a choice," Ernest said. Suzanne was amazed at this chap. For someone who seemed isolated out on the farm, waiting out his last days, he was more in tune with the goings on of

Headline than anyone. Suzanne knew he was part of a group of oldtimers who met every day at the Fox Den for coffee and chinwag.

"No, I guess I didn't in the early years," Suzanne said. "It was a tradition for Dad to go out to the Long Weekend."

"No doubt," Ernest said. "Your father wasn't a bad man, Suzanne. He even did the odd good deed in his day. He just had a hell of a monkey on his back. He came about it naturally."

"Yeah," was all Suzanne could think of to say.

"I doubt if he made growin' up much fun for you and them brothers of yers."

"No," Suzanne said. "I think we're all still recovering in our own way."

"Uh-huh."

"Of course, I went to the Long Weekend on my own that last year," Suzanne said, returning the topic back to where she wanted.

"You were out there?" Ernest said.

"Yeah, I was camping with Beatrice and Wade."

"Edwards?"

"Yeah."

"That's right," Ernest said, sinking back into memory. "Your father wasn't out there that year, was he?"

"He was in town. Then I called him to tell him about Mama and the baby and the fire..." As calculated as this conversation was, Suzanne still found this topic difficult to talk about.

"He was drivin' out to Thunder when..."

"The accident." Suzanne finished the sentence.

"Yep."

Suzanne watched the memory flash across the old man's face. She could tell it had been a long time since he had thought that particular thought. It took some careful searching through the shelves of his memory of find that one, and some heavy duty dusting to be able to read it. "You know, Suzanne Duncan, I was sittin' right here when that accident happened," he finally said.

"Really?"

"You betcha," Ernest took a long swig of lemonade and licked his Jabba the Hut lips. "I saw the whole thing."

Suzanne waited without saying a word. She had to hold herself back from pushing the old man for answers to the questions she knew he had. But she knew that he would get to it all in his own time.

"It all happened real fast I guess, but somehow in my memory now, it's all slowed down. I remember seeing Alf Fox's truck first. My first thought was that it was strange for old Alf to be drivin' so damn fast. He was the classic Sunday driver if you ever saw one. But that day, old Alf, or at least I thought it was him at the time, was really pushin' the pedal to the floor. I thought something had to be wrong for that old Fargo to be pushed so hard. I guess I was right.

Anyway, I was watchin' old Alf's blue Fargo, when all of a sudden, I heard another vehicle comin' from the other direction. I looked down the highway to the north, and I saw it."

"It was my father."

"Well, that's what I told the police," Ernest said slowly.

"What do you mean?" Suzanne said. "Isn't that what happened?"

"No, it isn't exactly what happened." Suzanne saw a man struggling within himself, deciding how much to tell.

"Can you tell me what really happened?" she ventured.

"I shouldn't, you know," he said. "I ain't never told anyone, not even the police. I eventually told Rebecca, but that was ten years after the fact."

"Why not?"

"Because nobody wanted the truth. The police, they wanted me to tell them what they wanted to hear. So I told them"

"I want the real truth," Suzanne gulped. She was suddenly very frightened.

"Yep, I bet you do," Ernest nodded. He seemed convinced he could go on with his story. "It most surely was not Ray Duncan that came barrelin' down the road. And you know, for a long time, I wanted to be wrong about that. But the more I thought about it, the more sure I was that I was right all along. It was not Ray Duncan's old clunker. At least yet. Nope, girl, that car cruisin' south down 65 was a little red Valiant."

"My God," Suzanne whispered. "Wade Edwards."

"You betcha," Ernest said. "And Wade was drivin' at a fair clip too, but not nearly as quick as the Fargo that was bearin' down from the south. Before I knew what to hell was goin' on, well, I heard another car. This time it was ol' Ray Duncan, drivin' the piss out of that shitwagon of his. He must have been goin' a hundred, straight up the ass of that car of Wade Edwards. I thought he was gonna drive right into that Valiant, but he pulled out to pass. Bang! Head on with Alf Fox's truck. There was one hell of a blast. The flame lept, hell, thirty feet in the air. I was completely in shock for a few minutes, I'll tell you. The noise, the fire, it all just echoed in my brain for a while. The thing that brought me out of the daze was the squeal of tires. That big hippy bus damn near piled right into the accident. Those damn dope smokers came within an eyelash of makin' a real mess of things."

"But what about Wade? Where was he?"

"I'll tell you, missy," Ernest said, rubbing his hands together. The memories cascading out of him were obviously very unnerving to him. "Things got a little hairy there for a while. One of those hippy guitar players came running up to the house to use the phone to call the cops and an ambulance. Then the police were out there, pulling bodies out of the wreckage and questioning the hippies and me. I just stood out there on the side of the road in my raincoat, watching the carnage and answering questions in a complete daze. My Rebecca, she kept callin' from the house for me to come in before I caught my death of cold. I told them what I saw, but I didn't say nothin' about Wade Edwards. They questioned me again and again about the accident, and I told them the whole story, except about the little red Valiant."

"Why not?"

"Like I said, I was in a daze. For starters, I wasn't so sure I had even seen that red car, and if I had, whether it was even Wade's car. There sure wasn't no sign of Wade or his little red bomb anywhere. If he had been there, why didn't he stop his car and help? So I kept my mouth shut. I'm just an illiterate farmer, and besides, the cops was pretty sure that old Ray Duncan had finally done it up good. I figured it was touch and go whether Ray Duncan ever drove on the right side of the road anyway, and if anyone ever earned a reputation for killing innocent kids, it was him." Ernest suddenly realized he was telling this to Ray Duncan's daughter, and jumped all over himself to take back what he had just said.

"I'm sorry, girl. I didn't mean to slander your father. I know he was a good man in a lot of ways..."

"It's okay," Suzanne managed to croak. She had heard so much, her brain had barely digested it all. It was difficult to even work up any indignity about Ernest's calumny. Besides, it was all true. "He was just as guilty of killing those people whether he was passing or just driving on the wrong side of the road. I've accepted the truth about my father. He was not a good man."

"There's more to your father than you think, young lady," Ernest said cryptically. "He's done the right thing on occasion."

"What do you mean?"

"I think you should ask your mother."

"But---"

"Ask your mother."

There was a long silence between the two. Suzanne absorbed the ghostly story she had just heard and Ernest took a long drink of lemonade. He hadn't talked so much in a very long time and his throat was parched.

"It wasn't until Wade Edwards was reported missing that I started to think that maybe I wasn't seein' things," Ernest finally continued his story. "It kinda fit that if the guy was cold and cruel enough to leave his pregnant wife behind without a word or nothin', he would be callous enough to drive away from a killer accident. By that time it was too late to say anything to the police. They woulda just been pissed off at me for not sayin' anything to begin with. Besides, I still wasn't sure about what I saw. I just didn't trust what I thought I saw. It all happened so fast."

"You said you only told Rebecca. Not the police, not your own family, no one. For twenty years. Why did you tell me? You said something about knowing I want the truth. How could you know that? You hardly know me."

"Because I have a pretty good idea what you're up to. You've been sniffin' around town a lot lately, talkin' to people about deadly car crashes on Highway 65. You even wrote that twentieth anniversary of Wade Edwards disappearance article in the Mail, in his widow's own paper. I tell you, that caused a bit of a stir. I figure you think Wade Edwards' disappearance has something to do with all these accidents, but you just haven't put it all together yet. That's why you walked up my driveway, pretending to have car trouble, when you just wanted to talk. You know, you just shoulda asked me, girl."

"But I---" Suzanne protested. Ernest lifted one hand to silence her. She stopped.

"I figure you saw something strange, or should I say, supernatural, in your own accident, and this new reporter job of yours gave you a chance to try to figure out what the hell you did see. I admire your guts. A lot of people saw the same thing you did and they just hid from it. They figured if they pretended it never happened, then it didn't, that it and all them nightmares would go away. I think you have it pretty well figured out too. Until you talked to me, you knew everything except what the hell happened to Wade Edwards, how was he killed and where was his car and his body."

"But I thought you said that Wade Edwards hit out of town, never looking back?"

"I thought that for a long time. Then, something else happened to me. You remember I told you it took me ten years to tell Rebecca. I may have never told her, except for something that happened one stormy night when Rebecca and I were drivin' home from visitin' one of the kids in town."

"Wade appeared in your car."

"You betcha. And let me tell you, girl, I nearly put the car in the ditch. I can see why so many people have either died or gone crazy after seein' that sight. Did you see him, Suzanne?"

"Just a silhouette. He was in the car that hit me."

"I tell you, it's not somethin' I would recommend. I damn near lost my water when I saw him there, flesh runnin' all over the upholstery and his clothes in tatters. I heard somebody screamin', then I realized it was me. Of course, Rebecca didn't see a thing and she thought I had lost my mind. So once I stopped the car and got my heart rate down, I told her the whole story. She was horribly distraught by it all, wanted me to turn around and go straight to the police, but I just couldn't. I knew that they wouldn't believe me. Maybe I coulda proven it by diggin' up other people who saw the same thing as me, but I'm an old man. I ain't got the time or strength for that nonsense. Nope, I just couldn't do it. It was to go on bein' a secret, I guess. Until today."

"So you think I should go on with this," Suzanne said. "You think I should find Wade and hopefully put a stop to this?"

"I think that's what you intend on doing, no matter what I say."

"I think you're probably right."

It wasn't much longer before Ernest Carruthers showed Suzanne to the porch door. She thanked him for the talk and the lemonade, but before she walked away, she stopped and turned.

"Mr. Carruthers?" she said.

"Yes, girl?"

"I only have one more question, a question I just can't seem to find the answer to."

"What's that?"

"Where is Wade Edwards? Not his ghost, but his body. His body and that old Valiant and the ice cream he was supposed to be taking to Beatrice?"

"That I don't know, girl," he said. "And don't think I haven't thought long and hard about that very question. You and I know more than anyone in Headline, but we don't know nothin' until we answer that one question."

"I guess I have a bit more investigating to do then," Suzanne said grimly.

"I'm sorry I couldn't help you more."

All the drive home, Suzanne was filled with both elation and disappointment. Elation at what she had found out from Ernest Carruthers, disappointment that she was no closer to finding Wade. In fact she was further away from the solution than an hour before. She had thought she had solved her father's death, believing that Wade had been the cause. But Wade Edwards had been alive at the time of Ray Duncan's crash. Suzanne felt as if she was going around in circles, never getting any closer to the nucleus, as imminent as she felt she truly was. For the first time in a long time, she had no idea where to look for clues.

Chapter 35

August 26, 1995

How many times it thundered before Franklin
took the hint! How many apples fell on
Newton's head before he took the hint!
Nature is always hinting at us. It hints over
and over again. And suddenly
we take the hint.

- Robert Frost

    The air was fresh and alive with the smell that could only be rain, and Suzanne turned her face up into the downpour, lightheaded. She did not know where she was, what day or time it was, but none of that seemed to matter. Dreams only tell you what you need to know.
    Through the pounding of the thunder and the raindrops, Suzanne could hear a small voice, calling out again and again. The voice wouldn't go away, and that annoyed Suzanne; she was having so much fun in the rain. She hoped against hope that the voice would go away, but it didn't. Irritated, she looked down from the sky. For the first time, she got a good look at her surroundings.
    She was sitting in the mud on the edge of a small pond, no, it was a dugout, it was the dugout in front of her sister's place out at Abbott House. She recognized it right away because the highway was right

beside it. The highway was silent now though. There were no cars whizzing by. That was not very surprising though. It appeared to Suzanne that it was the middle of the night.

"Hey! Hey, are you gonna come swimmin' or what?"

The voice drew Suzanne's attention away from the highway back to the dugout. There, in the middle of the water, bobbed a young boy, swimming easily around the pond. Though there was no rational reason for Suzanne to know it, other than this being a dream, she knew who the boy was. It was Justin Carruthers, the boy who had drowned here some sixty five years before.

"Come on, Suzanne," Justin Carruthers called. "Come on in. The water's great!"

"No, I don't think so, Justin," Suzanne called back.

"Please," Justin begged. "Pretty please."

"I'll just stay here and watch you."

"Wade's gonna be joining us," Justin cajoled.

"Wade?" Suzanne asked, suddenly alarmed. "Wade who?"

"Wade, you know Wade," Justin said. "I think I hear him coming right now."

Sure enough, Suzanne heard the sound of an approaching car. And it was advancing fast. Suzanne looked over at the highway, and there, approaching from the north, was a familiar red car. Even though she had not seen that car in twenty years, she knew it was Wade's. Further in the distance, she saw the lights of another car. She knew who it was, and as it came up behind Wade's car, her suspicions were confirmed. It was Ray Duncan behind the wheel of the battered old Chrysler.

Suzanne swung her glance over her shoulder, to the south, and there were some headlights heading straight for Ray Duncan, who was now passing Wade Edwards. Suzanne knew she was watching that horrible accident that had changed her life forever. The blue Fargo blurred in her vision, only to return as a big yellow school bus. The school bus was replaced by a blue Cadillac which was replaced by a shiny new 1990 black pickup which was replaced by a silver Tempo, her car! Suzanne was watching a parade of vehicles, all as much victims of this crash of August 31, 1975 as she was.

Suzanne heard laughter, and she looked back at the dugout. Justin was doing the backstroke now, cackling giddily at the moon. Suzanne saw that the water in the dugout had taken a devilishly red hue. She realized it was blood, boiling and turning within the mud banks. The red syrupy liquid licked at her toes, just inches from the water line. Suzanne screamed and tried to crawl backwards up the bank. But the mud was sticky and slippery at the same time, preventing her from any motion in the direction she was struggling towards. She just found herself slipping closer and closer to the lapping simmering blood.

There was an ear shattering crash behind her, followed by a fiery explosion that lit up the storm swept sky. Suzanne's screams became a long hoarse howl, as bits of metal and plastic and human flesh rained down upon her along with the raindrops, and the blood rose up, covering her feet completely. Her shrieks were drowned out by the roaring fire of the crash, and the hysterics of what now looked like two people now swimming in the blood-filled dugout. Before Suzanne woke up, she recognized who had now joined Justin. It was Wade Edwards, laughing and swimming and blowing mouthfuls of blood into the sky.

* * *

It wasn't until Suzanne turned the car down the familiar driveway that she even knew where she was going. After that fitful sleep the night before, interrupted by a startling nightmare that she couldn't even remember now, she had found herself in a strange distracted state all morning, abrupt and impatient with the kids. Even though it was Saturday, she wandered into the Headline Mail office, hoping to take the edge off her mood with some good old-fashioned work. But no go. Before she even wrote a complete article, she had found herself behind the wheel of the car, driving with no destination in mind. Until now. Now that she was here, she knew that this was where she had been heading all along.

The driveway into the yard looked just as it always had. To the left was the expansive lawn, now looking shabby and untended; to the right was heavy poplar bush. Somewhere back there amongst the foliage was the tree house she and her brothers had built when they were kids, a tree house that was now nothing more than a tangled mess of rotten boards and rusty nails. Ahead, it was all the same: the barn, the chicken house, the granaries. The only thing that was different was the house. Built on the foundation of the original house that had burnt down on August 31, 1975 was a newer, smaller house.

Suzanne didn't stop at the house though. She didn't know if Charley was even home, and if he was, he wouldn't want to see her anyway. Charley didn't have any use for anyone anymore, family or otherwise. Instead, Suzanne cruised down the narrow dusty road that led to the back buildings. More granaries, storage sheds, rusted machinery. And in a clearing off to the side, a half dozen wrecked rusted cars, all resting on flat tires or better yet, empty rims. This was where she was going. And now that she knew it, she could hardly wait to get there.

Suzanne parked the car a ways back from the Graveyard, as it had been affectionately called when she was growing up. Forbidden to even go near the collection of broken glass and sharp rusty metal for so long as a child, it felt strange to enter this grisly monument to Ray Duncan. The Graveyard consisted of all the vehicles that her father had managed to total during his stunning career as a drunk driver. Back in the years before such an act was considered any kind of a crime, more of a misbehavior, Ray Duncan had put together an impressive collection of twisted metal. Luckily, he only managed to hurt a few fence posts and road signs. That is until the final collision.

Suzanne spotted that old brown Chrysler right away. It was parked next to the old Oldsmobile with one light smashed out. Of course that car ended up with plenty more wrong with it than a busted headlight. Ray eventually hit an approach with the Olds and rolled it nearly flat. That had been when Suzanne was about thirteen years old. Right after the Oldsmobile was towed to the Ray Duncan Automobile Cemetery, they drove the brown Chrysler until its own untimely demise. These two cars, the Chrysler and the Oldsmobile were the cars that she remembered most clearly. Half of the cars Ray had smashed up were pushing up daisies before Suzanne ever entered first grade. She approached the old brown Chrysler with trepidation, almost expecting the driver's door to open, and Ray Duncan to pop out, slurring and cursing and drinking from a half empty bottle of rye whiskey. But there was no Ray Duncan. Only the wind blowing through the grass and through the smashed windows of the cars. Suzanne felt as if they were all staring at her with those unblinking headlights. Then she saw it.

The body of the Chrysler was crushed and burned almost beyond recognition, especially in the front where the horrible collision took place. But the back of the car was still almost intact; Suzanne could see the back seat and the trunk and the back fenders. She walked around the rear of the car, caught in her thoughts of years gone by. Then something caught her eye. There on the back passenger side of the Chrysler was something she had never noticed before. Not that she had ever been looking. Not that anyone, even the police, had been looking. But for anyone who had had their eyes open on that chilly rainy day twenty years ago, on the accident scene, towing the car away, someone should have, no, must have seen it. It almost looked like a wound. A scrape of red in the midst of brown. Suzanne reached down and touched the dent and the paint. The paint of the red car that had almost missed hitting the Chrysler. The metal was warm under Suzanne's fingers, heated by the summer sun. She almost felt soothed by the warmth. She so needed to be soothed, as the truth swarmed through her head, as the final pieces of the puzzle fit into place.

"Hello," a voice spoke. It was close, almost on top of Suzanne. She turned, expecting to see Ray Duncan. It was the next thing to him.

"Charley," she breathed. "You scared the hell out of me."

"I didn't mean to sneak up on you."

The brother and sister stood looking at each other for a long moment. Suzanne was crushed with memories of her dearest baby brother and their tormented childhood together. Of she and RJ and Charley, Suzanne knew Charley had been scarred the deepest by what had happened during their youth. RJ was tough as nails. And Suzanne always had the thunder. But Charley had nothing but his deep love for his mother and his father. It was this love, and the daily reminders of its imperfection that tore Charley to pieces. After the day he watched his house burn to the ground and his mother writhe in the pain of giving birth and then waited in a sterile hospital for bad news of his deceased father, Charley completely withdrew. He rarely spoke to RJ or Suzanne. He rarely even acknowledged his new baby sister, Roberta. Worst of all, he turned cold and angry to his mother, as if somehow this was all her fault. And maybe in some strange way it was. After all, she had married Ray Duncan to begin with. By the time he was fifteen, Charley quit school and left Headline. Reports came back that he was seen panhandling in downtown Edmonton. Then, suddenly he surfaced, returning to Thunder Ridge as if he had never left in the first place. Charley built himself a little house on the family homestead, right on the ashes of the old house. Like a phoenix. He proceeded to live the quiet life of a hermit farmer. No one ever saw or heard from Charley. The first few years after his return saw Isabelle and Suzanne and RJ and even Roberta serve futile attempts to include Charley in the family Christmases and such. But he would have no part of it. Charley had been hurt enough. There would be no more. He was making sure of that.

 Suzanne realized it had been nearly two years since she had seen her brother. It had been in the hardware store a couple of falls ago. She was buying light bulbs, he some nails. She had tossed out a cheery hello. Charley had mumbled some response and left in a hurry. Suzanne cried all the way home. She had tried so hard to protect her brothers when they were small, but she had failed. Ray Duncan was just too powerful for her. Every family function without Charley brought new shame to Suzanne, though it was nothing she could ever share with anyone. Myles would have laughed. The rest would have changed the subject. The secret shame only made Suzanne miss Charley more.

"It's good to see you, Charley," Suzanne finally said, her voice quavering. And it was. She almost felt whole again just seeing him with her own eyes. It was almost enough to chase away the ghosts that were flapping around her brain.

"You too," Charley said shortly, looking down at his feet. Suzanne knew that he didn't stay away from the family because of any spite or anger, more because of the pain it caused him. The pain of loneliness was easier for him to bear than the pain of the memories.

"How have you been?" Suzanne asked.

"Pretty good," Charley replied. "Good crop this year."

"I'm sorry I haven't been out to see you lately. I've been awfully busy lately and---"

"Yeah, I heard," Charley said. "You and Myles split up."

"I guess so."

"I think it's good."

"Myles is a good man, Charley," Suzanne said. "He's just an unhappy man."

"Sure," Charley said. "If you think so."

"I do," Suzanne said. She didn't know why she was defending Myles. For the first time since their separation two months ago, she felt a longing for the presence of her estranged husband.

"You got a job," Charley said, changing the subject.

"You heard?"

"You're the talk of the town."

"I didn't think you kept up on Headline gossip, Charley."

"You'd be surprised."

"I guess so."

"So why are you here, Suzanne?" Charley said. "It can't be to visit me since you didn't stop in at the house."

"I was going to on my way out, Charley," Suzanne babbled guiltily. "I had to check something out, and then I was going to come in for tea---"

"Slow down, Suzanne," Charley said. "You don't have to feel guilty. You take responsibility for everything that has ever gone wrong in your life, plus everybody around you. You really should let yourself off the hook, you know."

"I guess I should."

"So why are you out here?"

"I had to look at this old car, Dad's last wreck."

"Looking for anything in particular?"

"I didn't know what I was looking for when I came here, but I found it anyway." Suzanne indicated the red scar on the car's fender.

"Aha," Charley said. "So you found it. I knew you were looking for Wade after that article in the Mail. I wondered how close you really were to the truth."

"How close am I?"

"Pretty close, I'd say."

"I'd say," Suzanne said. "I'd say this is the last piece to the puzzle."

"I see."

"You know?"

"Yeah."

"When did you figure it out?"

"A couple of years ago," Charley said. "I was driving into town one day, and Wade dropped in for a visit. It didn't take much after that to figure things out."

"Why didn't you say anything, Charley? Don't you know that people are dying on that highway because of what Wade is doing?"

"When did you see him, Suzanne?"

"I didn't," she replied. "He was in the other car in my accident in May. I saw a silhouette. After I got my new job, I started digging into what had really happened that night. I had no idea it was going to snowball into this."

"That explains everything then."

"Explains what?"

"Explains why you are so brave and determined. If you had ever seen Wade, or at least the creature that Wade has turned into, you wouldn't be so courageous. If you saw what I saw, and what dozens of others have seen, you wouldn't be so confident. You would be scared stiff. Like the rest of us."

"Like the rest of who?"

"You probably think that most of the people that have seen Wade Edwards' ghost were killed in fiery car crashes, but that's not the case. There are plenty of us that survived our encounters---"

"Dwight Bowen, Uncle Morley, Ernest Carruthers..."

"So you have been talking to people."

"Yes."

"Those of us who met up with Wade on a stormy drive through the country and managed to walk away from the car, we had a lot to deal with. Some of us couldn't. Some went a little crazy, like Dwight. Some went really crazy like Jonah Belcourt who killed himself and his wife. Most of us though, just convinced ourselves it was a bad dream and tried to get on with our lives. It's easier that way. It's easier to just make believe it wasn't real than to face the reality of it all. And talking about it means admitting it was real. That's too much to handle and still stay sane. Now if you, dear sister, had actually met up with Wade in the, uh, flesh, you would understand."

"Maybe it's time someone who hasn't had the shit scared out of them figured things out. Then Wade Edwards can be pulled out of that dugout he crashed into and be put to peace once and for all."

"I'm sure it is. I was just telling you the reason why it wasn't me told Wade's story."

"I understand."

"No, Suzanne, you don't understand."

"No, I guess I don't, but I want to."

"I believe you do."

"Thanks."

"So what are you going to do?"

"I guess I'm going to get Matt Geary to go out to the dugout at Abbott House with me. See what we will find."

"God bless you."

Suzanne didn't take the time for tea with her brother. She promised to come back soon and share some more time with him. She just wanted to finish this saga she had been following for so long, too long. Charley agreed, and made her promise to come back soon.

It was only after she got back on the main highway that she saw the thunderheads building. Moments later, the raindrops were dotting her windshield.

Chapter 36

August 26, 1995

Let me be your shelter,
Shelter from the storm outside.
Let me be your shelter,
Shelter from the endless night.

- "Shelter"
Maria McKee and Steven Van Zandt

Suzanne was so excited, she barely noticed the sprinkles on her windshield were turning into huge raindrops. She had tried so hard for so long to solve the mystery of Highway 65 and of Wade Edwards' disappearance. Little had she known that these two mysteries were one and the same, and now, they were mysteries no more. For the first time, someone knew the truth and was not afraid to reveal it. Suzanne squirmed at the thought of Beatrice finally knowing the fate of her husband. She would finally be at peace.

"Suzanne..."

She heard the voice, and felt a chill freeze her body solid. She tried to tell herself that the voice was coming from inside her head, but she knew better. The windshield wipers were beating steadily now, and thunder and lightning was crashing all around her. She had wanted so badly to get back to Headline, find Matt Geary and take him to Wade's wreck. How could the inherent dangers of driving through a thunderstorm in this part of the country have slipped her mind? Upon hearing her name being whispered though, Suzanne knew that she was about to be reunited with Wade Edwards and she was more frightened than she had ever been in her life. Not even Ray Duncan had been able to wrench such fear in her heart. She thought of hiding in the thunder as she had all those times as a child, when Ray Duncan was on a rampage. But she realized what too much hiding in the thunder had done in the town of Headline.

"Suzanne, I need your help."

Suzanne held her breath and looked over to her right. There on the seat beside her, sat a decaying translucent human form. Even if she hadn't known who to expect, she would have recognized Wade instantly. In her nightmares, she had seen Wade's rotting corpse, still trying to act as if it was still alive, speaking with a lipless mouth, grasping with fleshless fingers. But no nightmare could have prepared her for what she now saw with her own wakened eyes. She now understood what Charley and Ernest Carruthers and Uncle Morley had been trying to tell her. Seeing Wade Edward's ghost was wishing you never had. Meeting with this sad phantom was something you would only want to rinse from your mind as soon as you could. That is, if you survived. Suzanne shuddered that this sight could affect her so deeply when she knew what to expect. What about all those unaware souls who were visited by Wade Edwards when they were least expecting it?

Suzanne touched around with her right foot, trying to find the brake pedal. She wanted to stop the car before the fright pushed her into the ditch. She pushed down with all her might, the car skidding to a howling stop.

"Suzanne, don't stop," Wade pleaded, reaching out to her. Suzanne recoiled back from his decomposing grasp. "I need a ride."

"I'll take you to wherever you want to go, Wade," Suzanne said, trying unsuccessfully to keep her voice from quavering. "Just relax. I can't drive when you're scaring me so."

"I'm sorry, Suzanne," Wade said. "I have to get back to Beatrice. She's waiting for this ice cream." Wade held up a mangled mess of paper and melted ice cream with a stick poking out the side. Twenty years ago, it had been a Fudgsicle. Wade didn't seem to notice anything amiss with the treat though, other than the fact he was late in delivering it. "She's gonna be pissed off at me."

"Where is she?"

"Out at Thunder River, Suzanne," Wade said, annoyed. "You should know that. You were just out there." Suzanne realized that in his 1975 consciousness, the last time he had seen her had been on the beach with Beatrice. She knew she would have to play along.

"Right," Suzanne said. "I just came out looking for you. Beatrice thought you got lost or something."

"Let's go then," Wade said. He had been trying so hard to get back to his wife, Wade was obviously relieved at finally finding someone who would co-operate in his quest.

Suzanne took her foot off the brake and pushed the gas carefully. She tried to keep her mind off her pounding heart and on the task at hand. She carefully turned the car around, and pointed it in the direction of Thunder River. It was only a couple of miles away.

Over the next two minutes, there was no conversation in the vehicle. Suzanne did not want to talk to the ghost of Wade Edwards. She didn't even look at him, knowing that the gruesome sight would only frighten her all over again. Wade was silent too, seemingly content to finally be on his way to his destination. Suzanne slowed to turn into the campground, and out of the corner of her eye, saw Wade lean forward in eager anticipation.

"I hope Beatrice isn't too mad at me," he said. His dank voice seemed to rattle around in his empty chest, bouncing around a cavity void of any internal organs.

"I don't think she is," Suzanne said as she pulled the car to a stop close to the river. She could see the expanse of the Thunder River in front of her now, calm and peaceful in the downpour. As she watched the scene in front of her, she noticed someone walking towards the water. Then she realized it was Wade. He had stepped out of the car without any concern for the locked door, anxious to get to his wife. He carried the remains of the ice cream in his hands. Suzanne wondered if it had been a mistake to bring Wade here. He wasn't going to find Beatrice here. Would that only make him more desperate, more urgent in his futile search? Suzanne shuddered at the thought. She slipped the car into reverse and backed away from the lake and Wade's vanishing form. He was getting further away from her and with the distance, he was only more luminous.

Suzanne sped away back down the campground approach, back onto Goldmine Road, back toward Highway 65. Now more than ever, she knew the urgency to get to Matt Geary and to Wade's body in the dugout. All the while she drove, she expected Wade's distraught form to appear in the seat beside her, exasperated in his search for his one true love. Finally she saw the lights of Headline, and relief washed over her like the rain. She was safe.

***

It was a sunny late August afternoon when the tow truck backed up to the Abbott House dugout and the divers went down below. Suzanne had insisted on it. She had been unable to drive during stormy weather since Wade had hitched a ride with her two days ago. As the hot sun beat down upon Suzanne and Matt Geary and all the other police officers and medical examiners and curious family members and friends of the late Wade Edwards, Suzanne felt quite safe for the first time in a very long time. Soon Wade's car would emerge from beneath the surface of the dugout, and his watery burial would be over. He could be put to rest alongside his parents, Jake and Peggy Edwards, in the Headline Cemetery. His name would finally be cleared and life could finally move forward for all those whose very being had been put on hold for twenty years. Morley Edwards and the family of Monica Andrews. All the

Carruthers relatives from Peggy's side of the family. Wade's friends, who outnumbered those in Headline who weren't. And Beatrice. Especially Beatrice.

Beatrice had been the first person Suzanne had contacted after she and Matt Geary had made their gruesome discovery in the bottom of the Abbott House dugout. It really wasn't that difficult of a find to make, once they knew that an old red Valiant was resting down there. Matt commented that Wade and his car would have been found years ago if that dugout had only been in use. But no one had drank or swam in that dugout since the Carruthers boy had drowned there so long ago.

Beatrice hadn't said much when Suzanne told her the news. She was speechless, really. But how does one react when told that one's vanished husband has been in the bottom of a dugout just eight miles from town for the past twenty years? One must ponder for a long while before reacting to news like that. Suzanne assumed there would be many emotions attached to such knowledge: relief, sadness, anger at a town too narrow in its focus to find such a grisly secret resting right under its nose for so long. Suzanne had not spoken to Beatrice since that conversation the day before yesterday. She had almost expected Beatrice to show up here today, when the car would be pulled out of the dugout, but then again, not really. This was not the place for a woman who for the first time in her life is really an honest-to-goodness widow.

Suzanne watched as the tow truck backed as far as it dared into the shallow edge of the dugout. The two divers then grabbed the hooked cable and pulled it down below the surface. She could almost see them working to attach the hook to the Valiant's rusty bumper, but the water in the dugout was now a mucky brown, as decades of sediment were finally being disturbed. Soon the divers emerged and walked up onto the edge of the water. The tow truck began to make its slow ascent from the water, pulling its rare cargo behind it.

Suzanne had expected the sight of the Valiant to startle her. For twenty years, it was a car she had been watching for on every highway trip she had ever made. It was the car she had always secretly hoped would pull up in front of her house or drive back into Headline with horn blaring. Now, she would finally see that red car that she had wanted to see so badly. Now she didn't want to see it at all. Because with the dead car came the dead Wade.

The front grill and hood and wheels of the Valiant emerged from the water, but they were barely recognizable as Wade's car. The red paint was covered in two decades worth of mud and muskrat droppings and green slime. Slowly, the tow truck sucked the car up further. The front windshield emerged, then the front doors and the roof. Suzanne closed her eyes for a moment. It really was Wade's car.

When she opened her eyes, the Valiant had nearly completely emerged. But she was no longer watching the flat tires or the rusted fenders. She was watching inside the car, inside the open windows of the Valiant. There was somebody in there! No, not just Wade Edward's decomposed body. There were several people in there, no, lots of people. Suzanne felt herself step forward in an attempt to see inside the car more clearly. She began to recognize faces. Terence Carruthers, Uncle Donald, Connie Sullivan, Buck Bowen, Monica Andrews, Jake Edwards, Fran Parker, Adam Abbott, Ryan Gass. They were all hanging out the open windows, over top of one another. And they were all speaking at once. Suzanne had to listen closely but she could not understand what they were saying.

The loudest voice of all was one lone screech from the driver's window. Suzanne recognized the rotting face she had seen two days ago. It was Wade, bawling like a baby.

"Beatrice!" he howled. "Where are you, Beatrice? I brought you your Fudgsicle and you weren't there. I'm sorry I was late, baby, but I'll make it up to you. Beatrice, where are you?"

Suzanne covered her ears and turned away. "No!" she screamed, drowning out the cacophony of voices that were assaulting her brain. She didn't want to see any of these dead people, all of Wade's unsuspecting victims. And she surely didn't want to see Wade, the unwitting murderer of dozens of people, all in the name of love and ice cream. "No, no, no," she chanted, falling to her knees in the mud.

"Suzanne!" Matt ran up behind her and pulled her to her feet. "It's all right."

Suzanne opened her eyes and looked into Matt's eyes. The voices were gone. She turned and looked over her shoulder. The faces inside the car were gone. All she saw was a rusted old car being towed from the bottom of a pond. She could not even see the remains of the car's driver behind the wheel. It all looked quite sane and quiet.

"Matt, I---" she began to speak, but she didn't know what to say.

"It's okay," Matt said. "This has been rough on you, Suzanne. But it's all over now. Wade Edwards can finally rest in peace."

Matt began to lead Suzanne away from the dugout. The ugly process of removing Wade's remains from the car was about to begin, something she should likely not witness. As Matt put her in the passenger side of his police car, Suzanne looked back again. No faces. No voices. Maybe she had imagined it all. Maybe she had even imagined Wade's ghostly haunting of her car during the storm the other day. Maybe. It was that maybe that Suzanne knew she would have to cling to if she expected to be able to sleep through the long dark nights ahead.

EPILOGUE

September 1, 1995

After a storm comes a calm.

- Matthew Henry

    Juggling clipboard and purse and jacket and tote bag and keys, Suzanne managed to slam the car door behind her with her hip. This was just another community event to cover for the Headline Mail, one that Suzanne knew she could have sloughed off onto another reporter. But there was no way Suzanne would do that because this event was special. It was the 21th Annual Headline Talent Competition and Myles was performing. Suzanne had been there for each of Myles' previous attempts at local fame and glory, and despite all that had happened between them, she was not going to miss this one.
    "Suzanne!" a voice called from across the parking lot. Suzanne looked up from her armload. She was surprised to see the very individual her thoughts had been occupied with. It was Myles, sauntering across the parking lot, his guitar case swung over his back. Suzanne felt a surge go through her that felt like electricity. She remembered a time so very long ago when Myles created that effect in her. It was bizarre that now, as the passion shot through her veins, Suzanne felt like a eighteen year old kid again, waiting for her beau to play a love song on his guitar.

"Hi, Myles," she managed.

"What are you doing here?" Myles shot back bluntly.

"I came to cover the contest," Suzanne replied. "Of course, I wanted to hear you play too--"

"Yeah, well, don't bother."

"Myles, what do you mean?" Suzanne was confused. After that rush of warm remembrance, it was doubly cutting to be met with Myles' equally characteristic cutting tongue.

"I mean, don't bother coming here looking for another excuse to rub my nose in the dirt."

"Myles..." Suzanne was confused. What was he talking about?

"Just because you find the long lost Wade Edwards and become the hero of Headline, doesn't mean I don't see you for what you really are?"

Suzanne felt such a deep and strong anger, it was impossible to believe that only moments ago she had actually felt some kind of desire for this man. But with anger, she regained her brains. And her voice.

"Which is?" she shot back.

"A bad mother. A disastrous wife. A traitor snuggling up with her childhood girlfriend."

"Myles!" As many times as Myles' had cut Suzanne to the quick with his words, even this was enough to shock her.

"You aren't worth those poor loving kids, Suzanne. They're all inside waiting to watch their dad play, but not because they know he is going to lose again, but because they really care. Unlike you. You fake this reporter interest in the "story" when everyone knows you don't have to cover these little events anymore. You're in the big time now, aren't you?"

"Myles," Suzanne said softly. "I am truly amazed. Every time I see you, I wait for you to kick in with some of that Myles charm and sweep me off my feet. There's a part of me that really wants that, that almost misses some of what we used to have together. But that old romantic poet Myles Gardner is gone. He died a long time ago from suffocation. Suffocation from a lack of dreams and art and fantasy. I don't even know why you are bothering to go on that stage today, because I cannot think of one thing you have to sing about. I feel sorry for you, Myles."

Before her flabbergasted husband could find his tongue, Suzanne spun around and walked away. She expected Myles to call after her, but he didn't. If she would have snatched a glance over her shoulder, she would have seen a very confused look come over his face. After a few puzzled moments, Myles would turn and walk inside the auditorium.

Suzanne did not know where she was walking. She had turned tail from the auditorium and her car and was now walking out into the middle of an empty parking lot. She was so angry and upset though, she could think of nothing to do but keep walking. After all, there was no way she was going to attend the contest now. It was a sharp horn blast behind her that finally brought Suzanne out of her muddled thoughts. She spun around to see Beatrice, smiling serenely from behind the wheel of her car.

Suzanne hadn't spoken to Beatrice in days, not since Wade's funeral on Tuesday. Suzanne had not known what to say to Beatrice after she had unraveled the mystery of Wade's disappearance. She figured that Beatrice would come to her as soon as she was ready. It appeared she was now ready. Beatrice parked the car and got out. She walked toward her friend.

"Hi, Bea," Suzanne answered absently, shaking off the effects of her encounter with Myles. "How are you?" she asked with genuine concern.

"I'm good," she said. "Actually I think I'm better than I have been in a very long time."

"That's good news."

"How about you? How does it feel to be the ace reporter who solved the biggest mystery in the history of Headline?"

"Sort of empty, really," Suzanne admitted. "It's kind of a let-down to have to go back to covering box socials and track and field." Beatrice laughed. "Besides," Suzanne added, "I don't think everyone considers me a hero."

"What do you mean?"

Suzanne told Beatrice about her confrontation with Myles.

Beatrice rolled her eyes. "I hate to tell you, Sue," she said, "but I never did like that guy. He wasn't good for you."

"Thankfully I know all about him now and I'm still young enough to get something out of life. I'm worried about the kids though. I hate to see him manipulating them."

"It's going to be hard for all of you. You're a good mother though. You will just have to stick together."

"Yes, we will."

"I talked to Annabelle," Beatrice said quietly. It was the first time Suzanne could remember Beatrice bringing up the topic of her daughter.

"Did you tell her about Wade?"

"I had to. He was her father," Beatrice said. "I put it off as long as I could, but I finally called and told her the whole story. She couldn't make it for the services. Classes started yesterday."

"How did she take it all?"

"Actually quite well," Beatrice said. "She never knew Wade. And I never told her much about him, about how fun and spontaneous and wild he was." Beatrice's voice caught. After twenty years, she still loved Wade more than anything. "I couldn't tell her because I was already going crazy. Anyway, she was quite happy to hear that her father hadn't deserted us after all. I'm sure it was a hell of a burden for a kid to carry, having a shit for a father."

"Yeah, I know," Suzanne said grimly.

"I'm sorry," Beatrice said. "I didn't mean..."

"I know," Suzanne said. "But just like you, it still hurts."

"I think you should give your dad a bit of slack though, Sue."

"Bea, you wouldn't say that if you grew up in the same house as him."

"Probably not," Beatrice said. "But there's something I think you should know. Something your mother should have told you years ago."

"What?"

"Did you ever wonder why your mom ever married Ray Duncan? She was from a good wealthy home. He was from way over on the other side of the tracks."

"I don't know," Suzanne shrugged. "I guess love is blind."

"Did you know that your mother was pregnant when they got married?"

"Yeah," Suzanne said. "I can do the math. I was born six months after they were married."

"Isabelle Bowen knew Ray Duncan only because he worked on the presses down at the paper. They chatted sometimes when she came around, helping after school and such. But Isabelle was heavily involved with Cameron Nelson. She got pregnant, and Cam headed for the hills, sure that his plans to be a doctor would go up in smoke as soon as a baby came into the picture. He was probably right. Isabelle was in a bad fix. She was seventeen and pregnant and now, suddenly alone. She went down to the paper to tell her parents the whole story, but chickened out. She ended up crying on Ray Duncan's shoulder in the press room. Two weeks later, they were married."

"I don't believe it," Suzanne said instantly. It was all too incredible to be true.

"Would I lie to you about something this serious?"

"How do you know this? Who told you?"

"My dad was Isabelle's brother. The whole family knows. Isabelle insisted that none of her children would ever know the truth though, especially you."

"My God," Suzanne said. She put down all her stuff on the hood of Beatrice's car and leaned heavily against it. Ray Duncan was not her father. She was not a Duncan at all. But somehow, knowing the solitary good thing her father had done, being a Duncan was not such a shameful thing after all.

"I'm sorry I had to be the one to tell you," Beatrice said. "I'm angry with your mother for not telling you. I guess she just figured you would really hate Ray Duncan if you ever found out he was not your real father. I think it would have the opposite effect though. At least you know he did one honorable thing in his life."

"I can't believe it, but I do," Suzanne said. "It all makes so much sense. Veiled comments and innuendo I never understood ever since I can remember. The whole town probably knows."

"I am sure word has got around," Beatrice said. "It was a heavily guarded family secret, but everything eventually comes out in Headline."

"Incredible."

There was a long silence between the friends. Beatrice began to fidget uncomfortably.

"I didn't come here today to lay this on you, Suzanne," Beatrice said. "I'm so sorry."

"I'm glad you did," Suzanne said. "There have been enough secrets in this town. It'll just take me a while to get used to this."

"I understand. I really do."

"So why did you nearly run me down in the parking lot?"

"I wanted to let you know I'm going to Vancouver."

"Are you coming back?" Suzanne said with trepidation. She would be lost if Beatrice left her life yet again.

"In a while," Beatrice said. "I'm going to spend some time with my daughter. I never allowed myself to get close to Annabelle all her life. I surrounded myself with work and single mother obligations so that I didn't have to encounter the face of Wade Edward's child every day of my life. It might be too late, but I want to try to be the only thing I ever wanted to be in life: a mother."

"That's wonderful."

"I also have some business things to tie up. I have to sell the house and get all my stuff together."

"Meaning?"

"Meaning Headline has been the only home I ever really loved. Vancouver was only exile. I want to end that part of my life and come back here where I belong. My family and my friends and the very best friend I ever had in my life are all here. I want to be here."

"And Annabelle?"

"I guess that's up to her. She's an adult just starting out on her own path. I can't even guess where her path is going. I just got my own finally figured out."

"When are you leaving?"

"Tomorrow."

"That quick? I guess you'll have to trust the paper to me then for a while."

"Actually," Beatrice paused. "I was going to ask Aaron Taylor to run the paper while I was gone."

"Oh," Suzanne managed through her shock. She thought she had been doing a good job of running the Headline Mail. "If that's what you want..."

"Of course I would prefer you to do it," Beatrice said, a peculiar grin emerging on her face, "but I figured you would be busy."

"Doing what?"

"Seeing the sights of course. There's Stanley Park and Gastown and the Vancouver Aquarium and---"

"Beatrice," Suzanne exclaimed. "What are you talking about?"

"Suzy, I want you to come to Vancouver with me. And don't say anything about the kids or the job or the house or Myles or any other excuse. Your mother and Michelle have already agreed to take care of your kids and your boss is giving you the time off, and face it, girl. You could use a vacation."

Suzanne knew nothing was truer than that statement. Never before in her life had she felt so bone tired. Everything in her boring but albeit stable life had turned upside down. She needed some time to catch her breath. And knowing Beatrice's tenacity, she was about to get her chance.

"Beatrice, I don't know what to say."

"Don't say anything. There's nothing to say. Hey, maybe you will love Vancouver so much you will pack up the kids and move out there yourself."

"I doubt it. I don't hate Headline anymore, Bea. I have learned so much about this crazy little town over the past couple of months, but most of all that there is no other place I would live."

"That's great to hear," Beatrice said, then she smiled and sang. "Baby, I love you, baby Susie-Q."

They sang their song and cried a little. Then Suzanne picked up her load, and made her way back across the parking lot.

She looked up into the bright sunny sky above her. They say that prairie skies are the biggest in the world. Suzanne grinned as she realized that she would soon be finding out for herself.

Printed in Great Britain
by Amazon